# ROYAL ESCAPE

## CONDITIONS OF SALE

# ROYAL ESCAPE

## GEORGETTE HEYER

UNABRIDGED

PAN BOOKS LTD : LONDON

First published 1938 by Wm Heinemann Ltd.
This edition published 1965 by Pan Books Ltd,
33 Tothill Street, London, SW1

ISBN 0 330 20101 8

*2nd Printing 1966*
*3rd Printing 1967*
*4th Printing 1968*
*5th Printing 1970*
*6th Printing 1971*
*7th Printing 1973*

PRINTED AND BOUND IN ENGLAND BY
HAZELL WATSON AND VINEY LTD
AYLESBURY, BUCKS

TO
NORAH PERRIAM

*At supper the king was cheerful, not shewing the least sign of fear or apprehension of any danger, neither then nor at any time during the whole course of this business, which is no small wonder, considering that the very thought of his enemies, so great and so many, so diligent and so much interested in his ruin was enough, as long as he was within their reach, and as it were in the very midst of them, to have daunted the stoutest courage in the world, as if God had opened his eyes as he did Elisha's servant at his master's request, and he had seen an heavenly host round about him to guard him, which to us was invisible, who therefore, though much encouraged by his undauntedness and the assurance of so good and glorious a cause, yet were not without secret terrors within ourselves, and thought every minute a day, a month, till we could see his sacred person out of their reach.*

(Colonel Gounter's *Last Act in the Miraculous Story of His Majesty's Escape.*)

# CONTENTS

# CHAPTER I

## 'THE CROWNING MERCY'

FROM the time of the King's ascending the cathedral tower, which he had done early in the morning, to observe the disposition of Cromwell's forces, the day had been dull, heavy with autumnal mists, as gloomy as General Leslie's face.

'Look well?' Leslie had said, weeks before, as sour as a lemon. 'Ay, the army may look well, but it won't fight.'

But the King had led the Highlanders out through the Sidbury Gate, with the best of his infantry, and the handful of English Cavaliers who pressed close about his person, and they had fought so well that Cromwell's Ironsides had been flung back at the foot of Red Hill. A charge of massed cavalry then might have won the day, but no cavalry came trotting up to support the infantry. Three thousand Scottish horse, under David Leslie, stayed motionless in the rear, while the foot soldiers, their ammunition expended, fought with halberds and the butt-ends of their muskets until forced to give way before Cromwell's reserves.

In Worcester, the citizens ran for shelter into their shuttered houses, for the battle was closing in on the town. To the south, Fleetwood had forced the passage of the Teme at Powick Bridge; west of the Severn, beyond Pitchcroft meadow, General Dalyell's brigade of Scots, with no heart in them for a losing fight on alien soil, began to lay down their arms; while on the main front the Fort Royal was being attacked. Guns barked and thundered; the atmosphere was acrid with smoke, through which confused, struggling forms loomed and faded as the ragged battle pressed nearer and nearer to the town.

Across the road before the Sidbury Gate, an ammunition-waggon lay overturned, blocking the entrance to the town. Two of its wheels were cocked up in the air, and the ammunition, spilling over the road, lay in a tangle of horses' guts. A tall horseman, in dulled and dinted half-armour, came riding up out of the murk and the mist, and was forced to a standstill, his horse's hooves slipping and stumbling amid the wreckage. Those by the gate caught the flash of a jewel as he alighted heavily, weighed down by his cumbering armour; and a glimpse of a young, harsh face under the brim of his beaver. Then he was hidden momentarily from their sight as some more horsemen surged up in his wake. Voices, sharpened by a sense of emergency, sounded in a confused hubbub; the tall cavalier broke through the press, and climbed laboriously over the waggon, into the town.

His gloved hands plucked at the straps of his breast-plate. 'Get this gear off me!' he commanded. His voice was husky with fatigue; he cleared his throat; and, as those who had followed him were slow in obeying, repeated more strongly: 'Get it off me, I say! You, Will Armourer! Duke, find me a fresh horse!'

Young Armourer tugged at the straps; his fingers were sticky with sweat, and trembling. 'The day's lost. They're closing in on us,' he muttered. 'Those damned Scots!'

The scarred breastplate was off, and flung down with a hollow ring on to the cobbles. The King stripped off the cuisses that guarded his thighs, and straightened himself with a gasp of relief. 'Not lost! Not lost yet!' he said, but a note of anguish rather than of conviction sounded in his voice. He turned, and seized the bridle of a big grey horse which Marmaduke Darcy had led up, and swung himself into the saddle, and dashed off up the steep street towards the cathedral.

General Leslie's troopers were drawn up in good order, but showed no disposition to take any part in the battle. The King rode up to where David Leslie stood in conference with some of his officers. The group parted to make way for him; he thrust between two officers mounted on fidgety chargers, and addressed himself hotly to Leslie. What he said only the General heard. A rigid look came into Leslie's face; he replied clearly: 'When your Majesty has had my experience of men, you will know when it is useless to expect them to advance.'

'Your experience!' the King said in a choking voice. 'Is this the way you use in Sweden?'

He did not wait to hear the reply, but wheeled about, and, snatching off his plumed hat, rode down the lines of the troopers, allowing them to see his face, and his tossed black lovelocks. 'Gentlemen, one charge for the King!' he shouted. 'Will you let it be said the Scots dared not face Cromwell's men? Which of you will strike a blow for Charles Stewart? You, Ned Fraser! – you, James Douglas!'

Leslie looked after him not unsympathetically, but shrugged as he heard him calling unavailingly on the men by name to follow him.

'Fine generalship!' said a drawling, insolent voice. 'Admire it, Talbot! Our friend deserves our compliments, oddsblood, he does!'

'For God's sake, leave that, Buckingham!' Talbot said. 'The rebels are in the town! General Leslie, on your loyalty, I charge you —'

'The men will not fight!' Leslie interrupted angrily. 'You cannot say I did not tell you how it would be! If you have interest with his Majesty, advise him that retreat is the only course left to us!'

A man with a mass of red hair, and a rough, spluttering speech, exclaimed with a strong Scotch accent: 'Mon, they're in guid order!'

'Ay, my Lord Lauderdale! In good order now!' Leslie retorted. 'Will you teach me my trade? I tell you, my lords, and you too, your grace! that if you try to make them engage in a fight they've no stomach for, there'll be no order left amongst them!'

Buckingham, to whom this speech seemed principally to have been addressed, merely lifted his arched eyebrows in an expression of disdain. The noise of the fighting by the Sidbury Gate was growing every moment more intense. Talbot exclaimed: 'My God, are they in? The King must be got away!'

He clapped spurs to his horse as he spoke, and so did not hear Leslie say: 'Let the King place himself amongst my men. I will engage to carry him safe back to Scotland.'

Talbot, with Lauderdale at his heels, and Armourer, Darcy, and another of the King's Bedchamber stringing out behind him, caught up with the King, and leaned out of the saddle to seize the grey's bridle. 'Sire, you must save yourself!' he said urgently. 'They're breaking in on all sides! There's no more to do here!'

The King tore his bridle free, and the grey reared up, snorting. 'Escape? No! But one charge and we may sweep them out of the town! Gentlemen, gentlemen, I implore you —'

'Sir, Hamilton, Douglas, Forbes are all fallen!' Talbot cried. 'You must save yourself!'

The King turned his distorted face to the ranks of the Scots. 'Will you not strike a blow for me?' he said fiercely. 'I would rather you would shoot me than let me live to see the consequences of this fatal day!'

The pain in his voice made the Lord Talbot grimace. Lauderdale thrust his horse forward, and in his turn grasped the King's bridle. 'Shoot ye?' he said, between pity and roughness. 'No, by God, sir, ye're too precious to this realm! Come awa'!'

A youth on a foaming horse came full-tilt upon them, calling out hoarsely that the Roundheads were in, and the King must fly or be taken. Some of Leslie's officers, who had tried to exhort the sullen troopers to charge, had gathered about him. The newcomer, another of the King's Bedchamber, said in jerks that the English horse had rallied in Friars Street, and were holding the rebels in check to secure the King's retreat. Lauderdale and Talbot almost dragged the King away as the Scottish troopers began to draw off.

The gabled house, which had been the King's lodging for nearly a fortnight, was situated at the end of New Street, and extended to the Corn Market. The street was narrow, a continuation of Friars Street, which led downhill to the Sidbury Gate. Here, as Mr May had described, a band of

English horse, rallying round old Lord Cleveland, Colonel Wogan, Majors Carlis, Massey, and others, was making charge after gallant charge. The street was a shambles, the dead and wounded trampled under sliding, plunging hooves, and blood running in the gutters. The little party escorting the King with difficulty made their way to New Street down one of the lanes that thronged with demoralized Royalist troops, and reached at last the big, half-timbered house at the western end. Here, the King, who had not spoken again after his last appeal to Leslie's brigade, dismounted, saying hurriedly: 'I will be with you presently. There is something I must do first.'

Only Talbot caught his words, drowned as they were in the noise of the fighting farther down the street. He shouted: 'Haste, haste, sir, for God's love!'

'Hold my horse!' the King said, pushing the bridle into his hand. 'My papers! I must destroy my papers!'

He vanished into the house. Darcy slid out of the saddle, and ran after him, pursued by Lauderdale's raucous voice bidding him hurry the King.

The uproar in the street seemed to be growing louder, caught and flung back as it was by the two rows of houses; and it soon became apparent to the anxious eyes that watched it that the fight was surging nearer. Reinforcements of Republicans were being poured into the town, and not all the desperate gallantry of the Cavaliers who again and again hurled themselves at the tide of red-coats could avail against the opposing weight of numbers.

Inside the house, the King had reached the room leading out of his bedchamber which served him for closet, and was feverishly searching through the mass of his papers, flinging first one document and then another to Darcy, who crammed them on to the embers of the dying fire. The King was absorbed in his task, but Darcy was sickeningly conscious of the sound of fighting, which soon seemed to be almost under the latticed windows. Once he begged the King to come away, but Charles paid no heed.

The door leading from the bedchamber on to the landing burst open; a hurried, heavy footstep came across the floor, and in another instant the doorway between the two rooms was blocked by the bulk of Lord Wilmot.

He was out of breath, and dishevelled, his florid, handsome face reddened by exertion; and, without wasting time on ceremony, he grasped the King's arm. 'Leave that, sir! In another minute they will be in! Your servants are holding the door! You must come at once!'

'Yes,' the King said. 'Yes, I'll come. One more, Duke! Blow up the flame!'

The last document flared up the chimney. Darcy scrambled up from his knees, stammering: 'Your gear – your jewels!'

'Oh, Duke!' The King began to laugh.

Wilmot flung open the door, and pushed the King through it. 'The back way! They wait for you there.'

To judge by the confused din coming up the well of the staircase from the ground-floor, the fight was by this time concentrated about the entrance to the house.

'Quick, sir! For God's love, will you be quick?' Wilmot hissed. He thrust the King towards the narrow back-stairs, but suddenly pulled him back again. 'No, wait! I'll go first: they may have got round the house by now!'

He pulled his sword out of the scabbard, and went swiftly but cautiously down the twisting stair. The King caught Darcy by the hand, who seemed as though he would remain heroically to guard the rear, and followed him.

Talbot, Lauderdale, Armourer, and Hugh May were all gathered about the back-door, and there was as yet no sign of a Republican soldier to dispute the King's escape. Talbot fetched a great sigh when he saw the tall, graceful form emerge from the house, and pressed forward immediately, leading the grey horse. 'Up, sir! Already we've stayed too long. Leslie will have marched out through the St Martin's Gate. We must follow him hard.'

'O God!' burst from the King. 'Flight! I *must* rally them. They *shall* follow me!'

Talbot, who had a bitter disbelief in the rallying power of men who had retreated, leaving their King to the mercy of his enemies, was silent; but Lauderdale said bluffly: 'Ay, we'll rally them, never fear! But ye'll need to catch them first, I'm thinking. On with ye, sir!'

The King set spurs to his horse; the little party closed in about him, and, trotting briskly, made its way along the narrow streets to the St Martin's Gate.

The struggle was now concentrated about Castle Hill, which was still held by Rothes and Sir William Hamilton; and in Friars Street, where the Cavaliers were being driven back with terrible loss towards the Key. As the King's party rode westward, the noise of the fighting became muffled in the distance. No Republican troops appeared to oppose the King's passage; and at six o'clock, in fast-gathering dusk, he galloped out through the St Martin's Gate on to the Wolver-hampton Road.

A mile beyond the town, at Barbon's Bridge, Leslie had succeeded in halting his brigade. With this imposing force of horsemen were also a number of English Cavaliers, who, finding the Scots horse retreating, and the King gone, had escaped in some confusion from the town. When the King rode up, a troop was hurriedly forming under Buckingham to break back into the town, and carry the King out of it in the teeth of his enemies. His arrival brought such a sense of relief to his friends that it was greeted with something like a cheer. He paid no more heed to it than to the saluta-tion of Buckingham, who rode up to him at once, a dozen questions on his lips. A hand motioned that beautiful young man out of the way; the King's eyes were fixed on Leslie's face. He said, with the good-humour that never wholly deserted him: 'You have them well together, General! It is not too late. A surprise attack now —'

'I have them together, as your Majesty perceives,' Leslie interrupted. 'But I can keep them together only in retro-grade movement. I must earnestly beseech your Majesty to abandon any thought of renewing hostilities.'

'Did you say *renewing*?' asked Buckingham, honeysweet.

Leslie ignored him, keeping his gaze on the King. 'Be-lieve me, I feel for your Majesty, but I should be failing in my duty to your person were I to counsel anything but retreat.'

Those near the King saw his hand tighten on the bridle. For a moment he did not speak, but after a pause he said in a low voice that was unsteady with some suppressed emotion: 'Do you know – do *they* know – that there are men back there in Worcester fighting to cover this shameful retreat?'

Leslie gave an infinitesimal shrug. 'The men you speak of are not Scots, sir,' he said dryly. 'These know that, at least.'

'Then you will do nothing?' The King's voice rose slightly. 'You are their General! They know you; they trust you! One word from you – the word you will not give, it seems —'

'I will give no order I cannot compel my men to obey, sir.'

The King uttered an impatient exclamation, and wheeled his horse about. Once more he showed himself to the troopers, calling on them by name, cajoling, almost imploring. It was useless; even this temporary halt was not to their liking; and men were already deserting from the ranks.

'This is not to be borne!' Talbot said under his breath, his heart wrung by the sight of the young King's despair.

His muttered words reached Lord Derby's ears. A flush had mounted to Derby's cheeks; his lofty brow was frowning; his eyes alight with contempt and a sense of outrage. 'It is not to be borne!' he echoed. 'Scottish scum!' He drove his spurs suddenly into his horse's flanks, and leaped forward after the King.

Buckingham would have followed, but found his way blocked by Talbot. 'Let be, my lord!' Talbot said. 'You can do no good there.'

Buckingham checked, but said with a scowl: 'Had I been given the command, these poltroons should have shown a different front!'

'It is useless to hark back to past grievances,' Talbot replied, curbing a little natural exasperation. The volatile Duke, though only twenty-four years old, and quite inexperienced in war, had been sulking for days because the

16

King had refused to give the command of the army to him. He had been brought up with Charles, almost like a brother, and enjoyed, besides the gifts of beauty, grace and wit, a greater share of the King's confidence than Talbot thought he deserved. He often presumed on his position and the King's easy temper, but though he looked sulky now, and for a moment obstinate, he did not push past Talbot, but sat flicking his embroidered gloves against his high boot, and looking angrily in Leslie's direction.

Wilmot, who had ridden after Derby, came back to join the knot of gentlemen gathered round Talbot. Talbot saw the glint of a tear on his cheek, and moved forward to meet him. 'It's a sleeveless errand, Harry: they won't fight, and every moment that we linger here puts him in danger!'

'He's distracted,' Wilmot said. 'I have never known him like this before.'

'Small wonder. This is a crushing defeat. I dare not think on the consequences.'

Wilmot sighed, but said, pursuing his own train of thought: 'To get him out of the country! There will be a price on his head. Oh, my God, what to do, Talbot? What to do to save that unhappy boy?'

Talbot was unable to answer, for the King had ridden up beside Lord Derby. In the gloom of twilight it was hard to see his face, half-hidden by the sweep of his hat-brim. He did not speak; nor, when an order rang out, and the brigade began to move northwards again, did he glance towards the ranks of the troopers. He reined in his horse at the side of the road, and remained motionless in the saddle, seeming to heed neither the steady trot of the squadrons passing him, nor the anxious consultation being held by his friends.

The last of the squadrons had not passed when the thunder of hooves approaching from the south sent hands instinctively to sword-hilts. But the oncoming cavalry was not riding in the orderly formation of Cromwell's victorious troops; the hoof-beats were irregular, approaching at full gallop; in another minute the King's party was lost to view in a sudden swirl of Cavalier horse, and the evening became loud with voices, sharp questions and disjointed answers tossed to and fro in almost indistinguishable babel.

The troop numbered from fifty to sixty horsemen, who had fought their way out of the town, after the wild turmoil in Friars Street. So great was the confusion in Worcester that the officers could give the King no very sure account of those of his followers who were missing from their ranks. The Roundheads were in possession of the town, but it was thought that the Scots lords were still holding out on Castle Hill, a position sufficiently impregnable to enable them to surrender upon terms. The English defence at the Town Hall had been overcome; someone had seen the Duke of Hamilton carried, mortally wounded, into the Commandery. Of Cleveland, Wogan, Carlis, Hornyhold, Slaughter, all engaged in the cavalry skirmish to secure the King's retreat, there was no news. At the end it had been each man for himself; nor, in the dusk and the appalling mêlée, had it been possible to discover who yet lived, and who lay dead in the reeking streets.

A sob broke from the King; he said wildly: 'We must go back, I tell you! I will not bear this flight! Better dead! Better dead!'

His words brought about a momentary silence. It was broken by Colonel Blague, who said bluntly: 'The day is lost, sir. We can do but one thing more.'

The King's eyes lifted eagerly to his face. 'What more?'

'We can preserve your person, sir, and that, God helping us, we will do.'

'My person!' the King exclaimed, with an impatient jerk of his head.

Derby's cool voice interposed. 'Your person, sir, which is to say, our honour. There can be no turning back. Your Majesty knows it as surely as I do.'

The King turned from him. 'George! Harry!' he said imploringly.

'Oh, sir, my Lord Derby is of course right: no question!' Buckingham replied.

Wilmot pushed up to the King's horse, and laid a hand over the ungloved one grasping the bridle. 'Alas, sir, think!,

What will become of us if you fall into Cromwell's hands? All is not lost while you live. Believe me, believe me, my dear master, the worst disaster that can now befall us who love you, and look to you to lead us again, is your death or your capture!'

The hand was rigid under his, but after a moment the King said in a quieter voice: 'You must forgive me, gentlemen: in truth, I am not myself. Let us go on.'

The last of the Scottish cavalry had ridden by; the King started after the diminishing squadrons, riding soberly, his cloak drawn round him, and his hat pulled low over his brow. The Lords Talbot and Wilmot joined him, riding one on either side of him; Buckingham, Lauderdale, and the Gentlemen of his Bedchamber closed in behind; and the remainder of the escort fell into some kind of order in the rear.

Leslie, who had waited to confer with the King and his advisers, ranged alongside the Earl of Derby, and began in his dry, rather expressionless voice, to explain the course he thought it proper to pursue. This consisted of an immediate retreat into Scotland, which, little though it might commend itself to one of Derby's proud temper, did indeed seem to be the only thing left to do. Both Buckingham and Lauderdale, who had pressed up close behind the King's companions, accorded the plan their approval, but the King, over whose apparently unattending head the discussion was held, did not utter a word, but rode on, jostled sometimes by the horses on either side of him, but aloof from their riders, his despair a barrier not even Buckingham cared to break through.

It was agreed that Leslie's itinerary should be followed, with Newport, in Shropshire, for the first objective. Leslie could not but believe that Cromwell would lose no time in pursuing the remnant of the King's army, but he trusted that by forced marches they might be able to reach the border before him.

He spurred on to join his own officers, leaving the King's friends to talk over his advice. The King's voice, now perfectly under control, but flat-toned, as though drained of vitality by the shattering of his hopes, interrupted the discussion. 'I will not go back to Scotland.'

The brief sentence surprised the four persons who heard it into a rather stunned silence. After a moment, Buckingham repeated: 'You will not go back to Scotland?'

'No.'

'But – oddsblood, sir, what else remains? You must seek your safety there!'

'I had rather be hanged.'

He spoke without passion, but so deliberately that it was evident his mind was made up. The crack of a laugh broke from Lauderdale. 'I warrant ye! But ye are bound to consider your safety, sire – or we for ye, forbye —'

'I think it absolutely impossible to reach the border. The country will all rise up on us once the news of this day's defeat is known.'

'Ay, maybe you're right at that,' Lauderdale conceded. 'But we've a matter of three thousand horse with us, I'll have your Majesty to bear in mind.'

'Men who deserted me when they were in good order would never stand to me when they have been beaten,' Charles replied.

Lauderdale found nothing to say. Buckingham, who had no reason to share his master's loathing of Argyll and his Covenanters, began to expostulate, but was silenced by the King's saying over his shoulder, with unaccustomed sharpness: 'Peace, George! My mind is made up. I do not go to Scotland.'

'Then, by your leave, sir, it is time to call a halt!' said Talbot. 'I shall not say you are wrong: indeed, I am with you, but this is a matter for consultation. Mr Lane! Pass the word to halt!'

Lane, one of Talbot's own levies, went galloping down the ragged line, and in a few minutes the troop was at a standstill, the King, with his attendant lords, and the chief amongst the officers, withdrawn off the road for a hasty council of war.

The light was by this time so dim that it was difficult to distinguish one face from another. The King, taller by half a head than any of those about him, addressed a group of shadows. He said: 'I have been considering, gentlemen. If we stay together we are enough to attract attention, not enough to withstand assault. All our hope lies in scattering.'

'Our hope is in your Majesty,' Derby said. 'Consider only your own safety, for nothing else is of any moment.'

This courtier-speech seemed to amuse the King. He said, with his irrepressible humour creeping into his voice: 'Oddsfish, does any man desire to feel a halter about his neck?'

'So only you were safe!' Wilmot said, trying to find his hand to kiss.

'I thank thee, Harry. My Lord Talbot, you are a native of these parts! Tell me, what good hope have I of finding honest friends here who will help me to safety?'

'The best, sir!' Talbot answered at once. 'But you will need to put yourself in some disguise. I too have been considering. Would your Majesty consent to counterfeit a country-fellow?'

'I will counterfeit what you please, but you will have remarked, my lord, that I have an odd, ugly face. Can you disguise that, think you?'

'More easily than your inches, sire. Will you be pleased to let us know your mind? What will you do? Where will you go?'

'To London,' replied the King, a ring of defiance in his voice.

His decision, as he had foreseen, provoked a storm of censure. To some it seemed the dream of a distracted youth; to others, a scheme, sound at core, but impossible to be put into action. Voices out of the dusk implored the King to abandon a notion so fraught with disaster, to trust in Leslie, to consider the difficulties to be met with, to be guided by older and wiser heads.

Talbot only seemed undecided, until Wilmot suddenly said, his light voice jumping a little: 'I agree with you, sir, and I will go with you.'

Buckingham, whose dare-devilry no man could deny, was nettled, and gave an unkind laugh. Wilmot flushed in the darkness, knowing his own soul's shrinking, but repeated: 'I will go with you. In London, they will never think to look for you; and in London you have faithful friends who will transport you back to France.'

'You amaze me, Wilmot, by God, you do!' said Buckingham.

'You should bear in mind, my Lord Duke, that I have the advantage over you of fifteen years' experience!' Wilmot flung back at him.

'Oh, hush!' the King said. 'Here is nothing to quarrel about, my good friends. My resolve is taken. Now I am in your hands, my Lord Talbot.'

'Leslie must be informed of this,' Talbot said, and again called up Cornet Lane, and sent him galloping up the road in the wake of the retreating Scots.

Derby said, with distaste vibrating in his voice: 'Your Majesty has scarcely considered what this project must mean! To put yourself into the guise of a country-fellow will require of you a behaviour which must be wholly against your birth, your breeding, your high estate! Your Majesty does not know – cannot know —'

'My lord, my dear lord!' interrupted the King, half-amused, half-soothing, 'my Majesty is not so nice, believe me!'

'Sire, you are a King.'

'I may be a King,' Charles replied, 'but I know something of how beggars live.'

This frank allusion to his financial straits made Derby, a nobleman of the old school, stiffen a little.

The King tried to see the faces about him. 'Well, gentlemen?'

Buckingham yawned audibly. 'Dear sir, you have told us your mind is made up. We await your commands.'

'I have only one left to give you. It is that you do now look to yourselves. You can do no more for me, and for what you have done, from the bottom of my heart, I thank you, gentlemen. I shall not forget.'

'So please your Majesty, before we look to ourselves we will see you to some place of safety,' said Colonel Blague.

'And where may that be?' enquired Buckingham.

Derby said reluctantly: 'If your Majesty is determined on this course, there is a house known to me where you may find safe shelter for a day at least. It stands retired, and is inhabited by a very honest fellow, one of five brothers who harboured me lately, after the defeat of my force at Wigan. My Lord Talbot, you should know it, I think. It is a hunting-lodge called Boscobel, in the parish of Tong in Shropshire, and belongs, they told me, to the Giffards.'

'I have one of the Giffards with me now,' said Talbot. 'But Tong must be forty miles from here!' He spoke hesitantly, thinking of the King, who had scarcely been out of the saddle since early morning.

'I like it well,' Charles said decidedly. 'Can you lead me there, my Lord Derby?'

'I dare not attempt it, sir. In this darkness, only a native of the country could hope to find his way.'

'Pass the word for Mr Charles Giffard!' Talbot commanded.

Before Mr Giffard could come up, Lane had cantered back to them, accompanied by General Leslie, who seemed, from the sound of his voice, to be in no very good temper. He spoke civilly, however, to the King, warning him that delay was dangerous, and begging that he would keep up with the brigade. When he learned that Charles had taken the resolution of separating altogether from the brigade, he was at first thunderstruck, and then coldly furious. He represented to the King in the strongest terms the folly of such a course, and made such an acid allusion to untrustworthy advisers that the hostility hitherto suppressed in the English lords' breasts flared up, and even some of those who had been most urgent with the King to escape into Scotland now supported his counter-plan.

An acrimonious dispute between Leslie and Buckingham caused the King to remark to the Lord Talbot somewhat bitterly that although he could not get Leslie's horse to stand by him against the enemy, it seemed he could not get rid of them now, when he had a mind to it.

His voice had a carrying quality, and as he had not

lowered it, it easily reached Leslie's ears. Leslie said, sitting rigidly upright in the saddle: 'Your Majesty may at least trust my men to carry you into safety!'

'I had rather trust to my own wits,' responded Charles.

'Your Majesty places me in an intolerable position. I am bound by honour to guard your Majesty's person.'

A melancholy smile crossed the King's features. As though his eyes, piercing the gloom, had seen it, Leslie said with difficulty: 'Your Majesty blames me for what no man could have prevented. If my life could be of avail you might take it with my goodwill.'

'But it is of no avail,' Charles said. 'I do not go with you to Scotland, General.'

'I beg that your Majesty will reconsider that most unwise decision,' Leslie replied, and saluted, and rode off without another word.

The King looked towards the troop he could perceive only as vague shadows in the gathering darkness. 'Let any who have a mind to try the chances of escape into Scotland, leave me now and follow General Leslie,' he said clearly.

No one moved. 'Your Majesty is answered,' Talbot said.

## CHAPTER II

## WHITE-LADIES

IN another minute Cornet Lane had ridden up with Charles Giffard at his heels. Talbot called Giffard to him, and led him to the King. A grave, rather awed voice assured the King that Giffard was his servant to command. Talbot disclosed briefly the King's immediate intentions, and after a moment's consideration, Giffard said that he thought he could undertake to be his Majesty's guide.

'Will you harbour me in a house of yours?' asked the King. 'I am like to prove a dangerous guest, bethink you.'

The direct question seemed to astonish Giffard. Again

he paused, but this time searching only for words, which tripped a little on his tongue. 'Sir – all I have – all my uncle calls his own – is at your Majesty's service. Chillington – my uncle's house – is sequestrated, and my uncle even now a prisoner, else I would lead your Majesty there, not to a poor hunting-lodge.'

'I would not have his Majesty go to Chillington,' Derby said decidedly. 'Boscobel is more remote, less likely to be searched. But can you be sure of leading his Majesty there in this darkness?'

'Yes, my lord. I have my servant Yates with me, who, I daresay, could find his way blindfold, being a native of Shropshire.'

'Does anyone know where we stand now?' enquired the King.

Mr Giffard knew. 'I judge that we are within a league of Hartlebury, sir. We should proceed through Kidderminster to Himley, where, if it please your Majesty, we must strike westwards, away from the great road.'

'It pleases me very well,' the King said. 'But tell me, Mr Giffard: which way will General Leslie's brigade take?'

'They must follow the great road, sir.'

'Then lead me off the great road,' commanded the King, 'for I have a fixed resolve to escape from the Scots, and that before they take it into their heads to set a guard about my person. Can you do that?'

'Yes, sir,' replied Giffard, 'but to do so we must leave Kidderminster on our left, and pass through Stourbridge instead.'

'Mr Giffard, I am in your debt. Lead on!'

'In good time!' Lauderdale said. 'Look ye, now, no more delays!'

'God send the man does not lead us astray!' Talbot muttered to Wilmot, as the cavalcade moved forward. 'Forty miles to ride, and the night upon us!'

'Weel,' said Lauderdale tartly, for although, being an Engager, he fully shared the King's detestation of the Covenanting party that ruled Scotland, he could not but regret Charles's decision not to make for the border, and was consequently in a testy humour, 'weel, Talbot, I'll call on ye to mind 'tis ain of your own gentlemen ye've delivered us to!'

A mile farther on, the road branched, and Giffard, who was riding ahead of the King, with his servant beside him, wheeled into the right-hand fork. The troop of horse was smaller than it had been, for some, too badly wounded in the last skirmish in Worcester to keep their saddles, had been forced to fall out and seek shelter in the countryside. The main body, in compact order, kept on, maintaining a steady trot. Faster, no one dared to go, for by this time there was scarcely light enough left for each man to discern the haunches of the horse in front of him. Giffard's servant had produced a lantern, and although its feeble glow did little to illumine the way, it served as a beacon, bobbing ahead of the troop like a dim guiding star.

The road was undulating, full of pits in which the water stood, stagnant and muddy. The country was so still that the thud of hooves, and the frequent splashes, sounded abnormally loud. From time to time, belts of great trees loomed up suddenly, but the greater part of the way lay through open country across which a chill wind, which carried with it a menace of rain, blew steadily and depressingly.

It was past eleven o'clock when the first straggling houses on the outskirts of Stourbridge warned the troop that they were approaching the town. Only a few lights in upper windows still burned here and there. A momentary halt was called, and the word passed back to walk the horses through the town. In this way, the party passed down the sleeping main street, so silently that no citizen awoke to the alarming noise of hoof-beats, or thrust his head out of window to spy upon the King's escape.

The Lord Talbot pushed forward to the King's side, asking anxiously: 'How does your Majesty?'

'Well,' the King answered, rousing himself from his thoughts.

'You have been in the saddle so long,' Talbot said compassionately. 'I wish —'

26

'I am not tired – only hungry,' said the King, with the ghost of a laugh.

The Lord Talbot remembered with consternation that the King had not touched food since early in the morning, when he had breakfasted. That he himself, and probably most of their companions, had been fasting for just as long seemed a matter of minor importance. He spoke to Lord Wilmot, whose voluminous form was just visible beyond the King. 'Harry, we must find food for his Majesty!'

'Oh, the devil! Where?' said Wilmot, in a voice drenched with sleep. 'Are you so hungry, sir?'

'I could eat an ox,' replied the King frankly.

'Pass the word for an ox for his Majesty,' murmured Buckingham, close behind.

That made the King laugh, but Talbot was too worried to see any humour in their predicament. 'We dare not let your Majesty stop in the town,' he said. 'I wish to God I knew where it may be safe to halt!'

'Safe?' said Wilmot. 'Nowhere!'

'I hope you may be wrong,' remarked the King, 'for if you are not I am as good as hanged already.'

The spectre, not indeed of a halter, but of an axe, hovered before the eyes of the three who heard him. No one spoke, until the King said cheerfully: 'But I think you are wrong.'

They had passed out of the town by this time, and once more set their horses at a trot. A mile on, lying at the foot of a steep hill, a solitary house stood by the wayside. A board swinging on creaking chains proclaimed it to be an ale-house, and a halt was called.

The host, roused from deep sleep by a thundering upon the door, soon thrust his head out of an upper casement, and demanded querulously who was there. He was with difficulty persuaded to come down, and when he did presently unbar the door, he was startled to perceive by the light of his lantern a host of horsemen in the road. He stood goggling, the lantern unsteady in his grasp. He heard the creak of saddle-leathers, the clank of spurred heels alighting on the road, and held the lantern higher to peer fearfully at men stretching cramped limbs, at weary, sweating horses, and, most fearfully of all, at a figure astride a great grey gelding. In the wavering lantern-light, the King seemed a giant to the bemused innkeeper, who stared up at him with starting eyes, and blanched cheeks.

Darcy's hand on his shoulder made him jump. He began to stammer out disjointed entreaties and protestations.

'Oddsfish! the poor man must think us a band of cut-throats!' said the King. He leaned forward a little, and asked: 'Friend, can you give us food and drink?'

The man's gaze, travelling round the dimly seen group, widened in a new horror. He shook his head, but presently, reassured by the Lord Talbot, found his tongue, only, however, to say that he had no provisions for such a company, no, nor enough for any one amongst them. In the end, he brought out ale, and half a loaf of bread, which Buckingham handed up to the King, saying: 'Your ox, sir.'

The King dug his strong white teeth into the crust. While he demolished the bread, some of his followers seized the opportunity to tighten bandages round flesh wounds, while others besieged the innkeeper for ale. The Lord Talbot, fretting to put more distance between the King and Cromwell, stood with enforced patience beside his horse until the last crumb of the bread had disappeared. The King finished his ale, dropped a gold piece into the tankard, and handed it down to Darcy, waiting at his stirrup. Talbot mounted his horse, saying: 'We have no time to lose, sir. We must go on.'

Hooves scraped and clattered on the road; before the innkeeper's wondering eyes the troop melted gradually into the night, until he was left, clutching the King's tankard in his hand, listening to the hoof-beats growing fainter in the distance, and still smelling the lingering scent of leather and of horseflesh.

The King's party rode on through the night. Occasionally a horse would stumble in some pit; a man would curse; or a trooper, reeling with weariness in the saddle, jerk himself awake; sometimes the way would be lost, and found again only after a halt exacerbating to nerves on the jump. For a mile or two beyond the ale-house, the King's spirits had seemed to revive, but very soon he grew silent, so deeply abstracted that when Wilmot spoke to him he seemed not to hear.

A few stars shone between the cloud-drifts overhead; once a watchdog barked in a farmstead crouching beneath the shoulder of a little hill.

Mile after mile slid past; Himley and Wombourn were left behind, and the road curved westwards towards the village of Upper Penn. Here Charles Giffard called a halt, and his servant, Yates, took on the leadership. The troop plunged into a lane so narrow that there was no room for more than two men to ride abreast. The clouds, parting, allowed the faint starlight to show the way. Once Talbot called sharply to Yates, asking whether he were sure of his direction.

At a hamlet, which Yates said was Wightwick, the road from Bridgnorth to Wolverhampton crossed the lane. They turned into it, and once more the straggling cavalcade closed up to ride four abreast. The horses were stumbling now from exhaustion; one or two were going dead lame, but were forced on.

Again Yates led the troop off the great road, into another lane bordered by banks and ragged hedges.

'God send this fellow knows where he is going!' remarked Buckingham, who had taken Wilmot's place beside the King. 'There is a damned reek of cow-byres. Are you awake still, sir?'

'I am not sleepy,' the King replied.

''Sblood, you're more than human, then!' Buckingham said. He shifted his bridle into his right hand, and laid the left on the King's knee. 'Shall I go with you, cousin?' he asked softly.

'No. Save yourself, George. I shall do best alone.'

'You cannot go alone: there must be someone to wait upon you. You are the King.'

'I shall keep Harry near me.'

Buckingham removed his hand. 'You know well Wilmot likes danger only until he comes face to face with it,' he muttered. 'Why do you choose him? Do you doubt me?'

'No,' the King said wearily.

'If you had trusted me today with the command that should have been mine, you would not now be flying for your life!'

The King was silent. Buckingham, who knew well that defensive taciturnity, fell back, and allowed Derby to ride by the King's side.

'Can I trust these men you are taking me to?' Charles asked abruptly.

'I believe them to be very loyal to your Majesty. This fellow who is conducting us is brother-in-law to them, Giffard tells me. They are poor Catholics, and have no cause to love the sectaries. I found them honest. There is, moreover, a secret place in the house, where your Majesty may lie hid.'

The King nodded, and said no more. The lane, which was twisting and very rough, plunged suddenly into the darkness of a great wood. A faint grey light in the east showed the dawn to be creeping upon them. Giffard saw it, and held a few moments' anxious discourse with his servant, at the end of which he begged the King to leave the lane, and take to the woods and the fields.

'It will soon be daylight, sire, and your Majesty must not be seen with this escort. I have spoken with my man, and if your Majesty would be pleased to follow us we will lead you to another house, not so remote as Boscobel, but, I dare pledge my faith, as secure.'

'How far is this house? Where is it?' Derby demanded.

'It is now only a matter of six or seven miles distant, my lord. The house is a manor in my uncle's demesne, called White-Ladies. It is mine own home; and a faithful kinsman of mine lodges there as well, also John and George Penderel, whom your lordship knows.'

'Oh! Two of the five honest brothers? Well, let it be as you advise – if his Majesty so wills it.'

'Do with me as you please,' the King said. 'I should like to come out of the saddle as soon as may be.'

'Only trust me, sire!' Giffard said, distressed by the fatigue in the King's voice.

'Why, so I do! Lead on, good friend.'

The King urged his reluctant horse forward as he spoke, and entered the skirts of the wood beside Giffard.

A tangle of bracken made the going difficult at first, and occasionally a low-hanging branch, unseen in the dimness, would sweep some unfortunate gentleman's hat from his head; but in a little while the trees grew more sparsely, dwindling towards the open, undulating country to the north. Up gentle hills, down into rich valleys, now thrusting through gaps in thin hedges, or fording swollen streams, the King's party pushed on, dreading lest the dawn should discover them to some labourer going early to work in the cow-byres.

The light was stealing above the horizon when they came again into very woody country. For the first time the King failed to hold his horse together when it stumbled. The grey recovered, and the King said, with a faint laugh: 'Fie, I must have been asleep!'

'Be of good heart, sire,' Giffard said. 'There is White-Ladies, straight before you.'

'Thank God for it!' Derby said, riding close beside the King. 'Your Majesty is spent.'

'No more than yourself, my lord,' the King retorted, with an effort at cheerfulness.

The Manor of White-Ladies, a half-timbered building erected beside the ruins of a monastery, was built in the form of a quadrangle, and enclosed by a wall in which an old gabled gate-house was set. Francis Yates had already dismounted, and was hammering on the solid oaken door. Presently the latticed casement above was opened, a head protruded, and a voice demanded sleepily: 'Who's there?'

'It's me – Francis!' Yates called up to him. 'Come ye down, George Penderel, come ye down, man, and let us in!'

'What has befallen? Who is with you?'

'Haste ye! It's the King!' Yates said.

'The King!' The voice sounded stupefied; and then grew sharper: 'I'll come! I'll come! Lord ha' mercy!'

The head disappeared; in a few moments the glow of a light shone through the casement, and then vanished.

Footsteps clattered down bare stairs, bolts and chains creaked and jangled. The door was opened by a man dressed scantily in a shirt and hodden grey breeches, and holding up a horn-lantern in one hand.

The King rode through the gateway into an open enclosure, and dismounted stiffly. In his wake streamed his escort, until the enclosure, which seemed to be partly wild and partly cultivated, thronged with men and horses.

A casement in the house was flung open, and a shrill female voice desired to know the reason for such a commotion. Yates shouted above the noise of trampling horses that it was the King, and Mrs Andrews must come down at once to let him in.

'A very faithful woman, sire: the housekeeper,' Giffard told the King.

A sharp exclamation broke from Mrs Andrews. She called: 'Then all must be lost! Wait till I slip on my kirtle! I will be with you anon. Woe's the day that brings his blessed Majesty here, for I know well what it must mean!'

She drew in her head, but others were awake in the house by this time, and the door was opened a bare couple of minutes later by a man wearing a frieze cloak over his night-rail, and with his feet thrust into odd shoes. He held a branch of candles aloft, and presented such a comical appearance that the King began to laugh.

Charles Giffard said quickly: 'George! It is the King!'

George Giffard's startled gaze sought his kinsman's face for an instant; his hand, holding the candlestick, shook, and a little hot wax spilled on to his fingers. The trifling pain seemed to recall his wandering wits. He pulled the door wide, trying to bow, to keep his cloak close about him, and to bear the candles steadily. 'Your Majesty!' he stammered. 'Forgive – I am all unprepared!'

The same shrill voice which had accosted the troop from the upper window sounded on the stairs; Mrs Andrews came stumping down, and across the raftered hall, scolding and commanding in one breath. Let them usher his sacred Majesty in immediately, addlepates that they were! Would none think to blow up the fire without telling? Must a poor

32

woman be everywhere at once, and not a man amongst them with more wit than might be trussed up in an eggshell?

She snatched the candles out of George Giffard's hold, and set them on the table, and began bobbing curtseys as the King came in, with Derby, Talbot, Lauderdale, Wilmot, Buckingham, and the Gentlemen of his Bedchamber crowding after him. The big hall was suddenly full of men. A boy who had crept halfway down the stairs to gape at the unexpected guests, rubbed his sleep-drowned eyes, as though to rub away the unquiet vision of faces swimming before him in the flickering candlelight. He had never seen such a noble company, and half-thought himself dreaming. The paved hall echoed to the clank of spurred heels, and the knocking of scabbards against the homely furniture. Everywhere he looked, he saw plumed hats, and lovelocks, rich baldricks, and fine lace. Then he became aware of Mrs Andrews dropping curtseys before a man who topped by half a head any other in the hall, and stared pop-eyed at the sight of that redoubtable dame mumbling kisses on to a white hand held out to her. It made him rub his eyes again to hear her say: 'God bless your Majesty!' for he thought that a King would wear a crown and robes, not a buff leather coat, splashed with mud, like this tall Cavalier, with only a blue riband and a great, sparkling jewel on his breast to distinguish him from any other in his train.

Then the King vanished from his sight, swept into the parlour by Mrs Andrews; and a fresh wonder burst upon the boy's starting gaze. A big grey horse, mired to the belly, was led into the hall. Bartholomew discovered, listening intently to the snatches of sentences, that this was the King's horse, and supposed that King's horses had to be more nobly lodged than their fellows. But soon he began to understand that for some reason the King's horse must not be seen by any outside the house. Mr George Penderel was eagerly questioning one or two of the Cavaliers; and Bartholomew, clutching the balusters, and leaning forward the better to hear, caught words and disjointed phrases that conveyed to his intelligence that somewhere there had

33

been a great battle fought, that all was lost, that the King's enemies were searching for him, and that in some way or other it was the fault of the Scots.

He was not allowed to stay any longer upon the stairs, for Mrs Andrews came bustling into the hall, and no sooner spied him than sent him running for billets of wood to lay upon the fire she had kindled in the parlour.

When he went timidly into the parlour with his burden, he found it overfull of gentlemen consuming biscuits and sack, and hardly dared to edge his way to the fireplace. They were talking very earnestly, all of them standing except the King, who sat in an armchair by the fire, leaning against his cloak, which was spread over the wooden back. He had a biscuit in one hand, and held in the other a pewter tankard, which quite shocked Bartholomew, for it was well known that the King ate off golden plates, and had meat at every meal. He seemed to be very hungry too, and when he spoke it was with his mouth full. Kneeling before the fire, his billets still hugged to his chest, Bartholomew gazed up at the dark, harsh-featured face, framed by a mass of tangled black locks, and realized that the King, incredibly, was a man, who could be hungry, and thirsty, and tired, and mud-stained, like any other man.

As he knelt, staring and wondering, the King glanced down at him. Bartholomew found himself to be looking into dark, heavy-lidded eyes that held his for an incurious moment, and then turned again towards the stout gentleman who stood nearest to him.

Bartholomew began to lay his billets upon the fire, and then to blow up the thin flame. He heard George Penderel's voice saying: 'Yes, my lord,' and 'No, my lord,' and screwed his head over his shoulder to look at him. A proud-seeming gentleman, whom the King addressed as my Lord Derby, was talking to George. It seemed that George must go at once, and secretly, to Hobbal Grange to fetch his brother Richard to the King. This seemed a very odd thing, for what could the King want of a poor wood-cutter? Perhaps George thought it odd too; his eyes were fixed earnestly on my Lord Derby's face, and his hands gripped his hat in front of him, twisting it uneasily between them. Next it appeared that William Penderel also must be fetched, from Boscobel House. Then a very alarming thing happened. A tall man was pointing at him, and saying: 'Send the lad for him: I warrant he will bring him fast enough.'

It seemed to Bartholomew that every head was turned towards him. He stayed on his knees, blushing, and pulling his forelock, as he had been taught to do when gentlemen accosted him.

Derby said: 'The risk is too great. A boy of his age can never keep a still tongue in his head. There's a priest in the house: let him be sent!'

'I had rather send young legs than old, my lord,' said Colonel Roscarrock. He nodded at Bartholomew, and said: 'Get up, boy! How far is Boscobel from here?"

Bartholomew scrambled to his feet, and muttered shyly: 'A little mile.'

'A little mile, eh? Could you find your way there, dark as it is?'

'Ay.'

'Do you want to earn a silver shilling for yourself?'

'Ay.'

'You may do so very easily, look you. Go to Boscobel as fast as your legs will carry you, and bid William Penderel hither on the King's business.'

'Are you mad?' Derby said. 'As well inform the whole countryside the King is here!'

'Fie, you wrong the boy!' the King was speaking. He looked at Bartholomew, and crooked a long finger. 'Come hither, boy. What do they call you?'

'Bartholomew Martin – please your Majesty,' answered Bartholomew, louting awkwardly.

'Would you like to serve me, Bartholomew?'

'Ay, please your Majesty.' He saw the smile in the King's eyes, and said firmly: 'I would!'

'Then you must go to this William Penderel, as that gentleman bade you, and tell him that I have need of him. But you must not tell any other that you have seen the King. If you should meet with a neighbour you must say that you are going upon an errand for Mr Giffard. Do you understand?'

'Ay. There's enemies after you – please your Majesty. Scotch 'uns,' he added, with a vague recollection of the snatches of talk he had heard in the hall.

A burst of laughter covered him with confusion; he ducked his tousled head, and ran out of the room.

Wilmot, who had been standing behind the King's chair, moved round it, and knelt with one knee on a joint-stool, his delicate hand grasping the back of the chair. 'Dear sir, do you indeed mean to go to London?' he asked.

'What think you, Harry?'

'Why, I like it very well – so you let me go with you. How many more?'

'None.'

'None!' Wilmot thought for a moment, his fair face inscrutable. Then he gave a little laugh. 'As you please! But bethink you, my dear master, you have not been used to fare forth by yourself. How will you do?'

'Very well, I trust. But I must be rid of these trappings.' A little gesture indicated his Garter-riband and the George of diamonds on his breast.

As though he had heard the low-spoken words, Derby crossed the room towards him, and said: 'Sir, if your Majesty's resolve is firm to put yourself into the guise of a country-fellow, is it your will that I should send Richard Penderel in search of fitting raiment? You cannot go from here in those garments and escape remark.'

'Yes, it is my will,' the King replied. 'But remember, I pray you, my lord, that I am a big fellow!'

'By good fortune, so is William Penderel a big fellow – bigger, I think, than your Majesty. I will advise with Richard when he comes.'

He moved away and went out into the hall. The King called for more sack, if it might be had. Buckingham came to fill his tankard from a great blackjack, walking across the room with the peculiar grace which was his. He stayed by the King's chair, looking down at him in some little trouble. The King murmured: 'What, George?'

36

Buckingham gave the blackjack into Colonel Blague's hold, and went down on his knees beside the King's chair, lightly clasping one long hand in both of his. 'Sire – nay, Brother Charles, let me go with you!' he said suddenly. His handsome, rather petulant face, was softened; he began to coax the King, enticement in his low-pitched voice, the allure of youth for youth in his heavy-lashed eyes. 'Were we not reared together? Did we not say we would go upon high adventures together one day? Charles, I am the man for your need. You know I would die for you, as haply my father would have died for yours. Do not bid me leave you!'

The King drew his hand away. 'I thank you, I thank you! My mind is made up.'

'The King is right,' Talbot said. 'His hope lies now in the common people, not in us. We can aid him best by departing from him.'

'Ay, though we would all of us die for your Majesty,' Colonel Blague said in his deep voice. 'But our deaths cannot help you. Yet if some of us fell into Cromwell's hands —' He paused, frowning, and then said, looking straight into the King's eyes: 'Sire, do not divulge to any one amongst us where you go. Let us know only that we left you here.'

Buckingham sprang to his feet. 'This is brave! Which one of us do you think a traitor, Tom Blague?"

'Under torture,' Colonel Blague said deliberately; 'men may be forced to tell what they may be damned for telling.'

No one spoke for a moment. Then Roscarrock said: 'You are well advised, sir.'

Darcy set his tankard down slowly on the table. 'What's this?' he demanded, shocked bewilderment in his face. 'You will not go without some at least of your Gentlemen, sir?'

The King glanced affectionately towards him. 'Yea, but I must, Duke.'

'Sir!' The ejaculation broke from several pairs of lips at once. Armourer, May, Street, all started forward.

The King got up out of his chair, stretching his long limbs. 'No, none of you,' he said. He looked sleepily round. 'What must I do?' he asked. 'I should be gone out of this house before day, I think.'

Derby, who had come back into the parlour, said: 'Richard Penderel has been here. I have sent him to fetch clothes for your Majesty to wear.'

'Is he willing to risk his life for my sake?' the King asked. 'What is he like, this wood-cutter who will dare so much for a man he has not seen?'

'He is an honest man, in no way remarkable,' Derby said.

'Oddsfish, I think he must be very remarkable to play at pitch-and-toss with his life for my sake!' the King said. He took off his Garter riband, and handed it to Darcy. Then he unpinned the George from his coat, and gave it to Colonel Blague, who chanced to be standing nearest to him. 'Here, Tom: keep that for me,' he said.

Blague took it, and wrapped it in his handkerchief. 'I thank your Majesty,' he said, with a good deal of feeling in his voice.

'I hope it may not serve to hang you!' observed the King, with a flash of humour. He pulled off the ring he wore, laid a gold spanner-string beside it on the table, and took his watch from his pocket, and stood holding it in his hand. 'Who will keep my watch for me?' he enquired.

'That's a heavy charge, sir,' Talbot said, trying to speak gaily. 'I am sure you would have the head of the unfortunate who lost it!'

'Give it to me, sir!' Wilmot held out his hand.

'You, Harry? No, that will not do, for you must go in disguise too, and my watch would sort very ill with a poor man's raiment.'

Wilmot shook his head. 'Oh, not I, sir! I should look frightfully in a disguise, I do assure you.'

'It would be safer,' said Talbot.

'Oh, do you think so?' Wilmot said, taking the watch out of the King's hand, and bestowing it in his own pocket. 'I am sure the countryside will so throng with distressed Cavaliers that I shall occasion not the least remark. Besides, I should not know how to play the part of a hind.'

'You think perhaps that the rôle will come easily to his Majesty?' drawled Buckingham.

The King called Darcy to him to help him out of his coat, and said with a chuckle: 'Harry, don't spare me! Say that I have a damned ugly face, fit for a low fellow.'

'Are you serious, my lord?' demanded Blague. 'Do you mean to accompany his Majesty in such shape as must instantly betray your condition?'

'Oh, let be!' said the King. 'I am going alone. My Lord Wilmot is to keep in touch with me, no more.' He shook his purse out on to the table, and began to pile the gold pieces into little heaps. 'I must not carry gold on me. My Gentlemen shall inherit all this wealth. There! never say you had never any money from me, Duke!'

There was a laugh from those who knew him best; Derby interrupted to say earnestly: 'Sir, you must make haste. I had word from Penderel that there is a troop of rebels quartered only three miles away, at Cotsall. Such a company as ours must not be seen in this neighbourhood.'

'Ay, that's well thought of,' Lauderdale said, setting his tankard down with a crash on the table. 'It's time the most of us were away.' He went to the door, and encountered there Mrs Andrews, who was coming to inform the King that William and Richard Penderel were both in the hall.

Derby hurried out after him. The King, standing on one side of the table in his shirt and grey cloth breeches, leaning his hands on it, was conferring in an undertone with Wilmot. After a few moments, Derby came back into the parlour, followed by two men, both dressed in country habits, and clutching their hats in their hands. As the group by the door parted to make way for them, Derby flung out a hand towards the King, and said: 'This is the King. You must have a care of him, and preserve him as you did me.'

The King turned his head and looked first at William, a giant of a man, with a long, rather severe countenance; and then at Richard, who looked back at him frankly, a little awe in his face, and some curiosity.

For a moment they measured one another in silence, the King seeing a stockily built man, with straight brown hair, and a tanned face not unlike that of a questing dog; the wood-cutter, a tall graceful figure in a white shirt, leaning forward a little with his hands on the table, a mass of black curls falling about a sallow face with great melancholy dark eyes, a jutting nose, and deep lines running down to a large, curling mouth.

'Richard Penderel, will you take me in charge?' the King said at last.

Richard did not reply except by a nod. He had discovered that the melancholy eyes could smile, and as he watched them, a slow answering smile crept over his whole face, until he stood broadly grinning and nodding at the King.

Charles Giffard's hand on his arm compelled his attention. He listened to Giffard's instructions, with a look of good-humoured tolerance, merely remarking at the end: 'I brought Will's breeches.' He turned back to the King, with the effect of ignoring every other man in the room, and said: 'Will and me have been a-talking, my liege, and seeing as there's a troop of rebels quartered hard-by, we say you'd best lie up in the wood yonder till night-fall.'

The King glanced beyond him to the elder Penderel, who, encountering that enquiring gaze, responded in a deep bass: 'Ay.'

'And, if it please your honour, we'd like well you should bustle,' added Richard. He pulled a bundle from under his arm, and dumped it upon the table. 'And here be the clothes,' he said.

'I thank you both.' The King stood upright. 'Leave me now, all but my Lord Wilmot.' He held out his hand as he spoke, and one after the other the lords and gentlemen attending him came up to kiss it, and to take their leave of him. The Penderels watched in stolid, yet attentive silence. Buckingham, the King embraced on the cheek, saying: 'Take good care of yourself, George!' Tears stood in the Lord Talbot's eyes; he said: 'God bless your Majesty, and deliver you from your enemies!' The King's personal attendants frankly wept as they kissed his hand. When all had gone, some to safety, Derby to his death, Lauderdale to long imprisonment, Buckingham to adventures as fantastic as his own puckish humour; and only Wilmot, Charles

Giffard, and the Penderels were left, the King stood for an instant looking towards the closed door with that in his face which made Wilmot catch his hand, and hold it to his lips for a moment.

The King gave a start, and looked down at Wilmot's bent head. 'Now what's to be done with you, Harry?' he enquired. 'Where shall you go?'

'I will go with you, sir.'

'No, that I swear you shall not!' the King said.

Charles Giffard interposed: 'Sir, my kinsman and I have spoken of this, and if my Lord Wilmot pleases, John Penderel will escort him to some place of safety in the neighbourhood.'

'John Penderel? Are there more of you, then?' asked the King of Richard.

'Ay, my liege. There be five of us, and one that's dead. Will, we'd best speak with John.'

'Ay,' said William, and opened the door.

As it closed again behind the two brothers, Wilmot exclaimed: 'I cannot leave you with such clods as these!'

'I like them very well,' said the King, stripping off his shirt. 'See what they have brought me to wear, Harry, and do not look so glum!'

The Penderels had brought the King a coarse linen shirt, a pair of old green breeches which, since they belonged to William, fell below the King's knees; a leather-doublet with pewter-buttons; a pair of down-at-heel shoes; a greasy, steeple-crowned hat, innocent of lining, and a green coat, which Charles Giffard told the King was called a jump-coat. Since stockings seemed to have been forgotten, the King wore his own with the embroidered tops cut off them.

He pushed his feet into the clumsy shoes, grimacing as he did so, for they were an ill fit; and bade Wilmot cut his hair short, after the country fashion.

Wilmot, already aghast at the appearance he presented, cried out against such a sacrifice, but the King said: 'Harry, do as I bid you!' and sat down on a stool to have his love-locks hacked off with a knife.

When it was done, he remarked that he was sorry there

was no mirror for him to see the figure he must cut, and bade Giffard summon Richard Penderel.

Richard came in with Mrs Andrews. Neither seemed to find anything to amuse or to horrify them in the King's changed looks, but Richard, after a moment's scrutiny, turned and walked out of the room; and Mrs Andrews said briskly: 'Well, and is there never one of you with the sense to hide those white hands of his blessed Majesty? The good-year! It needs a woman to attend to every tittle of business. Rare to let that lovesome boy go forth with his hands and face crying out, "I am the King!"'

The King laughed, and slid his arm about her waist. 'Is my face so white? When I was born, my mother cried out that God had sent her a black baby.'

'I warrant she was the proud woman that day! Nay, give over! Is this a time for merrymaking? Rub your hands in the soot back of the chimney! That a poor widow must think of all!'

He obeyed her, and, under her direction, smeared them over his face, protesting as he did so that there was never a lass would kiss him now.

She was busy rubbing the soot on to the backs of his hands, but glanced up to say shrewdly: 'Handsome is as handsome does: you'll never lack for lasses' kisses, I'm thinking – not with that pair of eyes! Fie on you, my liege! I'll have you know I'm an honest woman!'

Richard Penderel came back into the parlour with a pair of shears in his hand.

'Oddsfish, what now?' demanded the King.

'The noble lord has botched your hair, sir,' said Richard. 'It hangs all ends. Let your honour sit down, and I'll trim it.'

'Richard, I swear I love you well!' the King said, sitting down upon a joint-stool.

Colour rushed up into Richard's face. He snipped at the King's locks, without saying anything. When he had finished, he laid aside the shears, and said: 'It's daylight. We mun be going.'

The King rose, and gathered his discarded clothes into a

bundle. 'I'll throw these in the privy-house,' he said.

Mrs Andrews clawed them out of his hold. 'You'll not! George shall bury them, lazy lout that he is!'

'See it done,' the King warned her. 'They will bring you very ill-fortune if they are found.' He turned to Wilmot, and held out both his hands, and grasped Wilmot's delicate ones in them. 'At the sign of the Three Cranes, in the Vintry, Harry. God keep you safe!'

Wilmot fell on his knees, and kissed the blackened hands. 'God keep *you*!' he whispered.

'Your honour had best be stirring,' said Richard phlegmatically. 'We'll slip out by the back way, and no one the wiser.'

The King raised Wilmot, and clasped him in his arms a moment. 'You hear my careful guardian. Farewell! if I can contrive it, you shall hear from me. Lead on, Trusty Dick!'

In another moment he had gone. Wilmot put his hand into his pocket, and felt the watch there, and stood holding it, looking at the shut door.

CHAPTER III

A VERY RAINY DAY

Richard Penderel led the King out of the house by a back-door, no one observing their departure. A dull light – for although the sun was rising, the sky was overcast, with sullen black clouds in it promising rain to come – allowed the King to see the country to which he had ridden all through the painful night. It was a pleasant, kindly land, well-watered and as well wooded. White-Ladies lay secluded a little way down a rough track leading from the lane which ran north from the Newport highway to join the road linking Brewood and Tong. A mile farther up it, Richard told the King, Boscobel House was situated, over the brow of a slight hill. His own house, Hobbal Grange, lay a little way to the west of White-Ladies, but the wood in which the King was to spend the day stretched to the east, half a mile from White-Ladies, its outskirts clearly visible from the house across a succession of open hay and cornfields.

The crops had been gathered in, and the stubble made rough walking. The King's borrowed shoes hurt him a little. He said: 'I trust I may not have to trudge far in these shoes of yours, good Dick, for I find them very incommodious.'

Richard looked distressed. 'They be not fit for your liege to wear, but I had no better.'

'My liege is a scurvy ingrate,' remarked the King, shifting the heavy wood-bill with which Richard had provided him from one hand to the other. He saw by the doubtful look on Richard's face that he was not understood, but felt too tired to explain his words. He smiled instead, which seemed to satisfy Richard, for he smiled back at him, and volunteered the information that they had not far to go.

In a short while, the shelter of the first outlying trees of Spring Coppice was reached, and a few minutes later they had penetrated a good way into the wood, which was very thick, but without much undergrowth, the ground being covered with a tangle of tall bracken, rusted by autumn. The trees were mostly oaks, but some larches grew between them, with here and there a belt of dark spruce firs. The King remarked, as he followed Richard through the bracken which brushed his knees and clutched at his ankles, that the coppice seemed to be a very safe place. Richard was pleased, and said, yes, it was as safe as any other, since a man who did not know it might easily lose his way in it. He led the King into the heart of it, explaining that it was bounded on the eastern side by the road from Cotsall, where a troop of rebels was quartered. He was a little dismayed when Charles announced his intention of taking up a position within hail of the road, and tried to dissuade him. For all his bluntness, he was evidently very much in awe of his Royal companion, and when he found that his respectful representations failed to turn the King from his purpose, did not dare to continue arguing, but reluctantly led the way towards the lane.

'I like to see danger before danger sees me,' said the King.

'Ay, my liege, but I do mean to set brother Humphrey and Francis Yates to scout about for news, and so warn your honour of any danger.'

'What, another brother?' murmured the King. 'Yes, I do recall now that there are five of you. What does Humphrey do for a living?'

'Humphrey is a miller, please your Majesty. Francis is my sister Eleanor's good-man, and will be mighty sprag to serve you, I warrant you.'

They had reached by this time almost to the confines of the coppice. A good many bushes grew there, bordering the lane, which, as the King pointed out to Richard, would afford him excellent cover. Richard agreed rather dubiously, but found a resting-place for his charge at some little distance from the lane, and begged him so earnestly not to venture farther that the King laughed, and submitted. He sat down on a bank, and gave a sigh of relief. His whole body ached with weariness, and his feet, unused to rough and ill-fitting shoes, were already rather chafed. Richard hovered anxiously about him, thinking how pale he looked under the smearing of soot, and wondering whether he would swoon, and what to do for him if he did. He left him for a few moments to take a hasty survey of the road. There was no one in sight, and he went back to the King, who was sitting with his chin in his hand. In repose, his face set into haggard lines, and his dark eyes made Richard feel uncomfortable, so deep was their melancholy. He understood that the King was cast down by his defeat, and wished that he were a lettered man who would be able to offer words of comfort. For himself, crowns and kingdoms were so remote that he could not well appreciate what it must mean to be a King, and to lose both. All he could think of to say was: 'I do fear that your honour is very discomfortable.'

The King looked up, and forced a smile to his lips. 'No, I like it very well. I am only a little tired.'

'Ay, and if your honour would like to sleep I'll keep safe watch, only it would be best I fetch Humphrey and Francis first, I was thinking.'

45

'Do so, by all means. You have no need to fear for me: I shan't go to sleep.'

A disturbing suspicion that he ought not to be left alone crossed Richard's mind, but as his common sense told him that the wisest course would be to enlist his brother and Yates as scouts, he decided to take the King at his word, and to go as quickly as he could, and be back again before any but farm-hands could be expected to be abroad.

Accordingly, he took his leave, relieved that the King was so calm and, apparently, unafraid.

For a long time after he had departed, Charles sat motionless, his tired brain working over every stage of the previous day's battle. Until this moment, he had found himself unable to think clearly, for although he had ridden through the night in profound abstraction, his thoughts had kept the rhythm of the hoof-beats, and, instead of sober consideration, useless phrases had drummed repeatedly in his head. Voices had seemed to clamour ceaselessly all about him; and the need to keep his attention fixed on his horse, who at any moment might have stumbled and come down in the darkness, had precluded the possibility of consecutive thought.

Nothing could be more painful, or to less purpose, than a revision of his misfortunes at Worcester. From the moment of his realization that the Scots horse had failed him, events had moved with a tragic and irrevocable swiftness which seemed to set this hour and yesterday's same hour an age apart. Perhaps Leslie had been an ill-choice for General, yet whom else could he have appointed? 'A natural graceless man whom the Lord would never bless with success,' a fellow-officer had called him once.

But his misfortunes dated farther back than yesterday. The English levies, whom he had expected to join him upon his crossing the border, had hung back, His brain slid to the day of his muster at Pitchcroft, beyond the walls of Worcester. So few had come to the raising of his standard! The English did not like the Scots who accompanied him; they mistrusted the Covenanting part of his army. Massey was largely to blame for that. He had been sent ahead with his troop on the road south from Carlisle to recruit the English, but his stern Presbyterianism had caused him to flaunt the Covenant, and before he could be checked the mischief had been done.

The vista of ill-luck seemed to widen, to stretch slowly backwards, unfolding itself before the King's eyes. He lived again the moment of hearing of his brother-in-law's death, and, now that his desperate bid for his inheritance had failed, knew a feeling of blankness. William of Orange had been a good friend to him; indeed, to all his unhappy family. With a wry smile, the King remembered that it had been William who had paid for the mourning he had worn after his father's death. William's purse, William's wise counsel, had throughout been at his service. The future, bleak enough in all conscience, would be the bleaker for his death.

Dunbar: but that defeat had not seemed to him at the time an unalloyed disaster, for he had come by then to count Argyll and his faction amongst the chief of his enemies. He did not want to think of the bitter year he had spent in Scotland, but his brain could not be wrenched from it. There was no humiliation he had not been forced to bear before the Covenanters could be induced to crown him. He had done penances for himself, for his mother, for his father, until he had cried out, goaded beyond endurance: 'I think I must repent too that ever I was born!'

He remembered, upon his first coming into Scotland, how a poor woman, seeing him with Argyll beside him at Aberdeen, had shouted: 'God bless your Majesty and send you to your ain! but they on your left hand who helped to tak' aff your father's heid, if ye tak' na care, will tak' aff yours neist!'

His Chancellor ought to have heard that, he thought. Hyde had advised him steadily against trusting Argyll. None of the Cavalier party had wished him to embrace the Scottish plan. But the Queen, his mother, and all the Louvrians, had urged him to trust Argyll. Even the Engagers, who hated Argyll, had considered that in him lay the King's only hope of regaining his throne. He had allowed himself to be guided by them, for how could he sit still and dream out his life? Yet, in the end, that had been very much what Argyll had wanted him to do. Argyll wanted him for a figurehead, himself and his Covenant to rule Scotland. When he had visited the army, and Argyll had seen how popular he was growing with the soldiers, he had swept him off in a hurry. It was no part of Argyll's scheme to let the King make the army his own.

Argyll had forced him to part from his best friends. That had been known as the purging of his Court. The King's big mouth curled in a cynical smile as the recollection flitted through his head. A godly purging that could banish Hamilton, and leave almost alone amongst the gentlemen who had accompanied him from Holland the profligate Buckingham! The King had never known by what wiles Buckingham had insinuated himself into Argyll's good graces. It was possible that he had sold himself to Argyll with a promise to use his influence on the King. Argyll could not know that the sweet-tempered prince, who was always so docile, had learned to give his confidence to no man.

He had learned to swallow insults too, the petty as well as the great. He had never set much store by pomp, but until he set foot on Scottish soil he had not been called upon to deal with incivility to his person. He had soon discovered that there were no lengths to which the bigoted conceit of the Covenanting ministers would not carry them. He remembered, and could smile at the memory of his own astonishment, an incident that had occurred in the house of one of these ministers. When, upon his entering the parlour, the minister's wife had run to offer him a chair, 'My heart,' had said her austere spouse, 'he is a young man, and can help himself.'

Looking back, he knew that he should have realized by a dozen signs the trap the Scottish Commissioners had set for him when they came to Holland to invite him to go with them to Scotland. The stipulations that Rupert should not accompany him, and that Montrose should be commanded to lay down his arms would have been enough to warn anyone but a boy of twenty, pulled this way and that by conflicting counsels.

Montrose! As the name came into his brain, the King put up his hand across his eyes, as though to shut an unwelcome vision from his sight. 'I sent him warning!' he said, and started to hear his own voice breaking the silence of the wood.

His hand dropped, for no screen could shut out the vision of Montrose's calm, proud countenance, with the steady eyes that gazed so straitly into his.

But Montrose had had so many enemies; as many almost as Rupert, who was thought to possess a familiar spirit: it had seemed to be useless to risk all upon the chance of his prevailing against the Covenanters. But he had not meant to betray Montrose to Argyll. Argyll had sworn no hurt should befall him, and he himself had written to Montrose, twice, trying to explain his change of policy, and bidding him lay down his arms, and leave Scotland. It was not his fault the letters had been delayed, not his fault that Argyll had lied to him, and had delivered Montrose to a shameful death. And when the treachery had been accomplished, matters had been in too forward a train for him then to draw back. Too much had been at stake, and with Montrose dead there had seemed to be only Argyll left to whom he could look for help in his necessity. He had signed the Solemn League and Covenant, with not the smallest intention of fulfilling any one of its clauses; and those who had forced him to do it had known that he would never abide by it. But what none of them knew, least of all Argyll, was that one day he meant to have Argyll's head in exchange for Montrose's. He was not by nature a vengeful man, but even now, sitting in Spring Coppice, he renewed his resolve to have Argyll's head, if ever he should come to his crown.

A drop of rain, splashing on to his hand, which lay clenched upon his knee, recalled him to his surroundings. He looked up, and saw that it must have been raining for some while, for the leaves were thick above his head and the rain had only just begun to penetrate them.

He got up stiffly, for it was cold, and his limbs were

chilled. There was as yet no sign of Richard Penderel returning through the wood, no sound to be heard but the pattering of raindrops on the trees. He was quite alone, nor would anyone come to his call.

He began to walk up and down to warm himself, but his shoes hurt him, and his body cried out for rest, so he sat down again presently on the bank, choosing the most sheltered place he could find.

The noggen shirt he was wearing teased his skin unbearably; as he wriggled his shoulders he hoped that the clothes he had put on were not lousy. He did not think that he had been softly reared: his boyhood had been spent within sound and sight of war; he could not remember ever having had enough money for his needs; and latterly he had been put to such straits that he had even been obliged to borrow two hundred pounds to enable him to set sail for Scotland; but nothing in his experience had prepared him for the contingency he found himself in now. He had never sat in a wood, becoming slowly drenched with rain; he had never walked save for his own pleasure; nor had for his sole attendants a parcel of country-hinds. At the worst, there had been a house to call his own, servants to wait upon him, councillors to advise him, horses to ride, a bed to sleep on, and clean clothes to wear. The leather doublet Richard had brought him smelt of sweat, and the battered hat that was protecting his head from the rain was greasy and stained. He realized that he did not know where he was to rest that night, or where to find food, and for a few moments a feeling of helplessness, exaggerated by fatigue of body and mind, gripped him.

The sound, faint in the distance, of horses approaching along the lane jerked him from his mood of despair. He got up again, and moved cautiously towards the edge of the wood, taking cover behind a bush, through whose branches he was able to peep at the road.

The noise of the trotting hooves grew louder. In a few moments a troop of horse went by, riding steadily, apparently unconcerned with the presence of a possible fugitive in the wood. The King watched them till they drew out of sight, and then returned to his bank, to try to think what he ought to do next, and how make his way to London.

Presently he heard footsteps approaching through the wood, and, looking up, saw Richard Penderel coming back, with two other men following him.

He saw how anxiously they looked at him, and welcomed them with a smile, and a mild jest. 'Well, my new regiment of Guards? What news?'

Humphrey Penderel grinned appreciatively, but thought it proper to kneel to address the King. 'You may say it is good news, my liege.'

'I am right glad of it. Are you Humphrey the miller? Get up, man: my Guards don't kneel to me.'

'The news is not good,' interrupted Richard, with a rather severe look cast at his brother. 'Scarce an hour after your honour was gone from White-Ladies soldiers came into the village, asking if any had seen you. It was that made us late returning to you.'

'Yea, and I say it is good news, sith you were safely gone from the house, my liege,' asserted Humphrey.

A gleam of amusement lit the darkness of the King's eyes. 'Methinks you must be the wit of your family, friend Humphrey. Was it a troop of horse that came enquiring after me? I think I saw them but a short while ago, for a troop passed by the wood, riding northwards. As I judge, they were militia-men. They had not the look of soldiers.'

'It was a troop of horse,' Richard answered. 'They asked if any had seen your honour, but got no good by it. We told them —'

'We?' the King interjected.

Richard jerked his thumb towards his companions. 'Humphrey and Francis and me was there, my liege. We said there was a troop passed in the night, but whether your honour was amongst them we could not tell.'

He looked so wooden as he spoke that a laugh was drawn from the King. 'And what did they then, Dick?'

'They rode away,' replied Richard. 'Folk say as the Scotch lay at Tong last night, and are going north. Francis and me, we do think maybe the rebels will look for you amongst them.'

'Very like,' agreed the King. He glanced at Yates, who was standing at a little distance, worshipfully regarding him. 'Are you the man who led me to White-Ladies?' he asked. 'I thank you for it.'

Yates coloured to the ears, and moved his lips soundlessly.

'What is that you have in your hand?' enquired the King.

'It's a broom-hook, please your Majesty,' said Yates, shyly proffering it.

The King took it, and, finding it was less heavy than the wood-bill Richard had given him, asked if Yates would exchange it for the bill.

Richard, meanwhile, had been feeling with his hand the bank on which the King sat. He discovered it to be very sodden, which at once presented a new anxiety to his mind. He said nothing, however, and when the King asked him what had become of his friends, and whether my Lord Wilmot had got safe away, he lowered himself on to the bank beside Charles, and answered that the troop had ridden away in good time, and that my Lord Wilmot had been put in John Penderel's charge, who had it in mind to take him to the house of a very well-disposed man.

'Ay,' said Humphrey, 'but John would liefer care for your Majesty, that he would. He's as melancholy as a gibed cat, the noble gentleman. Besides, not a step will he budge without he has his horses and his servant go with him, as fine as a lord's bastard.'

'It's on account of his being a swag-bellied man,' said Yates thoughtfully. 'Such can't go afoot, not well, they can't.'

'I hope I may not be hanged before I see my Lord Wilmot again!' said the King, mentally treasuring up these remarks.

They did not understand that he was jesting, and looked gravely at him, evidently trying to find words with which to answer him. At last, Yates said very seriously: 'There's the three of us as'll hang first. Ay, and William too.'

A murmur of assent came from the other two. The King was touched, but answered with forced merriment: 'It's not hanging I fear, but drowning, good friends, if this rain keeps up.'

They could appreciate this, and grinned at him. Humphrey then nudged Francis, who muttered: 'It would come better from Richard, I was thinking.'

'Ay, it would,' Humphrey agreed, and nodded at his brother. 'You say it civil, as his honour ought to be spoke to.'

Richard drew a breath, and fixing his eyes on the King's face, blurted out: 'We'd like your honour to take the name of Will Jones, and to mend your speech, if your honour would be pleased to pardon us for saying of such a thing.'

'Why, with all my heart, so you tell me what you would have me do,' the King said.

'It's the way you talk,' explained Richard.

'The walk's not right neither,' added Humphrey. 'Anyone would know your honour was a King, no help for it. Francis and me, we'll be off to keep watch, and Richard'll learn your Majesty to speak the country-way.'

At the end of an hour he came back to report that all was yet well, and was at once called upon by the King to observe the progress he had made under Richard's teaching. But having heard the King utter some phrases in the dialect, and watched him walk a few steps, he sighed, and shook his head, and said that it would be best for him to travel by night.

'Alas!' said Charles, sinking down on to the bank again. 'I thought I was an apt pupil.'

'It's the way you hold yourself, so straight and easy,' explained Humphrey. 'Like as if you was a King and didn't care nobbut for nobody.'

'Like as if I was a King!' Charles repeated, dropping his head in his hands.

They stood looking at him in dismay. At length Richard ventured to say: 'Humphrey didn't mean to offend your honour, for all he spoke so free.'

'Nay, there's no offence,' the King said, with a mournful smile. 'Leave me alone awhile, good friends. I think I am too tired to profit by your teaching.'

The brothers went off together, leaving him seated under

the dripping trees. It was some time before Richard returned, but when he did come back it was with a blanket, which he spread on the bank for the King to sit upon, telling him it came from Yates's house.

The King thanked him, and bade him stay awhile, for he had questions to ask of him. Richard sat down on the bank, remarking as he did so, that it was not raining outside the wood.

'I begin to think I was born under an unlucky star,' said the King ruefully.

'It's well for you it does rain here, my liege,' replied Richard. 'They as is looking for you won't think to come poking and prying in the wood.'

'Are they searching for me already?'

'Ay, a few red-coats, but they don't know for sure you was ever in these parts. It's only that we be known Catholics, and Mr Giffard living here, and the Scotch passing so close, that sets them to suspicioning you might be a-laying up somewheres at hand.'

'I must get away from here,' the King said, half to himself. He saw that Richard had no suggestions to offer, but merely sat waiting humbly to be told his pleasure, and began to ask him a number of questions about the persons of quality whose houses were situated on the way to London.

It soon became plain that Richard knew nothing of the gentry outside his own immediate ken. He was quite unable to tell the King of any gentleman or yeoman who would be willing to house him in Staffordshire, and Charles, who was himself unacquainted with the district, sat silent for a moment, frowning. He knew the west country well, having lived there for some time in command of his father's western forces, but rack his brain as he might he could not call to mind any loyal gentleman living on the route to London.

'Is Mr Giffard still at White-Ladies?' he asked abruptly.

Richard shook his head. The King's easy temper was jarred for an instant by the sight of his stolidity. 'Then what the pox am I to do?' he demanded, his big underlip pouting a little.

Again Richard shook his head, but with such a look of apology in his face that the King choked down his ill-humour, and said: 'I must think on this.'

Richard, never talkative, said nothing, but sat gazing before him, chewing a blade of grass.

The sound of someone approaching through the wood presently brought Richard's head round, and an alert look into his eyes. He laid a warning hand on the King's arm, and got up to go and scout. The King was about to plunge farther into the wood when Richard stopped him. 'All's well, my liege. It's my sister Yates come with a mess for your honour to stay your stomach on.'

A little startled, profoundly mistrusting the ability of a woman to keep a secret, the King waited for Mrs Yates to appear, saying when she did: 'Good-morrow, good-wife. Can you be faithful to a distressed Cavalier?'

It was evident from the depth of the curtsey which she dropped, and the breathless note in her voice, that she was aware of his identity. 'Yes, master, I will die sooner than betray you,' she said very earnestly, and held out her basket to him.

He took it, and uncovering it, found that it contained something in a black earthen cup. He looked up, saying with a smile that set her heart fluttering: 'Is it milk and apples? I love it well!'

'Nay, alack, there are no apples, master. It is naught but a mess of butter and milk and eggs, not what your gracious Majesty is used to eat.'

The King set the basket down, and lifted the cup and a pewter spoon out of it, and tasted the concoction. 'It's very good,' he told Mrs Yates. He ate it nearly all, but gave the cup to Richard when he had taken the edge off his hunger, and invited him to finish it.

The rain continued. When Mrs Yates had gone, the King was left alone for some time, but presently Richard came back, and, after a little while, Humphrey and George. Once Richard asked him if he would not like to sleep for a while, wrapped in the blanket, but although the King's limbs ached, and his body felt strangely heavy, he could not sleep.

If he closed his eyes, unquiet pictures began at once to drift across his lids: faces, and battle scenes, and the monotonous jog-trot of horses.

Midway through the interminable day, unable to think of any safe way of reaching London, he decided to cross the Severn into Wales. There he had friends, and from Swansea, or some other sea-town, he might, he thought, find a vessel bound for France.

Richard, informed of this change in the King's plans, seemed to approve of it, and at once offered to conduct him to Madeley, where, he said, a very honest gentleman called Wolfe lived, and could be counted on to serve him.

The decision made, the King seemed to grow more cheerful, but his face, now that the grime had been washed away by the rain, looked so pale and drawn, that after a short consultation together, the brothers begged that he would go with them to Richard's home as soon as it could be considered safe for him to leave the wood, there to repose and refresh himself for a while before setting out on the nine-mile walk to Madeley. He agreed to it, and accordingly, at a little after five o'clock, all three of the brothers, with Francis Yates with them, escorted him to Hobbal Grange, which was about a mile from Spring Coppice, beyond White-Ladies.

The rain had stopped by this time, but a lowering sky gave no promise of a clear night to come. As they trudged along, sometimes over fields, and sometimes down narrow, deserted lanes, Richard and Humphrey, walking one on either side of the King, kept their watchful eyes on him, and from time to time reminded him to slouch his shoulders more, or to hold his head lower. Yates and George Penderel walked ahead to spy out the land, but no one was encountered during the short journey, and Hobbal Grange was reached without any other misfortune than the continual chafing of the King's feet in Richard's rough shoes.

Hobbal Grange was a cottage, situated three quarters of a mile south of the road from Tong to Brewood, and was approached by a lane little better than a cart-track. When Richard ushered the King into it, Charles stood for a moment on the threshold blinking in the light of the tallow candles, and looking curiously about him. The door opened immediately into a big kitchen, which seemed to be the only living-room the cottage possessed. A sharp-featured woman was bending over the open fire. She turned, as the King entered, and dropped him a rather perfunctory curtsey, looking narrowly at him as she did so. A little girl with straight, fair hair gathered into a cap, peeped from behind her skirts, a finger in her mouth. The King smiled at her, saying to Richard: 'Is the little maiden yours?'

'Ay, so please your honour,' replied Richard, gratified. 'Make your curtsey, Nan! And this is my wife, who is as glad as I be to serve your honour.'

A minatory note sounded in his voice. Mrs Penderel curtseyed again, but with her eyes cast down, and a forbidding look about her compressed lips.

The kitchen was not furnished with chairs, but the King pulled up a joint-stool to the fire, and sat down to warm himself, casting his hat on the floor beside him. Moisture began to steam from his clothes; he held his long, beautiful hands to the blaze, an action which drew from Mrs Penderel a muttered remark that the sight of them would surely betray him.

Richard told her sharply to hold her peace, and to bestir herself to provide supper for the visitor.

'There's naught but bacon and some eggs in the house, as I told you an hour agone,' she said. She looked sullenly at Humphrey and George, and Francis Yates, and added: 'Do you look to me to get food for them hungry good-for-naughts as well? I wonder your sister Nell would let her man go begging to a poor woman's house for his supper!'

'No!' Richard said, nipping her arm in his hand, and giving it a shake. 'For the King, woman!'

She said under her breath: 'You will ruin us by this! I'll be bound there's them as would give you a fortune for news —'

She stopped, growing rather white, for the look in Richard's eyes frightened her. He was breathing rather hard through his nose; she was afraid he would strike her, and

57

said quickly: 'I will get supper for him.'

She pulled her arm out of Richard's hold, and turned to find the King's heavy-lidded eyes fixed upon her. She coloured, and said defensively: 'I'm sure it's not me would be wishing harm to your honour, but we be poor folks, and if aught should befall my goodman I know not what must become of me and the innocent childer.'

'Get supper!' Richard growled, and said apologetically to the King: 'Never heed her, master! She is a poor, foolish creature. Your honour is safe in my house.'

'I do not doubt it,' the King said. He bent to unfasten the latchets of his shoes. 'What can be done to make these shoes of yours less discomfortable to my stupid feet?'

Seeing him fumbling unhandily at the latchets, Francis Yates ran forward, and knelt to help him. Nan Penderel's eyes widened to see her uncle drawing the shoes from the strange visitor's feet, and she uplifted her voice in a wondering question: 'Can that man not take his shoon off?'

A gleam shot into the King's eyes; he held out his hand to her invitingly. 'Nay, sweetheart, that is a home-question! I have been very ill-taught indeed.'

She drew nearer. 'Who be you?' she asked. 'I don't know you.'

'I am one Will Jones, a wood-cutter come in search of work in these parts,' responded the King, setting her upon his knee. 'Do you think any would hire me?'

She shook her head, saying with a quaint air of wisdom: 'These be very sickly times. There's no work for honest men. Why do you wear my father's jump-coat?'

'Faith, because I have no other, Mistress Sharp-Eyes!'

'You must needs be a very poor man,' she said.

'Yes, a very poor man,' he answered, sighing.

She tucked her little hand into his. 'Don't be sad. My father will have a care to you,' she told him.

'I never knew Nan so hang upon a stranger!' Richard said, a slow smile curving his mouth. 'But she must not tease your honour.'

'Let us be; we are in a fair way to a comfortable understanding,' replied the King.

Yates rose from his knees, saying: 'Nan will be a proud woman all her life to remember this day.'

'If she live to remember it!' muttered Mrs Penderel over her cooking-pan. She glanced over her shoulder at the shoes Yates was holding, and said grudgingly: 'If they irk his honour, put a bit of white paper in them, and I warrant he shall go the easier for it.'

By the time this advice had been followed, and the shoes squeezed again on to the King's feet, a supper of bacon and eggs was ready. The King commanded Richard to sit down with him at the table, and to share the meal, himself falling to with a gusto that made Nan open her eyes still wider.

'Poor Will Jones!' she said commiseratingly. 'Are you so hungry?'

'Yea, I have a very good stomach,' the King replied.

'I warrant you!' said his hostess, under her breath, watching the next day's provisions for her family disappear into his mouth.

When he had eaten and drunk, the King asked Richard to tell him more of the household for which he was bound, and, learning that Mr Wolfe was a Royalist, with sons who had all of them been engaged in the late Civil Wars, professed himself very well satisfied to entrust his person to his care. But, to their dismay, he would not permit either of the two other brothers, or Francis Yates, to go along with him to Madeley, saying that it was unnecessary, and would place their lives in needless jeopardy. They were quite taken aback, having meant to go with him as a bodyguard, but though he thanked them, they saw that he was obstinate in his resolve to take only Richard with him.

It was Yates who bethought himself of a possible need, and asked the King if he had money in his pockets.

'Money?' the King repeated. 'Yes – why, no! I had only gold pieces, and gave them to my servants.'

'If your Majesty would be pleased to accept of what I have, you are very welcome,' Yates said, pulling his purse out of the breast of his doublet. 'It was in my mind you had not as much as a groat upon you, seeing as Richard said you bestowed it all away, so I made bold to bring what I have.'

He shook his purse out into his cupped hand, and carefully spread a number of silver coins upon the table. His savings amounted to thirty shillings, which he seemed quite content the King should pocket. When the King took only ten of them, bidding him put the rest up, and keep it safe, he coloured, and said: 'I would like best your gracious Majesty would take it. It is very little.'

'I think it is more than was ever offered me before, since it is your all,' the King said. 'I am poor in thanks, friend, but I shall not forget.'

Richard, who had drawn back the shutters a little way to look out, closed them again, saying that it was now dark enough for them to venture forth. The King bestowed Francis Yates's money in his pocket, and replied that he was ready to go; but before he started, Humphrey, who had left the kitchen some few minutes earlier, came back into it, with a stout old dame leaning on his arm, and peering eagerly about her out of a pair of shrewd, bright eyes.

'Where is he?' she demanded. 'Let me but look upon him once, and bless myself to think of my sons being so singled out!'

'It's our mother, sir,' Richard explained. 'She is an honest woman your honour may be pleased to trust. Mother, here is the King.'

She stood for an instant, holding on to Humphrey's arm, and gazing with a slowly dawning smile of delight upon the King's tall figure. His shorn head almost touched the oak beam under which he stood. Dame Penderel let go Humphrey's arm to cast up both hands. 'Eh, the great fine lad that he is!' she exclaimed. 'He'll be as big as my Will, every inch! Eh, my liege, it's the happy day that sees your Majesty in my house! Let an old woman look into your face, master, for I once saw your royal father, of blessed memory, and I shall die a happy woman to have seen your fair face beside!'

A laugh sprang to the King's lips. He said: 'With all my heart, good mother, but I fear my face will grieve you, for I never yet heard any call it fair!' He moved towards her, and took her hand, and led her to the settle by the fire, and made her sit down upon it, and himself dropped gracefully on his knee before her, looking up at her with merriment dancing in his eyes.

She put out a gnarled hand, as though she would have laid it on his head, and then drew it back. 'Eh, my liege, what have they done to your bonny curls?' she asked him.

'Why, they cut them off, mother, that I might not be known.'

'I would I might have had one to keep!' she said. 'The good-year! the fine shoulders of you, and your royal father the little dainty prince that he was! Welladay! that I should have lived to be so honoured!' She ventured to put her hand on his shoulder, smiling a little tremulously. 'I bless God that He has allowed my sons to be the instruments of your Majesty's deliverance,' she said. 'I am the proud woman, yea, and they are proud men, to have so great a trust reposed in them. If they should fail you, my liege, they be no sons of mine.'

'Good mother, if all my subjects were as honest as your sons I had had no need to fight for my kingdom,' he replied. 'I know not how I can ever redeem the debt I stand in to you all, but here is Charles Stewart his pledge that redeem it he will.' He kissed her cheek as he spoke, and rose up from his knee.

'My liege,' she said, with tears dimming her sight, 'you have warmed this old heart of mine. God bless you and keep you safe!'

'Master, it is time and more that we budged,' Richard said. 'We have nine miles to go, and the night very dark.'

'I am ready,' the King answered, and put the battered hat on his head again, and picked up Yates's broom-hook. The three men whom he would not allow to accompany him knelt to kiss his hand, and bid him God-speed. Richard opened the door, and after looking cautiously up and down the lane, nodded to the King to pass out into the darkness.

## CHAPTER IV

## 'WHO GOES THERE?'

MADELEY was situated east of the Severn, and could be most easily reached from Hobbal Grange by the highway leading through Tong and Shifnal, but as Richard Penderel knew that some of the rebel troops were quartered in both these places he proposed to the King that they should make their way across the fields, and down the less frequented lanes with which the country was intersected. The King agreed to it, but it was not long before he was regretting his complaisance. At all times unused to rough walking, he found the journey over meadows and through coppices difficult. He was continually missing his foothold in the dark, or stumbling over a tree-root, or a mole-hill, and at every step the tightness of the shoes he wore caused him real pain. A little in advance of him, Richard plodded on, with his tireless, graceless gait, sometimes remembering to turn, and help the King through a hedge, or over a deep-cut ditch, but often forgetting that the King was not a country-born fellow, nor one whose body had been hardened from childhood to such exertions.

Charles made no complaint; he was, in fact, a little out of patience with himself for blundering so often, and for feeling so acutely the discomforts of ill-fitting shoes, and a rough shirt. Once he was compelled to call to his guide not to go so fast, for he had fallen behind and was in danger of losing Richard altogether; but when Richard stopped, and came back to lead him more carefully, he managed to crack a jest at his own expense.

Richard's dread of encountering some late wayfarer made him choose to go over the open country, even when a track offered. To the King, it seemed as though he selected the most difficult route he could find. Sometimes brambles would claw at his coat, or throw out long prickly stems across the path to entangle his feet, and tear holes in his stockings; at others, he would find himself walking into a tree that loomed up suddenly before him, or splashing ankle-deep through a puddle of muddy water. Once his hand brushed a clump of nettles, and the smart and itch of it was an added ill so petty and yet so maddening that he swore aloud.

Richard hushed him quickly, warning him that they were passing close by a cottage.

'The devil take the cottage and all inside it!' said the King savagely, licking the back of his smarting hand. 'I have put my hand into accursed bed of nettles!'

It was plain that Richard thought this a trivial matter. He said soothingly: 'The itch will soon go. If there were light enough, I would find a dock-leaf for your honour to rub on you. 'Tis wonderful how a dock-leaf eases nettle-sting.'

This remark exasperated the King, but just as he was about to return an acid answer, the humour of the situation struck him, and he began to laugh. Richard, forgetting the respect due to Royalty, grabbed his arm, and gave it a little shake. 'Give over, give over! Ye will have the neighbours out on us, as sure as check, my liege!'

They went on for another mile. The King found nothing more to laugh at, but had instead some trouble to keep himself from groaning at the pain of his cramped and blistered feet. He had never been so tired in his life; his head swam, and sometimes seemed to be a long way from his body, so that he walked uncertainly; his hat felt like an iron band, tightening about his forehead, and when he shifted it he got no easement thereby. He set his teeth, and limped on, but every step hurt him, and at last he was unable to endure it any longer, and called to Richard to halt.

Richard stopped at once, and turned to find that the King had sat down on the damp ground. He knelt beside him, anxiously asking if he were ill, or had hurt himself.

'No,' Charles said faintly. 'If you have a knife, give it to me!'

'A knife?' repeated Richard stupidly.

'Yes, a knife!'

'What would your honour want with a knife?' Richard asked, fearing for a distorted moment that the King was out of his senses.

'To slit these shoes, fool!'

Relieved, Richard put a hand into his pocket, and produced a jack-knife, which he gave to the King. Charles pulled off his shoes, and slashed them across and across. It cost him a good deal of pain to put them on again, but he managed to do it, gripping his underlip between his teeth as he pushed his raw heels down into them. He gave the knife back to Richard, and struggled up again, saying with an attempt at cheerfulness: 'Now I have room to move my poor toes. Lead on, Trusty Dick!'

'I do fear it be hard going for your honour,' Richard said, concerned for his evident exhaustion. 'You'll be glad of a bed at Mr Wolfe's, I warrant.'

'I shall indeed,' Charles replied.

They went on, the slits in the King's shoes at first affording his swollen feet some relief, but soon causing him a new pain, since they let in mud and small sharp stones.

After an interminable trudge up hill and down dale, during which Richard was occasionally at a puzzle to find the way, they came to a rough lane, which Richard recognized as a track joining the highway to Madeley at Evelith Mill. The hour was by this time far enough advanced for him no longer to fear meeting anyone on the road. For his own part, he would have preferred to have continued across country, but he thought the King would find it easier to walk along the highway, pitted with holes though it was, and so helped him over a hedge into the lane, telling him, to encourage him, that they had only five more miles to go.

The King did not answer him. He seemed to himself to be plodding through a nightmare from which he must soon awake. He was so remote from reality that when his struggling brain asserted, *I am Charles Stewart, King of England*, the phrase conveyed no meaning to him. It was a mere string of foolish words which drummed irritatingly in his head. From time to time, he made an effort to drag his mind from the only realities of his aching body, and lacerated feet, and to think of the future; but again his brain betrayed him, reiterating dully, *I must get me to France*, which seemed as wildly impossible a thought as that this weary frame could belong to that same Charles Stewart who had led an army into battle on Wednesday, the third day of September, in the Year of Our Lord, One Thousand Six Hundred and Fifty-one.

He tried to think how long ago that had been, and in the end was forced to ask Richard what day of the week it now was. When Richard replied that it was Thursday, he said fretfully that Richard was mistaken, but after he had thought it over for a while, he realized that Richard was right, and that it was indeed only twenty-four hours since he had been riding through the night with Wilmot and Talbot beside him, and Buckingham close behind, making some joke about an ox for the King's supper.

Richard, who was now walking beside him, suddenly touched his arm, and pointed ahead. A new moon, which had just risen, shone in a bare patch of sky like a sliver of silver, but it was not that which had attracted Richard's attention.

At the foot of the hill they were descending, the dark hulk of a building could be seen. A light shone through the chinks of the shutters on the ground floor, and the sound of voices could faintly be heard, mingled with the purling of the mill-stream.

'Go softly, my liege,' Richard whispered. 'Seemingly the miller has company. But so late as it is — Mind, master, if we come upon any stranger, do you stay mumchance!'

They trod on as quietly as they could down the hill to the wooden bridge across the stream at its foot. A gate gave access to the bridge; it scrooped harshly on its hinges as Richard pulled it open, and made him curse under his breath. He let it go, not daring to risk a second scroop as he shut it, but it was set at a slight angle, and swung to behind him with a clap that brought the miller out of his house, calling in a deep bass voice: 'Who goes there?'

Richard shouted over his shoulder: 'Friends, homeward bound!'

'If you be friends, stand and show yourselves!' commanded the miller, advancing towards the bridge.

Richard seized the King's hand, whispering to him, 'Run!' and set off as fast as he could up the lane on the farther side of the bridge. The sound of heavy-footed pursuit drove them on, splashing through deep puddles, and stumbling over the wheel-ruts, until the King, tearing his hand away, gasped: 'Over the hedge!' and himself, summoning all his remaining strength for the effort, leaped over the low hedge into a ditch on the other side, and lay prone there.

Richard followed suit, and for some minutes they lay recovering their breath, and listening for sounds of the miller's approach. When it became apparent that he had abandoned the chase, and gone back into his house, Richard became urgent with the King to continue their journey.

'I had rather you buried me where I lie,' Charles sighed, between jesting and earnest. 'I can go no farther.'

Richard sought his hand again, and tried to pull him up. 'Nay, nay, master, never say such foolishness! Come now, there's only a little way to go, and you may rest your fill.'

The King gave a groan, but struggled to his feet. The danger they had run into at Evelith Mill made Richard afraid to adventure farther along the highway. He again took to the fields, but he did not realize how spent the King was, and was presently aghast to see him sink down upon the ground, half-fainting. It was only with difficulty that he persuaded him to struggle on a little farther, promising him better going in just a few more minutes.

The rest of the journey was only accomplished thanks to Richard's dogged persistence. It was no longer a matter of King and subject between them. To Richard, the King had become just an exhausted young man whom by hook or by crook he was determined to bring to safe shelter. When he collapsed, saying that he cared nothing for his fate if only he might lie still, Richard coaxed him to his feet with assurances that they had only a few hundred yards still to cover; when he commanded Richard to leave him, Richard rated him for folly, and laughed to scorn his despair of ever making his way to France. The preservation of the King's person was to Richard a matter of such paramount importance that he was unable to comprehend the crushing sense of defeat which made Charles think himself better dead than wearing out his life in exile. Dimly he could perceive that a deeper agony than the pain of lacerated feet had the King in its grip; but since he could not comfort a grief he did not understand, all that was left for him to do was to care for the King's body.

It was midnight when at last they reached Madeley, and came in sight of Mr Wolfe's house, an old mansion standing beside the road through the town, and surrounded on three sides by fields, and great timber-barns.

The King, who had limped the last mile in silence, roused himself upon Richard's informing him that they had reached their goal, and bade Richard leave him in the field where they now stood, and go on alone to the house. Richard looked rather doubtfully at him, but Charles sat down in the lee of a hedge, saying wearily: 'You must discover first whether he is willing to receive so dangerous a guest in his house. Ask him if he will give shelter to a distressed Cavalier, a fugitive from Worcester. I will await you here.'

It seemed incredible to Richard that any loyal Englishman could be unwilling to shelter his King, but he had discovered by this time that there was a streak of obstinacy in Charles, so he did not argue the matter, but went off obediently to rouse the household.

All was in darkness, but the door was opened presently, in answer to his repeated knocking, by a thin woman with a cap tied under her chin, and a shawl huddled over her night-gown. She looked frightened, and her weak, kind eyes started at Richard in the light of the guttering candle she held in her hand.

He asked her respectfully to rouse Mr Wolfe, and to inform him that an honest servant of the King was wishful to see him.

The candle shook in her hold. She said in a whisper: 'I

am his daughter. Oh, do you bring news of my brother?'

'Nay, I know naught of him, mistress. I mun see Mr Wolfe.'

She said rather helplessly: 'He is abed.'

'I mun see him,' Richard repeated.

She let him come into the house, and softly closed the door behind him. 'I will rouse him. It is not ill news?'

'Nay.'

'Stay here,' she told him, and went away up the stairs like a troubled ghost.

In a few minutes, Richard saw a wavering light approaching down the stairs. An old gentleman with silvered locks came down, and held his candle up the better to scrutinize Richard.

'Who are you, fellow?' he demanded in a shrill whisper. 'I don't know you. Why do you come to this house at such an hour?'

'I be wishful to know whether your honour will give shelter to a distressed Cavalier,' replied Richard, painstakingly reciting his lesson. 'It's a gentleman as is escaping from Worcester fight,' he added.

Mr Wolfe gave a start that sent some of the wax from his candle spilling on to the floor. 'No!' he said sharply. 'Do you not know that I have a son even now clapped up in Shrewsbury prison? Take him to some other house!'

'There bain't no other house, master,' said Richard stolidly.

'It's nothing to me! It's too dangerous a matter to harbour anybody that's known. I'll venture my neck for no one unless it be the King himself!'

Richard looked at him, a bovine expression in his eyes, but with his brain slowly working behind them. 'Well, it is the King,' he said at last.

For a moment Wolfe stared at him, then he said: 'You lie, fellow!'

Richard shook his head.

Wolfe clutched at the baluster with one thin hand. 'The King himself? Where?'

Richard jerked his thumb over his shoulder.

'God, what ill wind blew him here?' Wolfe muttered. He came totteringly down the last stairs, and held the candle close up to Richard's face. 'Who are you? How came the King in your charge?'

'I'm Richard Penderel, master, from Hobbal Grange, over to Tong Parish.'

'Where is his Majesty?'

'Out yonder, in the orchard. He be wishful to pass into Wales.'

'Impossible!' Wolfe ejaculated. He stood biting his nails, while Richard watched him, a hint of scorn in his eyes. He looked up at last, and said testily: 'What do you wait for, clod? Bring his Majesty in! But softly, mind! I will have no one know he has been here!'

Richard gave him another of his long, ruminative looks, and then departed to find the King.

Charles was sitting where he had left him, leaning his head in his hand. When he heard Richard's step and presently saw his sturdy figure approaching in the moonlight, he straightened himself with a sigh, and said as soon as Richard came up to him. 'Well? Is he willing to shelter me?'

'Ay, he'll do it,' Richard answered. 'I did think him a better man, for sure, but there's no helping that.'

'Did you say what I bade you?' asked the King.

'Ay, I said it, but 'twarn't no manner of use. "I'll not risk my neck for anyone," he says, "save it be the King himself." So I up and told him it was you.'

'Told him that? Without leave?' Charles exclaimed. 'You had no right to do so! If that is the mind the man is in, I would not for the world have had him know my whereabouts!'

Richard was quite unmoved by this. He said reasonably: 'Seems I had to tell him. You mun get some rest, master, whether or no. Don't you be frumping at me: the old gentleman won't betray your honour, when all's said.'

The King got to his feet, saying fatalistically: 'What's done is done. In truth, I care very little what may become of me.'

'When you've had your sleep out, you'll maybe think different, my liege,' replied Richard.

By the time they reached the house, both Mr Wolfe and his daughter had partially dressed themselves, and were awaiting them in the hall. As soon as Richard knocked, Wolfe opened the door, and bowed punctiliously, saying in his prim, rather chilly way: 'I am sorry to see your Majesty here in such guise.'

'Oddsfish, you cannot be sorrier than I am!' said the King, his unquenchable humour rearing up its head for an instant.

He stepped over the threshold, and stood blinking his eyelids in the sudden candlelight. Ann Wolfe, in the very act of dropping a deep curtsey, could not forbear uttering a little scream at the appearance he presented. His ill-fitting clothes were splashed with mud, and stained with sweat; his torn shoes squelched moisture on to the paved floor; and his hat looked more fit for a scarecrow than a man. He pulled it off as she stared at him, a hand pressed to her mouth, and with a little sigh pushed the damp ringlets back from his brow. His eyes, which were bloodshot, and heavy with weariness, alighted on her. A faint twinkle came into them; he said: 'I must be a sight to frighten honest maids out of their wits.'

'Oh, sir! That your sacred Majesty should be put to such shifts!' she faltered.

Her father, who had been casting uneasy glances up the well of the staircase, intervened to say: 'We must not talk aloud here. If the servants were to waken and hear, we are undone! No one must know of your Majesty's arrival. Why, the town swarms with rebels! I know not what false counsel brought you here, sire, but I am very sorry for it. You have no more loyal subject than myself, yet there is nothing I can do to assist you. I am continually watched, and spied upon, and one of my sons is even now a prisoner at Shrewsbury. I daily look for news of his release, but if this were to become known I know not what might be his fate!'

'Oh hush, dear sir!' his daughter begged, pitifully watching the King, who was leaning on the carved back of a chair, an expression of ironic amusement in his drawn face. 'His

Majesty is forespent. Come into the parlour, sir! Indeed, indeed you are safe in this house!'

She caught up one of the branches of candles she had kindled, and led the way into a comfortable apartment in the front of the house.

As the King sank down into the chair she set for him, she looked shrewdly at him and exclaimed: 'Have you supped, sir? Would your Majesty be pleased to partake of anything? Alas, that we are all unprepared for this great honour! But there are some slices of cold meat in the larder, if you would condescend to such simple fare.'

The King threw her a grateful smile. 'Lady, I will be your bedesman all the days of my life for a plate of that cold meat.'

'If only the fire be still burning, I could toss up a fricassy for your Majesty!' she said. 'I will go at once, sir.'

Wolfe said quickly: 'No, no, Ann, cook nothing! The servants must discover it, and if they get wind of this night's work I cannot answer for the consequences. Bring in the meat, and some sack, and do it speedily, girl, do you hear me?'

'And for my faithful servant here, if you please,' said the King.

She withdrew, promising to be back in a very few minutes. Her father said earnestly: 'I would not have your Majesty think me unwilling to serve you. I will do all that lies in my poor power, but the best advice I may humbly give you is that you begone from these parts as speedily as you may.'

'Rest you, sir, I'll not let them take me in your house,' said the King. 'As soon as it may be safe to do so, I mean to go into Wales.'

'Sir, it is impossible! There is a guard set upon the bridge, and every ford is so strictly watched a mouse might not slip past unobserved!'

The King was silent for a moment, his underlip pouting a little. Then he gave a great yawn, and said sleepily: 'Odds-fish, then I suppose they will have my head at last! But not until I have had some rest. Is there any place hereabouts where I may lie hid?'

'Sir, you must know that I should count it an honour to give up my bed to your Majesty! For your own sake I dare not do it, no, nor let you remain under my roof! At any time the rebels may choose to search the place. There is only one thing I can think of, and God knows it is dangerous enough! I have a barn, full of hay, wherein your Majesty might lie till nightfall. I believe none would think to look for you there.'

'It likes me very well,' replied the King.

Richard, who had been standing behind his chair, now came round to kneel before the King, saying in his blunt way: 'We mun go back to Boscobel, my liege. Brother William has a very safe hiding-place, ay, and I warrant he will be right fain to serve you!'

The King looked down at him with a smile. 'Trusty Dick! Have you not yet had your fill of this grievous burden?'

'Nay, that's foolish talk, master. I'll lead your honour safe to Boscobel as soon as you have rested.'

'Richard, my feet will never carry me as far.'

'Yes, master, they shall do so,' Richard said stoutly.

Mrs Ann came back just then with cold meat and sack, which she set upon the table before the King. He thanked her, and beckoned to Richard to come and eat his share. Wolfe could not forbear saying in a shocked tone: 'The fellow may eat in the kitchen. Your Majesty will not have him sit down with you!'

The King looked up, with his mouth full of meat, a sardonic gleam in his eyes. 'You are out, sir. He shall sit at table with me.'

'As your Majesty pleases,' Wolfe said, with a stiff little bow.

He waited, fidgeting about the room, and listening from time to time for any sound from above-stairs, while the King and Richard ate and drank their fill. He was so anxious to convey them to the safety of his barn that he hardly gave the King time to set down his empty tankard before urging him to make haste out of the house. He bade his daughter fetch a lantern, and, with this in his hand, led his guests out into the yard by a back-door, and across it to one of the great barns they had seen from the field.

Inside, the barn smelt sweet with the scent of hay; a hen clucked sleepily from a nest in one corner; and a rat scuttered across the floor almost under their feet.

A bed was made for the King in the hay at the back of the barn. He lowered himself into it, murmuring that he would need no Venice treacle to send him to sleep. Richard spread an armful of hay over him, and stretched himself alongside. Mr Wolfe, after holding up the lantern to assure himself that neither man was visible, went away, shutting the door behind him.

'I do be sorry I brought your honour to this place,' Richard said.

'Richard, I am asleep,' responded the King drowsily.

In ten minutes this statement became true. Worn out with the exertions and the anxieties of the past two days and nights, the King sank fathoms deep into the sleep of exhaustion. Throughout the long day he continued so, yet Richard, dozing and waking beside him, could not think that the sleep refreshed him, for it was restless, accompanied by the twitching of limbs, and ugly dreams which made Charles mutter, and sometimes call out. Once, Richard was forced to wake him, for fear that his dreaming voice should betray him. The King stirred, and opened his eyes, murmuring the name of one of his Gentlemen. When the film of sleep cleared a little, he started up on his elbow, bewildered, and half-thinking himself in his bed at Worcester. The hay tickling his hand made him blink stupidly, but his eyes alighted on Richard's grave face, and he remembered where he was. 'What is it?' he whispered.

'Nay, my liege, you called out so loud in your sleep I was bound to waken you. 'Tis naught.'

'I have had bad dreams,' the King said, pressing his hands to his eyes. 'What o'clock is it?'

Richard shook his head. ''Tis full day, that's all I know, master.'

The King lay down again, and for a little while lay thinking of his future. It had been agreed at Hobbal Grange, on the previous evening, that word of his resolve to escape into Wales should be carried by one or other of the Penderels to Lord Wilmot; and it occurred to him now that he might by this time have lost touch with the sole friend left to him, for he had bidden the Penderels give a message to Wilmot that he was to save himself. His only course, now that his plan of crossing into Wales had miscarried, seemed to be to return to the neighbourhood of White-Ladies, as Richard proposed; and to try from there to make his way, either to London, according to his original scheme, or to Bristol, where he had a good hope of finding a vessel bound for France. Either town seemed to his weary brain almost impossible to reach, and as he lay looking with half-closed eyes at the rafters high above him, the harsh lines running downwards from his jutting nose to his mouth grew more clearly marked, and a sound between a sigh and a groan escaped him.

It brought Richard up on his elbow at once, concern in his face. 'My liege?'

'It's nothing,' Charles answered. 'Only my troubles weighing upon me.'

Richard, to whom Boscobel was a goal, not a mere stage in a journey, thought he was dreading the nine-mile walk and said: 'When your honour has slept again and eaten, you'll not care a button for the trudge, I warrant you.'

'I hope you may be right,' Charles said.

''Deed and I be so. Why, when all's said, it's naught! If you had been reared right, you would do it twice over in a night, my liege, and reckon naught to it.'

'Alack that I was reared so ill, then!' said the King.

The day wore on, the King sleeping and waking by turns. In the early afternoon, an elderly lady with a basket over her arm slipped into the barn, and, after looking back into the yard to be sure that no one was watching her, began to climb over the piled hay towards the corner where the King lay, whispering rather breathlessly as she came: 'Sire, Sire!'

''Tis the old dame, Mistress Wolfe herself,' muttered Richard in the King's ear.

Charles sat up, brushing the hay from his person. As

74

soon as she set eyes on him, Mrs Wolfe went down upon her knees. 'Alas to see your Majesty thus! Oh sir, forgive the harsh necessity that will not let me receive you into my house as I should. Indeed, indeed I dare not for my life!'

'Why, how is this?' Charles said. 'I assure you I do very well where I am.'

She began to spread a napkin on the hay and to lift out of her basket pasties, white bread, and a stone-bottle of wine, sealed with black wax. While the King ate and drank, she continued kneeling beside him, alternately bewailing his hard lot, and begging to know how she might help him. Since there was no way in which she could help him, he found her a little tiresome, but answered with great patience. At last, observing the whiteness of his hands, she exclaimed that that fault at least could be remedied, and promised to make a decoction of walnut leaves and water to stain his skin to a reechy complexion.

Later in the afternoon, her husband visited the barn, with a soldierly-looking man at his heels, who proved to be his lately imprisoned son, come home that very day upon parole from Shrewsbury. He seemed as though he would have been very glad to have helped the King, but as he was confined to a five-mile radius of his home there was no assistance he could render him. He was greatly shocked at the miserable clothing the King wore, and at the condition of his shoes; but being a slighter, smaller man, nothing in the way of a change of raiment that he could offer him would fit the King.

When darkness fell, he fetched the King out of the barn, and took him into the house, Mrs Wolfe having sent the servants out upon some pretext or another. Supper was laid before Charles, and when he had eaten, Mrs Wolfe found a pair of long white stirrup-stockings to put on over the torn pair he was wearing, and stained his face and hands with walnut-juice, telling him he need not fear to wash his skin, for the stain would not soon wear off.

While this was doing, Mr Wolfe kept watch, obviously, from the starts he gave at every unexpected sound, and his frequent glances towards the clock, dreading lest the servants should return before their time, or some late visitor arrive and discover the King under his roof. As soon as it could be thought safe, he conducted the King out of the house by the back way and took leave of him, and then, hardly waiting until Charles and Richard were out of sight, hurried back to see that no trace of the visit should be left.

The King was a good deal refreshed by his long sleep, and the food he had eaten, but his feet were if anything more painful than before, and covered with blisters. He could not help limping, but he made no complaint, and invariably answered Richard very cheerfully whenever he spoke to him.

They did not talk much, both being by nature taciturn, and the King just now weighed down by the burden of thoughts which Richard could not comprehend. He allowed Richard to lead him where he would, caring indeed very little where they went, so hopeless had the dream of his ultimate escape to France become.

By common consent they avoided Evelith Mill, but when, after about four miles of very rough walking, they came to the little river which ran past it, a new problem presented itself: how to cross it?

Richard, who had hitherto taken the lead upon all occasions, the King following obediently in his wake, was at a loss. Charles roused himself with an effort, casting a measuring glance athwart the stream. 'Can you swim?' he asked.

Richard shook his head. 'Nay, master, not I!' he said, with a shudder. 'Alack, what is to become of us? We be bound to go across the bridge at Evelith!'

'Nonsense, why should we?' said the King. 'It is but a little river, and since I can swim I'll engage to help you across.'

Richard, whose nerves on dry land nothing could shake, crossed himself with such a moan of dismay that the King burst out laughing. 'Nay, nay, I dursn't,' he said. 'I'll drown, for sure!'

'Drown in that rivulet?' mocked the King. 'Come, give me your hand, chicken-heart! I won't let you drown.'

He waded into the stream until he stood waist-deep in

the middle, and paused there, holding out his hand for Richard to grasp. Richard hesitated upon the brink, but upon the King's laughing at him again, set his teeth, and entered the water. It never came above their middles, and they soon reached the farther side, the King drawing his shrinking henchman on irresistibly, and Richard clinging to his hand with as frenzied a grip as though he were indeed on the point of drowning.

They squeezed the water out of their breeches as well as they could, and went on, but the discomfort of wet clothes clinging about his limbs was an added ill the King found hard to bear. If the journey to Madeley, with the prospect of a safe passage into Wales ahead of him, had been hard to accomplish, this backward journey was ten times harder. His swollen and bleeding feet forced him to go slowly, and it was near dawn when Richard paused in his tracks to say that they had come within sight of Boscobel House. 'And I do think, my liege,' said Richard, 'that maybe I should go on alone to be certain sure there's none but William and his good wife within. It would be a rare foolish thing to bring your honour all this way only to walk into a trap.'

'Do as you please,' the King said wearily.

'I'll leave your honour in the field alongside the house,' said Richard, 'and go wake William.'

The King returned no answer, but dragged himself on in Richard's wake through a hedge into a meadow smelling of cow-dung. Here Richard left him, under a tree, and went on as quickly as he could towards the wicket gate which led into the garden of the house.

The King sat down, leaning his back against the tree, and closed his eyes. It seemed a long time before he heard in the distance the click of the gate and the sound of a quick footstep. It sounded too quick and too light to belong to Richard, and he struggled to his feet, seized by swift alarm. The moonlight showed him the outline of a man approaching the tree, with two other, thicker outlines in his wake. He stood still, his hand clenching the broom-hook, which had served him all the way as a staff.

The foremost figure had reached him, and was holding

out hands that gleamed white in the moonlight. 'Sire, sire!'

The King let the broom-hook fall. He leaned forward, straining his eyes to see the newcomer's face. He put out his hands, and caught the ones stretched towards him, holding them in a hard grasp. 'Carlis?' he said incredulously. '*Carlis?*'

'Yes, yes, my liege! Oh, my dear master, what have they done to you?' Major Carlis cried, and dropped to his knees, carrying the King's hands to his lips, and bathing them with the sudden rush of his tears.

<br>

CHAPTER V

# ROYAL OAK

THE King bent over Carlis, still grasping his hands, himself much moved by this unlooked-for meeting. 'Carlis, Carlis, I thought you dead at Worcester! How came you here?'

'Faith, sir, by devious paths!' the Major replied unsteadily. 'I still wonder at finding myself alive, since I believe I and some few others were the last men out of Worcester. But there's no killing an old campaigner, as your Majesty knows!' He rose from his knees. 'Let us take you in, sir; here is my old acquaintance, Will Penderel, come to beg that you will be pleased to honour his house with your presence.'

'That is very prettily said,' remarked the King, his voice, though weak with fatigue, betraying a flicker of humour.

'Oh, I have often thought of turning courtier, sir,' the Major said, leading him towards the house, one hand still clasping his, and the other strong arm passed sustainingly about his waist. 'Run on, Will, and see if your goodwife is up yet, for I think we shall have need of her.'

William returned no answer, but forged ahead with long strides, while Richard brought up the rear of the little procession.

When they reached the house, they found that William had not found it necessary to bid Dame Joan come down to the kitchen. At the first word of the King's arrival with Richard, she had nipped up out of her bed, and by the time he stood upon the threshold, she had kindled a fire on the still-warm ashes in the fireplace, and slung an iron cauldron half-full of water from the big hook that dangled from the chimney.

Carlis brought the King immediately into the kitchen, which was a big low-pitched room, lit by a few tallow candles, and a lamp hanging from one of the massive oak-beams.

The goodwife, who was a neat, comely woman, with the ruddy cheeks and calm eyes of the country-dweller, bobbed a curtsey, at first a little shy of such an exalted guest; but when she dared to look up at Charles she saw how young he was, how wet, and muddied, and how haggard, and forgot that he was a King, and whisked about to pull a chair up to the fire, saying over her shoulder: 'Bring the poor lad to the fire, sir. Will'am, do you close that door, and see that the shutters be bolted tight! My sakes, did that feckless Richard lead you through a midden, sir? There, now, never fear? You are safe here.'

'You see, sir, that you are come amongst friends,' Carlis said, a gay note in his voice oddly at variance with the look of shocked pity in his keen eyes.

The King sank down into the chair, smiling with an effort upon his hosts. 'I thank you, I thank you,' he murmured.

Carlis, who had cast one swift appraising glance at him as soon as he had come into the lamplight, turned sharp on his heel, saying cheerfully: 'What have you in your larder, Dame Joan?'

'Little but bread, and some cheese, alack the day!' she replied.

'Why, that's food for a prince!' he said. 'I warrant when his Majesty has tasted of your cheeses he will desire no better. Come you with me, Richard, on a foraging expedition. Bustle about, man!'

'Ay and I will make a posset,' said Dame Joan, running an experienced eye over the King. 'I don't doubt you will have taken a chill, sir, as wet as you are. But a posset will drive it out, never fear! Will'am, don't you be standing gaping, but fetch a jug of small beer to me straight!'

'Where is my Lord Wilmot?' the King asked anxiously.

'He's safe enough my liege, in a very honest Catholic gentleman's house, over to Moseley. Will'am will be fain to tell you about him presently. Do you draw close up to the fire, now, and warm yourself!'

The King obeyed her, watching her as she moved about the kitchen, first setting a place for him at the table, then peeping into her cauldron, or snuffing a candle that had begun to gutter. She smiled comfortably at him when she chanced to meet his eyes, and when Major Carlis and Richard came back into the kitchen with provender from the larder, bade them place all upon the table, and pull off his Majesty's wet shoes and stockings. It was Carlis who performed this office for him. When he saw the condition of the King's feet, he stayed for a moment, looking down at them, his mouth rather grim under his neatly curled moustachios. Dame Joan came up with a basin of warm water, and told him to get up from the floor, for she wished to bathe his Majesty's feet. The Major rose, saying with determined cheerfulness: 'We must find a dry pair of shoes for you, sir.'

This, however, was easier said than done, there being none in the house to fit the King. In the end, having washed away the mud and the bloodstains, and cut the blisters, Dame Joan was forced to put hot embers into the old shoes to dry them.

Meanwhile, the King made a hearty meal, washing down the bread and cheese with a posset of thin milk mixed with small beer. At his request, William Penderel sat down on a joint-stool and told him as much as he knew of Lord Wilmot's movements. He spoke slowly, and at first seemed to hesitate a good deal, but when he found that the King only laughed at certain freedoms of speech, he grew more at ease, and very soon was giving Charles a graphic, though laconic, account of the whole affair.

It was evident that John Penderel had found my lord a tiresome charge.

'When your honour was gone with Richard into Spring Coppice,' said William, 'John carried my lord off, meaning for to take him to Shores', at Hungerhill, but my lord misliking the place, – 'deed, and it's a poor enough roof to set over a great lord's head – he bethought him that maybe John Climpson, which is an honest man, would shelter his lordship; and that failing —'

'How so? Would he not receive my lord?' interrupted the King, between mouthfuls.

'Ay, he would, and my lord have been as right as a ram's horn there, but his lordship would not condescend to it.'

The King's eyes gleamed. 'Was my lord so nice, then? Go on, man! Tell me the whole!'

William scratched his chin, saying diffidently: 'I be not wishful to offend your honour, but seemingly my lord's one as would find fault with a fat goose, by what John told us. He was hard put to it to get his lordship under cover for the night, his lordship scorning to set foot in the first dwellings John carried him to, and mistrusting Reynolds of the Hide, on account of his being a very poor man, and his house close upon the highway. So then John bethinks him of one Mr Huntbach, which is a gentleman mighty well-affected to your honour, and lives at Brinsford. Maybe his lordship would have been pleased to rest there, but by ill-hap, passing Coven, they had news of a troop of horse in the town, which put my lord into a fright, him being one as thinks every bush a boggard, as the saying is. Then they see some men on the road, which was friends, but my lord would have it otherwise, and got to thinking the countryside was rising on all your honour's party. A terrible time John had with him, for sure.'

'If I have not this tale from John's own lips, it will be too great a hardship to bear!' said the King.

'John would be proud to see your honour,' replied William doubtfully. 'Ay, and he will be amazed, I warrant you, him having got the notion great folks is all like my lord; but his gracious Majesty's no more like my lord than chalk is to cheese, I told him, and so he will find it. Not that we would be meaning any disrespect to his lordship,' he added. 'And, indeed, my liege, John was very diligent to serve him, and when my lord would not be at his ease with Mr Hunt-bach (besides which he was in a sweat over those horses of his, which was put up in an old barn, there being no other safe stable), John went off to Wolverhampton to find if he could hear of a better house for my lord to lie in. But finding no one he might trust, he was coming back when he met a priest who is very well-known to us for a good man and an honest, that is living with Mr Whitgreave of Moseley, by Wolverhampton, whom John accosted, telling him to his consternation that there was a great battle fought and lost at Worcester. Then he opened to Father Huddleston the business of my lord, to which the good Father replied he should go with him along to Mr Whitgreave's house, him being a staunch gentleman that fought for your Majesty's blessed father in the late wars. So John went along with him to Moseley, and Mr Whitgreave, hearing of the evil case my lord was in, straightway went back with him to Mr Hunt-bach's, and carried my lord out of that house to his own, with which my lord was well-satisfied.'

'And John too, as I should judge,' said the King caustically. 'When was all this?'

' 'Twas on the same Thursday that your honour set off by night for Madeley.'

'Where is my lord now?'

'Maybe he's with Mr Whitgreave still, my liege. John come home to White-Ladies yesterday, at cockcrow, my lord being wishful to get news of your honour. Which we told John you was gone with Richard to cross Severn into Wales, whereupon John goes back to Moseley, to carry the tidings to my lord. He'll be home today, if he was not returned last night, which I couldn't say.'

'Today?' the King said, frowning with an effort of memory. 'What is today?'

' 'Tis Saturday now, my liege, the sixth day of September, so please you.'

'Only Saturday!' the King exclaimed. He pressed his hands across his eyes for an instant. 'Is it possible?' he said, half to himself, his voice so mournful that William regarded him with a good deal of dismay.

Major Carlis, who had been standing behind the King's chair, while William told his tale, stepped forward, and with a little jerk of his head signed to William to draw back. He himself knelt on one knee before the fire, and picked up the King's stockings, which had been spread in the hearth to dry, and tested them with his hand. After a moment he said: 'It behoves us, sir, to think where we may best bestow you this day.'

The King's hand dropped to his knee. 'Like a bale of merchandise,' he said.

Carlis smiled. 'Very precious merchandise, sir.'

Dame Penderel paused in her work of clearing away the remains of the meal upon the table, to say in a low voice: 'You know we have two very safe hiding places in the house, sir. His Majesty might lie in either, sure!'

'If his Majesty will be guided by me, he will lie in neither,' said Carlis, looking at the King. 'There is danger here, sir, for these good people are much suspected, being Catholics, and very loyal to your Majesty. There have been some of Cromwell's soldiers searching diligently in the neighbourhood already, nor do I think we have seen the last of them.'

'My Lord Derby commended the secret place,' Dame Penderel said, unconvinced.

'My Lord Derby's sojourn with you likes me not at all, dame,' responded Carlis, lifting one of the King's feet on to his knee, and beginning to coax the stocking on to it. 'We do not know how many may have learned of it, and of your secret place to boot. Trust me, sir, I am not new to this game of hide-and-seek.'

'Where will you have me go?' asked the King, wincing a little as his foot was put into the shoe. 'Into the wood again, belike?'

'Nay, I have a better plan in my head than that, sir. You and I will go up into a very thick tree I know of, and there lie as safe as two mice in a cheese till evening, while William and Richard keep watch. If the rebels are still searching for fugitives from Worcester, and – as I think – for your Majesty in person – they will look very diligently through the wood.'

A smile crept into the King's eyes. 'So now I must spend my day perched in a tree! Oddsfish, my life has become so rich in experience I begin to lose all knowledge of myself. I like it very well, Carlis. But I will have John Penderel brought here to me, to go once more with a message from me to my Lord Wilmot.'

'That shall be done, sir, and at evening you may speak with him here.'

'Ay,' said William, from the shadows at the end of the kitchen. 'And his Majesty may lie snug in the secret-place all night, for the rebels will be likely tired out with searching, and not trouble us.'

The King turned his head. 'Fellow, have you considered how dangerous a guest I am? I would have you think well before you harbour me.'

'Ay,' said William placidly.

'Ay?' repeated the King. 'What may that mean? Have you understood me?'

'Ay. We mun serve your Majesty. There's naught to think on. Such is fiddle-faddling waste of time, and you should ought to be away out of the house before folks starts stirring abroad.'

'Very well answered,' said Carlis, rising to his feet, and going to the window to unbar the shutters.

The grey light of dawn already rather coldly lit the garden, and the fields beyond. Some distance to the south, the outskirts of Spring Coppice were just visible from the window, and a little way away, situated in the open ground lying between the house and the wood, stood a big pollarded oak, which Carlis pointed out to the King. One or two other trees stood at irregular intervals in the field, but none so sturdy, or so thickly covered with leaves. It commanded a view of the house, and the surrounding country, and from the fact of its standing outside the shelter of the wood, might be supposed to be considered by his enemies a very unlikely hiding-place for the King to choose.

As soon as the Major had made some small arrangements with the Penderels, the whole party escorted the King out of the house, Richard going ahead to spy out the land, and William bringing up the rear with a wooden ladder, by which means the King, who said, though gaily, that his feet were in no case to go a-climbing, was to ascend into the tree.

Carlis went up first, and finding a suitable branch, parted the leaves which hid him from the ground, and called to the King to join him. Charles mounted the ladder as nimbly as his hurt feet would permit and no sooner saw the leafy cave where Carlis was than he declared that he would defy all the rebel forces in England to discover him there. A cushion, provided by Dame Penderel's thoughtfulness, was handed up on the end of a long hook, and placed on a broad branch for the King to sit upon. The Penderels, fearing that some farm-labourer might be already abroad, then went away, promising to keep a strict watch, and to take word to John, at White-Ladies, of the King's return.

'I never knew such poor men to be so honest,' the King remarked, disposing himself more comfortably amongst the branches.

Carlis smiled a little. 'How should you indeed, sir? You have not known poor men. Yet I dare swear you might find an hundred and more as honest as these.'

There was a derisive gleam in the King's eyes. 'I should get great good from my adventures, then, for I am learning some things I knew not before. How came you to know these Penderels?'

'William sheltered me not as much as a year ago, when I was searched for very strictly, sir. My home is not two miles distant, at Bromhall, just across the border into Stafford-shire.'

'I had forgot. Did you come here at once from Worcester? Were you here that weary day I spent in the wood?'

'No, not then. When I escaped from Worcester, I rode first to the house of one Davy Jones, in the Heath, in Tong

Parish, and there lay for two days.'

'How did you escape from Worcester?' Charles demanded. 'Were you in the last fight in the street below my lodging?'

'To be sure I was, and a rare shambles we made of the street,' said the Major coolly. 'Had we had some few reserves, I believe we might even then have repulsed the rebels.'

The King gave a groan. 'Carlis, Carlis, I could not prevail upon Leslie's horse to budge! They would not follow me!'

'Would they not? The scurvy fellows! But the victory was ours, for we held the street while your Majesty made good your escape, and that, in sooth, was all our intent.'

'I should have died then, fighting!' the King said with suppressed violence.

'Nay, how should that avail us?' Carlis said. 'Do you think all lost because the dice fall once amiss? I shall live to see you at Whitehall, and that without help from the Scots.'

'If I come to my throne, it will indeed be without help from the Scots!' the King said, an ugly sneer curling his mouth. 'I should have known better than to have trusted Argyll, who sold my father to Cromwell! But they urged me so, all of them, save only Hyde —' He broke off, his brows lowering, the sneer more strongly marked. 'Well! I have learnt my lesson,' he said. 'A boy I was, but by God, I am not one now!'

'I dare swear you learnt other lessons in Scotland, sir,' said Carlis. 'Myself, I had never a liking for your Scottish Covenanter.'

A sharp crack of laughter broke from the King. 'What I could tell you of their beastly hypocrisy!' he said. 'You cannot imagine the villainy of Argyll and all his party! Indeed, it has done me a great deal of good, for nothing could have confirmed me more to the Church of England than being in Scotland, and seeing their hypocrisy!' The sneer vanished into a dancing smile of pure amusement. 'They bade me draw the blinds if I wished to take my pleasures on a Sunday! I have had as many as six sermons preached to me in one day, and by men so puffed up with pride it would turn your stomach to hear them! Yea, and

I have been forced to repent me of mine own sins of my father's wickedness – God save the mark! – of what they were pleased to call my mother's idolatry, – and all by men so bloody-minded and so bigoted —'

'And you did so?' Carlis interrupted, his pointed beard jutting belligerently.

The sneer came back, the great eyes glanced cynically towards him. 'Ay, I did so. What should I care for a few empty words, who had a kingdom at stake?'

Carlis said pitifully: 'Alas, that so sweet a prince should have learnt so grievous a lesson!'

The King laughed. 'So sweet a prince! I warrant, they thought me one! Carlis, here is a lesson from my book: give honey for gall, keep your counsel, and trust no man farther than his own interest!' He heaved a sigh, and leaned his head against the tree-trunk, saying: 'Alack, that I am not like to live long enough to profit by my lessons!'

'Why, what is this?' said Carlis. 'Do you lose heart, sir? I think you were not born to die with your head upon a block.'

'No, but I think I may very well break my neck falling out of this tree,' replied the King. 'I never knew how stupid a body I have, that craves so much sleep, and has legs that will not bear me nine miles without making me ready to weep with fatigue. Trusty Dick said that if I had been reared right I had not failed so grievously, and oddsblood, he spoke naught but the truth! Yet I did not think myself so softly reared. I had witnessed battles when other lads were busy over their hornbooks.'

'Comfort you, sir,' Carlis said. 'When John Penderel complained of my Lord Wilmot's being (he said) as soft as a cushion, William told him: "Then he is not like the King, for his Majesty is as tough as whitleather".'

The King chuckled. 'He had not seen my Majesty panting for breath in a ditch. A miller at some place on the road to Madeley – I forget – chased us till I bade Richard leap over the hedge beside the lane. It would have made you split your sides to have seen us!'

'It would have made me split the miller's sides, my liege,

but not my own,' replied Carlis grimly.

'Why, what a fierce fellow you are,' murmured the King, closing his eyes. 'For all the poor man knew, we were a pair of lawless vagrants.'

'If he, and others like him, had joined your Majesty's standard —'

'Oh, you cannot blame him that he stayed safe at home!' said Charles. 'I should not have come into England at the head of an army of Scots. I blame no Englishman for holding aloof from me.'

'I have some other thoughts on that matter,' replied Carlis. He shifted his position in the tree a little, and added: 'If you would lay your head in my lap, sir, I think you might sleep a while. You are so tired.'

'Oh no,' Charles said, his heavy lids lifting momentarily. 'I must learn to overcome this plaguey inclination to sleep. You have burdens enough to support without adding my head to the rest.'

'Put your head in my lap,' Carlis said, not as subject to monarch, but as a man to a boy. 'Come, do you think that is not a burden I would give my life to bear? Can you be comfortable so?'

Charles, yielding to the other's will, disposed himself along the branch, sustained by Carlis's strong arm holding him. 'Very comfortable,' he said drowsily. 'But you, my poor friend?'

'Also, sir.'

'I should warn you I think these clothes I wear are lousy.'

Carlis grinned. 'Never say so, sir!'

'Well, they stink,' said Charles. 'Odd rot you, do you laugh at my sufferings?'

'Yes, sir, to save myself from weeping,' Carlis answered, looking down at the stained face on his knee. 'Who made your Majesty's skin of that reechy complexion?'

'Mrs Wolfe, with walnut leaves. Old Wolfe was afraid for his life, so I stayed in a barn, in the hay. Mrs Wolfe brought food to us there.'

'I warrant you were glad of it.'

'Yes, I was always a very gross feeder,' said Charles.

'Well, it must needs take a deal to support this frame of yours, sir,' remarked Carlis. 'Do you know that you are an unconscionably big fellow, my liege?'

'Ay, for my sins. There have been many tall men in my family. My cousin Rupert is a very giant.'

'They say your Majesty's great-grandmother, the Queen of Scots, was a tall woman.'

'Talk not to me of any Scot,' said the King. He opened his eyes, and Carlis saw them brimming with amusement. 'Argyll had it in mind to match me with his daughter!'

'Oho! And how liked your Majesty that pretty plot?'

'Very ill. But I did not say so. I wondered that so godly a man should wish to see his daughter wedded to the depraved fellow I am.'

Carlis smiled down at him. 'So young and so depraved?'

'He thinks it. But when I wed, it will not be with a Campbell. Are you married, Carlis?'

'Nay, nay, not I, sir! I have been too busy fighting all my life.'

The big mouth curled. 'So? I'll swear you found time to beget a few bastards!'

Carlis laughed. 'Why, as to that, sir, I believe you may be right, but so far none have come forward to claim me!'

'You are a bad father,' said Charles, closing his eyes again. 'I have a fine son of my own. He is at nurse in Rotterdam. And that other one —' He roused himself with a jerk. 'What was I saying?'

'You are three parts asleep sir.'

'Oh, more than that!' Charles said. He lay silent for a time, until Carlis, wondering whether he had indeed fallen asleep, bent over him to look into his face. But the King's eyes were open, and he said: 'I wish I knew if Hamilton were alive. He was wounded, badly, I think. They told me he was carried into the Commandery.'

He sounded unhappy; Carlis replied: 'That was true, but what afterwards became of him I know not.'

'He was my friend,' Charles said, 'Argyll removed him, but he advised me to consent to his banishment, since in Argyll he thought all my hopes lay. I know now that there was never any hope for me with that party. Argyll would have shackled me so fast – why, when I visited the army, and Argyll saw that I was becoming too great with the soldiers, he carried me away in a fright! None but Argyll must be great in Scotland. And then they had another fast-day.'

'Why?' asked Carlis.

'Because of the army's self-confidence and profaneness,' replied Charles, in a voice drugged with sleep.

'My child, I think you are dreaming,' said Carlis softly.

'No, it's quite true. And when they had taken me away to Dunfermline, they set about the purging.' A little laugh shook him. 'Eighty officers, and four thousand men they purged from the army!'

'This sounds to me like madness, sir. Why should they do so?'

'Why, because they were ungodly, man! That was why Cromwell beat them at Dunbar – in part. He should not have done so. But the ministers were still busy with their purging, and Leslie —' He broke off; Carlis saw his face harden. After a little pause, he said: 'They scolded God for permitting His Covenanters to be defeated – those of them who did not blame themselves for not purging the army more strictly. But *that* was soon remedied. Also I repented me again of my many sins.'

The bitter mockery in his voice made Carlis lay a hand upon his short, tangled locks. 'Poor lad! Tales were told in England, but I think no one believed the half of them.'

'They sent away the chiefest of my advisers,' the King went on, in a voice thickened by drowsiness. 'And those whom I most loved, of course. It seems a long time ago. I remember I was very lonely, and repented me in good earnest that ever I had set foot in that bleak, unfriendly country. But I signed the Covenant, I swore to observe every Article; I listened to their sermons; and I was gracious to their canting ministers – all, all to one end, which at last they were bound to perform.' His eyelids were dropping, a smile played round his mouth; he said, so softly that Carlis had to bend over him to catch the words: 'They crowned me, at Scone, and that not even Argyll can undo.'

He did not speak again, nor did Carlis return any answer. Presently he knew by the King's deeper breathing that he slept. He sat very still, leaning his shoulders against the tree-trunk, one arm keeping the King from falling, and his attention divided between the dark head on his knee and the view of the surrounding country to be obtained through the thick foliage.

As the morning wore on, there was enough movement to be observed to keep him on the alert. The rough lane that ran from the highway from Tong to Brewood, past Boscobel House to White-Ladies, was visible from where he sat, and several people passed down it. He saw Richard plodding along, shouldering his wood-bill as though going about his rightful business; and a little while later caught a glimpse of Humphrey, the miller. Nearer at hand, Dame Joan was to all appearances busy with a nut-hook, collecting sticks for kindling, with William not far away upon the same errand. Then a troop of horse came into sight from the direction of Brewood. They did not check, but rode on towards White-Ladies.

Some time elapsed; the Major's right arm was aching from shoulder to wrist, but he dared not move it from about the King. He did what he could to ease it, but cautiously, for fear of waking Charles, who was sunk in a heavy sleep. He watched William Penderel work towards the edge of Spring Coppice, and presently disappear into it. William came back presently with a load of faggots, walking with a leisurely gait, and passed under the pollarded oak. He did not look up, but he said clearly: 'Soldiers searching in the wood.' Before long, Carlis caught sight of a red-coat amongst the tree-trunks. Shortly afterwards, one or two soldiers appeared, skirting the Coppice. They saw William and hailed him, and after gaping stupidly for a minute he shambled over to them. They were too far off for Carlis to hear what passed between them, but he saw William scratch his head as though puzzled, and then point towards Boscobel; and smiled to himself. Apparently the soldiers were satisfied, for William soon left them, and went on gathering his bundles of wood, roping them together, and carrying them across the field to the house.

By this time, Carlis's arm had ceased to ache, but a dangerous numbness was stealing down it, making it impossible for him to hold the King much longer. The soldiers, straying over the field in the indeterminate manner of men at a loss to know where to look for their quarry, were some of them close enough to the big oak tree to cause him a good deal of anxiety. He bent over the King, and softly spoke his name, but Charles did not stir. Finding him too sound asleep to be wakened by such gentle means, Carlis slid a hand over his mouth and with the little power remaining in the fingers of his right hand, pinched him shrewdly. The King woke with a start, and a half-dreaming exclamation, stifled by the hand clamped across his mouth. Carlis whispered: 'Quiet! There are soldiers near.'

The King's eyes, filmy with sleep, looked up at him, a little dazed. He blinked once or twice, and then raised his hand to Carlis's, and pulled it away from his mouth, and struggled up, holding fast to a stout branch. Having peeped through the leaves at his enemies, and ascertained that they were not close enough to overhear him, he said with a twinkle: 'Fie, what a way to use me! I thought Noll Cromwell himself had me in his grip.'

'I cry pardon, sir! I dared not speak loud enough to waken you, and so was forced to take the liberty of pinching your Majesty,' said Carlis, rubbing his benumbed arm back to life.

'I think that is lèse majesté,' remarked the King, cautiously parting the branches a little, to enable him to watch the movements of the red-coats on the outskirts of the coppice.

'I fear it, I fear it! But to have let your sacred person fall out of the tree, as I promise you I was in danger of doing, would have been a worse crime!'

'Oh, that would have been treason,' said the King. He made himself as comfortable as he could on his branch, and added: 'You should have wakened me before. Now if we had something to eat, how well-housed we should be!'

'But we have, sir,' said Carlis, thrusting a hand into the

pocket of his leather coat. 'Your Majesty forgets that I am an old soldier!'

'Carlis, I swear you shall be knighted for this!' the King exclaimed, watching him produce from his pocket some slices of bread and cheese, wrapped up in a clean cloth.

'When your Majesty comes into your own, I shall petition for the right to bear a coat-of-arms,' said Carlis, holding out the bread and cheese to him.

'It shall be granted to you,' promised the King. He took some of the food and waved the rest away. 'Eat it yourself – nay, that is a command, my friend! What will you have upon the shield?'

'An oak proper,' replied Carlis promptly. 'In a field – in a field or.'

'With a fesse gules charged with three regal crowns! And your crest?'

'Nay, your Majesty shall decide.'

The King took a large bite out of his bread. 'A garland, of course. An oaken garland with two swords – no, a sword and a sceptre, crossed through it saltirewise. And your name shall be changed from Carlis to Carlos, signifying Charles.'

'I am very willing. And my motto, sir?'

The King shook his head. 'Alas, I am no scholar. It should be in Latin. How like you Servant and Saviour?'

'What, with bread and cheese, sir?'

The King laughed, but said: 'I believe I was in despair when you came to me last night, Carlis, for it seemed that all my friends were lost to me.'

'Ay, you are partaking of adventures which I think no King of England partook of before you, sir,' agreed Carlis.

'I was reared as I'll swear no King was before me,' said Charles, with his mouth full. 'Did you ever hear how my brother James and I saw the battle of Edgehill when we were mere lads? We were in the custody of Dr Harvey at that time, James being nine years old and myself something over twelve. He withdrew with us under a hedge, being warned to have most strict care of us, as you may suppose; but, poor man, he was more interested in the cutting up of frogs and toads than in warfare, and soon pulled out a book from his pocket, and buried his nose in it! It was not till a cannon-shot came near to blowing us all to perdition that he remembered his charge, and where he stood. I leave it to you to imagine how swiftly we were whisked off then, the good doctor's hair verily standing on end with his horror!' He chuckled at the memory, and added: 'But it was not long before the King my father sent me into the west, to unboy me. I liked it best when I was in Jersey.' He finished the last of his bread and cheese, and said with a touch of youthful eagerness: 'Do you like sailing, Carlis? I could be well content with a bare acre of land, if only the seas and a stout yacht were mine. I had one made for me at St Malo, the perfect model of a pinnace! She was of great length fore and aft, with two masts and twelve pairs of oars. I would let none steer her but myself. Those were the happiest days I have known; perhaps the happiest I shall ever know.'

He ended on a sigh. Carlis said: 'Comfort you, sir; you will have other and finer yachts, besides a whole navy to call your own.'

'Maybe.' He looked down out of the tree, and saw that the soldiers were no longer in sight. 'They seem all to have drawn off. My good friend William is approaching us now.'

In a minute or two, William stood under the tree, and informed the King that the soldiers, after questioning him closely and observing that no watch was being kept in Boscobel House, seemed satisfied that he was not concealing the King, or any other fugitive, and had retired to prosecute more strictly their search through the woods. He thought, however, that the King ought not to descend from his hiding-place until dusk. Charles said promptly that he was willing to stay where he was, but that he was very thirsty. So William, after considering for a moment, nodded his head, and slouched off to the house. When he returned, it was with a bottle of sack, which he contrived to hand up to Carlis on the end of his nut-hook.

'And now,' said the King, deftly knocking the top off the bottle, 'we have nothing left to wish for. Your health, Carlis!'

## CHAPTER VI

# THE SUM OF ONE THOUSAND POUNDS

THE rest of the day passed uneventfully, soldiers being occasionally seen, but never near enough to the tree to cause the two in it any great anxiety. The worst the King had to bear were the discomforts of a hard perch, a rough shirt, and limbs aching from being for so many hours in a variety of cramped positions. He was very patient, making no complaint, but beguiling the time with cheerful conversation, and sometimes dozing a little, with Carlis's arm round him. Once he said, passing his hand over the black stubble that adorned his chin: 'I believe if my own mother were to see me now she would not know me!'

Carlis returned a jesting answer, but he thought that Charles spoke more truly than he knew. Those who had waved farewell to the youth who had set forth to try his fortune in Scotland, would see very little of that shy, slightly stammering boy in the taciturn young King who, in eighteen bitter months, had found his manhood, and had learnt to trust no man beyond his own interest.

When he slept, the lines of his face were softened; he looked younger, and strangely defenceless. Carlis watched him, trying sometimes to see a likeness to the little stately King, his father; at others, wondering what the future held for him. An ugly young man, Carlis thought, smiling under his moustache. He was swarthy, harsh-featured, his countenance melancholy, his full underlip inclined to pout. Almost a repellent young man, one would have thought; yet with such a magic in his smile, in the very look in his dark eyes, that even a hardened soldier felt his heart warm to him.

It was not until the daylight had quite gone that William Penderel came with his ladder to the tree, and told the

King that it was at last safe for him to come into the house. The King and Carlis descended somewhat stiffly, Charles discovering as soon as he stood upon them, that his feet, instead of having benefited by his rest, were rather more painful than before, having swollen a little. He was glad to lean on William's arm, and had not covered more than half the distance to the house when he announced that come what might he would go no farther upon his journey that night.

Being arrived at the house, he was escorted immediately to the parlour, where a fire burned, and a brave number of tallow candles cast their light on to the oak wainscoting and made the plaster mouldings of the ceiling assume grotesque, mask-like shapes. The King sat down in a chair by the fire, saying that he had not dreamed of such entertainment; but after he had rested for a few minutes, and warmed himself, listening lazily to the low-voiced discussion that was being held between William Penderel and Carlis, he pulled himself up and asked to be shown the secret-place in the house.

There were, in fact, two hiding-places; one approached through a sliding panel in the best bed-chamber, which was above the parlour, and having a way of escape down the wide chimney and into the garden through a door hidden by a thick creeper; the other, a square hole under the floor of the cheese-room upon the top floor. This one, Carlis and William considered to be the safer of the two, the priest-catchers being more likely to suspect the wainscoting than the floor; and after the King had descended into it and found that by drawing up his legs he could lie in it without too much discomfort, he declared himself to be so well satisfied with its security that he was resolved to spend the night there.

He was then conducted down the two flights of stairs again to the parlour, where Joan Penderel had by this time spread supper upon the table.

'Roast chicken, as I live!' the King said, sniffing the air. 'My Dame Joan, I warrant you, I think William a lucky man!'

'Oh, my liege,' she said, smiling and blushing, 'it is all I have to offer your Majesty, and little enough, alas!'

He sat down in the chair at the head of the table, telling her that it was a very ample supper, though he would engage to leave nothing of it but the bones; and picking up the carving-knife, commanded Carlis to sit down with him, and fall to.

'I will wait first on your Majesty,' Carlis replied.

'Sit down, man, sit down!' said the King. 'Oddsblood, have you perched all day on the same tree-branch with me only to stand upon ceremony now?'

'Please your Majesty, I will wait upon you,' said William. 'And if your Majesty is wishful for to see my brother John, he is in the kitchen, and I will fetch him in to you.'

'Have him in,' said the King. 'Where is my Trusty Dick?'

'Dick and George do both be on guard, watching the highway,' replied William. 'And Humphrey has gone to Shifnal for to get news, and will be back anon.'

'Why, it seems I have a bodyguard!' said the King, digging his teeth into the flesh of the drumstick.

'It's best some of us should be on the watch,' William said.

He went away to summon John to the parlour, and presently came back with him, giving him a thrust towards the King, and saying: 'Go one, and speak up; there's naught to scare ye, man!'

John, the second of the brothers, was a sturdy woodman, with a pair of serious grey eyes, which he kept fixed on the King's face. He looked a little bashful, but upon the King's beckoning him with a movement of the half-eaten drumstick in his hand, a grin dispelled some of his gravity, and he stepped forward.

'John, where is my Lord Wilmot?' demanded the King.

'If he's not gone, he should ought to be at Moseley, your honour,' responded John. 'But, 'deed, there's no foretelling but what he may have gone off somewheres, for he's as fidgety as a maggot – saving your Majesty's presence.'

'Did you tell him I was gone with Richard to Madeley?'

'I did so, and right glad his lordship was to hear it. But what he might take it into his head to do is more than I can tell your honour. His horses was sent over to Colonel Lane, at Bentley Hall, which, seemingly, is a gentleman which served under my lord in the late wars. Maybe he would help my lord to escape – for all Moseley Hall is a very safe hiding-place.'

'Will you go once more to Moseley with a message for my lord?' asked the King.

'Ay, I'll be off first thing in the morning, and gladly. Not but what it's not me would be trusting your Majesty to that one,' he said disparagingly.

'Fie, John, his lordship is a very faithful friend of mine.'

'Ay,' said John. 'He do be mighty anxious to get tidings of your Majesty, I'll allow. But the way it takes him, jumping about as wanton as a calf with two dams, puts me in fear he'll yet be the cause of your Majesty's being caught by them rebels.'

'I'll take good care of my skin,' replied the King. 'I must prevail upon my lord to put on him a disguise.'

'He'll not do it,' said John. 'Nor he'll not budge without he has his horses, which put Mr Whitgreave in a taking to know where to hide them, the stables at Moseley Hall being hard by the road.'

The King laughed. 'My lord is too fat a man to go a-walking, friend John. He never does so.' He pushed his chair back from the table, and stretched his long legs out before him. 'Dame Joan, my stomach is now so well-lined that I am in a mood to defy all my enemies. But I should like to be rid of this beard,' he added, stroking his bristly chin.

'Well, and there's not a bit of need for your Majesty to go unshaven,' said Dame Penderel. 'Will'am, you could shave his Majesty.'

'Ay,' William agreed. 'I could.'

'Will you let him, sir?' Carlis asked, bending over the King's chair.

'Why not?' said Charles. 'William, I desire you to shave me.'

'Ay,' said William, and went off to get his razor.

John followed him, remarking when the parlour door was

shut behind him: 'You'm right, Will: he's not like my lord, not he! Lordy, to think of him a-sitting in the parlour as cool as you please, and the whole pack of them rebel soldiers a-hunting him to have off his head, like they had his blessed father's! But as for my lord being the one to go along with him – well he's not worthy to carry guts to a bear, and that's the truth!'

When the Penderels had withdrawn from the parlour, the King leaned his head against the back of his chair, the smile fading from his face, and leaving it drawn and rather desolate. Carlis, watching him, was impelled to take one of his hands, and to hold it in both his own strong, square ones, for comfort. The King's drooping eyelids lifted, and the eyes themselves faintly questioned.

Carlis smiled at him: 'One day you will look back upon these adventures of yours, and laugh, sir.'

'If I live to look back on them I shall certainly laugh,' agreed the King.

In the tree, slipping into sleep, his reserve had been lowered, but he was awake now, and hidden from Carlis behind the fence of his charm. He smiled and jested, made light of his troubles, and set his hosts at their ease by his own ease of manner; but what thoughts struggled in his brain, what sick despair, or crushing loneliness, made his eyes so sombre, were secrets known only to himself. Carlis could only kiss his hand, saying: 'You must have rest. After, the world will not look so grey.'

The King replied with a gleam of amusement: 'I doubt I seem to you a poor creature.'

'No,' Carlis said.

'I am not used to this life I find myself leading,' the King said, not in complaint, but matter-of-factly. 'The people are strange to me. But they seem to wish me very well.'

'Well enough, I daresay, to give their lives for you, sir.'

'I do not know why they should,' the King said, yawning. 'They know nothing of me, after all.'

Just then William came back to shave him. He took great pains over it, but was unskilful enough to provoke Carlis into saying with a twinkle: 'I am afraid William is but a mean barber, sir.'

'I was never shaved by any barber before,' remarked the King.

When the stubble had been removed, he said that he felt more like himself; and upon William's asking him respectfully if he would permit him to trim his hair, he said that he was very willing.

William, accordingly, cut his hair short on the top of his head with a pair of scissors, leaving it longer, however, about the ears, which was, he assured the King, more after the country-fashion. When he had finished, he knelt down to pick up the fallen black locks, gathering them into a handkerchief. The King, observing this, and perhaps guessing that William meant to keep the hair, said warningly: 'It must all be burned.'

One of the short wiry ringlets had curled itself round William's finger. He did not look up when the King spoke, nor did he answer him, but when Charles repeated: 'It must be burned. Throw it on the fire, man!' he said gruffly that it would make a nasty reek in the room, and would be better disposed of in the kitchen. He removed the lingering hairs from about his finger, adding, ' 'Tis strong – like it was alive.'

'Yes, strong enough to hang you,' said Charles.

Before he could insist upon his command being obeyed, John Penderel came into the room bringing Humphrey, the miller, who had that instant arrived from Shifnal. The King's attention being thus diverted, William discreetly withdrew with his relics.

Humphrey grinned broadly at the King. 'I don't know whether to be glad or sorry to see your honour again,' he confessed. 'That was a rare misfortunate journey you had, and us thinking you safe into Wales! Ay, and there's a mort of news hereabouts. Wait while I tell your Majesty: I warrant you'll get a good laugh!'

'Tell me then,' the King said. 'I shall be glad to laugh.'

'Well, I went off to Shifnal, like it was agreed betwixt me and Will. There's a Captain of the Rump there, which was used to be a heel-maker, and, thinks I to myself, that's the man for my need. So I up and took twenty shillings with me for the pay of a man in this new militia, which was all right and tight, it being for my mistress, and honest business, true enough. And being come to this Captain Broadway, I got to talking with some of the men there, but without much good got from it.'

'Get on, man, get on!' said Carlis. 'Tell this story with a better grace!'

'Why, so I will, master,' Humphrey said, rather reproachfully. 'For now's the marrow, mark you! Whiles I was there, there comes in a Colonel of the rebels for Captain Broadway, being wishful to know what search had been made at White-Ladies for the King, which the Captain said he knew no more than was rumour.'

'They traced me there?' the King interpolated.

'Ay, sure enough, for the Colonel told Broadway the story of your honour's coming there with a great, great company. But 'twas mostly lies, him not having the full sum of it – nor like to, I says to myself. So then the Captain bethinks him of me, and calls me up to tell what I knew to the Colonel.'

'What said you?'

'Why, that your honour had been to White-Ladies, which was nothing, seeing they knew it before; but the Colonel took it kindly, saying I was an honest man, and should be rewarded for my pains. Then he asked me where was your Majesty now – misnaming you, which made me mad. But I said how would I know the like of that, me being but a poor man, and not one your Majesty would be speaking to? And you talking to me so free in Spring Coppice, and eating your supper in Dick's house! Laugh! I could ha' split my sides! But when the Colonel said to me, was not your honour hid at White-Ladies still, I stood a-gaping at him like I was amazed. "Nay, how should that be?" I says, in a seeming puzzle. "There's three families living there and all at difference one with the other. There's no likelihood for him to stay there." That made him glum, I warrant you. However, he says he doubts not within a day or two to have your honour delivered into his hands, him having had tidings from London that there was a great reward to be got by any who could catch your honour, ay, or would tell where you lie hid. "The sum of One thousand pounds", he says to me, mighty solemn; which fair took me aback for 'tis a mort of money, so 'tis.'

He broke off, the grin fading from his face, for it was evident that the King was a good deal disturbed by his news. He had been lounging in his chair, but the mention of the reward had made him stiffen. He said slowly: 'A mort of money. Yes; a fortune, to a poor man.'

Humphrey stood staring at him with his jaw dropping. The King got up and walked away to the other end of the room, biting his nails. Carlis watched him for a moment, and then went over to him, leaving Humphrey crestfallen by the fire. 'What is it, sir?' he asked.

Charles shot him a look under his brows. 'I should not have put myself in the hands of such poor men. A thousand pounds to a man who earns a few shillings a week is too great a temptation!' he replied in a low voice.

'If it were one hundred thousand pounds it were to no more purpose, sir,' Carlis said. 'I will engage my soul for the truth of these same poor men!'

Charles did not speak. Humphrey, unable to hear what had been said, and not comprehending the cause of the King's discomposure, feared that in some way he had been indiscreet, and stood looking unhappily towards him. 'I do be sorry if I've done wrong,' he faltered.

Carlis turned his head. 'A large sum, Humphrey, one thousand pounds! A man could be snug for life with such a fortune, could he not?'

'Ay, surely.'

'*You* could earn it very easily, could you not? You have but to go again to Shifnal, to speak half-a-dozen words in the ear of this rebel Colonel, and you may be a rich man. Now tell his Majesty – have you a mind to do it?'

The miller's face turned slowly crimson. 'Blood-money?' he said. 'Me touch such? You should ought to know we'm honest men, sir!'

'I do know it.'

Humphrey's smouldering gaze went past him to the King's face. He said haltingly: 'We do be poor men, my liege, but not rogues! There's not one of us would betray your honour, no, not for a hundred times a thousand pounds! Lord ha' mercy, you wouldn't never think that of us? I'd not have told you, but for the jest of it!'

'No, no! I don't think it!' the King said quickly. He lifted a hand to his brow, pressing it as though it hurt him. 'I ask your pardon. I did not know such loyalty existed.' His hand fell, he forced a smile, and came back to the fire. 'In truth, I am over-tired and not myself. But I wonder that you should count me worth the loss of a fortune, indeed I do, for I have brought no good to this country.'

'Ay,' said Humphrey doubtfully, 'but – but I'd not sell any man for dirty gold, my liege, let alone your honour, which is my King – for all those damned rebels miscalled you the King of Scots! I'd give 'em King of Scots!'

The King laughed at that. His laughter banished the discomfort that had hung over the room since his hasty rising from his chair. Humphrey drew a deep breath of relief. By the time William came back into the room, which he did a few minutes later, his angry flush had faded, and he was regaling the King with a pungent description of the rebel troops he had encountered in Shifnal.

William was looking very serious, and at once drew Carlis aside to confer with him. The King glanced enquiringly at them. Carlis smiled at him, and said: 'Here's a weighty matter, sir. Will and Dame Joan would like to know what your Majesty would be pleased to eat tomorrow.'

'I should like some mutton, if it might be had,' replied the King without hesitation.

This simple request seemed to fill both the Penderels with consternation. William looked worriedly at Humphrey, who shook his head. Seeing their perplexity, the King said: 'It's no matter: I will eat what you have in the house.'

'Ay, but you've done that, my liege,' explained William bluntly. 'And tomorrow being Sunday, we mun make provision.'

'So we will,' said Carlis briskly. 'If his Majesty desires

mutton, mutton he must have.'

'I allow he should ought to have it, but I dursn't go to buy such in any market hereabouts, master. 'Twould set the neighbours a-talking, for they do know I don't use such, being a poor man.'

'God help the man who has me to feed!' remarked the King. 'Let it go, let it go, I will eat bread and cheese.'

'No, sir, you shall have your mutton,' said Carlis, a laugh in his eyes. 'You forget that I am an old soldier. I will take counsel with William presently. Meanwhile, my ambition is to see your Majesty safely bestowed for the night.'

'Ay,' agreed William. 'I've put a decent pallet in the priest's hole. Humphrey and Dick and George and me will take turns to watch. John had best get some rest, seeing he do have to go to Moseley in the morning.'

'I shall be glad of a bed,' said the King. 'But mind, Carlis, I'll not have these men's lives put in jeopardy for the sake of mutton to fill my belly!'

'Oh, content you, sir! It's only a sheep's life which is in jeopardy,' replied Carlis, picking up a candlestick from the table. 'Will your Majesty be pleased to seek your bed?'

The bed in question was a straw-pallet, which had been spread in the priest's hole. The steep attic-stairs which led to the cheese-room were shut off from the rest of the house by a door; at the head of these, a trap-door had been lifted out of the floor, disclosing a dark cavity, five foot square. The cheese-room, part of which bore evidence of having been used as a chapel, was long and low-pitched, with windows at either end of it, one commanding a view of the highway from Tong to Brewood, and the other overlooking the garden at the back of the house. The King lowered himself into the hole, remarking that it was well that he liked the smell of cheese; and Carlis and William, having seen him as comfortably settled as the constricted space would allow, left him to get what sleep he could while they kept watch.

He spent an uneasy night, for the dimensions of the hiding-place would not permit him to stretch out his long legs. The brothers took it in turns to keep watch throughout the night, and at daybreak Carlis stole out with William to a neighbouring sheepfold. Here the fattest wether of the flock fell a victim to the Major's dagger, while William stood by, not a little dismayed at such high-handed conduct. The Major did his work neatly and well, and straightened himself, wiping his dagger on his handkerchief. 'Hoist it on to your back, Will,' he said cheerfully. 'His Majesty shall have his mutton.'

'Ay, but it's downright robbery, master!' replied William. 'I'll have to pay Mr Staunton for it, so I will, for he's an honest gentleman, and I wouldn't like to have it on my conscience I'd thieved one of his best wethers.'

'Be easy, the blame is mine. Hoist it up, now: we will bestow it in the cellar, and his Majesty shall have some slices for his breakfast.'

The King, meanwhile, unable to bear his restricted quarters any longer, had climbed out of the priest's hole; and, after spending some time at his prayers, stretched his cramped legs a little by walking up and down the cheese-room. He told Richard, who, at the first sounds of movement, had come up the attic-stairs to discover if he needed anything, that he thought himself in a very good look-out place, indicating with a wave of his hand the window at one end.

'Ay, 'tis good enough, but there'll be none stirring yet awhiles,' agreed Richard. 'I would bring your honour down to the parlour, only that the Major did say to keep you close till he came back.'

'Came back? Where has he gone?' demanded the King.

'He's taken Will off with him to Mr Staunton's sheepfold, to get some mutton for your honour,' replied Richard.

The King burst out laughing. 'I swear I love that man! A whole sheep for my diet?'

'Ay,' said Richard severely. 'And not honestly come by, master. Will is sadly put about over it, but seeing it's for your honour, and Mr Staunton mighty well-affected to you, he said he'd go along with the Major.'

'And the others? Where are they?'

'Francis Yates and George be on guard, master. Humphrey's gone off to his home, and John to Moseley, to find my lord. Will's wife she do need me to chop a bit of wood for the parlour fire, so if your honour will be pleased to stay here safe I'd best be budging.'

The King gave his word to remain close by his hiding-place, and Richard clumped down the stairs again. It was not long before a lighter footstep sounded, and Major Carlis came up to the cheese-room. The King welcomed him with a smile. 'My friend, what villainy have you been about?'

Carlis kissed his hand. 'Why sir, you must know that you cannot keep a soldier from plunder!' He looked keenly at the King. 'Alas! You have not slept, sir.'

'Not very much. It is irksome in that cavern to one of my inches. It is also devilishly stuffy. What have you done with your corpse, Carlis?'

'I've bestowed it in the cellar, sir, to grow cold. Meanwhile, a fire awaits you in the parlour. Will you be pleased to come down?'

'Very pleased,' said the King, with a comical grimace. 'Did I tell you that I liked the smell of cheese? I lied then.'

Carlis laughed, and went down the stairs before him to open the door at the bottom. Both William and Richard Penderel were in the parlour, Richard feeding the fire, and William waiting to discuss with the Major the measures to be taken for the King's safety throughout the day.

'I'm thinking the oak tree is maybe the surest hiding-place,' he said. 'Only his Majesty might not be wishful to spend another day in it.'

'I am not at all wishful to spend another day in it,' said the King, sitting down beside the fireplace.

'There's the coppice,' suggested William doubtfully.

'And there it may stay,' said the King, thrusting a hand into his leather doublet, and pulling out a coarse handker-chief. 'I'll none of it.'

William scratched his head. 'Will you bide in the priest-hole, then, master?'

The King was holding the handkerchief to his nose, and said in a muffled voice: 'I'll go into it, if I'm forced, but I'll not stay there.' He removed his handkerchief to add: 'Cromwell's godly men won't search for me on the Sabbath, I'll be sworn.'

He pressed the handkerchief to his nose again, but not before Richard, kneeling in front of the fire at his feet, had seen the blood on it.

'Master!' Richard exclaimed, aghast. 'Master, what ails you? Will – your honour!'

'Peace, peace! It's only my nose begun to bleed!' said the King.

Carlis, who had sprung forward to his side, bent over him, an expression on his face of considerable anxiety. 'Sir, are you sure you are not ill? Tell me!'

'It's the hardships his honour's borne so patient!' Richard said, wringing his hands.

'Ay, you shouldn't ought to have taken him to Madeley,' said William. 'I knew it were not fit for him, so dainty-reared and all!'

The King stretched out his free hand. 'Oddsfish, don't look as though you thought to see me fall dead at your feet! I tell you it is but my nose bleeding. It often does so.'

This reassurance, though it did not entirely set his hosts' minds at rest, allayed a little of their alarm. They continued to hover about him, suggesting remedies, to all of which he shook his head, and could none of them be induced to go about their several businesses until they had satisfied themselves that the bleeding had quite stopped. He was touched, and a good deal amused by their concern, but when he was at last able to restore his blood-stained clout to his pocket, Carlis said: 'This is the outcome of too much hardship, even as Richard says. Would to God I could devise some way —'

'Would to God you would not make such a piece of work about nothing!' interrupted the King.

'Ay, but isn't there naught we can do for your honour?' begged Richard.

'You can get me some breakfast,' said the King.

This request put William in mind of the carcass in his cellar, and he at once bore Richard off with him to cut it up into joints. Dame Joan being busy about the farmyard, the King commanded William to bring a frying-pan and butter into the parlour. This being done, he cut some collops off the leg of mutton William had brought him, and set about cooking them himself.

William, shocked to see the King performing such a menial task, would have gone out to summon his wife, but the King forbade him, saying merrily: 'Do you think I don't know how to cook? Carlis, we must have more butter!'

Carlis brought it and dropped it into the pan. 'You will roast yourself as well as the mutton, sir. Let me hold the pan!'

'You would ruin all,' replied the King. 'When I give the word, you may turn the collops. 'Tis I who am master-cook here. Get me a trencher for when my breakfast shall be ready, William!'

William went away, shaking his head. The King, sitting on a joint-stool close to the fire, held the frying-pan over the flames, giving it a little shake now and then, and laughing at Carlis's efforts to turn the slices without burning his own hand in the spitting fat.

'Courage, my hardened campaigner!' he mocked. 'If you splash me, I shall drop the pan!'

'I warrant you will, sir! – The devil! I'd rather face a charge of cavalry than this plaguey fat! Now who is the master-cook? Your Majesty who but holds the pan, or I who have turned the slices?'

'Scullion's work, I promise you,' said the King. 'Who cut the collops? Who measured what butter was needed?'

When William returned with a trencher and a loaf of bread, the mutton was done (the King said) to a turn.

'And even some of it to a cinder,' added Carlis, spearing a somewhat charred slice on the point of his knife.

'Your portion,' said the King.

'I thank you – master-cook!'

'Fie, are you still envious? *My* master-cook shall give judgment between us – one day.'

By the time the King had eaten the collops, and washed

them down with some sack, the autumn morning-mist had lifted from the fields, and the sun had pierced the clouds. Humphrey came in to bring the news of a fine day to come, and no rebel troops to be seen abroad. The King was so sure that the day would be spent by all Puritans in godly exercises that nothing the Penderels urged could prevail upon him to go into hiding. He elected to sit with a book in a pretty little arbour in the garden, which was set upon a mound and so commanded a view of the neighbouring countryside. Carlis, having begged him unavailingly to retire to some safer place, said with the hint of a smile: 'With submission, sir, I must say that I find your Majesty very obstinate.'

The King's eyes rolled towards him, in a look half of drollery, half of penitence. 'Nay, you wrong me.'

'I am very sure I do not,' said the Major dryly. 'But if I allow you to have your way, sir, you shall first make me this promise, that upon a word from me you will retire without question into the secret place.'

The King said pensively: 'Allow?'

'Yes, my child: allow,' repeated Carlis. 'For when your life is at stake, look you, I dare not stand upon terms with you. Come! You may clap me into the Tower later, but be guided by me now!'

'You need not use me so harshly,' protested the King. 'I begin to think myself back in Scotland.'

Carlis smiled. 'Dear sir, you may have my head to play at pitch-and-toss with, but not your own.'

The King laughed. 'A soft answer! Well, I will swear to obey you. But as you love me do not send me to my damned uneasy dungeon without good cause!'

'Oh, trust me, sir, I will not! I think you are perhaps right, and they will not search very strictly for you today. But I shall be glad to get you safe away from here, and that right speedily.'

'Yes,' the King said sardonically. 'Each one of my subjects must be glad to see me safe out of his house. I should have got myself killed at Worcester. I should certainly have preferred to die in battle than upon a scaffold, as I seem likely to do.' He opened his book, and began to flick over the pages. 'My father lived a King, and died a gentleman. I desire to live a King, and although I think it makes little odds how I die, I own I should not choose to be dragged out of some hiding-place to my death.'

Carlis replied with a little difficulty: 'Your Majesty will not die so. You must escape, if only to cheat your enemies.'

'Of all the reasons that have been shown me why my life should be preserved, I never heard one that appealed to me more strongly than that,' said the King.

## CHAPTER VII

## THE WEIGHT OF THREE KINGDOMS

THE morning passed quietly, the brothers, who were mounting guard, raising no alarm to send the King into hiding. He remained for the most part in the arbour, sometimes reading, sometimes talking to Carlis; and occasionally stretching his legs in a rather painful walk about the garden. A very little of this exercise was enough to convince him that his feet would not carry him far. He was, moreover, so mentally and physically fatigued that even to converse was an effort; but the sleep which he needed was driven away by care; and although he lay down upon a bed for some time, he could get no rest, his brain continuing obstinately to worry over its problems, and his body suffering all the pains of over-exertion.

Major Carlis had worries also. Very little more was needed, he thought, to make the King really ill; but since every moment that he spent in the neighbourhood of White-Ladies was dangerous, ill or well he must be got away. When noon came without anything being heard of John Penderel, a still greater anxiety was hidden beneath the Major's invincibly cheerful manner. Moseley Hall lay some eight or nine miles to the east of Boscobel, but since

John had set out at daybreak to walk there, he must, if he had found Lord Wilmot, have had time to have delivered his message, and to have brought back an answer. As the hours crept on, the possibility of Wilmot's having left Moseley before John could reach him began to assume the aspect of a certainty. If Wilmot, believing the King to be in Wales, was gone past recall, the King would be in a perilous predicament. Beyond their own district, the Penderels could be of no service to him, and Carlis, who would have liked nothing better than to have become his escort, was too well known throughout all the neighbouring countryside to be anything but an added danger to him.

The Penderels, who thought with Carlis that John's continued absence boded very ill, conferred amongst themselves at great length, but were unable to offer any other suggestion than that Richard should immediately set out for Moseley Hall, to discover what had gone amiss, and, if necessary, to disclose the secret of the King's presence at Boscobel to Father Huddleston, in the hope that he might be of assistance.

This plan Carlis rejected without hesitation, since John, whether he found Lord Wilmot or not, was bound to return to Boscobel.

Another hour passed. The King enquired what the time was, and upon being told that it was nearly four o'clock, looked a little startled. 'So late? Is it far to Moseley?'

'Nay, 'tis a bare nine miles, master,' Richard blurted out. 'We be afeard of a mischance.'

'My Lord Wilmot must have departed from Moseley.'

'We do not know that, sir,' interposed Carlis.

The King glanced from one grave face to the next. When he saw how anxiously the Penderels watched him, he said lightly: 'Well, if he has, he should not be difficult to trace, judging from what I hear of his progress! Do not look so glum: if I must, I shall do very well without my lord.'

'Of course you will,' said Carlis. 'It is merely that we must make a new plan for your Majesty's safety, and that is easily done, once we bend our minds to it. For the present, we must wait in patience for John's return.'

They had not much longer to wait, for at half-past four John came in. He was greeted with a warmth that betrayed anxiety, and, having touched his forelock to the King, said in his serious way: 'I do be powerful sorry I've kept your honour waiting. But seeing my lord was gone away to Colonel Lane's, I was bound to trudge after him.'

'You found him?' Carlis said quickly.

'Ay, to be sure I did,' John replied, faintly surprised at the question. 'You should ought to know I'd not be here else, master. I found him, and 'tis all arranged betwixt us that his Majesty shall meet him at Mr Whitgreave's this night.'

'You are the trustiest of envoys, John!' said the King. 'I thank you.'

'John does be the one as takes pains,' agreed William, looking proudly at his brother. 'We was afeard my lord was gone past recall, John.'

' 'Tis God's mercy he were not,' said John. 'For my lord made off to Bentley Hall yester-night, Colonel Lane having visited him privately on Thursday evening for to tell him that Mrs Jane Lane, which is his sister, had procured a pass from the Governor of Stafford for herself and a servant to go to Bristol. And the Colonel, bethinking him that my lord should travel with her as her servant, did greatly urge him to it, which my lord refused till he should know what had befallen your Majesty, but begged the Colonel to stay his sister's going till he should hear from him again. And me bringing my lord news of your Majesty's having gone with Richard towards Severn, for to pass into Wales, my lord, accordingly, next morning, which was Saturday, sent to Colonel Lane's for his horses, and at midnight took leave of Mr Whitgreave, and went off to Bentley. But Mr Whitgreave, which is a very honest man, and the good Father being sadly anxious to get news of your Majesty, they took the notion to walk to White-Ladies this day, to learn what they might. And they was a-walking together on the backside of the orchard this morning when I come suddenly upon them.' John's solemnity was momentarily lightened by a slow smile. 'I warrant you, they did not look to see me, and when I up and asked them mighty urgent, *Where is my lord?* they was sadly put out of countenance. *He is gone*, says the good Father; whereat I was in a consternation, and told them we was all undone, for your Majesty, finding the passages over Severn all guarded, was come back to Boscobel, and we knew not what to do with you, or how to dispose of you. And further I disclosed to them that your Majesty was hid in an oak-tree with only the Major here for guard, and much dejected, wherefor you had sent me to find my lord, that he should take some speedy course for your removal and security.'

'Alas, poor Wilmot!' murmured the King, much entertained by this ingenuous recital. 'He must be repenting him of having saddled himself with such a charge!'

'Nay,' said John seriously. 'Myself, I did think my lord a poor meacock body, but I'm bound to tell your honour I found him mighty sprag to come to your aid. For Mr Whitgreave, look you, being much moved by your danger and calamity, took me along with Father Huddleston to Bentley, for to find my lord; which being done, and me having told my lord in what case I had left your Majesty, my lord instantly bade the Colonel stay his sister's journey yet longer, and concerted with me how he should best contrive your Majesty's safe escape. And the long and the short of it is, master, that we Penderels, and Francis Yates beside, will conduct your honour to Moseley this night, and there meet my lord at midnight, or as near as maybe.'

'But I cannot walk nine miles,' said the King.

This statement, tossed so casually into the midst of John's plans, was productive of a dismayed silence. Having made his announcement, the King leaned his head against the high chair-back and sleepily regarded his odd little court. It was evident he awaited further suggestions. Carlis, looking down at him as he sat there, entirely at his ease, neither his abominable clothes nor his cropped head disguising his indefinable air of majesty, was suddenly betrayed into a laugh.

This brought the King's eyes round to his face. He said with less than his usual good humour: 'Let me share this jest, if you please! I should be glad to discover what there is to laugh at in my present condition.'

Carlis shook his head. 'Alas, there is nothing, sir! Nay, do not look so crossly at me! Must I not laugh to see you transform this parlour into your council chamber, and us, your poor servants, into a court?'

The King looked blankly at him. 'God he knows what you mean, Carlis; I do not. Here is neither King nor court, but a wretched fugitive with sore feet, sitting with his very good friends.'

'Nay,' said Richard. 'Your honour is graciously pleased to say so, but 'tis like I told you in Spring Coppice: there's no mistaking what you be, do what I will to learn you different.'

'A plague on your carping!' said the King. 'You said I trod too proudly, but that is a fault I'll swear you can no longer find in me, since I limp along now like any footsore hobbledehoy.' He added with a note of finality in his voice: 'But I will not nor I cannot limp nine miles to Moseley, and so I tell you.'

'No, your Majesty is in no case to walk half that distance,' said Carlis. 'We must contrive a little.' He glanced at the three Penderels. 'Is there no horse hereabouts that we could come by?'

William shook his head; Richard said doubtfully: 'There's my lord's horses. Happen I could fetch one of them for his honour to ride upon. 'Tis a pity John didn't think to bring one back along with him.'

'God send you more wit and me more money!' replied John scornfully. 'A rare trick that, to go a-leading a blood-horse of the like of my lord's about the countryside, ay, and all them rebels after it for to see where I'd be taking it!'

'No, that won't serve,' Carlis said decidedly. 'There must be some neighbour who owns a nag you could borrow upon some pretext.'

'"A horse! A horse! My Kingdom for a horse!"' murmured the King.

'I'll not do it,' John replied. 'If we had need of a horse we should take up Humphrey's from grass, and so all the neighbours know full well.'

'What's that?' Carlis said. 'Do you say that Humphrey owns a horse? Then in God's name, man, why could you not tell us so before?'

'I did bethink me of it,' answered John, 'but 'tis a pitiful old nag, in no ways fit for his Majesty to ride upon, being but the mill-horse, master. I wouldn't durst offer such to his Majesty for that he would disdain it.'

'Oddsfish, what case am I in to disdain even a mill-horse?' demanded the King. 'Will he bear me?'

'Ay, that he will, master, no question.'

'Then one of you go and take him up from grass,' ordered Carlis. 'Meanwhile, his Majesty waits for his supper.'

This reminder was enough to send William off at once to seek his wife; and, after discussing with the Major the time the King should be in readiness to set forth, the other two departed.

The King spent the evening in the parlour with Carlis, before the fire. He spoke very little, but sat with his elbow on the arm of his chair, his head supported on his hand. The flickering fire-light showed Carlis that he was awake, but he sat very still, gazing with heavy eyes into the heart of the fire. Once he said: 'When must I set forward?'

'Not before nine o'clock, sir, if you are to be at Moseley by midnight. I fear you will find the journey very rough and tedious. Humphrey's horse is indeed a sorry beast.'

'No matter, if I find my Lord Wilmot in the end.'

'Be sure you will, sir.'

'I lose count of the days. It seems a long time since I parted from him, and the others who were with me. I would I knew that they were alive still.'

'Why, sir, they had a better hope of life than your Majesty, and you are alive.'

'True. But I greatly fear for them. Many of my friends must have died in Worcester, in that last fight. I wonder how many fell there? It is in my mind, Carlis, that I shall not see Hamilton again.'

'You have at least one faithful friend left to you in my Lord Wilmot, sir. And you will be glad of his company. Do you think I do not understand what it must mean to you to be cast amongst strangers who have never been alone in all your life before?'

'Carlis, Carlis, do you call yourself a stranger?'

'Nay, sir, but a poor soldier; not one who has been used to wait upon a King.'

'I was never so well-cared for, I promise you. But I am ashamed to be such a grievous a burden upon your shoulders.'

'My liege, if I should die tomorrow it would be happily, since so sweet a prince entrusted his life into my hands for two precious days,' Carlis said unsteadily.

The King turned his head. 'Why, what is this? You go with me to Moseley, surely?'

'No, sir. We must part here. I am too well-known in this country to go with you. For your sake, I dare not do it.'

'Alas!' The King's voice sounded disconsolate. 'I had thought you would remain with me. How shall I fare without you, Carlis?'

Carlis slipped from his chair to his knees, and, taking the King's hand in his, kissed it. 'You will fare very well, for the Penderels will take good care of you, sir, and bring you safely to my lord.'

'Yes, but —' The King broke off. 'You are right, I suppose. Yet I am sorry that I must part from you. What shall you do?'

'I shall make my way to France, sir, and there kiss your Majesty's hand again.'

The King smiled faintly. 'Yea, God willing.'

He relapsed into silence again, from which he was only roused by the arrival of Richard, who came into the parlour to warn him that it was time to start upon the journey to Moseley.

When he had taken his leave of Dame Joan, which he did very charmingly, thanking her for all her care, and kissing her cheek with easy familiarity, he went out with Carlis to where all five Penderels and Francis Yates awaited him in the yard. He checked upon the threshold when he saw them, a laugh springing to his lips, for they presented a comical appearance, being armed each one with clubs and bills.

'Oho, you mean to sell my life dearly, I see!' he said. 'But indeed I have no need of such an escort, good friends. I will take two, and no more.'

'So please your Majesty, we would like all to go with you,' replied John firmly. 'Will and I will trudge ahead for to see the road clear, and Francis and George here come along behind lest there be spies following, which we can't tell.'

'Let it be so, sir,' said Carlis. 'We know not whom you may meet upon the road. Six men are better than two.'

'What, do you foresee a pitched battle?' mocked the King. 'Well, do as you please. Indeed, I am much beholden to you.'

Humphrey then led up his mill-horse, a slow-plodding beast, fat from having been at grass, and accoutred with a ramshackle saddle that had long since outworn its irons, and a bridle that looked as though it might at any moment part company with the rusty bit.

'Lend me your knee, Trusty Dick,' said the King, observing the absence of stirrups. 'I am in no vaulting humour.'

'By your leave, sir!' Carlis said. 'Set your foot in my hands, and I will mount you.'

This being done, and the King settled in the saddle, which he complained was the strangest he had ever encountered, William and John went out into the lane to be sure that no one was within sight, and Humphrey and Richard took up their stations, one on either side of the horse, Humphrey holding the bridle, and Richard shouldering a stout hand-bill.

The King leaned down to give his hand to Carlis to kiss. 'Fare you well, my good friend. I pray you, have a care to yourself!'

'Never fear for me, sir: I shall be in France as soon as your Majesty. God have you in His keeping, sir!'

A low whistle from William told of a clear road ahead, and Humphrey began to lead the horse away from the house. The King turned in the saddle as he reached the gate, and waved his hand. Carlis lifted his own hand in answer, and for several moments after the King had disappeared from sight remained standing quite still, his face rather grim, and in his mind the vision, not of a shabby figure drooping a little on the back of a mill-horse, but of a straight young man with plumes mingling with his black lovelocks, a blue riband swept across his buff coat, and a diamond George sparkling on his breast, who sat a plunging charger as though he were a part of it.

Dame Joan's voice recalled him; he turned, saying with an effort: 'Ay, what is it?'

' 'Tis like it was all a dream, master,' she said. 'Only that William has his precious hair put by safe I wouldn't believe 'twas real!'

The Penderel brothers, meanwhile, led the King away from the Brewood highroad, a little way down the lane that led from Boscobel to White-Ladies. His steed's gait was awkward, and he soon discovered that to add to the discomforts of a bad saddle and a shambling horse, the Penderels were determined to proceed down by-lanes which were pitted with holes in which the horse every now and then plunged a clumsy forefoot. He was thus very much jolted, but after protesting once, and being told that his escort dared not take the risk of leading him down the better but more frequented roads, he sighed and relapsed into silence, bearing the many stumbles with great patience, and resolutely shutting his lips on the exclamations of exasperation which rose to them at the repeated halts which were made to enable William and John to scout well ahead of him.

The way seemed interminable, and was indeed very circuitous; and to make matters worse the storm-clouds, which had been gathering all the evening in the sky, soon obscured the moon. After about an hour's tedious going, it began to rain, a circumstance which made the King repeat his request to be conducted along easier roads, since the rain might be supposed to have chased Royalists and Roundheads alike within doors. But the Penderels, themselves impervious to rain and rough walking, were so much obsessed by the sense of the responsibility that rested on their shoulders that they could not be brought to agree to this.

'You shouldn't ought to ask it of us, master,' Richard said.

'God's truth, it's my life that is at stake, after all!' said the King.

'Nay, 'tis all our lives, my liege. Look you, if you be taken through any fault of ours we mun go hang ourselves.'

'Ay, that's so,' agreed Humphrey. 'No help for it.'

'I see not the least necessity,' said the King. 'But lead on, lead on!'

The night had by this time become so dark that it was very difficult to make out the way. More than one false turning was taken, and the mill-horse presently stumbled so badly that the King was almost thrown over its head. His annoyance momentarily getting the better of him, he said angrily: 'God's body, can you not lead the brute so that he does not bring me down with him in the mire?'

'I do be mortal sorry, master,' replied Humphrey apologetically. ' 'Tis tricky, you see, me not being able to spy the holes very well. But the horse'll not let your honour down, I promise you.'

'It's the heaviest dull jade I ever rode upon!' said the King.

Humphrey looked up slyly into his face, and said with a grin: 'My liege, can you blame the horse to go heavily when he has the weight of three kingdoms on his back?'

The King gave a reluctant laugh. 'A wit, i' faith! I think he will soon sink under me.'

'Nay, not he, master. Why, he's carried six strike of corn in his time, and none the worse for it.'

'A strike? How much is that?' enquired the King, idly curious. 'I never heard the word before.'

'No?' said Humphrey, surprised. ' 'Tis common in these parts. How much would a strike be, Dick?'

Richard, after due consideration, measured a space in the air with his hands. 'It would be like that, maybe.'

'I suppose it is a bushel,' remarked the King. 'But I am not learned in such matters.'

'Ay, that'll be it,' Richard agreed.

They plodded on, the brothers only speaking when it was necessary to confer together about the route to be followed, and the King becoming lost once more in his own unquiet thoughts. The rain, which kept falling in fitful showers, dripped off the brim of his steeple-crowned hat, and soaked the green jump-coat he wore over Richard's leather doublet. He made no further complaint, however, but suffered the Penderels to lead him where they chose.

It was past midnight when a halt was called in a valley where a mill-stream burbled over the pebbles on its bed. William and John were waiting beside a stile for the King to come up with them, and as soon as George Penderel and Francis Yates had caught up with the rest, the brothers held a low-voiced conference amongst themselves. At the end of it, Richard came to the King's knee and said in his stolid way: 'Master, Will and John they do think it be unsafe to go farther along the road with the horse, we being come to Pendeford Mill, which is hard by Moseley, and Mr Whitgreave being a Catholic like ourselves, and mightily suspected. We be wishful to lead your honour by the Moor, so as none will see you.'

'Richard, Richard, do you mean to lead me through bogs and hedges yet again?' said the King.

'Nay, 'tis easy walking, master, and three of us to help your honour.'

The King smiled wryly in the darkness. 'I know you, fellow: you would cozen me on with false promises as you did before. Tell me the truth, how far must I walk?'

'Master, as I am a Christian, 'tis no more than two miles.'

'Country miles, I'll be sworn. Well, do with me as you will.'

William and John, being informed of the King's docility, heaved audible sighs of relief. To facilitate his descent from the saddle, they led the mill-horse into the ditch beside the stile, on to which the King dismounted. Richard helped him over it into a stubble-field, and he remarked as cheerfully as he could that it was a relief to alight from such an incommodious saddle.

'Your feet do not pain you too much for the trudge, master?' Richard asked anxiously.

'No, no, let us go on! It must be long past midnight, and my lord, I daresay, thinking me dead, or a prisoner.'

He took a few steps forward as he spoke, but stopped

when he perceived that only three of his escort were with him, and realized that the others were going no farther on the journey. He turned and went back to where William and Humphrey and George were still standing beside the stile, and held out his hand, saying simply: 'My troubles make me forget myself: I thank you all!'

They fell on their knees on the sodden ground to kiss his hand.

'If ever I come into England by fair or foul means, I will remember you,' he said. 'Let me see you, whenever it shall so please God!'

The rest of his journey lay over open country, and was rather painfully accomplished. His impatience to find Wilmot carried the King forward, even when the sharp stones working through his slit shoes hurt him most. John told him that Father Huddleston had directed him to meet him at the Pit Leasow, which was a dry limestone pit by a little grove of trees in a close behind Moseley Hall. This was approached from the Moor by the narrow avenue in which John had found the Father and Mr Whitgreave walking together earlier in the day. Owing partly to the darkness, and partly to the King's halting progress, it was nearly two o'clock in the morning when at last John sighted the grove. A few more steps brought them up to it, and not one but two figures emerged from the shelter of the trees to meet them. The stockier of these stood hesitating, while the other unshrouded the lantern he carried, and held it up so that its light fell on the faces of the King and his escort.

It was the priest who held the lantern, as John informed the King in a brief whisper. His companion, Mr Whitgreave, looking from one shabby figure to another, could not tell which was the King, but John at once greeted Huddleston, saying with an expressive jerk of his thumb towards the King: 'We've fetched his Majesty safe, Father, and he be mighty wishful for to see my lord.'

'He is within doors, most eagerly awaiting your Majesty,' Huddleston said. He had a quick, vibrant voice, and seemed as far as Charles could discern in the feeble light, to be grey-haired and elderly. He bent the knee to the King, but said almost at once: 'Your Majesty will forgive this unseemly reception. We thought it not safe to bring you in by the front way. Indeed, I beg your Majesty will not linger even here, but come in straight to my lord.'

'I care nothing for my reception, so you bring me to my lord,' the King replied.

He sounded exhausted and leaned heavily upon the staff he had taken from Richard. Huddleston said with swift compassion: 'Sire, you shall be with my lord in an instant. John, where are your wits? Lend the King your arm, and bring him in! We have been sadly anxious, sire, fearing some mischance had befallen you.'

The house lay only a few hundred yards from the Pit Leasow, and was soon reached. A door gave on to a kitchen-yard and, being opened, disclosed a short flight of narrow, steep stairs immediately within the house.

'Straight up, sire, and softly!' whispered Huddleston, holding the lantern on high. 'We must not wake the servants.'

A door creaked on the landing above, and a shaft of light shone across the floor. A bulky figure appeared at the head of the stairs, and, seeing it, the King went quickly up. A pair of warm hands caught his; Wilmot's voice whispered with a break in it: 'My dear master! Safe! Safe!'

'Harry, thank God I have found you!'

Wilmot flung an arm round him, and swept him across the landing to the open door and through it into a panelled bedchamber in the front of the house. The curtains were drawn close across the window, a fire burned in the grate at the foot of the bed, and a number of candles lit the room.

The King pulled off his battered hat, throwing it aside. Wilmot, seeing the ravage of his face, gave a choked exclamation, and knelt down, embracing his knees, ready tears springing to his eyes.

The King bent, and pulled him to his feet, and kissed his cheek. 'Harry, what of Buckingham, Cleveland and the others?' he asked urgently.

'I know not – I have heard nothing. But *you* are safe! What else signifies? Alas, alas, what you have suffered, my dearest liege!'

The King managed to smile. 'Nay, 'tis only the walnut juice staining my face that makes you think so. I am well – very well.'

He heard footsteps on the landing, and turned his head as the priest, followed by Mr Whitgreave, came into the room, and paused diffidently upon the threshold.

No two men could have been more dissimilar. Father Huddleston, who was dressed very simply as a private gentleman, was a sparely built man, with a hatchet-face that had humorous lines carved in it, a pair of lively brilliant eyes deeply set under rather over-hanging brows, and a coarse pugnacious nose. He was over forty years old, but seemed less, having a certain impetuosity of manner, and a quick way of moving. He wore his clothes carelessly, and his grey hair waved loosely back from his face. Beside him, Thomas Whitgreave looked neat to the point of primness. He was a younger man, but more sedate than the priest, moving and speaking with deliberation, his hair brushed smoothly into ordered curls that just reached his shoulders, and every detail of his dress arranged with precision. His nose was slightly aquiline, the firm mouth under it rather small, and his eyes very calm and direct.

Wilmot, on whose cheeks the tears still glistened, said in a moved voice: 'My good friends, though I have not disclosed the truth to you, yet I think you know it. This is my master – your master – the master of us all!'

'Yes, my lord we did know it,' Whitgreave said. 'Sire, the honour your Majesty does me in trusting your sacred person to my care makes me barren of speech.'

'We are your Majesty's humble servants to command!' the priest said.

The King gave them his hand to kiss, saying: 'Indeed, gentlemen, I have received such an account of your fidelity to my lord that I shall never forget it.'

'It is very true, sir; I owe them a debt I can never repay,' said Wilmot. 'You must know that Mr Whitgreave fought throughout the late wars in Captain Giffard's troop, which formed a part of my brigade.'

'Is it so? I am indeed come amongst friends,' the King replied. 'I need not ask whether you who fought for my father are willing to conceal his son.'

'Sire, I am very willing.'

'Mr Whitgreave knows how earnestly I desired, whilst I lay here, that my friends were with me. I never saw so secure a hiding-place, I do assure you, sir.'

'Yes, the hiding-place!' said the King. 'Where is it?'

'It is here, sir,' Whitgreave replied, going to the wall beside the fireplace. The panelling slid open under his fingers, disclosing a cupboard. A trap-door in the floor of this gave access to a small brick chamber, into which the King immediately lowered himself, to test its dimensions. Being informed by Whitgreave that the cavity in one corner was a portion of a chimney that led down to the brewhouse, rude steps being cut in the bricks to afford footholds, he expressed himself well content with the place.

'But I trust I may not be obliged to seek refuge there, for it is very dank and stuffy, I think,' he remarked, climbing out of it, and coming back into the room. 'You must know, Harry, that I spent a very damnable night in the priest's hole at Boscobel, and was like to have died of cramp there.' He found that his nose was beginning to bleed again, and pulled out his already bloodstained handkerchief, saying as he sat down on the edge of the bed: 'A pox on this plaguey nose of mine that will not give me any peace!'

Father Huddleston went to him, trying to make him lie down upon the bed. When he observed the condition of the wretched clout the King held to his nose, he was a good deal concerned, and said in his quick way: 'Your Majesty is absolutely spent! Such persistent nose-bleeding is very bad, and must be stopped. My lord, the King must rest, ay, and he must eat! Mr Whitgreave, we are sadly remiss to stand gaping here!'

Mr Whitgreave, however, was not gaping. He had, in fact, upon closing the cupboard in the wall, told Wilmot quietly that he would go down to the buttery to fetch refreshment for the King, and had left the room. Huddleston went after him, returning in a few minutes with one of his own handkerchiefs, which he gave to the King, removing the stained clout from his grasp.

While the King sat still upon the bed, waiting for his nose to stop bleeding, Huddleston, whose keen eyes had not missed one detail of his deplorable costume, busied himself with the preparation of warm water for the bathing of his feet, and fetched into the room clean stockings, and a fine flaxen shirt to take the place of the noggen one which continually fretted the King's skin. As soon as the King was able to remove his handkerchief from his nose, Huddleston requested Wilmot to bring him to the fire, where a comfortable chair awaited him. The King sank into it and while Wilmot hovered beside him, Huddleston knelt own before him to strip off his shoes and his mudsoaked stirrup-stockings.

The sight of the King's feet, which were still very swollen, and in some places raw, affected Wilmot profoundly. He dared not trust his voice, but wetted the King's hand with his tears. Huddleston, not less moved, but by far more practical, bathed and dried the feet. He found that the paper which had been put into the King's shoes to give him greater ease had rolled itself between and under his toes, and was responsible for more than one blister. He exclaimed wrathfully at the folly of Richard's wife, when the King explained how the paper came to be there, and was careful to remove every scrap of it before putting clean stockings on to the King.

'And now if your Majesty will stand up, we may remove these wet clothes, and put you into a softer shirt. Ay, it irks you sadly, that rough noggen, does it not? The Penderels should think shame on themselves to suppose you could be comfortable in such coarse stuff!'

'Nay, how should they bring me better? They gave me what they had, and I was grateful.' He let Wilmot tie the strings of the shirt at his throat, and added: 'Where are they? I do not desire them to leave this place until I have seen them, and thanked them for their great care of me.'

'No, no, they will not do so, I promise your Majesty! Mr Whitgreave took them to the buttery, and will give them a good supper. Do not trouble your head over them!' replied Huddleston.

He spread the King's jump-coat before the fire to dry as he spoke; hung the greasy leather doublet over a chair near by; and began to remove the bowl of water and the cloths. The King sat down again in his shirt and breeches, and shut his eyes, and in a few moments Mr Whitgreave came in with some sack for him, and biscuits.

The King roused himself at a beseeching word from Wilmot, and smiled at his host. 'I thank you, I thank you! I am very hungry indeed.'

The food and the wine revived him. His face began to look less haggard under its stain, and when Wilmot asked him tenderly how he did, he replied in a stronger, more cheerful voice: 'Why, so well that I am now ready for another march. And if it should please God once more to place me at the head of but eight or ten thousand good men – of one mind, and resolved to fight,' he added with a flash of mordant humour, 'I shall not doubt to drive these rogues out of my Kingdoms!'

<br>

**CHAPTER VIII**

### 'SOLDIERS, SOLDIERS ARE COMING!'

WILMOT, who was unable to shake off the dismay with which the King's appearance had filled him, was anxious to put him at once to bed, but Charles, revived by his supper, and very much more comfortable now that he had shed his shoes, and had exchanged his noggen-shirt for Father Huddleston's flaxen one, said that he felt no extraordinary fatigue, but was desirous of talking over the plans for his escape. Mr Whitgreave made a sign to Huddleston, and they were both about to withdraw when Wilmot called sharply after them that provision must be made for keeping a strict watch about the house while the King lay in it.

Whitgreave replied that it had been already arranged that he himself would stand guard within the house, while Huddleston remained outside to warn him of anyone's approach.

'We should take it in turns to keep watch outside, but Mr Huddleston is very obdurate,' he said, with a slight smile.

'Obdurate! Ay!' exclaimed Huddleston. 'Your Majesty must know that Mr Whitgreave is only just risen from a sick bed. He would not tell you so, but it is right you should be informed of the cause that kept him from joining your Majesty's army at Worcester.'

'Indeed, I am sorry,' the King said.

'I thank your Majesty, but I am quite well now – very well,' Whitgreave replied. 'My lord, you need be under no apprehension. If you should desire to speak with me, I shall be in my study: you know the way.'

He bowed and went out, closing the door softly behind him. The King said: 'I wonder to find so many people well-disposed towards me that never before set eyes on me. It would have amazed you, Harry, to have seen the exceeding great care that was taken of me by these poor Penderels.'

'That I could have left you in their hands! I knew, I *knew* that I should not do so! I begged you not to bid me leave you!'

'Why, yes,' Charles interrupted. 'But I am still of the same mind, Harry, and if you think I mean to ride about the country with you, while you go so proudly, looking as my friend Humphrey informed me, as fine as a lord's bastard, you are much mistaken.'

'But my dear sir, you would not have me put on a disguise!' Wilmot protested. 'No, no, I assure you I could not do it! I am too old for such masquerades, and should certainly betray myself. But you shall not again persuade me to leave you.'

'The truth is we acted a trifle hastily,' remarked the King. 'For the future, I will have you stay within my reach. But go with me I swear you shall not! I never saw so palpable a Cavalier in my life. Tell me about these people: am I safe in this house?'

'I would stake my life on Whitgreave's fidelity. I fancy, besides, that Huddleston is a Catholic priest – though it is not admitted. He is here in the guise of a tutor to Whitgreave's nephew, young Sir John Preston, who has been sent here to keep him hidden from the Puritans, they having sequestrated all his father's property. There are two other lads also staying in the house, to share his studies. Besides these, there are the servants and Whitgreave's mother, a very honest dame, as I believe.'

'So many?' The King looked a little startled. 'I wonder the house will hold them all, and me besides. I must not linger here.'

'No,' Wilmot agreed. 'Not above a day or two, I trust. I have been concerting with Lane, sir, and we think we have a plan to carry you safe to Bristol. Would you consent to counterfeit a servant? Colonel Lane – a good, honest soldier, and one who served under me: I know him well – mislikes the notion of asking you to perform so mean a rôle – yet can hit upon no better plan. I said I was very sure you would not disdain it.'

'If *you* did not, how indeed should I?' murmured Charles.

'Now you are laughing at me! Be serious, my dear master, I do beseech you! Your task would be to convey Mrs Jane Lane to Bristol. She must ride behind you upon a double-gelding, of course. A kinsman of Lane, one Henry Lassels that was his Cornet in the late wars, would go with you. I know your Majesty will be pleased with Mrs Jane, for she is a most beautiful young woman, and entirely devoted to you.'

'Is she so indeed?' said the King. 'Then I am sure I stand in no need of Cornet Lassels's escort. In fact, I shall do very much better without it.'

Wilmot laughed. 'No, no, that will not answer at all! You will have, besides, Mrs Jane's sister and her husband, who mean to ride as far as Stratford-upon-Avon with her. They are at present upon a visit to Bentley Hall, but we have not disclosed the truth to them, nor shall not do so. Will you go, sir?'

The King's eyes gleamed under his drooping lids. 'My

dear Harry, you offer me a beautiful young woman to be my escort, and ask me if I will go! Where are your wits, man? Be sure I will go!'

'I see that your troubles have not in the least chastened you,' said Wilmot, smiling at him with deep affection. 'Will you attend to me now, and leave jesting? Lane awaits your answer to this proposal, and I must carry it back to him at once. It will be more convenient, besides, for me to lie at Bentley, since our good host here cannot stable my horse with any safety. There are some matters that must be arranged before we fetch your Majesty to Bentley, notably the procuring of a suit of clothes for you to wear. I think the hiding-place in this house so secure that I could not wish to see you in a better refuge. Therefore, if you agree to it, I shall ride back to Bentley as soon as it is light, and we will keep John Penderel to go between the two houses at need. I have found him a very good sort of a fellow, and one that grudges no pains upon your service. Yet if you prefer me to remain with you —' He broke off, his handsome irresolute countenance flushing suddenly with a little rush of emotion. He knelt down beside the King's chair, and said in a shaken voice: 'Yes, yes, I must remain! I dare not leave you again! Ah, sir, if you knew the agony I have suffered on your behalf! And to see you thus, so spent and buffeted —'

'Oh, peace, peace!' the King said, yawning. 'I don't doubt I look like a scarecrow, but it is not very courtier-like of you to put me in mind of it. Go to Bentley: I think myself in good hands in this house. As for John Penderel, I hope he may not be wishing us both at the devil by this time.'

'Sire, you forget what I am very sure he does not: you are the King!'

'You comfort me, Harry. I feel like a vagrant.'

'If you dislike to keep John, I could employ my man, Swan, upon the business,' said Wilmot. 'Yet I think John would occasion less remark, Swan being —'

'Wilmot, do you tell me that you have kept your servant with you?' demanded Charles.

Wilmot blinked at him. 'But, my dear sir, what else could I do? There are my horses to be cared for, bethink you.

Besides, how should I contrive without him? Really, I could not stir a step!'

'Oh!' gasped the King in a paroxysm of laughter. 'Oh, why is not George here to share this jest with me? *I* trudge my feet raw with none but a poor woodman to be my guide, while *you* ride with your servant at your heels! Odd rot me, I have not laughed so much since I left Holland!'

Wilmot said in rather an injured voice: 'It was your choice, not mine. You *would* go, and how should my wandering about in a like case help you? You know I could never walk far, sir. Now, be still, I implore you! You will rouse the house if you laugh so loud!'

The King's full-throated laughter had already brought Whitgreave into the room. A smile lurked in Whitgreave's eyes, but he said gravely: 'I am glad your Majesty is merry, but I do most humbly beg of you, sir, to be more careful!'

'I will, I will,' the King promised, mopping his eyes with Father Huddleston's handkerchief. 'You must blame my lord for this commotion; indeed, it was not my fault!' He pulled himself up out of his chair, and said, still with a quiver in his voice: 'Put me to bed, Harry. Oh, do not look so much affronted, or you will set me off laughing again.'

Wilmot caught his hands and held them tightly. 'Yes, I will put you to bed, sir. How could you think yourself servantless who have me to wait on you? Come, a truce to this! You are falling asleep where you stand.'

The King suffered himself to be led to the bed and lay down upon it. Wilmot covered him with the quilt, while Whitgreave began to extinguish the candles.

'Are you comfortable, dear sir?' Wilmot asked, bending over the bed.

'So comfortable!' sighed the King.

Wilmot laid a hand on his head, smoothing back his tangled curls. 'Sleep well,' he said softly. 'Sleep well, my dear. You are quite safe.'

The King returned no answer; the candles were all put out, but a leaping flame in the hearth showed Wilmot that he had already closed his eyes, turning his head a little on the pillow. Wilmot tucked the quilt in more securely, and followed Whitgreave out of the room and into the adjoining chamber.

This was a pleasant apartment, which was used by Huddleston and his pupils for their work. Leading out of it, and built over the front porch, was Whitgreave's own study, a tiny square room overlooking the Wolverhampton road. This had a triangular trap-door let into the floor, through which it was possible to drop down into the porch immediately beneath it.

Whitgreave, who had spread some cushions on to a daybed, suggested that Wilmot should lie down upon it, and try to get some sleep.

Wilmot, however, shook his head impatiently. His spirits were evidently much agitated. He began to walk about the room as though he could not bear to be still, and ejaculated in answer to his host: 'Sleep! Do you think I could sleep while his Majesty lies there, in peril of his life?'

Whitgreave considered this quite seriously, replying in a moment: 'Nay, he is in no danger at this present, my lord.'

Wilmot scarcely attended to him. He said, wringing his hands: 'It breaks my heart to see him reduced to such straits! Shall I ever bring him safe to France? The whole countryside up and searching for him – himself so spent and ill – and all, all upon my shoulders!' He turned his face towards Whitgreave, his dreamy eyes haunted by fear, his sensitive mouth quivering. 'And you bid me sleep! Sleep – my God! Shall I ever sleep until this fearful charge is removed from me?'

'I feel for you, my lord, but you should consider that while the King lies under my roof I am as responsible for his safety as yourself. I beg of you, do not torture yourself with hideous imaginings! No one may approach the house without my being forewarned. If danger were to threaten, the King will have ample time to conceal himself in the secret place. I do most earnestly counsel your lordship to rest while you may.'

Wilmot sat down upon the day-bed, saying with a forced laugh: 'Do not heed me! I think myself participating in some nightmare from which I must soon awake. His changed looks, his feet – what he must have undergone! Oh no, no, it is the dreadful truth, and there he lies, trusting in me to save him from his enemies! Whitgreave, Thomas Whitgreave, he is a boy, unused to such hardships, accustomed all his life to be waited upon, cherished, surrounded by friends who love him! It is a miracle that he is here this night. Could any man mistake that face, that great height? How dare I let him adventure his person with Jane Lane as we planned? He must be recognized. Yet carry him to the coast I must!'

He began to bite his nails in an agony of indecision. Whitgreave, who, from the moment of the King's arrival had been forcibly struck by the contrast of his coolness with Wilmot's quite understandable dismay, said soothingly: 'No one will look for his Majesty in the guise of a serving-man. I am not acquainted with him as your lordship is, but I do think that his courage will carry him farther than all our endeavours. Tired he was, when we brought him in, but I never saw a man so unconcerned with the thought of his own peril.'

This drew a smile from Wilmot, but he sighed too, and said: 'Alas, I know him so well that his very courage fills me with misgiving! He will turn all to a jest, and care nothing that he is an anointed King, no ordinary man! You have seen how he can put aside the King. Judge how it will be when he hazards his precious life, as though —'

'I did not see it,' said Whitgreave. 'As he sat there in his dirt and his rags, the thought came to me that no disguise you might put upon him would serve to hide his kingship. I do not think, my lord, that he forgets it, but I will not conceal from you that I fear that air of majesty that clings about him more than I fear his height, or the cast of his countenance.'

Wilmot said wretchedly: 'Is it so plain? My God, my God, what hope has he, then? Yet he is easy, he does not love pomp; indeed, how else could he have borne to disguise himself thus? His father would never have done so!'

'No,' said Whitgreave, the very thought of the late King in his son's plight startling him by its fantastic improbability. 'No, indeed!'

Wilmot sank his head in his hands, but raised it presently

to say in a calmer tone: 'Whitgreave, in case of an alarm, his Majesty must go into the secret chamber, and I into the cupboard that leads to it. If soldiers should come to search the house you will discover me first to them. Haply they will be satisfied and search no farther. You understand me?'

'I understand you perfectly, my lord, and will do as you bid me,' replied Whitgreave, looking at him with a certain sympathetic respect. 'Yet I trust that no such need will arise. And now, since your lordship is to ride at dawn, may I once more beg of you to repose yourself for a little while?'

Wilmot, who was indeed quite worn out by the fret of his own nerves, consented to lie down upon the day-bed and, in spite of his own certainty of being unable to sleep, was soon gently snoring.

Nothing occurred to disturb his slumber until Whitgreave roused him soon after five o'clock, telling him that it was now daylight, and the King awake, and waiting to bid him farewell.

Wilmot found the King sitting up in his bed with Richard Penderel and Francis Yates kneeling beside it to take their humble leave of him. He gave them both his hand to kiss, and reminded them that they were to present themselves at Whitehall, if it should please God ever to restore him to his Kingdom.

'And let me not forget that I owe you ten shillings!' he told Yates, with a twinkle. 'All I can give you now is my thanks. As for you, Trusty Dick, I charge you, keep the memory of the miller at Evelith in mind, for I promise you I shall, and we will enjoy a laugh together over that craven flight of ours when we meet again!'

They were too much overcome to do more than stammer a few disjointed words in answer to him, but they kissed his hand very fervently, and went slowly out of his presence, turning at the door to take a last look at him.

When they had gone, the King nodded at Wilmot, saying cheerfully: 'Harry, I now think I have a reasonable hope of escaping out of this country. And, meanwhile, I have a bed at my disposal, which, in truth, is all I care for. God speed you, my friend, and don't wear that glum face for my sake, for I am very well content to be here, I assure you.'

'Promise me that you will be guided in all things by Thomas Whitgreave, sir!' begged Wilmot. 'Remember how precious to your people is your life!'

'It is a deal more precious to me than to my people, from what I can discover,' retorted the King. 'You have not the least need to fear for me: I do not mean to fall into my arch-enemy's hand, I promise you.'

'Before that happens I shall be dead!' said Wilmot.

The King lay down again, snuggling his cheek into the pillow. 'Harry, don't be tragical!' he said with sleepy amusement. 'You are too fat for it, and I have an empty stomach.'

There was no more to be got out of him, and as Whitgreave came into the room just then to hasten my lord's departure, Wilmot tore himself away.

When he had ridden away on the short journey to Bentley Hall, Whitgreave and Huddleston consulted together on the measures proper to be taken for the King's safety. It was finally agreed that all the servants but the Catholic cook-maid should be sent to work out of the house, and that she should be told that the guest in the parlour-chamber was a friend of Huddleston, escaping from Worcester fight. There remained the three boys, still peacefully sleeping in their chambers at the top of the house. Whitgreave was not inclined to repose much confidence in these striplings, but Huddleston thought he could depend upon their loyalty to himself, and proposed to make use of them by giving them a holiday from their books, and posting them in the look-out chamber above Whitgreave's study, to keep a watch on the road.

'Do not breathe a word to them of his Majesty's presence!' Whitgreave said, not quite liking the plan.

'No, no, they shall think it is my life they guard!' promised Huddleston. 'I will tell them that I have had word brought me that the priest-catchers have got word of my true estate. That will serve very well, for in case of soldiers coming to search the house, the lads, if forced to betray me, may very likely thus preserve his blessed Majesty's life.'

His pupils, when informed a few hours later how they were to spend the day, consented to his plans with joyful alacrity. To some, a prolonged sojourn in an extremely tiny attic might have seemed a dull prospect, but to three striplings, conscious of an ill-prepared lesson, it seemed nothing short of a reprieve. The notion that the house might be invaded by the enemy did not in any way abate their pleasure, for although they would be sorry if any ill befell Mr Huddleston, such an unlooked-for excitement (carrying with it, as it did, a delicious pang of fear), could not come amiss to three young gentlemen all in the best of health and high spirits. They clattered upstairs as soon as they had eaten their breakfasts, Sir John Preston having constituted himself (though not without argument) the Captain of the Guard; and it seemed probable, to judge from their remarks, that the day's duty would be rapidly converted into a sport that would keep them pleasurably occupied till dinner-time.

The King slept far into the morning, Mr Whitgreave making it his business to watch over him, continually creeping into his room in case he should have awakened, making up the fire, once softly drawing back the curtains lest a passer-by should see them closed and wonder at it. With the departure of the servants, upon various errands, and the withdrawal of the boys to the top floor, the house had become very quiet. A log falling out of the fire on to the hearth at last woke the King. As Whitgreave knelt down to replace the log, he heard the bed creak, and Charles give a mighty yawn. He rose to his feet, anxious to reassure the King if he should be momentarily startled by his sudden awakening, and found that Charles was lying with his hands linked behind his head, placidly regarding him.

Mr Whitgreave was himself a man of calm temperament, but he found the King's unconcern with any thought of possible danger remarkable. As he looked, hesitating whether to approach the bedside or to wait until he was summoned, Charles smiled, and said: 'Is it late? I have not slept so well since I lay at Worcester.'

'That is very good hearing, sire,' replied Whitgreave. 'Would your Majesty be pleased to get up now? I do not anticipate any sudden surprise, yet if soldiers did come to the house it would be better that this bed should not seem to have been too lately slept in.'

The King sat up. 'Indeed you will find me very biddable, Mr Whitgreave,' he said. 'I will get up at once. But I should like some water to wash with, and a razor, if you please!'

'I will bring it to your Majesty immediately. May – would your Majesty permit me, or Mr Huddleston, to shave you?'

The King looked suspiciously at him. 'Have you ever shaved a man before?' he demanded.

'Well, no, sire!' confessed Whitgreave, with a smile.

'Then I will shave myself, and so preserve you from the fate that awaits those who cut their King's throat,' said Charles, throwing back the quilt, and swinging his long legs to the ground.

By the time he had washed and shaved himself, Mr Whitgreave standing by all the time, holding the bowl of water, Huddleston had come up from the buttery with some breakfast for him. The King fell upon this with avidity, conversing so cheerfully and easily with his two attendants that Whitgreave was emboldened to ask whether his mother might have the great honour to be presented to him.

'Why certainly, if she will not turn from such a shabby figure in disgust!' responded the King, with a grimace.

But Mrs Whitgreave, ushered presently into the room by her son, showed no sign of doing any such thing. She was a little over-awed, and made the King a very low curtsey, scarcely daring to look up into his face. But by the time the King, who never failed to captivate old ladies, had saluted her, placed her in a chair by the fire, and sat himself down on a joint-stool beside her, and confided to her the great discomfort of his feet, she had almost forgotten his exalted station, and began to treat him very much as she would have treated any young man for whom she felt a marked liking. No housewife worthy of the name could fail to possess a cupboard bursting with salves, ointments, and cordials, all of her own distilling, and the King had no sooner spoken of blisters, than Mrs Whitgreave was up on her feet and bustling out of the room to bring out from her store of pots and bottles a certain remedy for every kind of gall, blister or open sore, which, she assured the King, was infallible, the recipe having been handed down from her great-grandmother. Could any clothes have been found in the house to fit the King, she would have followed up the anointing of his feet by insisting upon his exchanging Richard Penderel's doublet for a more seemly garment. He told her that he would not dare to put off his mean clothes for fear of being surprised by his enemies, but it was evident that she set very little store by any Parliamentarian.

'A pack of ignorant rebels!' she said, scornfully disposing of all Cromwell's forces. 'I warrant you, my son will know how to send *them* about their business, dear sir!'

When the dinner hour came, the King insisted that she should sit down at the table with him, while Whitgreave and Huddleston waited on them. She was a chatty old lady, and she made the King laugh a great deal, particularly when she told him that a rumour was flying about amongst the country-people that he had not only beaten his enemies at Warrington Bridge, upon his retreat, but that no less than three Kings had come to his assistance.

'Three Kings!' he exclaimed with a droll lift of his brows. 'Surely they are the three Kings of Cologne come down from heaven, for I can imagine none else!'

'Yes, and I will tell your Majesty another thing,' she nodded. 'When Mr Huddleston called the boys down to their dinner just now, and they not having the smallest notion of your being within twenty miles of us, my great-nephew, John Preston, claps his hands, and sings out to the others: "Eat hard, lads, for we have been on life-guard, and hard duty this day!" I warrant you I was near to dropping where I stood!'

'It was said in innocence,' Huddleston interposed, from behind the King's chair. 'Sir John will be a proud man when he learns – as one day I hope he may – how truly he spoke.'

The rest of the day passed without incident. The King had arrears of sleep still to make up, and went early to bed, his host and Father Huddleston standing guard as before. The following morning, which was Tuesday, September 9th, he arose betimes, and found his feet so much easier that he was no longer content, as he had been on the previous day, to sit quietly in his own chamber. Mr Whitgreave had scarcely had time to despatch all the servants but the cook-maid out of the house before the King came out of his chamber, pleading that he must stretch his legs a little. The door into the room adjoining his being open, he went in, and began to wander about it, picking up a Latin Grammar that belonged to one of Huddleston's pupils, and looking through it with a comical grimace of distaste. He was not, he confessed, at all skilled in Latin. 'But I learned mathematics of Mr Hobbes,' he added. 'Also Dr Harvey instructed me in physics. I have more aptitude for science, I think, than for classics.'

The door, curiously placed between the windows, that led into Mr Whitgreave's study, next attracted his notice, and he desired to be told what lay beyond it. Whitgreave at once opened it, and he stepped into the tiny room, and was so charmed by it that he declared his intention of remaining in it, and from its commanding window watching the traffic along the road. Both Whitgreave and Huddleston remained with him, taking care that he did not draw close enough to the window to be seen by any passer-by.

Of these there were many, a great number of them being Scottish soldiers who, escaping from the shambles at Worcester, were painfully making their way northwards in the forlorn hope of winning to safety across the border. There were many pitiable sights amongst them, and more than one wounded Highlander came up the neat garden-path to the front-door to beg for food, or a plaister for his hurt. Some were so hungry that they had been reduced to eating cabbage-stalks, and even leaves that they had picked up by the wayside. None of those who summoned up the courage to knock on the door of Moseley Hall was sent away without relief. Mrs Whitgreave cared nothing for Cromwell or the Parliament; she knew her duty as a Christian; and spent the entire morning distributing food, and binding up festering wounds.

The King watched the sad procession in silence for a time,

and with a lowering brow; but presently he said in a harsh voice, as though the words forced themselves from him: 'It need not have been! No, it need not have been!'

'Such sights are inevitable in time of war, sire,' Huddleston said gently.

'Could I but have prevailed upon Leslie's Horse to follow me – the Scots have dealt very ill with me – very ill!' the King said, his face sombre and glooming.

After a little pause, Whitgreave ventured to ask: 'Did the Scots fail your Majesty at Worcester fight?'

The King gave a crack of sardonic laughter. 'The Scots' Horse would not budge, even though we had broken through Cromwell's lines! The foot-soldiers were fighting with the butt-ends of their muskets at the end, waiting, waiting for the Cavalry to finish what they had so well begun! But Leslie and Middleton —' He broke off, shutting his lips tightly on further confidences, but when Huddleston begged him presently to tell them a little about the battle, if it would not be too painful to him, he complied with his usual good-humour, greatly praising amongst the Scots, the Duke of Hamilton, and Lord Lauderdale; and all those English Cavaliers who had rallied so gallantly to cover his retreat from the town. When he came to the account of his own adventures, the brooding look quite vanished from his face, for he was always very quick to perceive the ridiculous, even when it related to himself. His audience might be aghast at the tale of his hardships, but his inimitable way of describing all the unpleasant circumstances of the past week made them laugh in spite of themselves.

When he grew tired of looking out of the window, he got up and began to inspect the books upon the shelves, greatly delighting his hosts by pulling out Turberville's Catechism, and reading a little of it. 'This is a very pretty book,' he said decidedly. 'If I may, I will take it with me.'

'Indeed, sir, I should be glad!' Whitgreave said.

The King put the book in his pocket, and finding next a manuscript, written by one Richard Huddleston, and entitled *A Short and Plain Way to the Faith and Church*, he ask if this Richard were a relative of Mr Huddleston? Upon

Huddleston's bowing, he said that he should like to read the manuscript.

Huddleston was too shrewd a man not to suspect the King of a little graceful duplicity, but he smiled, and put the manuscript into his hand. Charles read it through very attentively, remarking when he came to the end that he had never seen anything more plain and clear on the subject. 'Indeed,' he added, 'the arguments are so conclusive, I do not conceive how they can be denied.'

'Your Majesty is a theologian?' said Huddleston, with a lurking smile.

The King looked up at him sharply. What he saw in the priest's face brought a twinkle into his eyes. 'Nay, not I!' he confessed. 'But indeed I found the manuscript very interesting.'

'Your Majesty is not prejudiced against our faith?'

'I am only prejudiced against the Covenant!' retorted Charles. 'If ever I come to my Crown, I shall use my endeavour to procure liberty of conscience for my subjects, which I think a thing most necessary.' He saw Huddleston give his head a quick little shake, and said: 'You are a priest – you need not fear to own it to me, I do assure you – so I must not look to have you agree with me.'

'With submission, sir, I must say that your Majesty is young yet, and has not thought deeply enough on this question. By prayer, and by —'

'Mr Huddleston,' interrupted the King demurely, 'my first Governor, who was, I think a wise man, bade me beware of too much devotion for a King; for (said he) one may be a good man, but a bad King.'

The priest could not help laughing, but said: 'Ah, sir, I think you twist those words to mean something your Governor did not intend. But I am not here to lecture you! Indeed,' he added, 'if it were my duty to look for faults in you, I could not find any. I have seen only a very gracious prince, with a sweetness of temper and an infinite patience which is an example to us all.'

'Alas, how little you know me!' said the King, amused, but having the grace to blush under his tan. 'I fear I have a number of shocking faults, Mr Huddleston, but I will not destroy your good opinion of me by telling you what they are.'

He went back soon after to his own chamber, and during the afternoon lay down upon the bed with a book in his hand. He was sliding softly into sleep when he was jerked wide awake by hearing the gate on to the road clap to, and a woman's scared voice call out: 'Master, soldiers! soldiers are coming!'

It was the cook-maid, returning from the village, whither she had gone to buy provisions. Whitgreave met her at the door, and pulled her into the house, bidding her be calm, and tell him exactly where she had seen the soldiers. She answered him in gasps, for she had run all the way home. A troop of rebels had ridden into the village, but for what purpose she had not stayed to discover. 'And oh, master, they do say that one Southall, which is a notorious priest-catcher, is amongst them, and has been questioning the blacksmith very strictly what Catholic houses there be hereabouts! I do be afraid for the good Father's life!'

Whitgreave consigned her to his mother's care, bidding both women go and busy themselves in the stillroom, and himself went swiftly up to the King's chamber.

He found Huddleston already there, and the hidden door of the wall-cupboard standing open. The King, having caught up his jump-coat, and his hat, stepped into the cupboard, and dropped down through the trap-door into the brick chamber. Whitgreave quickly replaced the trap, and, having shut the cupboard, helped Huddleston to straighten the bedclothes.

'Father, do you set every door in the house wide!' he ordered. 'Let there be no appearance of concealment. And do you keep out of sight! I am going out to meet these soldiers.'

'Mr Whitgreave, if they search the house, you must give me up to them!' Huddleston called after him.

Whitgreave returned no answer. He went down the stairs, and pausing only for a moment to assure himself that his dress was as neatly ordered as usual, walked out of the front door, and strolled down the path to the gate.

A few minutes later, a small troop of horsemen came trotting up the road from the direction of the village, and halted. Mr Whitgreave, looking prim and sedate, was nipping off the withered heads of a few late roses. He paused in this occupation when he saw the soldiers dismounting outside his gate, and bent a mildly enquiring gaze upon them.

The leader of the troop shouted to him: 'You, there! Is your name Whitgreave?'

'Why, yes,' said Mr Whitgreave. 'Do you seek me, friend?' He opened the gate as he spoke, and stood holding it as though inviting the Captain to step inside.

'Friend, do you say? Ha, that won't serve!' said the Captain. 'You're a damned Papist, and one that was at Worcester fight!'

Mr Whitgreave found himself hemmed in by troopers, two of whom laid ungentle hands upon him, thrusting him forward to confront their Captain. He did not resist; he merely looked a little bewildered, and said in his quiet way: 'Gently, gently, if you please, my good fellows! You are strangely mistaken, sir. I was not at Worcester fight. Indeed, I have not been away from home these several months, as my neighbours will testify.'

'You lie!' barked the Captain. 'You're a notable Royalist, and so I know you to be!'

'But I was not at Worcester fight,' said Whitgreave with unruffled placidity.

'It will be best for you to confess the truth, Master Papist,' said the Captain menacingly. 'Now then! Out with it!'

Mr Whitgreave glanced down at the barrel of the long pistol that was being pressed against his chest. He shook his head. 'I think you confuse me with some other man,' he said. 'If I had wished to do so, I could not have been present at Worcester fight, since I was not then risen from my sick-bed.'

A murmur arose from the knot of villagers who had followed the troop along the road. 'Ay, that's the truth,' said a man in a leather doublet. 'Powerful ill, you did be, master.'

'Us thought you was like to die,' agreed an aged man in a smock.

The Captain of the troop glanced round him with just enough indecision in his face to convince Whitgreave that his accusations had been nothing more than shots at a venture. He said: 'If you doubt me, I will have you carry me before a proper tribunal, if you please, where I will answer faithfully whatever questions may be put to me.'

The Captain scowled at him, but instead of pursuing the subject, said: 'If you weren't at Worcester, I'll be sworn you're concealing fugitives under your roof – maybe the traitor Charles Stewart himself.'

Whitgreave, who, out of the tail of his eye, had seen the sergeant and two men go into the garden, replied patiently: 'No, but I have given such poor alms to a few wretched wounded men that begged of me, as lay in my power.'

'Ha, assisting traitors to the Commonwealth!' exclaimed the Captain.

'Were they so? I did not know it. I but did what I would do for any fellow Christian in distress.'

'Ay, you've a mighty smooth tongue in your head,' growled the Captain. 'If I find not a Malignant hiding in the house, trust me never!'

'Ho, ho, come forth, and flee from the land of the north, saith the Lord!' suddenly remarked one of the troopers. 'For I have spread you abroad as the four winds of heaven, saith the Lord.'

'Peace, fool!' snapped the Captain, not unreasonably annoyed by this interruption.

'The wicked in his pride doth persecute the poor,' groaned the trooper. 'It is written: woe unto him that buildeth his house by unrighteousness!'

'It is also written: I will purge out from among you the rebels, and them that transgress against me!' retorted the Captain, with some ferocity.

Mr Whitgreave stood with a graven face; a quotation was in the trooper's eye, but the return of the sergeant from the garden created a diversion. He whispered in the officer's ear. The only words Whitgreave caught were 'all open: nothing secured', but these were enough to satisfy him. The rebel captain glared at him, blustered for a few moments, but finally signed to the soldiers to let him go. The troop remounted, and rode off. Mr Whitgreave went back into his garden, where he continued to tend his roses until he was satisfied that none of the soldiers had returned to spy on him. After that he went into the house, and up to the parlour-chamber.

The King emerged from the secret place, remarking as he did so: 'Oddsfish, I am glad I am not a priest! You should provide that dungeon with cushions, Mr Whitgreave. Am I safe?'

'By God's grace, and Mr Whitgreave's exceeding great courage, you are, sire!' said Huddleston.

The King noticed his host's dishevelled appearance. 'They handled you roughly, did they?'

'They did me no hurt, sir. Nor do I think they had any notion of your Majesty's being in these parts. They would not so easily have been satisfied had they suspected me of more than of being at Worcester fight.'

The troop did not return, but at dusk John Penderel arrived from Bentley Hall, and was conducted at once to the King's presence. He was looking more than usually serious, but the news he brought was good. He told the King that, all being arranged for his journey to Bristol, Colonel Lane would bring a horse for him that evening, to convey him to Bentley. The Pit Leasow was named as the meeting-place, and the hour appointed was midnight.

'You have done very well, John,' Huddleston said approvingly.

The King's slumbrous eyes were still fixed on John's face. 'What else?' he asked.

John shook his head with a wry smile. 'Ay, your honour's mighty sprag to see through the chinks in a man. I did come by some tidings which was discomfortable, but maybe there's naught to worry us, and the whole's a parcel of lies.'

'Come, man, come! Be brief with me!' the King said, authority creeping into his voice.

'I happened on a neighbour, which was going towards

Wolverhampton,' said John. 'Seemingly, the rebels caught a Cornet which was with your honour when you come to White-Ladies, and so constrained him that he told of your Majesty's going there.'

The King's mouth took on an ugly twist. 'Well?'

'They do say that he was put to some torture,' said John. 'Anyways, if the tale's true, there was a party of rebels rode up to White-Ladies this afternoon, and called for Mr George Giffard, which is a gentleman known to your honour. And he being come out to them, they put a pistol to his breast, and bid him confess where your honour was hid, or he should die. But Mr Giffard very steadfastly denies knowing any more than that a company of Cavaliers came to the house on Wednesday night, and ate up all the provisions, but he knew not who they were. Whereat they told him he should surely die. And when he begged leave to say a few prayers, they told him if he would not confess where your honour was hid he should say no prayers. Then, Mrs Andrews coming out to them, they used her in a like fashion, but could not affright her, she being a very redoubtable woman, as your honour knows, and berated them in such sort that they were put in a fury, and set about ransacking the house, pulling down the wainscot, and I know not what beside. But not finding your honour, and Mr Giffard and Mrs Andrews standing to it they knew naught of you, they presently fell into a rage with the Cornet that betrayed your honour, and beat him with their belts, thinking he had but told them lies.'

'He came by less than his deserts!' said Whitgreave. He glanced at the King. 'If they are persuaded the unhappy man lied, sir, you must still be safe. Yet I own the pursuit draws too near the scent for my liking. I never thought to say that I would you were out of my house, but I think it now too perilous a hiding-place for you, and must thank God Colonel Lane comes to-night to fetch you away.'

'Poor man!' said the King. 'He should be warned that it is an ill-business to have aught to do with me. I am sorry, John, to have been the cause of such trouble at White-Ladies. You will tell Mr Giffard and Dame Andrews that I thank them for their loyalty. Indeed, I shall never forget it.'

'Master,' said John, reddening, but looking him squarely in the face, 'when I tell them how your honour took thought of them, and you so beset as you are, and they but poor folk, they will think themselves right well rewarded, and so I promise you!'

## CHAPTER IX

## 'THAT ROGUE CHARLES STEWART'

THE King supped in his chamber, waited on as usual by his hosts. He did not seem to be much disquieted by the tidings John had brought, but to them the hours dragged past, and every sound heard in the road caused them to break off whatever they were saying to listen with straining ears for the whistle of warning it had been preconcerted that John should give.

After he had supped, the King, who seemed restless, suddenly asked Huddleston to show him the chapel, adding with a slight smile: 'You know you may trust me.'

Whitgreave was a little taken aback, but Huddleston was delighted, and, as soon as he had assured himself that his pupils were all in bed and asleep, conducted the King upstairs to a set of rooms on the top floor of the house. One of these, approached through delicately carved oak double-doors, was furnished as a chapel. Huddleston showed the King the secret-place into which candlesticks, altar-cloth, and crucifix could all be swept away in case of a surprise visit from Puritan priest-catchers. Charles inspected everything, remarking seriously at length: 'It is a very decent place. Yet I hope that if it shall please God ever to restore me to my Kingdom you will not need such privacies. I had an altar, and crucifix, and candlesticks of mine own – till my Lord Holland brake them.' He added with one of his sardonic smiles: 'Which, however, he has now paid for.'

At midnight, Whitgreave went with John to meet Colonel Lane at the Pit Leasow. The Colonel came punctually, leading a spare horse, and upon Whitgreave's stepping out from the shadow of the trees, he dismounted, saying: 'Mr Whitgreave? I trust his Majesty is safe, and in train to set forth immediately?'

He had rather a loud voice; it held a note of disapproval, and was more the voice of one accustomed to shouting orders to a regiment of soldiers than of a conspirator. He was fond of describing himself as a plain man, which meant that he disliked new ideas. He suffered from a profound mistrust of Papists, as Whitgreave was perfectly well aware; and had indeed been quite disgusted with Wilmot for having stayed a moment longer in a Papist household than had been strictly necessary.

He spoke curtly to John, bidding him mind the horses, and followed Whitgreave across the fields to the stile that led into the orchard behind the house. He was a fleshy man, and trod heavily, his spurs jingling as he went. He wore a sword at his side, and, when Whitgreave begged him to go more softly, said that he should know how to account for any prying rebel knave. He declined accompanying Whitgreave into the house, on the score of its being dangerous to risk being seen there; but Whitgreave, smiling to himself in the darkness, thought that his real reason was a disinclination to enter a Papist's dwelling.

Whitgreave left him tapping his riding-whip impatiently on the top-bar of the stile, and himself went on to apprise the King of his arrival.

Charles had pushed his feet into his slashed shoes again, and had put on the old green jump-coat. Father Huddleston was with him, and looked round anxiously as Whitgreave entered the room.

'All is well, sire,' Whitgreave said. 'Colonel Lane is here, and awaits your Majesty at the orchard-stile.'

'Does he?' said Charles, standing still while Huddleston buttoned up his coat. 'What ails him that he does not come in to me?'

'The Colonel thought it might be wiser not to risk being

seen, sir,' replied Whitgreave tactfully.

'A careful man!"

Huddleston said with a smile: 'I fear the good Colonel suspects me of being a priest, sir. He is mightily prejudiced against our religion.'

The King laughed, and moved towards the table. He picked up from it a paper, on which the ink was barely dry, and held it out to Whitgreave. 'Mr Whitgreave, it is in my mind that if your part in this adventure were to become known, you and Mr Huddleston here would fare very badly at the hands of my enemies. I have drawn a bill of exchange on a certain merchant of London, whom you may trust. If you should be forced to go into hiding, make your way to London, and present this paper. The good man will advance you moneys, and arrange your passages to France, or to Holland.'

Whitgreave took the paper, bowing very deeply. 'Your Majesty's concern for our safety so much overwhelms me that I know not how to thank you,' he said, in a moved voice. 'I did not look for such kindness.'

'Mr Whitgreave, you know very well how much I am beholden to you. What kind of a scurvy ingrate do you think me, that you are surprised I should do the little that lies in my power to ensure your safety? Let us have no more words, but put that bill up securely.' His sombre eyes smiled suddenly. 'If you be found with it upon you, it will certainly serve to hang you. You will then think yourself very damnably repaid for your loyalty!'

'Never that, sir!' Whitgreave said. 'I desire death as little as any other man, yet since die I must, soon or late, I should choose that I should die serving your Majesty.'

'And I,' Huddleston said. 'But we stay too long! Your Majesty should make haste to Bentley. We forget the poor Colonel by the orchard-stile!'

'He can wait,' said the King. 'Will you bring your mother in to me, Mr Whitgreave? I desire to take my leave of her.'

'Sir!' said Huddleston impetuously, 'every moment that you tarry here may endanger your life!'

The King looked at him, his brows raised in faint surprise. Huddleston, recognizing the expression, stepped back, and bowed. 'I crave your Majesty's pardon!'

Whitgreave went out to summon his mother. She had been hoping to be sent for, and so had not gone to bed. When she came into the parlour-chamber it was with a scallop-dish full of sweetmeats, which, knowing that the King liked such things, she had prepared for him. He ate a St Catherine's prune, and a dried grape, praising them highly, and permitted her to stuff the rest into his pockets, saying, though with a pronounced twinkle in his eye, that he should be very glad of them. He would not suffer her to kneel to him, or to kiss his hand, but bowed over hers instead, thanking her for her entertainment of him. At that she quite forgot he was not a son of her own, and put her hands on his big shoulders, and kissed him, and blessed him. He seemed to like this usage very well, folding his arms about her, and saluting her on both cheeks, and telling her that he should never forget her kindness.

He was then led out of the house down the narrow back-stairs, Whitgreave going before with a lantern, and Huddleston hurrying after with a cloak of his own, which, fearing that the King might be cold on this sharp autumn night, he had run to fetch for him.

The Colonel was standing by the stile when they came to it. Mr Whitgreave at once presented him to the King, to whom he bowed, with a sweep of his feathered hat, saying in his strong, firm voice: 'Sire!'

'I am very glad to see you, Colonel,' said the King. 'I hope you have brought a stout horse for me to ride?'

'If your Majesty would be pleased to walk to this place they call the Pit Leasow, the horses will be found there, sir. Mr Whitgreave thought it not advisable to fetch them closer.'

'Let us go, then,' the King said.

John Penderel was walking the horses up and down in the grove by the Pit Leasow. He held the stirrup for the King, who, however, would not mount until he had spoken a few last words to Whitgreave and Huddleston. The night was cold enough to make him glad of Huddleston's frieze cloak, which, he promised, should be returned to him from Bentley Hall.

'Certainly!' the Colonel said. 'It shall be strictly attended to, Mr Huddleston. I am grieved I did not bring a cloak for your Majesty. I had not fully understood the condition in which your Majesty stands. My lord did indeed speak of the mean raiment that you had been forced to put on you, but I did not dream – could not believe, sir, that you were reduced to such straits!'

He was evidently much shocked by the deplorable appearance of his sovereign; there was even a suggestion, in his tone, of amazement that any man could demean himself by wearing such a disguise.

The King gave a chuckle, and bent to give his hand to John Penderel. 'Farewell, my faithful friend! From my heart, I thank you. If it please God to bring me to my Crown, let me see you!'

He gave his hand in turn to Whitgreave and Huddleston, bidding them have a care to themselves; again thanked them; and only then signified to the Colonel that he was ready to start.

There was enough moonlight to enable them to see their way. They rode side by side, the Colonel sitting very erect in the saddle, and keeping a sharp watch ahead. The King did not speak for a minute or two, but presently he enquired how far they had to go, and upon being told, four miles, remarked that it was the shortest journey he had yet undertaken.

'I wish it were shorter, for your Majesty's sake,' the Colonel said.

'Why, I am very well able to ride as far as I must,' Charles replied. 'These two days I have lain at Moseley have quite restored me.'

'I would your Majesty had been the while at Bentley!'

'You are kind, Colonel. But I have been in good hands.'

'I must own, Thomas Whitgreave seems to be a very honest man,' admitted the Colonel. 'Yet I could not but deplore your Majesty's being taken to a Papist's house, and wonder at my lord's thinking it in any way safe. Such people are much suspected, sir.'

'So I see,' said the King rather dryly. 'But tell me, if you please, what measures for my escape have been concerted between my lord and you. Am I to have the honour of riding with your sister to Bristol?'

'Sir! If your Majesty will be pleased to consent to it, the honour will be my sister's, which she is very conscious of, I do assure you.'

'I hope she is also conscious of the danger she courts,' said the King. 'Is she willing? I will have no woman constrained to aid me to her own undoing.'

'Your Majesty need be under no apprehension. My sister, I warrant, would count it a blessing to die in your service.'

'My dear good friend, that is very nobly said, but I do not desire anyone to die in my service. When must we set forth upon our journey?'

'If your Majesty pleases, it is arranged that you shall leave Bentley in the morning, so that you may lie to-morrow night at the house of a relative of mine, one Mr Tomes, of Long Marston. And, for better convenience, we think you should go by the name of William Jackson, the same being a poor tenant on my father's estate. To this end, I have procured a decent, plain suit. Upon reflection, neither my lord nor I thought it well your Majesty should go as a servant. As William Jackson, you may command fitter lodging upon the journey than would be deemed proper for a waiting-man.'

'It likes me well,' said the King.

'Furthermore, sir, we have admitted a young kinsman of mine, that was my Cornet in the late Wars, into the secret. Your Majesty will find him very trustworthy, nor will he leave you until you are safely embarked for France.'

'I thank him, and you, Colonel.'

'There is one other circumstance of which your Majesty should be informed. My sister, Withy, and her husband, one John Petre, of Horton, in Buckinghamshire, are staying at Bentley upon a visit to my father and mother, and do intend to ride a part of the way with my sister Jane, upon their return to Buckinghamshire. It is unfortunate, for although Mr Petre is a very honest man, neither I nor my lord feel it meet that he should be informed of the secret. Yet to put obstacles in the way of his setting out with Jane must, we fear, occasion suspicion in his breast.'

'Will he know me?' enquired the King.

'Nay, sire, he has never seen your Majesty, nor concerned himself greatly with what lies beyond his own demesnes.'

'Then I see no harm in his going along with us. But my lord I will not take with me.'

'If it please your Majesty, my lord and I mean to ride abreast of you upon another road, with our hawks upon our wrists, and a couple of dogs at our heels, as though upon a day's sport. We may lie tomorrow night at Sir Clement Fisher's house, at Packington, and so be within reach of your Majesty.'

'You have thought of everything, Colonel.'

'Sire, my earnest desire is to serve your Majesty. If there is aught that mislikes you in our schemes, I will instantly order it better.'

'My dear Colonel, there is nothing I would have altered, save only a certain small matter. And that is that you will bear in mind that I am now become a poor tenant on your estates. Majesty me no Majesties, for if you do not speedily rid yourself of that trick, I am very sure you will betray me.'

The Colonel did not answer for a moment, but presently he said, picking his words: 'I ask your pardon, sir. You are very right. The truth is, I was bred in the old school, and find it hard to treat your – to treat you as any other than my King and master.'

'When you have seen me in a better light you will not find it so hard,' said the King, a quiver of amusement in his voice.

But this was a subject in which the Colonel was unable to see any humour. He said with strong feeling: 'I am not glib of speech, sir, else I could tell your Majesty of my dismay, my horror, at the disasters which have befallen you! Sir, do you blame us, your English subjects? I swear to you that I, and a hundred – two hundred! – like me would have rallied to your standard with all our forces, had we but been apprised of your coming into England! When the dreadful tidings of the defeat at Worcester reached us, I was even then marching to join your Majesty at the head of my own men. Sir, I did my possible, but there was no time! no time to muster our men, no time —'

'Peace, I blame no Englishman!' the King said. 'The Covenanters would not let my letters to you go out of Scotland.'

'Would not *let*!' the Colonel exclaimed. 'You were the King, crowned and anointed!'

'Oh yes, I was the King. Also I was a prisoner, but no matter for that.'

They rode on in silence, the King wrapped in melancholy, the Colonel fuming with indignation at the effrontery of the Scottish Covenanters. In a little while they had reached the confines of Bentley Hall. Entering, not through the great wrought-iron gates, but by a farm-gate reached by way of a miry lane, they rode for some distance across a deer-park, arriving at length at the house, which was a large mansion, set in well-ordered gardens, and displaying imposing rows of windows along its extensive façade.

The Colonel led the way past the house, skirting its gardens, to the silent stables, where he begged the King to be pleased to dismount. A stately figure emerged out of the shadows, and bowed deeply.

'Robert Swan, my lord's man,' explained the Colonel.

The King laughed.

Robert Swan, who, though not as portly, was quite as dignified as his master, held the King's horse while he dismounted. He was one who had been accustomed all his life to wait upon exalted personages, and not by the smallest sign did he betray that he found anything at all out of the way in the arrival of the King at such an hour, and in such a guise. His punctilious manner seemed to people the deserted stableyard with a throng of courtiers and lackeys. He went backwards before the King into the stable, and ushered him into the harness-room as though it had been an audience chamber. Not even when Charles stepped into the light of a lantern hanging from the roof, and he was able to see his cropped head and stained skin, did his countenance lose one jot of its lofty impassivity.

'Before I escort your Majesty into the house, I will discover whether all is quiet there,' the Colonel said. 'My father is sometimes wakeful, and we think it best he should not know of your Majesty's presence, since he is an old man and in failing health.'

'Oddsfish, is the sight of me as bad as that?' asked the King.

'Sir! Your Majesty mistakes! No such thought was in my mind!'

The King perceived that he had to deal with one who did not share his own love of a joke. He glanced from the Colonel's concerned face to Swan's rigid one, and choked down the laugh that rose to his lips. 'I know, I know!' he said. 'Go and do your scouting, Colonel; I will await you here, I promise you.'

The Colonel bowed, and took a step backwards to the door. As he reached it, a footfall sounded outside, and a moment later, a girl had entered, so lightly that it seemed as though the wind had blown her in. She wore a gown of some pale stuff, and over it, caught carelessly round her shoulders and held together by one hand, a dark, flowing cloak. An oval face, faintly tinted with colour, a lovely, proud mouth, and glowing eyes under the sweep of drooping lids swam before the King's vision. In her left hand she carried a lantern of gilded tin. She held it out to her brother, but not looking at him. Her gaze was fixed on the King, and as the Colonel took the lantern from her, she released her cloak, letting it fall in a heap upon the floor, and sank down in a profound curtsey.

'Sir, I beg leave to present my sister to your Majesty!'

The King stepped forward, and raised Jane Lane. As his brown hand closed on her wrist, she lifted her head and looked up into his face. He noticed that her hair, which was of a light, lustrous brown, lay on her forehead in ethereal ringlets, and that her expression was one of sweet seriousness. He put out his other hand to take hers, and she bent her head to kiss it before suffering him to pull her upright.

He withdrew it gently, saying: 'Mistress, I am one William Jackson.'

'Pardon, sire!'

Her voice was low-pitched, a pretty, youthful voice, not shy, but grave.

'Jane, is all safe?' demanded the Colonel. 'I would not keep his Majesty standing here!'

'Oh no!' she agreed. 'Everyone is asleep but my lord. Will you come in, sir? Indeed, all is secure.'

'Yes, I will come in, so you will lead the way,' answered the King. He bent, and picked up her cloak from the floor, and put it round her shoulders.

She said simply: 'I thank you, sir,' and took the lantern again from her brother. 'Will your Majesty be pleased to follow me?'

She went out of the stables before him, flitting across the yard like a spirit. He followed with his long stride, and reached the side door into the house almost on her heels. It stood open, and she stood aside for him to pass in.

'Go in, sir; my lord is awaiting you,' said Lane's deep voice behind the King.

Charles stepped over the threshold. The Colonel led him down a long passage to a door that opened from it into the main hall. It was lit only by one branch of candles, which cast their light in a dwindling circle in the centre of the room. In the dimness beyond, a shadowy staircase rose in broad, shallow flights to an upper floor.

Jane Lane moved across the hall to set her lantern down upon the table. Her gown whispered over the black oak boards like autumn leaves drifting across the ground. Her voice was muted, but very clear. 'My lord went upstairs to see all in readiness for his Majesty's arrival. I will fetch him.'

Her brother stayed her with a gesture. 'No, it will be well if I escort his Majesty immediately to the privacy of his chamber. Go you to bed, Jane: you must be up betimes. His Majesty will excuse you.'

The King had pulled off his hat, and Jane was able to see his face more distinctly. She curtseyed again. 'I will bid your Majesty good night, then.'

'Good night, Mistress Jane Lane,' he responded.

'This way, sire!' whispered the Colonel.

The King went up the stairs in his wake. My Lord Wilmot was discovered in the Colonel's bedchamber, which had been prepared for the King, that none should know that any other guest than his lordship had slept at Bentley that night. As Lane ushered the King in, Wilmot heaved himself out of a chair by the fire, and started forward with his hands held out. 'My dear sir! God be praised you are come, and safely!'

The King embraced him, and stood warming himself by the fire, looking round with a quizzical expression on his face at the size and style of the apartment. It was a large room, with a sparver-bed of crimson velvet, a fine carpet on the floor, carved cupboards, chairs, and chests, and a suit of crimson hangings embellished with Venice twists, and lined with taffeta.

Wilmot, watching him, held one of his hands, and patted it, saying fondly: 'There, sir: now at last I can see you housed as befits your state! You may be comfortable again, who have fared so ill throughout this unhappy week.'

'I think I sort very damnably with such state,' said the King somewhat ruefully. 'My dear Colonel, you do me too much honour, indeed you do!'

'That is not possible, sire. Let me assure your Majesty that you may lie here in perfect safety. We do not boast secret priest-holes, but it will go hard with any upstart knave of a Puritan who dares force his way into Bentley Hall. If your Majesty would be pleased to cast off those clothes, my lord's servant will be here presently with water, and a bed-gown, which I hope you will condescend to put on you.'

'There is nothing I desire so much as to be rid of these clothes,' said the King. 'I have not put them off the whole week. I think I must stink as much as they do.'

The Colonel's eyes started with horror, but Wilmot burst out laughing. 'You *would* assume that low disguise, my dear master! Now you must own that I was wiser than you! But the suit my good Lane has procured for you is at least clean, though very mean, alas!'

As he spoke, his fingers were busy unbuttoning the King's jump-coat. He pulled it off Charles, and cast it into a corner of the room. The leather doublet followed it; and as soon as Swan, having stabled the horses, came into the room with a silver ewer and bowl full of hot water, the patched, ill-fitting breeches were also discarded.

The King let them draw Huddleston's shirt off over his head, and stood stark naked before a mirror, laughing at the sharp line round the base of his throat where the walnut stain ended, and the natural whiteness of his skin began.

Twenty minutes later, washed from head to foot, dressed in a bedgown with a cloak over it, and with his damp, short ringlets combed free of tangles, he stood in front of the fire, sipping a glass of wine, and discussing with Wilmot and Lane the details of his projected journey. Robert Swan had withdrawn, taking with him, to be burned, all the discarded raiment. It seemed that nothing could shake Swan's lofty calm. That his master and his sovereign should both be escaping by stealth from the country offended his sense of propriety, but he contrived to bear the humiliation by ignoring it. He was not in the least afraid of the Parliamentarians, for that would have been beneath his dignity, since he considered them to be a set of vulgar, ill-conditioned rogues; but the thought of the King's riding all the way to Bristol in the guise of a yeoman-tenant came as near to disturbing his peace of mind as anything could. He wished to know who would wait upon his Majesty, and upon being told that his Majesty would wait upon himself said simply: 'That, my lord, is not possible.'

The King, overhearing, laughed at him. Swan said gravely: 'Please your Majesty, I will make what provision I can, but I fear if neither my lord nor I are to go with you, your Majesty will be very uncomfortable.'

The King had said a very shocking thing. He had said: 'My good fellow, if I cannot contrive to shave and dress myself without aid, I must be less of a man than I knew.'

Swan had bowed, and withdrawn, because he knew his duty too well to point out to this disturbing young giant that he was not a man, but a King. After a little consideration, he betook himself to Mr Lassels's bedchamber. That young gentleman, roused out of a deep sleep, found that he was being given very precise instructions how to wait upon the Royal traveller. He sat up, blear-eyed amongst his pillows, and listened in a kind of fog to Swan's monotonous voice, initiating him into every detail of etiquette.

It all sounded extremely complicated, and Mr Lassels could not help wondering, in his bemused state, how the King's disguise was to be preserved if he must never be permitted to do anything without assistance. When morning came, and Colonel Lane took him to be presented to the King, he felt so nervous that he dared not raise his eyes to Charles's face. He went down on to one knee, upon the Colonel's announcing him, and stayed so with bowed head until a lazy voice startled him by saying: 'Mr Lassels, if you and I are not to quarrel, kneel not to me!'

This, after Swan's nocturnal discourse, was so unexpected that Mr Lassels looked up in quick surprise. What picture of Royalty he had nourished in his brain he did not quite know, but he certainly had not thought to find himself confronting a tall, brown-faced young man in a plain grey suit, with a cropped head, and an ugly mouth curled in irresistible laughter. He rose to his feet, and stood staring at the King.

Charles was eating his breakfast. He favoured his new escort with one of his lazy yet penetrating looks, enquiring after a moment: 'Well, Mr Lassels, are you willing to take charge of me?'

'Yes, sir, I am very willing,' responded Lassels promptly.

'I thank you. I am now very hopeful of reaching Bristol, and think it will be an odd thing if between us we cannot contrive to cheat my enemies.'

'We pray to God you may do so, sir,' said the Colonel, but in a rather grave voice. 'It is more hazardous than I like, depending upon your Majesty's being able to enact a part which, alas, is wholly beneath your dignity.'

'But I am a shocking low fellow at heart,' said the King.

Mr Henry Lassels caught the gleam in his eye, and realized that the heavy charge laid upon him was going to be no care-ridden duty, but the greatest adventure of his life. He gave a spontaneous laugh, which brought his kinsman's frown to bear upon him.

'It must never be forgotten, Henry,' said the Colonel, 'that though harsh necessity compels us in public to treat his Majesty as though he were indeed a man of inferior degree, in the privacy of his chamber he is the King of this realm.'

The King's eyes rolled expressively towards Lassels. 'So there's for you, Mr Lassels,' he observed.

Wild visions of dying heroically in defence of this King swirled across Lassels's imagination. He stammered: 'I c-could never forget that, sir!'

The King drained his tankard, and got up. 'I am much obliged to you. See you do not forget in public that I am one William Jackson. I shall be a very unhandy servant, I fear. I look to you to instruct me. What must I do?'

'But it is so difficult!' complained Wilmot. 'One has never been a serving-man! You will have to stable the horses, I am sure. My dear master, bear it in mind, and do not – *do not* betray yourself by waiting upon every occasion for someone else to do the task to your hand! Mr Lassels, if you find the King backward in unstrapping the baggage from your saddle, or some such like thing, do not fail to nudge him! It were better by far that you should forget his Kingship in private than remember it in public!'

Colonel Lane agreed to this, but with a sigh. The King having finished his breakfast, he thought it advisable to conduct him immediately to the stables, and there to instruct him in the duties of a serving-man. Charles took an affectionate leave of Wilmot, drew a grin from Lassels by commanding him to be very high-stomached with him when next they met, and went off with the Colonel.

An hour later, mounted on a double-gelding, and leading Lassels's horse by the bridle, he rode up in the wake of a groom with another double-gelding for Mr and Mrs Petre to the front of the house, where Lassels, the Colonel, and old Mrs Lane were already awaiting him. He touched his hat, which he wore pulled low over his brow. The Colonel said in the bluff, authoritative tone he used towards his servants: 'Good-morrow to you, Will. Now, mind that you have a care to my sister upon this journey!'

'Yes, master,' said the King.

His voice made old Mrs Lane peer sharply up at him, but her brain was too much preoccupied with the details of her daughter's journey, and with the messages she desired Lassels to convey to Mr Tomes, of Long Marston, to permit of her wasting more than a moment's curiosity upon him. She turned back to Lassels, and a few minutes later Jane Lane came out of the house, followed by her sister and Mr Petre.

All three were dressed for travel, the ladies in long cloaks with hoods held close round their heads by drawstrings, and Mr Petre in a drab suit, with heavy boots, and a formidable brace of pistols stuck into them.

John Petre, a small man, seemed to be possessed of a fussy, nervous disposition. He bustled about, issuing a great many orders to the groom, insisting that his portmanteau should be more securely strapped, and saying repeatedly that he trusted they might not encounter soldiers upon the road. Of these he stood in not uncommon awe, having once suffered at their rude, predatory hands. While he created all the stir of which he was capable, Jane Lane stepped up to the King's knee. She raised her eyes to his, and smiled in her sweet, calm fashion, saying in a low voice: 'I am ready, Will.'

Here an unforeseen difficulty presented itself, the King never having taken up a lady to ride pillion behind him. The Colonel, who, while seeming to attend to his brother-in-law's discourse, had never ceased to keep an eye upon Charles, said instantly: 'You must give my sister your hand, Will.'

But the King gave her the wrong hand, which made Mrs Lane burst into a cackle of laughter, and demand shrilly of her son what goodly horseman her daughter had got to ride with her.

Withy Petre's coming up to the old lady at that moment to take leave fortunately distracted her attention. By the time she had kissed and embraced Withy, and had seen her safely up behind her husband, Jane had mounted into her pillion, and the King's sudden flush of discomfiture had faded.

After Jane had had her skirts rearranged by her mother,

and had promised not to forget to give all the old lady's messages to Mrs Norton, to whose house at Abbotsleigh, by Bristol, she was bound, the whole party set forward upon the journey.

The road being narrow, Henry Lassels fell behind to let the sisters ride abreast. Withy Petre, a placid woman, too much taken up with home-interests to spare much thought for anything outside them, paid no heed at all to the King. Her pleasant, unimaginative voice was upraised in a gentle monologue for some miles, as she recounted for Jane's edification numerous details of her children's health and precocity. Her husband from time to time interrupted her, expressing his misgivings that they had not started soon enough, had chosen the wrong road, would not reach Horton within six hours of the appointed time. To all such complaints, Withy responded with unruffled good-humour. Jane said little, but the few remarks which she did make seemed to the King to be distinguished by their good sense. Once, when the road dwindled to a narrow causeway between great pools of stagnant water, and obliged the party to ride for some distance in single file, Charles was able to exchange a few words with her. He said softly: 'I have only one complaint to make.'

'Is it something I can put right, sir?' she asked.

'Not yet, alas! I cannot see your face.'

He thought she must be smiling from the sound of her voice. 'Ah, when you spoke it came into my mind that you were jesting, sir.'

'But you wrong me! I am not. It seems to me a very damnable piece of work to put me up on this clumsy horse with my back turned upon the gladdest sight mine eyes have beheld these many weeks.'

'Not glad till I know you are safely embarked for France, sir,' she said seriously.

The absence of any coquetry in her amused him. 'Why, I am sorry, for you must know that *I* am very glad to find myself in such company.'

Again she seemed to be unconscious of his gallantry. She said wonderingly: 'Are you never afraid, sir?'

'Are you, Jane?'

'Yes, for you.'

'Not for your own danger?'

'I do not think of that.'

'You are a very loyal subject,' he remarked.

'Yes, sir.'

'Do you think that when we see each other face to face that demure tongue of yours will wag more freely?' he enquired.

She answered simply, but with a touch of shyness: 'No, sir. I think it will be tied fast.'

'Oddsfish! Am I so displeasing to you, or has your brother been preaching sermons to you on the deference due to my Majesty?'

'He had no need, sir. I think – I think your Majesty hardly understands.'

'Expound then, and I promise I will do my endeavour to understand.'

She hesitated. 'My family has always served the King. Your Majesty knows that my brother fought in the late Wars. But I never thought it might come to me, who am only a woman, to serve you as now I do.'

'Yet you wanted to serve me?' he asked, catching the note of worship in her voice.

'Truly, sir. But though maids have all their dreams they do not look for them to be fulfilled. I think myself dreaming still, for it seems strange and awesome to me to be riding thus, behind my King.'

'But I am no dream,' said the King.

'I shall know it indeed when I see you face to face, sir.'

'And that will tie your tongue fast?'

'Yes, sir.'

'Jane Lane,' said the King, 'you shall know me better before we come to the end of our travels.'

'Yes, sir,' she said obediently, 'but my sister is looking round at us, if you please.'

In another few minutes the condition of the road improved sufficiently to allow of the party's riding once more abreast. The King enjoyed no more conversation with Jane, but became presently the subject of Withy's solicitous interest. She had been looking curiously at him from time to time, until he, aware of her scrutiny, began to fear that she had recognized him. She had not, however; her interest had been aroused merely by his haggard appearance. She suddenly remarked to Jane: 'Your man looks sickly. I do trust he has not a fever?'

Jane replied quietly: 'He has been ill of a tertian ague.'

This seemed to satisfy Mrs Petre, and beyond asking the King a few searching questions on the nature of his ague, and prescribing a number of excellent remedies, she paid no further heed to him.

Having made an early start, and their route taking them away from the main road, they for some time met few people on the journey. As the weather was fine, and the Petres were anxious to reach Horton with all possible despatch, it had been decided to brave the fatigue and discomfort of long hours in the saddle for the sake of reaching Stratford-on-Avon at least by nightfall. All went well for the first twenty miles, but just as the straggling village of Bromsgrove came into sight, the King's horse cast a shoe, a circumstance that put Lassels momentarily out of countenance. But the glance he tried to exchange with Jane was intercepted by the King, who said blandly: 'If my mistress would be pleased to dismount at this village, and take some rest and refreshment, I will lead the horse to the stithy, sir.'

'Yes,' said Lassels, a little uncertainly. 'Yes, we cannot go further till he is shod.'

'Well, for my part, I shall be glad to dismount for a while,' declared Withy. 'You too, Jane, I'll be bound.'

Jane assented, but upon the limping gelding's falling a little behind the Petres, the King felt a light touch upon his arm, and turned his head. A pair of troubled eyes peeped over his shoulder at him. Jane whispered: 'I am sore afraid. This is a very fanatical part of the country. Yet if my cousin were to go to the blacksmith in your stead it would look oddly.'

'Of course it would,' replied the King. 'There is not the least need for you to be afraid. Your sister has stared me well-nigh out of countenance without recognizing me, and if she knows me not, why should the blacksmith?'

She could not be quite so easily reassured, but since there was no alternative to his going to the stithy she said no more. The village was soon entered, and the travellers dismounted at a neat little inn not far from the blacksmith's. Mr Petre pulled out his watch, and discovered that the hour was more advanced than he had supposed. He bade the King make haste upon his errand, saying that it was the greatest piece of ill-luck imaginable that the horse should have cast a shoe, though for his part he was not surprised at it, since in such times as these, when knaves ruled England, no honest man could be surprised at anything.

The King said respectfully that he would bid the smith make haste, and led the horse away, leaving Mr Petre to remind his wife that this visit to her father's house had been undertaken wholly against his judgment.

By good fortune, the smith was able to shoe the horse at once. He glanced indifferently at the King, remarking as he began to blow up his fire: 'You'm strange to these parts, bain't you?'

'I come from Staffordshire, but I was bred in London,' replied the King.

'Ah, I knew you weren't a countryman,' said the smith. 'London, eh? I warrant that's a rare, sinful city.'

The thought of it seemed to absorb him; he plied the King with questions, shaking his head over the answers, but evidently wishing very much that he could see the sinful city with his own eyes. He picked up the red-hot horse-shoe with a pair of tongs, and plunged it hissing and smoking into a tub of water. While he nailed it into place, the King held the horse's foot up for him, asking: 'What news is there? I have been sick of an ague these several weeks, and have heard nothing.'

'News?' said the smith. 'There's none that I know of, since the good news of the beating of those rogues the Scots.'

'Oh, that!' said the King. 'Were there none of the English taken that were with the Scots?'

The smith drove home another nail. 'I haven't heard of

that rogue Charles Stewart's being taken,' he replied. 'They do say some of the others were, but not Charles Stewart.'

'Well, if that rogue were taken he deserves hanging more than all the rest, for bringing in the Scots,' remarked the King cheerfully.

The smith glanced approvingly up at him. 'You speak like an honest man,' he said.

Mr Lassels, who had ridden up to the forge in time to overhear these remarks, thought it well at this point to intervene. He called the smith's attention to himself by demanding impatiently if the horse were not yet shod, and upon being told that the task was nearly accomplished, stayed by the door of the forge, engaging the smith in idle converse.

When the King presently mounted the gelding, and the two men rode off together up the street, Charles said in a tone of mock-complaint: 'What the pox did you mean by interrupting me in the middle of my talk with that worthy fellow?'

'Worthy!' exclaimed Lassels, his eye kindling. 'A dis-affected knave, sir! And you said – I *heard* your Majesty say —'

'I said I deserved hanging for bringing in the Scots, and so I do, by God!'

'Sir, I was afraid every instant he would look more closely at you, and discover you!'

'Lassels, if you are going to see a wolf at every turn, we shall certainly fall out,' remarked the King.

'Indeed, I am sorry, sir, but – but what would become of me if you were discovered?' asked Lassels. 'Your Majesty must know I could never lift up my head again.'

'If it comes to that,' retorted the King, 'I could never lift up my head again were I discovered, for the very good reason that I should have no head to lift. But I don't mean to put myself in a sweat over it, so why should you?'

'Yes, sir, but for you it is – it is just *your* head, and – and for me it is the King's head.'

'I promise you I will take good care of it. I must remember to tell my lord of my new title. It will make him laugh.'

'It made me want to knock the knave's teeth down his black throat!' said Lassels.

'Oddsfish, if that is the humour you are in you *will* put me in a sweat!' replied the King.

Lassels looked at him in surprise. 'Sir, did it not make you angry? Not at all?'

The King burst out laughing. 'Angry with the poor man for saying I was a rogue? My dear Lassels, what kind of a fool do you think I am?'

'I fear 'tis I who am the fool, sir,' replied Lassels, abashed.


CHAPTER X

A POOR TENANT'S SON

WHEN the travellers left Bromsgrove, they rode on with-out incident for some thirteen miles, following the main highway through Headless Cross to Alcester, and on through Great and Little Alne towards Stratford. The road being in a fair state of repair, they were able to push on at a smart trot. Mr Petre was, in fact, beginning to talk quite cheerfully of their being easily able to reach Long Marston that day, when, a few hundred yards short of the little village of Wootton, a very unpleasant thing occurred. Mr Petre was chatting to Jane, when an old woman, who was working in a field beside the road, called out in a warning voice: 'Master, master! Don't you see a troop of horse before you?'

The mere mention of soldiers was enough to make John Petre jump in his saddle. He peered ahead, and saw to his dismay that the woman was speaking the truth. Rebel soldiers were certainly in possession of Wootton. A number of red-coats could be seen, and horses, straggling over the road in front of a small inn, the troop having apparently halted there to water their horses, and get refreshment for themselves.

'I daresay they will not do us any hurt,' said Withy in her comfortable way.

'Not do us any hurt!' exclaimed her husband. 'They will have our horses as soon as they clap eyes on them! We must turn back and go into Stratford by another way! I would not for the world expose you and Jane to their rude manners! We must turn immediately! Jane, you hear me? Jackson, stop this instant!'

The King obediently reined in, but whispered over his shoulder: 'Let him not go back! It were fatal to be seen making off!'

'But, sir, what shall we do?'

'Ride on as though we had nothing to fear,' he replied under his breath.

Her good sense told her that his plan was the best, but the risk he must run of being recognized frightened her. Her voice shook as she answered John Petre. 'Do not let us turn back, I beg you! Withy and I are not afraid.'

'You know nothing about it,' he said impatiently. 'I have already suffered at the hands of these Parliamentarian rogues, and I'll take good care I run not upon them again!'

She looked imploringly at Lassels, who, realizing that she must be acting under the King's orders, immediately said: 'Consider, sir, how suspicious we must make the knaves if we turn, and ride off! Then indeed they might be moved to pursue us!'

'You may do as you please,' replied Petre. 'For my part, nothing would induce me to go on. I shall take Withy into Stratford by the other road, and if you have a particle of sense, Jane, you will go with us!'

'I have pride,' she said gently, but with sufficient reproof in her voice to bring a flush into his cheeks.

'I wish you joy of it! You are an ignorant girl, and so I tell you! Now, are you coming, for I warn you, I will not stay to dispute with you longer?'

'I shall ride on,' she answered. 'Harry will go with me, even if I cannot prevail upon you to do so.'

He muttered something about headstrong women, and wheeled his horse about, ignoring his wife's mild expostulation. Jane made no further attempt to persuade him to change his mind, but said: 'Please to go on, Jackson.'

The big horse moved forward; Lassels, lingering only to watch John Petre ride off as fast as he was able, trotted up abreast of the King. He said anxiously: 'Will you take my pistols, sir? If you should be known —'

'I shall not make bad worse by engaging in a shooting match,' replied the King. 'And do not you either!'

A breathless voice spoke behind his shoulder. 'We must try to converse together, Harry. Say something to me. I cannot think of anything, but I will answer you.'

They were already almost within earshot of the soldiers gathered in front of the ale-house. Lassels took his cousin at her word so instantly, and with such an air of light-hearted unconcern, that she felt some of the constriction in her throat relax, and was able to respond with a fair assumption of ease.

Their party had naturally attracted the soldiers' attention. They were aware of being scrutinized as they drew towards the lounging group, but it was Jane's beauty that held the soldiers' eyes. The troop-horses taking up the whole width of the street, the travellers were forced to halt. A fat fellow with a tankard of ale in one hand, and a hunk of bread and meat in the other, ogled Jane, and another called a somewhat ribald greeting to her. Lassels pushed forward, saying sharply: 'Make way, if you please!'

'There's a lusty young gamecock for you!' remarked one of the men. 'Now, who would ha' thought to meet such a rare, pretty lass in these miserable parts?'

Jane blushed faintly, but said in her quiet way: 'Please to let us pass, good fellow!'

Several of the troopers had strolled up to her: one of them said with clumsy gallantry: 'You don't need to be in such haste. Where might you be off to, mistress?'

At this moment, an officer came out of the ale-house. He was a stern-looking man, very neat and soldierly in his bearing, and as soon as he perceived the travellers, and the uncomfortable situation they were in, he rapped out a sharp order. The troopers gathered round Jane's horse drew back in a hurry.

'Clear a way there for the lady to pass!' commanded the officer. 'Your pardon, madam; I am sorry for it if you have met with any discourtesy.'

'Thank you, sir, but I think none was intended,' she replied, smiling faintly at him.

'I am obliged to you, sir,' said Lassels, doffing his hat. 'Go on, Jackson! The road is clear now.'

The horses moved forward, the officer taking off his hat and making Jane a bow as she passed him.

She did not speak until they were out of the village, but as soon as they emerged again on to the open road, she said with a note of bewilderment in her voice: 'He was very civil to us!'

'Ay, we were lucky to chance upon a gentleman in command of that troop,' said Lassels. 'He looked to be a good sort of a fellow.'

'But, Harry, a rebel! a traitor!' she said.

The King laughed. 'Did you think there were no decent, gentlemanly fellows amongst mine enemies, Jane? Alas, I fear there are many!'

'Yes, sir, and the more shame to them!' said Lassels roundly. 'I pray God I may live to see them come by their deserts!'

'Why, what a fierce fellow you are!' remarked the King.

'Shall you punish your enemies, sir, when you come to your throne?' asked Jane.

'What, be revenged on every poor devil that had the bad taste not to like me? No, child: if I could do it, which I am very sure I could not, I would not.'

'I hoped you would say so,' she replied. 'If your enemies knew you as I do, I think they could not be any longer your enemies.'

'Those are very comfortable words, Jane, but at this present I am giving thanks that my enemies do not appear to know me at all. I think this disguise of mine must be better than I had hoped. We have now only one care left, and that is how to come up with poor Mr Petre again.'

'For my part, sir, I think we shall be well rid of him,' said Lassels.

'Yes, you are a very ruthless man, my friend. I promise you, I fear you!'

A laugh quivered in Jane's throat.

'How now, Jane?' promptly demanded the King.

'Sir, placed as I am between one ruthless man and one reckless King I must wonder at it if I find not myself clapped up presently in prison.'

'Why, what have I done?'

'Sir, you chose to ride straight through that troop of rebels, and you did not even make shift to hide your face from them, for I watched you, and saw you looking the soldiers over as though they had been your own.'

'There was nothing reckless in that. They were not paying any heed to me. Their eyes were fixed on that face which I cannot see, and small blame to them! If we find not your sister and Mr Petre in Stratford, we had best await them at a decent inn there. I suppose they will look for you in the town.'

This suggestion, however, Jane rejected, nor could any argument advanced by the King in favour of his plan induce her to change her nay to yea. She thought that the Petres would very likely catch them up on the road to Long Marston, and begged the King not to court discovery by lingering in a disaffected town. Accordingly, they passed through Stratford without a halt, and, having crossed the Avon, proceeded by the Pebworth road towards Long Marston.

It was agreed between them that although Mr Tomes was a man of undoubted loyalty he should not be admitted into the secret of Will Jackson's identity, and so, when they drew rein at last outside a half-timbered manor-house, standing a little retired from the highway, only Jane and Lassels alighted, the King remaining in the saddle to lead both horses to the stables.

His appearance excited no curiosity there, for however unhandy he might be in helping ladies into pillion-saddles, there was very little he did not know about the care of horses. When he presently shouldered the baggage, and made his way towards the house, he had rubbed both nags down, assisted by one of Mr Tomes's grooms, had watered and fed them, and seen them bedded down for the night. He had also enjoyed a desultory conversation with the groom, who ascribed his voice and accent to his supposed Staffordshire breeding, and thought him a very pleasant fellow.

He entered the house by way of the kitchen, where a harassed and consequently short-tempered cook-maid was preparing dinner for her master's unexpected guests. She looked at him with disfavour, and upon his asking her to direct him to Mr Lassels's chamber, told him that it was not for the likes of him to go trapesing about the house unbidden.

'But I must carry the baggage up, must I not?' said the King.

'Set it down: there's others as'll 'tend to that. A nice thing it would be if every great overgrown gowk out of the stables was to go where he pleased in a gentleman's house! And don't stand about there in my way, and me with dinner to get, and not so much as half-an-hour's warning of company!'

'It smells very good,' remarked the King, putting the saddle-bags down by the door.

'It may well! And me withouten any to give a hand! Company! Ay, it's always company when that lazy slut Joan's ill a-bed. Do you do somewhat to earn your dinner, and wind up that jack, 'stead of standing there like a great maypole!'

'Why, with good will!' said the King, stepping forward, and grasping the handle.

He found, however, that there was more to this seemingly simple task than he had supposed, a certain knack, which he did not possess, being required. His efforts exasperated the cook-maid. She thrust him away, and winding the jack up herself, demanded scornfully: 'What kind of a countryman are you, that you know not how to wind up a jack?'

'I am a poor tenant's son, of Colonel Lane in Staffordshire,' replied the King meekly. He added with a heart-rending look: 'We seldom have roast meat, but when we do, we don't use a jack.'

She subjected him to a sharp scrutiny, but answered in

a mollified tone: 'Ay, and you look as though you'd never seen a good dish of meat, that I will say! Well, you can eat your fill here: there's no stint, and all of the best.'

The butler came into the kitchen at this moment, and, at sight of the King, said: 'You're to take up the baggage. It seems nothing will do for your master but he must have his own servant to wait upon him. I'm sure it's naught to me, and he may have it as he pleases, for all you look to me more fit for the stables than a gentleman's bedchamber.'

'Mr Lassels can never bear to have a stranger near him,' explained the King. 'I'd best go to him at once, or he will fly into one of his passions.'

'I warrant he will!' said the butler. 'A mighty high-stomached young gentleman, so full of fads and fancies as I never did see! Well, pick up the bags, and I'll lead you to him before he can come down shouting for you himself.'

The King once more shouldered his burdens, and followed the butler out of the kitchen. When they reached Lassels's bedchamber, that young gentleman, who had evidently flung himself into his part with a good deal of zest, greeted them with an exclamation of pent-up impatience.

'The devil! What have you been about all this while? Set the bags down, and unstrap them! I want a clean handkerchief directly.'

'Yes, master: at once!' said the King.

The butler withdrew. Lassels waited until the sound of his footsteps grew faint upon the stairs, and then said: 'Forgive me, sir! I knew not how else to bring you away from the kitchen.'

'A mighty high-stomached young gentleman!' mocked the King. 'I think you have made an enemy for yourself in that poor butler. As for me, I fell into very ill-odour in the kitchen. How do you wind up a jack?'

'I don't know, sir.'

'Nor I. I thought the cook-maid would have boxed my ears. But she has promised me a good dinner, which I shall eat in the buttery.'

'We must contrive!' Lassels said, beginning to pace about the room. 'You cannot dine with the servants, sir. It is not to be thought of!'

'Content you, I shall fare excellent well. I shall divulge to the butler what an ill master to serve you are, and for very pity I daresay he will cut me some slices of the mutton you are going to have for your dinner.'

Lassels stopped his pacing, and said with a grin: 'Are we going to have mutton, sir?'

'To be sure you are. Also Joan is ill a-bed.'

'Good God! Who is Joan, sir?'

'I know not, but she is always ill when there is company.' He lounged across the room to where a mirror stood upon a chest, and meditatively studied his own reflection. 'She said I looked as though I had never seen a good dish of meat. Would you say I was an overgrown gowk, Lassels?'

'No, sir, I would not!' replied Lassels emphatically.

'That is because you know your duty,' said Charles. 'But I am hearing some home-truths from those who know me not.'

A soft scratching upon the door made him turn his head. Lassels went to the door and opened it. Jane Lane stood upon the threshold, and said in an anxious whisper: 'The King?'

Lassels stepped back to let her pass into the room. 'He is here, Jane. All's well!'

She came in. She had shed her cloak, and tidied her ring-lets, threading a ribbon through them. She curtseyed to the King. 'Sir, I came to consult with my cousin how we may contrive to have you fittingly bestowed this night. You must not sleep in the servants' dormitory.'

The King moved towards her, and as she rose from her curtsey, took her face between his long, brown hands, and held it tilted a little upwards. 'Now at last let me look at this face I have yet seen so fleetingly,' he said.

She stood perfectly still, looking gravely up at him, not afraid to meet his gaze, but with a suggestion of humility in her quiet.

Something glowed behind the smile in his eyes. 'Such a pretty face!' he said under his breath. His hands seemed to her to harden; he bent his head and kissed her.

Colour leapt up under his fingers; still holding her, he had an odd fancy that she had sprung suddenly into life. He looked up and saw Lassels watching him, a little trouble in his face. He laughed, and let his hands fall on to Jane's shoulders. For a moment they rested there; then he slid them down her arms to her wrists, and lifting her hands, carried them one after the other to his lips. 'My Life!' he said, caressing her with the careless magic of his voice and smile. 'I shall hereafter call you so, since you hold it between these little hands.'

'It is a proud title, sire,' she said. 'Indeed, I am proud to bear it.' She slightly bowed her head as she spoke, and drew her hands out of his hold.

'Touching this question of where your Majesty is to sleep,' began Lassels, 'I have been considering that I should request Mr Tomes to set up a truckle-bed in this room.'

'Well, you have made yourself so troublesome to the household already that I daresay no one will be much surprised,' remarked the King, moving away to lean his elbow upon the mantelpiece. 'I think I must not go to bed with the servants, for, as I remember, Richard Penderel told me that I called out in my sleep.'

'Of course your Majesty cannot go to bed with the servants!' said Lassels. 'Upon all counts it would be unthinkable! I will tell John Tomes that I am used to have my man sleep in the room with me.'

'It were better you should tell him what my sister already knows, that his Majesty is suffering from a tertian ague,' said Jane. 'He will not think it odd then that you should desire better accommodation for one whom he believes to be but a poor man.'

'And if he should object that I seem not to have any fever, you will say that it is in the intermission today,' interpolated the King. 'Is your sister come yet, Jane? I hope Mr Petre fell not into another ambush upon the way to Stratford!'

She shook her head. 'They did not meet any soldiers. I think Mr Petre is a little ashamed that he did not go along with us. We shall part from their company tomorrow.'

'I am right glad of it,' said the King, 'for you will thus be able to talk to poor Will Jackson. I thought myself sadly neglected upon our ride today, I can tell you.'

Her gravity was dispelled by a sudden smile that gleamed in response to the teasing light in his eye. 'Comfort you, sir! If I did not talk to you, for very fear, at least you were not once out of my thoughts – nor out of Harry's, either, I dare swear.'

'I care nothing for being in Harry's thoughts,' said the King. 'But I am certainly much comforted to know I live in yours. Tell me, what sort of a fellow am I there?'

'My liege,' she said, in a low voice.

'Alas! As well say a crowned puppet! Mr Lassels, I am well aware that I do not fill your notion of what a king should be, but for all that I am one, and I will not brook being frowned upon.'

Lassels reddened to the ears, exclaiming: 'But, sir, indeed, indeed you do, and I was not frowning upon you! I was – I was wondering how to contrive that you should not be called upon to eat your dinner in the buttery.'

'Is that all? Frown no more, then, for I am going to eat in the buttery.'

He spoke with decision, so that there was nothing for Lassels to do but to acquiesce, though with many inward qualms. He could not conceive how even the stupidest scullion could fail to perceive that the King was no common fellow, and said as much to Jane presently, when he found himself for a few minutes alone with her in the parlour.

She listened to him, but said calmly: 'Perhaps the servants might suspect him of being other than he seems, but I think they will not dream he could be the King. Did not even we look for some stiffness, some haughtiness in his bearing which is not there? Were not you surprised to find him so easy, and – and merry?'

'Ay, it's very true.' He stole a glance at her, and then lowered his gaze to his own boots, saying with a little constraint: 'One forgets that he is the King, because he delights in laying his Majesty aside.'

'I do not forget it.'

He went on studying his boots. 'Well, I am glad to hear

you say it. You know, cousin, I don't desire to busy myself with what doesn't concern me, but Cousin John in some sort entrusted you to my care, and there's no denying that the King has a way of making himself so generally pleasing that – in short – no one could help loving him.'

He looked up with an apologetic smile as he ended. Jane replied quietly: 'I understand you, Harry.'

'I should not like you to regret this adventure,' he blurted out.

'I shall not.'

'You know, it's said that he is something free with women. I do not mean that I believe it —'

Her eyes darkened with amusement. 'I do!'

He was a good deal taken aback by this. 'Why, cousin!'

She repeated: 'I shall not regret, Harry. You spoke of our journey as an adventure. Indeed, it is one, and I have thought that since the King is merry we should be so too. We shall never have another adventure like to this, you and I.' She moved her hands. 'He will go his way, and we ours, but this will be a little part of our lives that we shall remember always, like a fairy-tail told us in our childhood. You are anxious because the King kissed me, but you need not fear for me. I am not for him, since I am not a princess to whom he may offer marriage, and not a trollop whom he would make his mistress.'

'Jane,' said Lassels uncomfortably, 'Kings – well, kings are not quite as other men are. They – they do sometimes take what they want, thinking it a Right Divine.'

'Not this king,' she replied. 'In my heart, I know him for an easy lover, but no ravisher.'

She spoke so serenely that he began to think he had been indulging absurd fears. He said in his boyishly blunt fashion: 'I'll tell you what, cousin: you're a wise woman, not one to have your head turned. To be sure, he is very ill-favoured, is he not?'

She looked at him with a blankness in her gaze. She was not aware of the King's dark ugliness, though vaguely she could remember her first impression of him as a swarthy, coarse-featured young man. But then he had smiled upon her, and spoken, and she was aware only of a beautiful deep voice, and of a presence that filled her vision to the exclusion of all others. She said slowly, fumbling for words: 'Is he? Yes, I do recall I thought so.'

'It's a mighty queer thing,' remarked Lassels, 'but for all I have not known him above a day, I've a notion life will seem an empty business when he goes away from us.'

'Yes,' she said. 'Yes. An empty business.'

His words seemed to cast the shadow of the future across the room. She said no more, but moved away to snuff a candle that was guttering.

She did not see the King again that evening. Mr Tomes readily caused a truckle-bed to be set up in Lassels's chamber: so readily, in fact, that Lassels suspected him of guessing that Will Jackson was not what he seemed to be, and privately informed Jane of it. She was sure, however, that although her kinsman might suppose the King to be a Cavalier, he had no inkling of his true identity. It was evident that he did not wish to be taken into their confidence, for upon Lassels's beginning to tell him of Jackson's tertian ague, he said quickly: 'I ask no questions. I know only that your serving-man is in feeble health, and that is not a matter that concerns me.'

Lassels went early to bed, and was soon joined by the King, who came up from the buttery, declaring that they fared much better there than in the dining-parlour.

Lassels bolted the door, and knelt down before Charles to pull off his boots. 'Was it very rude and uncomfortable, sire?' he asked anxiously.

The King smiled sleepily down at him. 'You know, you are as proud as a cock on his own dunghill, Lassels. I wonder you will jaunt about the country with a low fellow like myself. I was right well-entertained in the buttery, and have been exchanging bawdy stories with the butler this hour and more. He is an honest man, and wishes I may escape from mine enemies.'

'But he did not know you, sir?'

'Nay, he called on me to drink mine own health, which I did very willingly. Also he pitied me that I must lie upon

177

a truckle-bed in your chamber, and said it was strange that a young man with so kind a countenance should be so exacting a master as to expect to be waited on by night as well as by day.'

Lassels helped him to take off his coat, remarking with a grin: 'I dare swear you spun him a mighty fine tale of my harshness, sir.'

'I did,' said the King, casting his shirt on to a chair. 'If they do not reckon me very good company in the kitchen, trust me never!'

'We think that John Tomes suspects you of being a Cavalier in disguise,' said Lassels. 'But there is no need to fear him, sir.'

The King got into bed, and lay down. 'Very well, I won't give him a thought,' he said, closing his eyes. 'I hope you will not find that pallet very hard.'

'Be sure I shan't, sir.'

'I am reasonably sure that you will,' said the King. 'The butler told me I should.'

'Sir,' said Lassels, 'I do not anticipate any sudden danger in this house, but in case the need should arise, will you have one of my pistols beneath your pillow?'

'Good God!' murmured the King. 'Are you at that again? You are too dangerous a man for me. Put up your pistols, and go to bed!'

Lassels said, 'Yes, sire,' in an obedient voice, but having assured himself that the King's eyes were still shut, slipped both pistols under his own pillow.

Nothing occurred during the night to cause him to draw them out from this hiding-place, but although all was quiet in the house he several times awoke, and fancied that he heard sounds. The King slept peacefully, a circumstance that filled the young attendant with a kind of wondering admiration. He did not call out in his sleep, though once he muttered some indistinguishable words. When morning came, Lassels was obliged to rouse him. He woke then with a start, and for a moment seemed bewildered, blinking up at Lassels, and saying in a voice thickened with sleep: '*One* charge! I beg of you – I beg of you, gentlemen!' He broke

178

off, as the dream receded, and sat up, pressing his hands to his eyes.

'Sire, you are safe at Long Marston,' Lassels said, a little timidly.

The King's hands fell. 'I do remember. I thought – no matter: it was nothing to the purpose.' He flung back the bedclothes, and got up, saying cheerfully: 'Help me to dress, Lassels. I think your servant would fetch hot water for you to shave with, would he not?'

The King ate his breakfast in the buttery, and went out immediately after to the stables. As soon as Jane had taken her leave of the Petres, who set off at an early hour, Lassels sent to command his horses. The King brought both up to the house; the saddle-bags were strapped on, and Jane Lane put up into her pillion. Mr Tomes came out to speed his guests on their way, but beyond casting one searching glance at as much of the King's face as he could see for the shading brim of his hat, paid no heed to him.

It had been agreed that the second night should be spent at Cirencester, which lay some twenty-four miles from Long Marston, and they rode there by easy stages, encountering nothing on the way to occasion them the least alarm. The King seemed to be in excellent spirits, declaring that the only blot upon his enjoyment was the necessity of twisting his head over his shoulder every time he was desirous of looking at Jane. The indulging of this desire upon a very rough part of the road nearly resulted in their both being tumbled in the mud, for the King had let his bridle hang loosely, and the big gelding stumbled badly, setting a foot into a deep pit full of water. Jane clutched the King about the middle with a gasp of dismay, but the gelding recovered his footing, and the danger was past. Releasing the King, Jane said severely: 'Indeed and indeed my mother was in the right of it! What goodly horseman have I to ride before me?'

The King, whose first governor had been the finest horseman of his day, said meekly: 'But I was taught horsemanage by my Lord of Newcastle.'

'Then I must say that he taught you very ill, sire, or you

were a dull pupil.'

'He was used to say I could ride his horses better than he could himself,' pleaded the King. 'But being but a lad I was not set up before a lady whose face I most earnestly desired to see.'

'Being but a lad, sir, you would most heartily have despised it,' returned Jane.

'Oh no!' said the King. 'I do assure you I had always an eye for a pretty face.'

'Fie upon you, sir! You must then have been a bad, odious little boy.'

'I doubt I was,' agreed Charles. 'An ill-favoured urchin, to boot, and one that halted in his speech. My brother James is generally held to be greatly my superior, being fair to look upon, very graceful in his bearing, and with plenty to say for himself.'

She smiled. 'And you, sir?'

'Oh, I sit mumchance, and devour good mutton when I should be partaking of French kickshaws. I can tell you, they would give you no good account of me at my cousin Louis' court. In particular, la Grande Mademoiselle looks upon me with disgust, thinking me a great boor.'

'Does she, sir?' Of what like is she, I wonder?'

'Her teeth stick out,' said the King.

Laughter quivered in her voice. 'Oh! If my teeth did so, I think I might find you – a great boor, sir.'

'The unhappy cause of my ill-success with Mademoiselle,' said the King primly, 'is my unlucky tongue, which cannot master the French language.'

'*You* cannot converse in French?' she said, momentarily astonished.

The King turned his head, and cast her a sidelong, wicked look that spoke volumes.

She gave a little chuckle. 'Sir, sir, I think that smith spoke truly who called you *that rogue, Charles Stewart!* Shall you marry Mademoiselle?'

'Oddsfish, no! Do you think Mademoiselle would wed a penniless adventurer, my Life? You are sadly out!'

Her face became troubled. She asked: 'What will you do,

when you come safe to France, sir?'

'Listen to a homily from my good Chancellor,' replied the King flippantly. 'Lassels, at the next inn we come to, we will alight, and take some refreshment.'

'I am very willing, sir,' said Lassels, 'but do you think we should? Mr Tomes had some bread and cheese put up for us.'

'I have had enough of bread and cheese to last me the rest of my life,' said the King. 'As for my being recognized, if that is what troubles you, I begin to think myself a match for all my enemies.'

But no one betrayed the least interest in him at the inn which he presently chose to honour with his patronage. His conversations with the butler at Long Marston had informed him that a gentleman's groom, travelling with his master, was generally a pert, swaggering fellow, and this rôle he enacted with such zest that his anxious companions' hearts seemed several times to miss a beat. When they expostulated, he was quite impenitent, and, indeed, conducted himself with so much assurance at the Crown, at Cirencester, where they arrived at dusk, that they began to think that their fears for him were wasted.

As at Long Marston, a truckle-bed was set up in Lassels's bedchamber. Both he and the King passed an undisturbed night, setting out again upon the last stage of the journey at an early hour on the following morning.

Going by way of Chipping-Sodbury, they reached the outskirts of Bristol in the late afternoon, crossing the Avon at the Rownham Ferry, and entering the town by Lawford's Gate.

Neither Jane nor Lassels was familiar with Bristol, and the King, who had blithely engaged to lead them safely through it, found it so much enlarged since his sojourn there some years previously, that he soon confessed himself to be at a loss to find the way. The circumstance of the town's being extremely disaffected, the castle being held by a strong Parliamentarian garrison, made both Jane and Lassels nervous of lingering in it. The streets were full of people, and a great many red-coats were to be seen. A small party of obvious travellers did not attract much attention in a sea-port, but when the King, who had been looking about him with great interest at all the changes to be seen in the town, insisted on riding up to the castle and all round it, Lassels could not contain himself, but implored him not to behave so rashly.

'Consider, sir, what must be your fate if any should know you! This is a veritable stronghold of the rebels!'

'Alas!' said the King. 'I did like this town very well, as I remember. How all is changed! It is become very fine and large. I think I may certainly find a vessel here to carry me to France.'

'Ay, or a strong guard to carry you to London, sir!' retorted Lassels.

'What you mean is a tumbril,' said the King.

'No, I do not, sir,' replied Lassels, missing the laugh in the King's voice. 'They could not carry you all the way to London upon a tumbril! Besides, even rebels would not do so!'

'Oh, then, I have nothing to fear!' said the King. 'Let us go on. I once dwelt within those walls, Jane. My cousin Rupert, too. I would give a fortune to see the Governor's face if he knew that I was even now riding round his fortress.'

Jane laid her hand on his arm. 'Dear sir, I am afraid,' she said. 'They will haply kill me if they find you out.'

This gentle reminder made the King say remorsefully: 'Why, what a careless knave I am! Lassels, have done with this junketing about the town, and enquire the way to Abbotsleigh!'

This being done, and the party directed towards the Redclyffe Gate, they were soon out of the town, descending the precipitous hill to the river again, which ran through a magnificent limestone gorge. The road wound sharply up to Leigh Down upon the south side of the Avon, and by the time the travellers arrived at Abbotsleigh it was nearly dusk.

The house, which was a large, rambling building erected in a previous age, and much added to, commanded wide views, and had before it a bowling-green, upon which some men were finishing a game. A number of spectators were gathered round, greatly to Jane's discomfiture, but since there was no other way of approaching the house, she was obliged to acquiesce in the King's decision to go boldly on.

Accordingly, they rode forward at a gentle pace. The men by the green were too much interested in the game to bestow more than a few casual glances upon them, and Jane's heart had just resumed its normal beat when the King gave a sudden exclamation under his breath, and pulled his hat low over his brow.

'What is it, sir?' Jane whispered.

'Do you see that fat fellow sitting upon the rails? He is Dr Gorges, who was one of my chaplains.'

Her hands gripped the skirts of his coat. 'Sir, what shall we do? Is it safe to disclose yourself to him? Is he honest?'

'He may be honest, but there was never a fool that blabbed more,' said the King. 'Ride on the other side of me, Lassels, that he may not catch any glimpse of this accursed face of mine.'

Lassels pushed forward at once, but said: 'If he is your friend, sir, surely he would not —'

'I thank you, at this present, I had liefer come upon mine enemies than my friends!' retorted the King sardonically.

## CHAPTER XI

## 'I KNOW IT IS MY LIEGE'

They had arrived by this time, skirting the bowling-green, at the house. Lassels at once dismounted, and lifted Jane down from the pillion; and the King, without losing any time, led the horses away to the stables, where, it had been hastily concerted between himself and Jane, he would await a summons from her.

Scarcely had he departed, when Mrs Norton, a pretty

young woman, just now heavy with child, came out with her husband to welcome her guests. She clasped Jane in her arms, kissing her repeatedly, and besieging her with affectionate questions, while her husband took Lassels in charge. It was some time before any opportunity offered of mentioning Will Jackson and his tertian ague, for Mrs Norton, besides being very chatty, was so hospitable that she set the whole household in a bustle, fetching refreshments for the travellers, removing their cloaks, and running to be sure that their rooms were in readiness for them.

'You dear, dear thing!' she cried, clasping both Jane's hands in hers, and beaming upon her. 'The comfort it is to have you with me! How kind it was of Madam Lane to spare you! Oh, and to send me that cordial! I have been so low, you would scarcely credit it! And then that tiresome Dr Gorges – not that I mean to complain, for indeed he is perfectly amiable, but for ever talking, till my head is like to split.'

'Dr Gorges?' Jane repeated, feeling a little chill in the pit of her stomach. 'Is he staying in the house, Nell?'

'Oh yes! And a worthy good man, that was a cleric, only now, you understand, he dare not own to it, but has taken up the study of physic. But he leaves us tomorrow, for which I am so thankful!'

George Norton, a sensible-looking man, as quiet as his wife was vivacious, overheard these words, and broke off in the middle of asking Lassels what route he had come by, to say with a reproving smile: 'Eleanor, for shame! You must know, Jane, that the good doctor is a distant relative of hers, and very welcome in this house.'

'Well, and said I not he was a worthy, good man?' protested Mrs Norton. 'But while I have my dearest Jane I want no other company! I should have warned you, dear heart, that George so loves to entertain our acquaintance that the house is for ever full of visitors. Oh yes, indeed! I never have the least notion how many will sit down to dinner with us: it is quite abominable! While as for the buttery, you would say it was a common inn, for every poor man in the world comes into it. The broken meats that go out of this house! But George is so generous he will never turn a soul away!'

Mr Norton, who had reddened a trifle, was spared further embarrassment by the butler's coming in with the refreshments he had been bidden to bring to the parlour. Mrs Norton at once became busy pressing canary upon Jane, and urging Lassels to tell her without hesitation if he would prefer a glass of sack. 'Pope will get it for you on the instant!' she assured him. 'If there is aught you wish for at any time you have but to tell Pope. You must please to think yourself perfectly at home. Now do, do inform me of *everything* you would like!'

'Indeed, you are very good, madam, but there is nothing, really nothing!' said Lassels, quite oppressed by her hospitality.

Jane set down her glass of canary, and said in as natural a voice as she could: 'Oh, Nell, there is only one trifling matter which I had well-nigh forgot! The serving-man who came with me is suffering from a tertian ague, and I am very wishful to see him housed as comfortably as may be. He is a tenant of ours, an honest man whom my brother thinks very well of, and he is not quite used to sleeping in the common dormitory, besides being sickly.'

'Poor man!' exclaimed Mrs Norton. 'Pope shall see to it that he is put into a bedchamber, and I will send my waiting woman – you remember Margaret Rider, I'll be bound, Jane! – and she will have a very good care to him, I promise you.'

'Oh, no need for that, madam!' said Lassels hastily. 'The fellow can sleep upon a pallet in my room. Do not put yourself out, I beg of you!'

She began to protest that he should not be put into the same room with a sick man, but Jane at once intervened, saying with a smile: 'Dear Nell, you are quite out! My kinsman will not own it, but ill or well he must always have his servant within call. He will not thank you for putting William in a room apart.'

'Well!' said Mrs Norton. 'It is very odd of him, but it shall be just as he pleases. Pope will see to it, and this

William of yours shall have a good bed in his chamber.'

'Yes, mistress,' said the butler. 'And will your honour take a glass of sack, or the canary?'

'Yes – I mean, no! I'll take canary!' Lassels replied, wondering what his Royal master was doing, and what hope there was of his escaping detection in a house that seemed, by all accounts, to be teeming with casual visitors.

Jane's cool voice recalled his wandering wits. She had drawn off his host's attention by asking him some question about his estate. Lassels forced himself to drink his wine, and to attend to Mrs Norton's rippling and inconsequent chatter; but when, after what seemed hours, it was suggested that the travellers might like to be taken to their bedchambers, the alacrity with which he jumped up from his chair was marked enough to make Jane frown upon him.

Mrs Norton herself led the way up a flight of graceful stairs. The sight of an elderly woman in a plain stuff gown and a mob-cap, crossing the landing at the head of the stairs, made her remember her friend's serving-man, and she called out: 'Margaret, Margaret, here is Mrs Jane Lane! And how is that poor man? You must have a care to him, for Mrs Jane is not to want for a groom, you know.'

Margaret Rider, dropping curtseys, replied that 'deed she would make the poor fellow a carduus-posset, for he was feeling mighty aguish, and looking for all the world like a ghostie, so pale he was, which anyone could see, for all his tan. She pointed out Lassels's bedchamber to him, and told him that William was laid down upon his bed there, adding, as Mrs Norton conducted Jane down the passage to her own room: 'Ay, sir, and 'tis a sick man he is, and quite forespent, or I know naught of the matter. All this hard riding, and him as should ought to have been in his bed, poor overgrown lad that he is!'

This suggestion quite alarmed Lassels, and he entered the bedchamber with such an anxious expression on his face that Charles, who was stretched on a cupboard-bed against the wall, with his hands linked behind his head, opened his lazy eyes at him in surprise. 'Oddsblood, what disaster has befallen us?'

'Oh, none, sir, none!' Lassels assured him. 'But that woman said you were forespent, and it put me in mind of the hardships your Majesty has undergone, and the way I have never given them a thought, but let you spend all day in the saddle, as though you were not indeed ill, as she says you are!'

The King, who had listened to this tumbled speech with his brows lifted, broke in on it, saying in a tone of considerable amusement: 'What the devil ails you, man? I promise you, I was never better in my life! Even my feet are in a fair way to healing, so what is all this pother about?'

'The waiting-woman said how pale your Majesty was beneath that stain, and now I see that it is very true!' Lassels said, conscience-stricken. 'Only your Majesty never complained, and I did not think —'

The King swung his legs to the ground, and stood up. He took Lassels by the shoulders and shook him slightly. 'Peace, peace! What if someone were listening outside that door while you stand there babbling of my Majesty at every second word? What the pox has put you in such a taking?'

Lassels gave an uncertain laugh. 'I ask your pardon, sir! But I wish we had not come to this place, for it is full of strangers, besides that Dr Gorges is a guest here, and I know not how to keep your – to keep you concealed! We have contrived that I am to lie in your chamber, but I dare not remain to guard you by day as I should, for fear of its giving rise to suspicion, yet how may I leave you alone where you are like to be discovered at any moment?'

'But there is not the least need for all this distress, I do assure you!' said the King, still amused, but rather touched. 'I think myself reasonably safe here. I have encountered a multitude of grooms and scullions and cook-maids, and not one of them favoured me with as much as a second glance. As for the waiting-woman you spoke with, I told her I had been ill many weeks, and she has promised me a carduus-posset of her own making. If I were ten times King of this realm, she would not care a button for it. Do you know so little of women? I tell you, if a man will but declare himself to be ailing, they will think of naught else but how best to cosset and cure him. Go and tell her I am the King! She will say, *Ay, is he so? The poor lanky lad that he is, and he with the fever still upon him! I will put a warming-pan between his sheets this instant.*'

His mimicry was exact enough to make Lassels laugh. He could not, however, be at ease, and although he was obliged to leave the King presently to go down to supper, his mind persisted in flitting back to him, and so many horrid possibilities presented themselves to his imagination that he had several times to pull out his handkerchief and wipe the starting beads of sweat from his brow. His hostess, observing this, feared that the log-fire discommoded him, and begged him to change his place at the table.

Jane, who was seated beside George Norton, and had Dr Gorges opposite to her, was herself a little troubled to know how to convey a good supper to the King. She guessed that in such a large, haphazard household the meats that would ordinarily be carried up to a sick serving-man would by no means suit the King's appetite, and when a bowl of broth was brought to the table, she desired the butler, in a low voice, to bring her a little dish that she might fill it for William. He did so, and she ladled some broth into it, and gave it back to him, saying: 'Please to have it carried up to William, and tell him he shall have some meat presently.'

She had thought Dr Gorges's attention to have been fixed upon his host, but no sooner had Pope taken the dish from her than the worthy cleric turned his inquisitive gaze upon her, and demanded: 'Is that for your servant, the same whom I am told is suffering from the tertian ague?'

'Yes, sir,' Jane replied tranquilly.

'Well, it is a fortunate thing you have chanced upon me, Mrs Lane!' said the doctor, with a consequent little laugh. 'You must know that I have a considerable knowledge of physic, and I shall be very happy to do what I can for your servant.'

'I thank you, sir, but we believe William's sickness to be mending.'

'The more reason to have a care to him. These fevers are

not generally understood, and much harm may result from them. Now, tell me: how long has the ague been gone?'

'A full two weeks, sir,' replied Jane.

'Two weeks? Ay, very good, very good, but has he been purged since it left him?'

'Yes, indeed, sir.'

Lassels, who had been listening in an agony to this interchange, tried at this point to engage Dr Gorges's attention, but without success. The doctor continued throughout the meal to ply Jane with questions, and to describe the various methods used in treating such disorders. She answered him to the best of her ability, but was very thankful when supper was at last over, and Eleanor Norton bore her off for a cosy chat with her in the winter-parlour.

Several gentlemen from the neighbourhood had sat down to supper at Abbotsleigh, and when the two ladies went away together, the conversation soon came round to sport. Mr Norton desired the opinion of one of his friends on a fowling-piece which he had just purchased, and most of the men, including Lassels, went off with him to inspect it. Happily for what little peace of mind was left to Lassels, he did not observe Dr Gorges presently withdraw from the group.

The doctor, who was no sportsman, was still considering the case of William Jackson, and had decided to see the sick man with his own eyes, and, if necessary, to prescribe for him. A waiting-man readily directed him to Lassels's bedchamber, and up went the doctor, puffing a little as he mounted the stairs.

The King, who had just finished his supper, heard the heavy footsteps halt outside his door, and quickly got into his bed, drawing one of the panels a little, to shut out the light of the candle on the table near by. When he saw who was entering the room he shifted his position until he lay as near the wall as he could, with his face in deep shadow.

The doctor came up to the bed, saying kindly: 'Well, my poor fellow, and so you are sick! I am sorry for it, and will do what I can for you. Let me take a look at you!'

His hand had already grasped the candlestick, but the King groaned, and begged that the light might not be brought close, since it hurt his eyes.

This did not at all surprise the doctor; he had met with such cases before, and assured the King that the weakness in his eyes would pass, if he would but follow his directions. He then possessed himself of the King's hand, and felt his pulse. He seemed a little disappointed to find it so strong, but said that he could detect a flutter in it.

The King, who thought this extremely probable, said that he had a great desire to sleep.

'Ay, I daresay, and so you shall presently,' replied the doctor, pulling up a stool to the bedside, and sitting down upon it. 'You have been ailing a long time, have you not? That hand has not done any work this many a day, I can see. But you shall soon be hale again, I promise you.'

The King withdrew his betraying hand. 'Ay, master, but indeed I am well-nigh recovered. I would not be wishful to trouble your honour.'

But Dr Gorges, securely mounted upon his hobby-horse, told him to put such qualms out of his mind, and began to question him very searchingly upon the nature and duration of his disorder. The King, who knew as little about agues as any other healthy young man, took refuge in weary groans, and when pressed, complained that his head ached so that he knew not what he was saying.

The doctor left him at last, promising to tell his mistress of an excellent remedy for him, and warning him against eating too much red meat.

He encountered Jane upon the staircase, and hailed her immediately, saying: 'Well, mistress, I have just come from Jackson's bedchamber!'

A man less preoccupied with his own importance might have wondered to see the colour recede from Jane's cheeks. Dr Gorges noticed nothing, not even how her hand gripped the baluster, nor how the pupils of her eyes dilated.

'Yes?' she said, her voice a mere thread of sound.

'Ay, I have this instant come from him. Poor fellow, he is very sick still, and cannot bear to have the light fall upon his eyes, which is a common symptom of his disorder. But we will speedily amend all. He must keep his bed, and take a strong posset before sleeping, to induce a sweat, which will greatly relieve him.'

A tiny sigh broke from her. 'Yes. I thank you, sir. You are very good.'

He disclaimed, detained her a few moments longer to listen to his instructions, and then went off to direct Margaret Rider how to prepare the posset. Jane, who had first felt ready to faint, and then sick with the surge of relief, waited until he was out of sight, and sped down the passage to the King's chamber. She scratched upon the door, calling softly: 'May I enter?'

'Come in, my Life!' he answered.

She slipped into the room, and shut the door securely. The King had risen from his bed, and was standing in the middle of the floor. She looked across at him, her breast unquiet, and, hardly knowing what she did, went towards him with her hands held out. 'Sir, he knew you not!' she managed to say.

The King took her in his arms. 'Why, my Life!' he said gently, feeling how her limbs were trembling. 'Why, sweetheart, what is this?'

The cause of her agitation was suddenly forgotten. She stood still, her cheek laid against the King's chest. His hand caressing her bare shoulder made her shiver. Her fainting reason, struggling against the insistent tingling of her body, grew stronger. She said with a little gasp of breathlessness: 'No! No, my liege!'

The King loosed his hold. If she were willing, he would like, he thought, to lie with her. She was beautiful, though not, his cynical mind reflected, of that type of bold handsomeness which most appealed to him.

He watched her, half-waking desire in his expressive eyes. He knew too much of women not to know that he could have his way with her, if he chose to exert his power a little. But the profligate in him could never, all his life long, quite overmaster the gentleman, any more than his lusty, urgent body could subdue his brain. His brain was working now, telling him that he would be a knave indeed to seduce this gently-bred girl to whom he owed his life. Suddenly he laughed.

Jane looked quickly, questioningly, up at him. 'That rogue, Charles Stewart!' he quoted ruefully. 'Alas, sweetheart, I am not rogue enough to satisfy my needs.' He put his arm round her waist, and kissed her cheek. 'Be of good cheer, Jane! He did not know me.'

She did not immediately answer him, but after a little pause she said: 'No. But his visiting you made me afraid. He will go away tomorrow. Yet this house is over-public. I know not how my lord may contrive to come to you here without exciting remark.'

'Let Wilmot grapple his own problems,' said the King carelessly. 'If he is in this neighbourhood he will certainly come to me.'

She agreed, but could not share his unconcern, for until Wilmot was once more in touch with the King nothing could be done towards hiring a vessel to carry him to France. Presently, when Lassels joined them, she spoke to him of this anxiety. He, feeling even more strongly than she the danger of allowing the King to remain long at Abbotsleigh, said instantly that if nothing were heard of my lord upon the following day, he would himself go into Bristol to try for a vessel. The fact of his being little more than a boy, quite inexperienced in such matters, made her look upon this resolve with considerable misgiving, but she acquiesced in it, taking comfort from the King's evident belief that Wilmot would surely come.

The King slept soundly that night, and, waking early in the morning, got up and dressed himself before Lassels opened his eyes. Lassels had slept only fitfully, the encounter with Dr Gorges having taken such possession of his mind that he could not rest. As the dawn crept over the horizon, however, his youth cried out, and he sank into a deep sleep of exhaustion from which he was only aroused by the King's sprinkling drops of cold water on to his face from the tips of his fingers. He started up then in instinctive alarm, but the King was wiping his hands upon a towel, and laughing at him, so he knew, even in his bemused state, that no danger threatened.

'You need not get up,' said Charles. 'I woke you only to

tell you that I am hungry, and so am going down to the buttery to get me some breakfast.'

'Oh, do not, sir!' begged Lassels. 'It shall be sent up to you here!'

'No,' replied Charles. 'That would be folly, nor will I stay prisoned in this room all the time I remain at Abbotsleigh.'

'But, sire, it is well-known that you have an ague!'

'It is in the intermission today,' said Charles.

He was gone before Lassels could advance any further arguments against his exposing himself to the scrutiny of the household, and, drawing his hat over his eyes, found his way presently to the buttery.

There were several strangers present there, in addition to the regular servants. Those near the entrance gave the King good-day, but no one appeared to take any particular interest in him, except Pope, the butler, who was dispensing bread-and-butter and ale, and who looked rather suspiciously at him from under frowning brows. As he handed him a plate with a slice of bread on it, he asked: 'Where might you come from? Where were you reared?'

'In Staffordshire,' responded the King, taking a bite out of his bread. 'I am a tenant of Colonel Lane's, of Bentley Hall.'

'Your master's an honest man, I know well,' said Pope. He picked up the blackjack at his elbow, and poured out a tankard of ale, and pushed it across the table towards the King. 'But as for you, Jackson (or whatever your name may be), you look to me like a Roundhead.'

'Not I, i' faith!' said the King. 'I was never of that stamp.'

'Well, I will try what metal you are made of,' Pope said, still frowning, but reaching out his hand for his own tankard. 'Will you drink to the King's health?'

'Ay, with all my heart!' replied Charles. 'Here's wishing his Majesty a safe deliverance from his enemies!'

The toast caught the ear of a man at the other end of the buttery, who was the centre of a small and interested group of serving-men, all of whom seemed to be hanging upon his lips. He called out: 'That's a good toast, but I warrant you the King will mighty soon be taken prisoner, and so you would say also if you knew him like I do.'

Charles shot a glance at him from under the brim of his hat. He was a rough-looking man, dressed in a leather doublet and patched breeches, but he wore his hair long, in imitation of his betters, and the battered beaver on his head had a brave, rakish cock to its brim. He was evidently held in some esteem by those gathered round him, for they all watched him admiringly, and one of them begged him to tell them some more about Worcester fight. He was nothing loth, but straddled his legs, and at once took up his interrupted tale, saying: 'Well, lads, there was we, way out beyond the Sidbury Gate, and the ammunition all gone, and us fighting with the butt-ends of our muskets. Ah, and I accounted for a round dozen of red-coats myself. We had 'em on the run, I promise you, but the Scots – the black vomit on them for a set of lily-livered canting Covenanters! – they was a-laying down their arms fast as they might, and the King a-riding up and down the lines, so heedless and all he was like to have been cut down, only that I sees the red-coats round him, and I catches a pike like this, and smites 'em hip and thigh, as they'd say themselves, and so he got away.'

A murmur of approbation sounded. The King picked up his tankard from the table, and strolled towards the group. A man in an otter-skin waistcoat said: 'And the King warn't killed in the battle? Folks do say as his body was found, all cut up horrid.'

'It's a lie, for I was there myself, ay, and in the thick of it, and I say he got clean away. But for all that they'll have his head off yet, because he's a tall man, and one nobody could mistake.'

'A thousand pounds they do be offering to any as'll help them to catch him,' observed a groom. 'It's a lot of money, so 'tis.'

'They'll have him,' asserted the swashbuckling gentleman. 'Why, if I was to see him, I'd know him the instant I clapped eyes on him, no question.'

'Ah, but you was one of those as was close to him!' said an obvious sycophant.

'Close? Ay, I warrant you!'

From the other end of the buttery, Pope said with a scornful laugh: 'Braggart's talk! The likes of you don't come nigh to princes. If you saw him once in your life it's the most you did.'

The swashbuckler's chest filled. 'I've seen the King twenty times!'

'What was your regiment?'

The sudden question came from the King, and brought him under the gaze of six or seven pairs of eyes.

'The King's regiment, my bully!'

'Colonel King's regiment? I have heard there was such a regiment.'

'Ho, you have, eh? May be you'm right, but when I says the King's regiment, the King's regiment is what I means! I was of his own Guards, in Major Broughton's company, and them as says I don't know him lies in their teeth!'

The King's mouth was full of bread-and-butter; he washed it down with a draught of ale, and enquired: 'What kind of a man is he, then?'

'A tall, black man,' responded the soldier. 'He rode a great grey charger at Worcester fight, and put on him a steel corselet over his coat, which was of buff leather. Ay, and he had a blue ribbon 'cross his chest, and a great jewel beside!' He added, critically looking the King over: 'If you be wishful to know, he's not so unlike yourself, which is to say, remarkable ill-favoured. But he's a matter of four fingers taller than what you be.'

'A big fellow,' said the King, and, turning, walked away from the group to set down his empty tankard on the table. The rest of the company became absorbed again in the soldier's conversation, and the King sauntered out of the buttery into the main hall of the house.

There, by ill-luck, he came upon Mrs Norton, who, with Lassels, and a gentleman whom the King did not know, was walking towards the open front door. The King was forced to stand aside to let her pass, and to pull off his hat. As he did so, he became aware of Pope standing quite close to him, and realized that the man must have followed him out of the buttery.

Mrs Norton nodded kindly to him, and hoped he was better of his disorder. He answered her civilly, aware all the time of Pope's gaze, which remained fixed on his face. As soon as Mrs Norton passed on, he put on his hat again, and went up the stairs to his bedchamber.

It was a little while before Lassels could escape from his hostess, for she took him into the gardens, and led him all over them; but presently they were joined by Jane and Mr Norton, and he was able to withdraw unobtrusively towards the house.

There was no one in the hall but the butler, and Lassels was about to go up the stairs when he saw that Pope was coming towards him.

'Sir!'

Lassels stood still, one foot upon the first stair, his hand grasping the baluster. 'Ay, what is it?' he asked.

'I am wishful to speak to your honour.' Pope cast a glance up the stairs; there was no one in sight, but he lowered his voice. 'How long has William Jackson been in your service, sir?'

'Jackson?' Lassels repeated. 'He is a tenant of Colonel Lane, my good fellow.'

'Sir, I know it is my liege,' Pope said earnestly.

Lassels burst out laughing. 'You are mad to think so. I assure you, you are quite out!'

'I served under Colonel Bagot at Lichfield, in the late Wars, and I know this man for the King, sir.'

'You know more than I do then, fellow, for I tell you it is not so.'

Pope looked at him in silence for a moment, and then said: 'I am an honest man, sir, and one that fought for the late King. You need not fear me. But I know full well it is my liege, and I would like to do him a service.'

'You have taken a silly fancy into your head, and had best forget it,' replied Lassels.

Pope said no more, but drew back with a bow. Lassels went on up the stairs, and along the passage to his bedchamber.

The King, who was reading by the window, looked up, and, seeing Lassels's face of concern, laid down his book.

'Now what's amiss?' he enquired.

'Sire, what shall we do?' Lassels said. 'I am afraid Pope knows you, for he says very positively to me that it is you, though I have denied it.'

'I thought he looked very hard at me,' remarked the King. 'What kind of a man is he? Is he honest, or no?'

'Indeed, sir, I believe him to be a very honest fellow, and one that was always upon our side. I would trust him with *my* life, but —'

'Well,' interrupted the King, 'if he is honest I think we had better trust him with mine too, than go away leaving him with that suspicion upon him. Bring him up to me.'

'Yes, sir, I will, and at once,' said Lassels, more cheerfully. 'For I do think him anxious to serve you.'

He went off downstairs again, and came back in a few moments with the butler at his heels. As soon as Pope saw the King, he knelt down in the middle of the floor, saying in a much moved tone: 'God bless and preserve your Majesty, sire, and forgive me that I misdoubted your Majesty!'

'So I look like a Roundhead to you, do I?' said the King, with a smile.

'Your Majesty's hair!' stammered Pope. 'Indeed, I ask your Majesty's pardon!'

'Nay, I trust others may think the same. How came you to know me in the end? That fellow that was in my regiment of Guards did not, though he described me very exactly.'

'It is God's mercy that he did not, sire!' said Pope gravely. 'He is a bragging, untrustworthy rogue. When I looked more closely at your Majesty, I thought I did recognize you, for I did once see your Majesty every day, when you dwelt at Richmond, and I was falconer to Sir Thomas Jermyn, that was a gentleman of your Majesty's Bedchamber.'

'What, were you a servant of Tom Jermyn?' said the King. 'Why, then, I am very glad to meet you here, for it seems we are old acquaintances. Get up from your knees, man! I think I may well trust my life to you.'

'Ay, my liege, and I am happy I know you, for otherways you might run great danger in this house.'

'I knew it!' Lassels exclaimed.

The King lifted a finger at him, but said, with his eyes on Pope's face: 'How so? Is not your master honest?'

'Yes, my liege, he is so, and my mistress too; but there are one or two in the house that are very great rogues, and would sell your Majesty for half the sum the rebels have offered for your apprehension. But I think I can be useful to you, if you would condescend to tell me of your gracious intentions.'

'My design is to get a ship at Bristol to carry me to France, if that be possible,' replied the King. 'If you will serve me, go into Bristol, and discover what ships are bound for that country, and whether any of their masters would be willing to carry two Cavaliers thither.'

Pope said at once that he would do so, but upon the King's next mentioning to him that he expected my Lord Wilmot to come to Abbotsleigh that day, he looked perturbed, and said it would not do, since there were several persons in the house who would certainly recognize him.

But after all it was not Wilmot who came to Abbotsleigh that morning, but Robert Swan, his servant, who arrived, while Pope was still with the King, to discover whether it would be safe for his master to visit Charles.

From him they learned that Wilmot had parted from Colonel Lane, and was at the house of one John Winter, at the village of Dirham, a few miles distant from Abbotsleigh. It was then arranged that Swan should go back to Dirham, and bring Wilmot to meet Pope at an honest man's house, not far from Abbotsleigh, there to stay until nightfall, when Pope engaged to conduct him to the King.

Neither Jane nor the King could imagine why the Colonel and Wilmot had parted company, but as Robert Swan was unable to tell them where or why the Colonel had gone, they had to be content to wonder at his departure until Wilmot should arrive to elucidate the matter.

The King did not see Pope again until much later in the day, when he returned from Bristol with the news that he could discover there no vessel sailing for France for at least a month. These were gloomy tidings, and made the King thrust out his underlip a little.

'I was thinking maybe your Majesty would have better fortune at one of the southern sea-ports,' suggested Pope.

'How the devil am I to reach a southern sea-port?' demanded the King.

Jane spoke out of the shadows that were deepening in the room. 'We reached Bristol, sir.'

'Yes, my Life, for we had this house to come to, where you are known. Without some sure hiding-place at my journey's end, I must be undone.'

'There must be surer hiding-places than this, I think, for although Pope is faithful, I do not count this house safe.'

'No, mistress,' Pope said in a worried voice. 'You are in the right of it: it is not safe.'

'Very well, then,' said the King, with a shrug of his shoulders, 'I *am* undone.'

Jane got up and went across the room to where the King was seated, and knelt beside his chair. 'How should that be, while we are here to serve you, sir? Something we will yet contrive.'

He glanced down at her, but for a moment did not answer her. She saw how harsh his face had grown, how sombre his eyes. His thoughts, which he would let no one share, seemed to creep between them like a chill, intangible barrier. She bowed her head, clasping her hands tightly before her upon the arm of his chair, for her heart yearned towards him, yet could not reach him, and it made her throat ache with unhappiness to meet that look of his that rested on her face without seeing it.

Suddenly his hand was laid over her clasped ones, lightly yet strongly emprisoning them. He said cheerfully: 'I don't doubt I shall come safe off. But I must take counsel with my lord before I can decide what were best to do next.'

'Please your Majesty, I will bring my lord to you by the back way as soon as it is dark,' Pope said.

The King nodded. He still kept his hand over Jane's, and when Pope had left the room, he said with a note of caress in his voice: 'Troubled, my Life? Do you fear for me? You need not, for I am very sure God has not preserved me for so many days, only to let me fall at last into the hands of mine enemies.'

'Not that,' she answered, keeping her eyes lowered. 'I have foolish thoughts, sire, nothing worth. I know your Majesty will win free.'

'What are these thoughts?' he asked.

She shook her head, but looked up, and managed to smile. 'Ah no, they are mine, sir, as yours are yours alone. Must I not be cast down when your Majesty frowns?'

'Did I so? But not at you, I swear.'

'Not at me, but at your troubles, which now you make light of that I may not suspect they irk you,' she said wistfully.

He did not tell her what was in his mind, that women were made for loving, not for counsel. He said instead: 'The truth is, I am an impatient fellow, that cannot stomach the least check.'

She rose from her knees. 'Nay, for you are a prince, sir, and all unused to the checks that fall in common men's paths.'

That amused him. 'Oddsfish, am I so indeed? I thought my path had been all checks!'

'Great checks, sir, not little. For princes there is always someone to prepare the way. But you have no one to depend upon, save only yourself.'

'Fie, Jane, I have you, and Lassels, and John Pope, upon whom I do depend absolutely.'

'A woman, a boy, and a serving-man!' she said.

'Also my Lord Wilmot,' he added.

'My Lord Wilmot!' she repeated. 'Do you look to him to save you from your enemies, sir?'

'Faith, no! I look to my own wits, Mistress Disdain.'

'It is as I said: you have only yourself. And you are weary, with great cares upon you, as well as the little ones of this strange, rough journey you are forced to go upon.'

'My Life,' said the King, with a droll look in his eye, 'care and I are never bed-fellows for long, I fear me!'

## CHAPTER XII

## 'FRANK, FRANK, HOW DOST THOU?'

Lord Wilmot was brought into the house soon after night-fall, and led up the backstairs to the King's bedchamber. He was very glad to see his Royal master, but having embraced him he began at once, in his light, bored voice, to complain of the exigencies of travelling about England in disguise. No one, listening to his frivolous speech, could have guessed that under his façade of insouciance my lord was deeply, coldly afraid. His nerves had been on the stretch for ten days; and, not being by nature an intrepid man, he was obliged to hide his haunting fears under a studied nonchalance, and to court absurd risks merely to prove to himself that he was not afraid. The King, being seventeen years younger than his lordship, endowed with strong nerves and a lusty constitution, and concerned only with his own safety, suffered only from a healthy young man's normal desire to escape imprisonment and death. Wilmot, who could lead a cavalry brigade into battle with dash and gallantry, felt his soul shudder at the thought of death upon a scaffold, and faint within him when he envisaged the possibility of the King's capture. Sometimes, with a burning sense of wrong, he thought that no one, not even Thomas Whitgreave, realized the horror of his position. When he looked down at the King, sprawling in a chair by the window, heedless of his danger, a little storm of anger shook him. It was so obvious that Charles spared not one thought for the hideous weight of care upon his shoulders. Charles could face death with his cynical smile; but Charles did not realize that if he died his chosen companion must die too, or live out the rest of his life in shameful seclusion, because never again could he dare to face his world.

He managed to overcome his irritation, and to say with

a flutter of his expressive hands, and an absurd air of ill-usage: 'But, my dear sir, how can you say I do not wear a disguise when I have taken such pains to ride with a hawk upon my wrist, besides calling myself Mr Morton, which is a name, I assure you, I do not easily answer to?'

'Wilmot, what have you done with Colonel Lane?' demanded the King, broadly grinning.

Wilmot cast a look round the room, but Jane and Lassels had left him alone with the King. He said confidentially: 'My dear, it would not do! A worthy fellow, and one that is a very good soldier, but I could not – no, I could not spend any more days in his company! I sent him to London to try whether he could procure a pass for two gentlemen to go out of England into France. Now you are laughing again! Will you be still? *You* have the sister to go with you, but I can tell you the brother is another matter.'

'But, Harry, Pope can discover no vessel sailing for France or Spain from Bristol within the next month,' objected the King.

'Oh, pooh! nonsense!' Wilmot said. 'What does he know about it? I shall go myself into Bristol tomorrow, with my good host, John Winter, who knows how to set about such things. Meanwhile, are you comfortably bestowed here? Do they take good care of you? Does anyone suspect you of being the King?'

'Oddsfish, I don't know! Pope recognized me, though he had not seen me for eight years; yet a fellow who served in my regiment of guards at Worcester knew me not.'

'I wish you will take heed how you expose yourself!' Wilmot exclaimed.

'I will, I will!' said the King, yawning. 'But find me a vessel, Harry, for I cannot, nor I will not, remain in this house a month.'

'Oh, don't bother your head, sir! I shall certainly find a vessel, and return here tomorrow night to tell you of it.'

This airy promise was destined to remain unfulfilled. The following day was a Sunday, and when Wilmot was once more taken up the backstairs to the King's bedchamber his florid countenance was overcast, and there was a pronounced look of strain in his eyes. He bowed over the King's hand, which was carelessly held out to him, but said without any preamble: 'Sire, I can hear of no vessel bound for France. We are utterly undone!'

'Why, what are these strange tidings that you bring us, my lord?' mocked the King.

'It is as this fellow told you, sir,' Wilmot said, indicating Pope with a jerk of his head.

'Ay, so I knew. What now, my Life? Instruct me!'

Jane, who was standing by the window, turned, and said with her grave smile: 'Nay, how can I, sir? I have no skill in instructing princes.'

'But we will obey you, sir!' Lassels said. 'Here are four of us ready to serve you. It cannot be but we shall yet bring you off!'

Wilmot turned his harassed gaze upon him. 'Very prettily said, young man. Four of us against the world!'

Amusement rippled in the King's voice. 'No, faith, you do me less than justice, Harry! I am not as much hated as that, I swear!'

'Good God, sir!' said Wilmot, aghast at his own words. 'What have I said? Nay, but this is no time for laughter! We are in a damned parlous coil, if you would but realize it!'

'Oh, I do!' the King assured him. He held out his hand to Jane, and when she moved across the room to stand beside his chair, took her hand, and began to play with her fingers. 'What say you, Jane? I think I must not stay in this house.'

'No,' she agreed. 'That at least is sure. But there are other sea-ports.'

'There are many. But how to reach them?' He appeared to be intent on the foolish task of doubling her fingers one by one, but the smile had faded from his face, leaving it harsh and brooding. He raised his eyes after a moment, and turned them towards Pope. 'Rehearse me the names of any honest gentlemen that are known to you in Somerset, or Devonshire,' he said. 'I had friends once in the west.'

The butler hesitated. 'My liege, those that wished your Majesty well have suffered greatly, in the west as elsewhere.'

'I know it. But cudgel your brain a little! Have I no friends left there? Did you ever know Colonel Frank Wyndham?'

Pope's face brightened. 'The same as was Governor of Dunster Castle in the time of the late Wars, sir? Ay, very well!'

'What has become of him?'

'Why, sir, he was married to Mrs Anne Gerrard, that was daughter and heiress to Mr Thomas Gerrard, of Trent, in Somerset, and is gone there to live, as I hear.'

'Where is this Trent?'

' 'Tis midway betwixt Yeovil and Sherborne, my liege, and lies south of Castle Cary. You might reach it in two days, and less.'

'That is very good hearing,' said the King briskly. 'I will go there.'

'Wyndham?' said Wilmot. 'Well! I have nothing against him; indeed, I believe him to be an honest man; but we know not how he may be situated these days, after all.'

'Odso, snugly, if he is married to an heiress!'

'Ay, very like, but of what political complexion may she be? I do beg of you, sir, not to hazard your person unadvisedly! If you will go to Trent, I must go before you to learn Wyndham's mind.'

'Content you, I know Frank Wyndham's mind as I know mine own. But he must certainly have notice of my coming to his house.'

'Then I will set out tomorrow to go there,' said Wilmot. 'When I have discovered whether it may be safe for you to trust yourself to Wyndham, I will send Swan back to you with a message.'

'I thank you, I shall be upon the road by that time. I will give you a day's grace, Harry, and set out myself on Tuesday.'

'You will not go alone, sire!'

The King glanced up at Jane, still standing with her hand lightly held in his. 'Nay, I think not. Will you go along with me, my Life?'

She saw her journey's end taking gradual shape through the mist of the future. 'I will go with you, while I may. You will not need me long.'

He did not deny it; he had turned his head towards Pope, and began to enquire the way to Trent. Presently Jane drew her hand away; it slipped from the clasp of his long fingers as easily as the thought of her from his brain.

Wilmot took his leave a little while later. His mind misliked the uncertainty of this new plan. He professed a profound ignorance of the country lying between Bristol and Trent, but this objection was met by a suggestion from Pope that he should take Mr Winter's servant, Henry Rogers, with him as guide, Rogers (Pope said) being a very honest man. A little more discussion revealed to his lordship that a man who was well known to him was living at Castle Cary Manor House, as steward to the Marquis of Hertford. These tidings had the effect of dissipating some of the fretful gloom that had settled on his lordship's fair countenance. He sighed, and supposed that the King might lie at Mr Edward Kirton's with as much safety as could anywhere be found in a country bristling with danger.

'Ay, but will this Kirton be willing to receive such a perilous guest as I am?' demanded the King.

Wilmot looked blankly at him. 'Be willing?' he repeated. 'My dear sir, naturally he will be willing! How should he be otherwise! I assure you, he is perfectly loyal. I shall instruct him to prepare against your Majesty's arrival at Castle Cary upon Tuesday. If by some ill-chance he should be away from home, I will despatch Swan to inform you of it.'

'Why, this is such devotion to my person as I did not dream of, Harry! What would become of you without Swan?'

'My dear master, do not give that a thought! You forget that I shall have John Winter's man, Rogers, with me,' Wilmot said earnestly.

The King's shoulders began to shake. 'Oh, Harry!'

Wilmot accorded him a rather absent smile, but was feeling too careworn either to appreciate the cause of his mirth or to wonder at it. He turned from the King to draw Lassels aside, and having laid his instructions upon that young man, kissed the King's hand, and went away, escorted by Pope.

The King turned his head. 'Well, Jane, my affairs seem to be in good train. Tell me now how we may beguile the time until we set forth again upon our travels.'

'I had rather tell you how to remain safely hid from curious eyes, sir,' she replied, smiling.

'That is a lesson I have by heart. You would have me keep my bed. But I had never a liking for a lonely bed, look you!'

She shook her head. 'No, I would but have you keep away from the bowling-green, and such places, sir. My cousin told me that you walked out there, and were accosted by a man who asked you to play.'

'But I said I had no skill in it,' pleaded the King. 'You are too fearful, my Life. Think, if you were a man playing at bowls in such a little village as this, would you look to see the King at your elbow?'

'I should not, indeed, but you know full well, sir, you are above the common height, and very dark, which are circumstances the Parliamentarians have warned all men to look for most particularly. Be patient, sire! In one more day we shall leave this house.'

But upon the following day, the 15th September, very early in the morning, the household was stirred into sudden commotion. Footsteps scurrying along the passages; voices raised in urgency, or hushed to shocked whispers, roused the King and Lassels from sleep. The same thought leapt to both their minds. It made the King turn a little pale under the walnut-stain, but he remained rigidly still, raised in his bed on his elbow, his eyes fixed upon the door. Lassels got up with scrambling haste, and could scarcely wait to pull on his breeches before assuring himself that his pistols were ready to his hand.

'If there were danger, Pope would have found the means to warn me of it,' the King said. 'Go out, and see what's toward, but leave those pistols here.'

Lassels laid his pistols down on the table within the King's reach, and went over to the door. The King propped his head on his hand, and waited for his excitable henchman to return.

This Lassels soon did. One glance at his countenance was enough to make the King stretch himself out upon his pillows again, saying with a yawn: 'Well, what is it?'

'No danger, sir! It is very shocking, however, for they say Mrs Norton is taken ill, and is very bad. Jane is with her, and Margaret Rider too.'

'I wish her a fair son,' said the King, preparing to go to sleep again.

'Ay, but she has not gone her full time, and they greatly fear a mischance, sir.'

A little while later he was back again with the news that his hostess had miscarried of a dead child, and was very ill.

'Poor woman!' said the King, who was shaving himself. 'Have they called in a physician to her?'

'Ay, and Jane is continually with her. I do not know how it will end. George Norton is sadly distracted.'

'I am sorry for him: it is an ill thing to be a husband when women lie-in.' He began to wipe his razor, adding as he did so: 'Discover for me who is in the buttery, for my stomach cries out for breakfast.'

'Everyone is quite overset by this trouble,' said Lassels. 'But I will find Pope immediately, sir.'

Throughout the morning, the King kept his room, enquiring from time to time of Pope or of Lassels how Mrs Norton did, and, indeed, showing an easy sympathy that endeared him more than ever to them. But at noon Jane Lane contrived to slip out of the sickroom, and to visit the King, and what she had to say caused him to forget Mrs Norton's perilous condition. For Jane, who was looking pale and anxious, raised her troubled eyes to his face, and said: 'She is very ill, but that is not the worst. I do not know how I may leave her to-morrow, sir, as we had planned.'

His brows went up. 'Sweetheart, are you so skilled a midwife?'

'No, sir, indeed, but I am her friend, and how may I desert her now?'

'On my business!'

There was a faint stress laid upon the pronoun. The shadow of a smile touched Jane's lips. 'She knows not that, sir. If I leave, it must be for no apparent cause. How may I do so?'

He said: 'You must do so. Since I came here in the guise of your servant I cannot go hence except in attendance upon you without occasioning some suspicion in the minds of all these people.'

'I will obey you in everything, sir,' she responded, faltering a little. 'Yet will it not seem strange to Mr Norton that I should go away thus, without good reason, who call his wife my dear friend?'

The logic of this appealed to him as Mrs Norton's plight did not. He said, frowning: 'We must use some stratagem to lull suspicion. If a letter were brought you from Bentley summoning you to return instantly because your father, say, was ill, would you not be bound to go?'

'Yes, sir, but who will bring me such a letter?'

'Trust me for that!' he answered. 'Lassels, procure me ink and paper! Who writes, Jane? – Your mother? Nay, I think I cannot counterfeit a woman's hand.'

'The steward,' she said, as though against her will. 'Poor Nell! Oh, poor Nell!'

'It will be poor Charles if I escape not from this coil,' retorted the King. 'Mistake me not, my Life: I am sorry for Nell, but your duty is to me.'

'Yes,' she said, clasping her hands together. 'Indeed, I do know it, sir, and would not have it otherwise. I will do as you bid me.'

She lingered only until he sat down at the table to write, and then, seeing that Lassels was well able to instruct him in what language to use in this supposed steward's letter, stole away again to Mrs Norton's room.

The letter was delivered to her at supper-time by Pope, who told her that it had been brought by a serving-man from Bentley. Nervousness made her hand shake as she broke the seal, and her voice fail a little. 'Why, what can this mean?' she said. 'I do trust – oh, Harry! My father!'

'Not ill-tidings, Jane?' exclaimed Lassels, jumping up from his chair, and coming round the table to her side.

She held out the letter to him, saying faintly: 'Read!'

He took it from her, and perused it. She saw from the light in his eyes that he was enjoying himself; certainly he played his part very well, enacting so much concern over the false tidings in the letter that George Norton was roused from his own anxious reflections, and began to ask a great many questions about old Mr Lane's seizure. When Jane said that she felt herself bound to return to Bentley, Norton agreed without hesitation, and entered at once into her plans for departure early on the following morning. The thought of her own duplicity made her blush, but when, later, she told the King how uncomfortable she felt, he only laughed, and said teasingly: 'Fie, would it make you less so to see my head upon a charger? Moreover, if I reach not Trent on Wednesday, my Lord Wilmot will certainly believe me a prisoner.'

'I hope to God my Lord Wilmot will find the place, ay, and this Colonel Wyndham as well!' Lassels said, suddenly perceiving the danger of travelling into unknown country without any very certain asylum to go to.

But the King refused to consider the possibility of my lord's failing to reach Trent. 'He will arrive there, be sure. Though, if the way be as rough as Pope warned us, I would give much to hear his remarks upon it.'

The way which Rogers led Wilmot was difficult enough to reduce his lordship, at the end of the first day's ride, to a state of peevishness which was only partially dispelled by his finding his old acquaintance, Edward Kirton, residing at Castle Cary, and perfectly ready to do all that lay in his power to assist the King. Castle Cary, a little grey town, steeply climbing cobbled streets, lay only six miles to the north of Trent, but thinking that it would be safer to approach Colonel Wyndham's house after dusk, Wilmot did not set out again upon the following day, which was Tuesday, until an advanced hour.

As he rode towards Trent, his spirits began to lighten, for every mile that he covered seemed to carry him farther into a dreaming countryside that was remote from the turmoil of the world he had lately been living in. Hollow lanes, so narrow that two packhorses could scarcely go abreast, led twisting through a rich land of pastures, or dipped into the shadows of deep woods. Scarcely anyone was encountered upon the road, Rogers taking care to skirt the few hamlets. The lanes were very rough and dirty, smelling of cow-dung, which strove successfully with the scent of the meadowsweet growing by the ragged hedges. Wilmot wrinkled his aristocratic nose, and Robert Swan rode silent and disapproving behind him.

But there was nothing in Trent itself to offend the most fastidious taste. A lovely, lost village, it nestled amongst trees, its houses, built of oolitic stone, softly grey against a background of green and russet foliage. At the southern end of the village was the Church, and close by, secluded from the road by a grey wall, and deep gardens, the manor house itself.

The size and style of the manor made Wilmot at once fearful lest the household should be too large a one for safety; and when he came to the front door, and dismounted, he would not go in, but sent Rogers in his stead, to draw Colonel Wyndham out to him.

This caution seemed to be justified, for the butler who presently opened the door led Rogers across the hall to a large parlour where several people were assembled.

Perceiving that the Colonel was entertaining guests, Rogers stayed diffidently by the door, but the butler crossed the room to his master's side, and spoke to him, whereupon the Colonel looked round, and seeing Rogers, who was known to him, came towards him, a pleasant smile warming his eyes.

He was a tall man, and very thin, with a long, sensitive face. His brown hair, which he wore in Cavalier ringlets, receded from a lofty brow, and his cheeks fell into hollows beneath his cheek-bones. When he smiled, a number of little wrinkles appeared about his eyes and mouth, and the eyes themselves, which, though not dark, were remarkably fine, lost the faint look of strain which was nearly always in them. He greeted Rogers kindly, saying in his light, well-bred voice: 'Well, Rogers? – it is Rogers, is it not? What is your errand to me? Have you come from Dirham to find me?'

'Yes, sir.' Roger's gaze flickered past the Colonel to the knot of gentlemen behind him, and returned again to the Colonel's face.

The significance of this glance was not lost on the Colonel. He went a little apart with Rogers, and said in a lowered tone: 'What is it? Is it some weighty matter?'

'Sir, I am sent to acquaint you that a gentleman, a friend of yours, desires this favour of you, that you will be pleased to step forth and speak with him.'

The smile had quite faded from the Colonel's face; he looked suddenly very alert, but on his guard. 'Who is this gentleman? What is his business?'

Rogers shook his head. 'Nay, sir, I know nothing, only that he is called by the name of Morton.'

The Colonel looked hard at him for a moment, but asked no more questions, merely saying: 'Very well; I will come.'

Outside, the twilight was heavy with the scent of musk carnations, and late roses, and the sharp sweetness of lavender. There was at first no sign of Wilmot, but upon the Colonel's walking towards the stable, where Rogers informed him that his unknown visitor would be waiting, he soon saw, pacing up and down, a portly figure, half enveloped in a cloak, and bearing a hooded hawk upon his wrist. He stopped short, staring with narrowed eyes, and then strode quickly forward. 'My Lord Wilmot!'

Wilmot, who had turned at the sound of his approach, awaiting him with his hat drawn low over his brows, gave a start, and said in a somewhat chagrined tone: 'You know me, then?'

'Know you?' repeated the Colonel. 'My dear lord, how should I not know you? You are not altered in the least degree since the day when I first enrolled under your command!'

'Not altered!' exclaimed Wilmot peevishly. 'I do not know how you can talk such nonsense, Wyndham! Can you not see that I am travelling in disguise?'

'Nay, I see no disguise. My lord, how may I serve you? I thank God you are safe! What news —'

'But this hawk, man! the lure I have here! these clothes

I wear, which are so travel-stained I do not know myself in them!' Wilmot interrupted.

'I should have known you anywhere,' replied the Colonel. 'But your news, my lord, your news! You were surely at Worcester fight!'

'Of course I was at Worcester fight!' said Wilmot. 'I am now seeking to escape from England, and have sought you out to open to you a very dangerous, secret matter. Wyndham, I know I may trust you!'

'You may certainly do so. Be plain with me, my lord, for I am still as ever your man! Do you seek my aid?'

'Ay, for the King!' Wilmot said, sinking his voice to a whisper.

'The King? The *King*?' Wyndham seemed for an instant to be stunned. Then he grasped Wilmot's right wrist in his bony fingers. 'He is not dead?'

'Dead? No!' Wilmot replied. 'He is one day behind me upon the road to this place, and looks to you to give him aid and shelter.'

The uncomfortably hard grasp on his arm was removed; the Colonel put his hand up to shade his eyes for an instant, saying in a shaken voice: 'We believed him dead. He was reported slain at Worcester. My lord, these blessed tidings you bring quite unman me!'

'So report has slain him!' said Wilmot. Some of his natural sprightliness came back to him. 'It is very well! Indeed, nothing could be better! But for all I wish the rebels may continue to think him dead, he is very much alive, my dear Colonel, and will be with you tomorrow, unless you can show me good cause why he should not venture here. Will you receive him into your house? for I must tell you that he knows himself to be a perilous guest, and will go nowhere save his host be willing to run that risk which he must incur.'

'Willing to receive him! You should know, my lord, that for his preservation I value neither life, nor family, nor fortune! But come you in! What am I about to keep you standing here? In truth, you have set my thoughts in such a whirl I scarce know what I am doing!'

He called to one of his grooms, who was speaking with Robert Swan some little distance away, gave my lord's hawk into his charge, instructed him to see the horses stabled, and led Wilmot towards the house.

Since Wilmot had never been known to any of the gentlemen gathered together in the parlour, the Colonel thought it would be best to introduce him to them, under the name of Morton, as though he had been an ordinary visitor. Accordingly, he led him into the parlour, and had the satisfaction of seeing that not one of the three honest squires there showed more than a casual interest in him. They made him welcome after their own blunt fashion, and would have been pleased to have engaged him in conversation about the state of the crops, the prospects for the season's fox-hunting, or the shocking state of the country, had he been less aloof. But his lordship, who had never consorted upon equal terms with small country squires, found their talk tedious, and their opinions commonplace. The faint hauteur which dwelt in his eyes, and the curve of his mouth, grew more marked, and caused the Colonel to feel some misgiving. Fortunately, his fellow-guests were more interested in their own concerns than in his lordship's manners, and beyond deciding that he was a proud, townified fellow, wasted no thoughts upon him.

When the company was presently summoned to supper, Wilmot for the first time encountered the Colonel's lady, who, with a young kinswoman of the Wyndhams, Mrs Juliana Coningsby, met the gentlemen in the dining-parlour.

A very short time spent in Mrs Wyndham's company was enough to assure Wilmot that the Colonel had not married a Parliamentarian. An elegant, well-bred woman, with a thoughtful brow, and mild, steadfast blue eyes, Anne Wyndham would have scorned to conceal a political opinion that was to her almost a religion. Lord Wilmot was soon satisfied that there was nothing to be feared in admitting her into the secret of the King's identity. He found her pleasant to talk to, but had a horrible suspicion that she was bookish, a quality he abominated in women. He supposed some would call her handsome, but to his eye her body was too slender, and her countenance lacked sparkle. Mrs Juliana Coningsby, who was seated opposite to him at the table, was far more to his taste. His gaze rested approvingly on the swell of plump breasts rising in lovely white mounds from the confinement of a low-cut dress of red brocade. Her neck, with its thick creamy throat, might be a trifle short for perfection, but he considered that her head was charmingly set upon it, and liked the artless way her hair was arranged in glossy, chestnut-coloured curls that bobbed on her shoulders with every movement of her head. No need to fear bookishness in Juliana: his lordship would have been willing to stake his fortune on those roguish eyes never having wasted more time upon a printed page than they had been forced to do. A warm, seductive armful, thought his lordship, and wondered what his Royal master would make of her. She was not a bold, luscious beauty like Lucy Barlow, his mistress, though her ripe mouth invited; there was a suggestion of fastidiousness about its curves, which Mrs Barlow's lips quite lacked; but she had a way of looking through her lashes, and a peeping dimple, that made a man's blood quicken and tingle in his veins. My lord, whose thoughts were just now far from dalliance, was himself conscious of it, and hoped that the King would not find this fruit too inviting to be left unplucked.

He discovered presently that Juliana resided at Trent in the position of waiting-gentlewoman to old Lady Wyndham, who, the Colonel explained, was confined to her own apartments that evening with a slight indisposition. Both Juliana and Anne Wyndham retired upstairs before the company finally dispersed and the Colonel was at liberty to enter into private discussion with Wilmot. As soon as the last of the three neighbouring squires had left the house, he took my lord into a small parlour, and, having carefully shut the door, begged him to give him an account of the King's movements since Worcester fight. Wilmot's description of his adventures during the first days of his flight moved him so much that he was obliged to get up, and walk about the room to conceal his emotion. When he heard of the part being played by Jane Lane, his quick sympathies were at once roused, and he said impulsively: 'She must be a noble woman! I am right glad she is on her way to my house. Anne will delight in her!'

This led Wilmot to enquire what security there was for the King at Trent House. The Colonel replied: 'The best, for there is a secret hiding-place opening into one of my mother's apartments. I have been considering that one of those rooms would be fittest for his Majesty, since they are in a way secluded, and not commonly visited by any of the servants other than two Catholic maids who wait particularly on her. Both of these wenches I believe we may trust; also (and for certain), Henry Peters, my own man. But more of this when we have consulted with my mother! Meanwhile, I must devise some means of dispersing the rest of the household tomorrow morning. This village, my lord, is a hotbed of the most beastly Puritanism, and I want no eyes that I cannot vouch for to spy upon his Majesty's arrival.'

Lord Wilmot regarded his finger-tips. 'I do not ask you if you can trust your lady, Colonel; but I must ask you if you can be sure that a woman's – ah – natural alarms – may not lead her to look with misgiving upon your harbouring the person of his Majesty?'

He looked up to see a radiant smile in the Colonel's eyes. 'She shall speak for herself, my lord,' Wyndham said simply.

In the morning she did so, the Colonel having brought Wilmot into his mother's private parlour, upon the first floor, where she was. She moved forward to greet him, holding out her hand to him. 'My lord, how shall I thank you – the harbinger that brings such glad tidings to us?'

He took her hand, bowing with remarkable grace in one so portly. 'You have a brave spirit, madam. I do not doubt but that his Majesty will think himself fortunate in having you for his friend.'

She said earnestly: 'When it was related to me, by my husband, what dangers his Majesty has lately passed through, the thought – nay, the most devout belief! – that the arm of God stretched out from Heaven to his rescue – possessed my poor mind. It is surely a story in which the constellations of Providence are so refulgent, that their light is sufficient to confute all the atheists in the world!'

'Ah – indeed and indeed, madam!' said Wilmot vaguely.

He was rescued by his host, who stepped forward to lead him up to old Lady Wyndham, who had risen from her chair by the window, and was standing leaning a little on a long ebony cane, and regarding him out of a pair of cool, shrewd eyes.

'Lord Wilmot, madam,' said her son.

She extended her hand. 'So I perceive,' she replied. 'You are heartily welcome, my lord. I remember you very well.'

He kissed her fingers, replying with the ready address of a courtier: 'And I you, madam.'

She looked amused. 'You are extremely gallant, Lord Wilmot. I shall not distress you by requiring you to recall where or when we had the happiness to meet.'

'Was it not at Oxford, madam?' he asked, throwing all upon one cast of the dice.

She chuckled. 'Very good! You are acquainted, I believe, with my niece?'

He cast an appreciative glance at Juliana, demure beside Lady Wyndham's chair. 'I had the honour of meeting Mrs Juliana Coningsby last night.'

'She is a foolish girl, but honest,' Lady Wyndham said. 'You may trust her.'

Juliana fixed her glowing eyes upon his lordship's face, and said, with her hands clasped at her breast: 'Oh yes, yes! Believe it, my lord! If I might serve his Majesty, I think my heart would burst with happiness!'

'H'm! yes,' said her aunt dryly. 'We must guard against such untoward contingencies. Sit down beside me, my lord. We are agreed that it will be more prudent for you to remain within doors than to go with my son to meet his Majesty. You and I must renew our old acquaintance.'

He professed himself to be very willing to do so, and after a short discussion with the Colonel, took a chair beside Lady Wyndham, while Juliana was despatched upon an errand to the stillroom, and the Colonel and his lady went away to stroll in the fields at the back of the house.

It was some time before they saw anyone approaching, but a little before ten o'clock two horses appeared in the dis-

tance, one bearing a double load, the other ridden by a tall
shabby figure, with a portmanteau strapped to the saddle
behind him.

Anne Wyndham's clasp on the Colonel's arm tightened.
'Is it?' she whispered. 'Is it indeed his blessed Majesty?'

The Colonel was watching the horsemen's approach between puckered eyelids. 'Before God, I cannot tell!' he said.
'It must surely be he, and yet —'

He broke off. The travellers were now within hail, and as
his anxious gaze went from one to the other of the men, the
single rider called out to him in a voice he knew well: 'Frank,
Frank, how dost thou?'

The Colonel let go his wife's arm, and started forward.
The King swung himself out of the saddle as the Colonel
reached him, and grasped him by the shoulders, saying
merrily: 'My old Frank! I swear you have not altered one
jot since last I clapped eyes on you! You dare not say the
same of me!'

The Colonel could not immediately trust his voice. He
looked up into the King's dark, laughing face, thinner than
he remembered it, with deep lines carved in it, and bitter
experience dwelling behind the smile in his eyes; and with
an inarticulate exclamation, pulled one of Charles's hands
from his shoulder, and caught it to his lips.

Charles felt a tear upon his hand, and said in a rallying
tone: 'Why, what's this? Do you weep at the sight of your
King, traitor? Nay, but I thought you loved me well!'

'So well, sire, that to see you thus, so changed, so grievously
entreated – nay, this is womanish folly, after all! I thank God
you are here, for in my house I swear you may lie safely!
Come you in, sir, I beg of you!'

'Why, so I will, but you shall first let me present you to my
good friends here.'

He turned, to find that Lassels had lifted Jane down from
her pillion. She came to him obediently when he stretched
out his hand to her, but although she curtseyed slightly to
the Colonel, she said: 'Let such matters wait until you are
hid from prying eyes, sir, I do entreat you!'

'When my Life entreats, I ask nothing better than to

please her,' he replied, with one of his irresistible smiles. 'Yet I do desire that I may be made known to one whom I guess to be my old friend's lady.'

'Ay, sir, my wife indeed, who bids you welcome with as full a heart as I do.'

'Sire!' Anne Wyndham said, raising her serious eyes to his face. 'I would I might tell your Majesty how much I am your servant. Let me add my entreaties to Mrs Jane Lane's (though they cannot have that power with your Majesty which hers so greatly deserve), and beg that you will lose no time in seeking the shelter of my husband's roof.'

'Lead me there, Frank, lead me there!' said the King gaily.

Anne turned towards Jane Lane, and took her hand. 'May I bid you welcome too, mistress? Oh, surely you must be the best and most blessed of women!'

'The most blessed, madam,' Jane said. 'An unworthy instrument, honoured far beyond my deserts, beyond my dreams.'

Anne heard the forlorn note in her voice, and saw how her gaze followed the King, as he walked away from her, deep in converse with Wyndham. She pressed her hand, saying in a low tone: 'His Preserver! You must be proud indeed!'

'His Life, madam!' said Lassels. 'You heard him call her so, and I can tell you he does so with good reason.'

The colour crept into Jane's cheeks; she shook her head. 'It is his pleasure to call me that, but it is not true. I am one of his humble servants, no heroine, believe me, madam.'

## CHAPTER XIII

## 'THOUGH THE CROWN SHOULD HANG UPON A BUSH'

THE King, being arrived at the house, was led immediately upstairs by Colonel Wyndham to the rooms prepared for him. Here Lord Wilmot awaited him, greeted him with fondness and relief, and saying, with the King's hand held between both his own: 'At last, at last, my dear master, we see the sky through the clouds! You are come amongst friends, and the end of your troubles is in sight. Wyndham you may trust, as you would trust me.'

'But I told you so, Harry!' said the King. He cast off his hat, and pushed his fingers up through the coarse, short ringlets that clung damply to his head. 'Did I not say I knew his mind as I know mine own?' He took the glass of wine which Wyndham had poured out for him, and rewarded him with his sleepy smile. 'Get me away from this ungrateful kingdom of mine, Frank.'

Wyndham's eyes were fixed on his face, searching its haggard lines for traces of the heavy, yet shrewd, boy he had known. He said: 'It shall be done, sire. All my desire is to serve you. It is my duty, my pleasure, and was further laid upon me by my father as a strict charge I dare not (if I would) neglect.'

'How is this?' enquired the King. 'I had thought your father died before I was breeched.'

'Ay, sir, he died fifteen years ago, in '36, but ere he departed this life he called unto him his five sons, and discoursed to us of some things which puzzled us sorely. Of the loving peace and prosperity this kingdom had enjoyed under its three last glorious monarchs, he spoke; and of the miseries and calamities which lay upon our ancestors, by invasions and rebellions. After some further speech, he disclosed to us his fear that the garment of peace would shortly be torn in pieces through various causes, but most particularly the prevalence of the Puritanical faction, which (if not prevented) would undermine the very pillars of Government. He said to us, very earnestly: "My sons! we have seen serene and quiet times: but now prepare yourselves for cloudy and troublesome. I command you to honour and obey our Gracious Sovereign, and in all times to adhere to the Crown. And though the Crown should hang upon a bush, I charge you forsake it not!" Thereupon he arose from his chair, and left us in deep consultation what the meaning should be of *the Crown hanging upon a bush*. His words made so firm an impression in all our breasts that nothing, I promise you, sir, can raze out their characters.'

'A true prophet!' said the King. 'But if I can but escape from mine enemies at this present, I have a strong notion the Crown shall not long hang upon a bush. What good chance have I of finding a vessel at Lyme, or at Plymouth, to carry me to France, Frank?'

'I hope, the best, sir, and have been considering how we should set about the matter. Your Majesty must know that I am not long released from Weymouth prison, upon my parole; and, being but newly come here from Sherborne, the jealous eyes of our Somersetshire potentates have scarce found me out.'

'Ay, but being upon your parole, can you move about unmolested?'

'Most freely, sir,' responded the Colonel, with a smile. 'For my pass will save me from being stopped. You may say it is a protection rather than a hindrance. But I believe there is one who may more easily serve you than I in this matter of procuring a vessel to carry you to France. Does your Majesty recall Sir John Strangways, who gave his two sons to your Royal father's service, both being Colonels, and, I think, known to you?'

'Ay, he was always very loyal to the throne.'

'Strangways? Strangways?' said Wilmot. 'Oh – ah! Yes, I fancy I recall the man.'

'A gentleman of great fortune and interest,' said Wyndham. 'He lives at Melbury, some ten miles from here. I think, if I were to call upon him, he might render your Majesty powerful assistance.'

'Why, then, do so, by all means!' said the King. He drank up his wine, and began to take stock of his surroundings, remarking that he liked his lodging very well. Upon Wilmot's excusing himself presently, and leaving him alone with his host, he stretched himself out in a chair by the window, and rolled an enquiring eye towards Wyndham. 'Something mislikes you, Frank. What's in your mind?'

The Colonel shook his head. 'A medley of thoughts sir. Mostly I grieve to see you in such straits as these.'

'It is well that you saw me not a week ago, then,' said the King. 'I was a sorry sight, I pledge you my word. But that is long past. Indeed, I think I was wet, and footsore, and hungry, and exceeding dismayed in another life, not in this.'

'Do not speak of it, sir!' the Colonel said, with a shudder.

'If it irks not me it need not irk you,' remarked the King. 'I assure you, it does not. I have learnt much since Worcester fight. For I never knew, look you, until the Scots deserted me in that battle, and I was forced to seek refuge amongst the country-people, how many poor men there were who, owing me nothing, would willingly sacrifice their lives for my sake. I remember that when I lay at Boscobel my mind misgave me that I had done ill to entrust my person into the hands of such poor men. Well! no man shall say of me that I do not profit by my lessons. I hope I am not to be so easily affrighted now.'

'Yet there is such danger threatening you!' the Colonel said. 'On all sides – even here, under my roof!' He drove one clenched, impotent fist into the palm of his other hand, and began to pace about the room, saying with a good deal of agitation: 'Myself a prisoner at large! All who served the Crown spied upon, trammelled! While every dog of an up-start, Puritan knave – Ah, God give me patience, and the means to aid your Majesty!'

'Oh, amen to that, my friend!' said the King. He watched the Colonel's quick, fretting movements with a somewhat sardonic smile, but presently he stretched out his hand. 'Nay, be still, Frank, be still! You make my head to spin with all this marching up and down!'

The Colonel came to a halt beside his chair, and said with a fleeting smile: 'I should be still, and calm, and careless while you are in danger, should I not?'

The King took hold of the fringed end of the Colonel's scarf, and began to flick it idly backwards and forwards over his fingers. 'You have been talking to my Lord Wilmot, Frank. You are thinking every bush a boggard, as my honest friend William Penderel would say.'

'I cannot find it in me to blame my lord for being fearful,' replied Wyndham. 'Yet —' He hesitated, looking down at the King, and then said impetuously: 'Sire, why, out of all men, chose you my Lord Wilmot to go with you upon such a journey as this?'

'Nay, I am sure you wrong my lord,' murmured Charles. 'He loves me well.'

'Is that wonderful, sir?'

The King raised rueful eyes from the sash's fringe. 'Frank, Frank, you behold me disguised and forced to escape by stealth from this my realm, and yet you can ask me that? I have grown more used to dwell amongst those who wish me ill than with friends who love me.'

'Sire!' Wyndham exclaimed. 'That I cannot believe!'

For a moment he saw in the King's eyes a look that shocked his own warm heart. Charles was still smiling, but coldly, as though in cynical enjoyment of a jest he did not choose to share. The expression was swiftly gone, but it left Wyndham disturbed and sorrowful.

'Ah!' said the King. 'But you do not know my Scottish subjects, do you, Frank?' He gave a little laugh, and released the Colonel's scarf-end. 'Touching this question of my choice of my Lord Wilmot, when I took the resolve to go to London (as I at first intended, look you), only he offered to go with me, though I am very sure he thought me mad to think to reach London. You account him a fearful man, but I tell you this, Frank: I might have his life for the mere asking.'

'Fearful! I know not that! I had rather have called him foolhardy! When I saw him all undisguised, and called to mind whose harbinger he was, his confidence really begat admiration in me. I marvel that such folly has not betrayed you, sir!'

The King only laughed, and said: 'I take good care not to travel in his company.' He turned his head, for the door had opened; and when he saw my Lord Wilmot ushering into the room an elderly lady leaning on an ebony cane, he rose at once to his feet, and stepped forward to meet her.

Wilmot begged leave to present Lady Wyndham, who swept the King a curtsey that at once conjured up memories of Whitehall and happier days. He raised her at once, and led her to a chair, and sat himself down beside her. She was at first very punctilious with him, but he had a knack of shedding his kingship which made it difficult for ceremony to obtain when he chose that it should lapse. It was not long before they had reached a comfortable understanding.

'You have been fortunate, sir, in your travelling companions,' said Lady Wyndham, regarding him with a sapient, benevolent eye. 'I have had some discourse with Mrs Jane Lane, and find her a very good sort of a girl, concerned just as she should be with your preservation. We have decided that for better convenience she shall be thought a cousin of ours while she remains under this roof. That, however, will not be for long, since upon all counts it will be best for her to depart with Mr Lassels tomorrow morning.'

'So soon?' said Charles. 'Nay, you are right: she must not remain here, for it might give rise to some suspicion. I would not have her run into danger for my sake. But where is she?'

'She is with my son's wife, sir, and will come to you presently. Meanwhile, if your Majesty will be guided by an old woman, we will take counsel together.'

'Instruct me, madam. I shall certainly obey you.'

She smiled. 'It would be well for you if you would, sir, for by all accounts you are too careless of your person. Now, this household numbers upwards of twenty persons. We think our servants trustworthy, but we can be sure only of three, two of whom are Catholic, and confirmed in their abhorrence of the Puritans. The third is my son's man, Henry Peters, who may yet prove to be of great use to your Majesty. For the rest, we desire they shall neither set eyes upon you, nor know of your presence in the house. Can you be content to remain in two rooms, sir?' She added with a twinkle: 'We will have no visits to butteries or bowling-greens, if you please!'

'I said I would obey you, madam, and so I will, but I must tell you that I find myself very much at home in butteries,' said Charles meekly.

She was amused, but she did not doubt him. She saw that he was of that easy nature that could be at home in any surroundings. She found it increasingly hard, every moment she spent in his presence, to believe that he could be his father's son. When her niece came into the room with Mrs Wyndham, and Jane Lane, she was struck by yet another difference between the first and this second Charles. That roving eye alighted upon Juliana, and kindled with undisguised appreciation.

Juliana blushed under the King's gaze, but though she hung her head in maidenly confusion, she could not resist peeping at him through her lashes.

Lady Wyndham watched the smile curl Charles's lips, and said in a dry tone: 'My niece, sire, Mrs Juliana Coningsby.'

'I am right glad to know Mrs Juliana,' said the King, holding out his hand.

Juliana went forward in a rush, sinking down in a billow of skirts, and fervently kissing his hand. 'Sire!' A girl's awe filled her voice; she stole a look up into his face, a doubtful, surprised look (for his dark ugliness came as a shock to her); then his smile made her forget his swarthiness, and his coarse features, and she ventured to smile back at him. 'Oh, *sire*!'

The King glanced up, and saw that Lady Wyndham was watching him. His smile changed to one of somewhat mischievous comprehension; he got up, drawing Juliana to her feet. 'Do not kneel to me, mistress,' he said lightly. 'That is a custom I desire all who wish me well to rid themselves of.' He walked across the room to Jane, and took her hand, and led her to Lady Wyndham. 'Madam, I commend my Life to you, and think I have no need to solicit your kindness for her.'

'No need,' she said, receiving Jane's hand from him, and holding it. 'You are come in good time, Mistress Jane. I wish you will add your counsel to mine, that his Majesty will be pleased to remain in these apartments, which have been prepared for him, until my son has contrived to hire him a vessel to go overseas.'

'That I will certainly do, madam,' Jane replied. She raised her eyes to Lady Wyndham's, and added: 'I am happy to leave his Majesty in such careful hands. I think him safe now, for the first time since I had the great honour to be of service to him.'

'So you are to leave me, Jane?' the King said, 'and so soon!'

'Why, yes, sir,' she replied. 'My part is played. I can no longer be of use to you, and I think I should return to Bentley, lest it become known that I did not go there from Abbotsleigh.'

Her voice was tranquil; she wished to be gone from Trent, for the King, who had depended upon her for more than a week, was now amongst his own friends, and she felt a little desolate. She thought he would soon forget her, not knowing that whatever, in after life, this careless King might conveniently forget, all those who had rendered him aid in these dark days would always live in his memory. When she went with Lassels the following morning to take leave of him, she found him teasing Juliana, under the world-weary eye of Lord Wilmot. Her heart ached dully in her breast, but when he saw her he dismissed Juliana, and Wilmot too, saying abruptly: 'Give me leave, mistress, and you too, my Lord Wilmot!' He took Jane's hands, and said: 'Going, my Life? Alas, that I dare not, for your sweet sake, bid you remain!'

She shook her head, answering him in the ghost of a voice: 'Better not!'

'I know it. Yet I shall miss you sorely.' He released one of her hands, and held his own right one out to Lassels. 'You, too, my exacting master! I hope you may never have so clumsy a servant again! Nor one, indeed, who will put you so often in a sweat of fear! Will you do be a last favour, Harry Lassels?'

'Anything, my liege!' Lassels said, dropping on his knee to kiss his hand.

'If ever I come to my throne, let me hear from you! I am a King so deep in debt I may never repay the whole. Yet there are some debts I shall certainly repay. I charge you, do not forget!'

Lassels gulped, but could only say rather thickly: 'God preserve your Majesty!'

'I thank you, and do not doubt, since He has put such faithful friends in my way, He will do so. Leave me now:

Mistress Jane shall join you presently.' He turned to her, almost before Lassels had withdrawn, and said, half-mournfully: 'I can find it in me to regret that I am not even now strapping your baggage on to the saddle. This is a sad leave-taking, my Life.'

'Yet hopeful, sire!' she whispered.

'For which I have you to thank. How shall I thank you, Jane? I think there are no words.'

She raised her face, mutely inviting him to kiss her. Tears hung on the ends of her lashes, but her heart had warmed, and she could smile through her tears.

'That, yes,' Charles said. He took her face between his hands, and kissed her. 'Do not weep, sweetheart! This parting is but for a little time. We shall meet again, in happier days.' He kissed her once more, and let her go. She seemed for a long time to feel the pressure of his fingers on her cheeks. He said: 'I have been thinking, Jane, that you may be placed in some danger, if my enemies should discover the part you have played in my escape. It mislikes me a little that my lord should have sent your good brother to London. Heed me well, now! If suspicion should fall upon you, do not tarry in this country, but come to me, wherever I may be! If you can find a vessel to carry you to France, set sail immediately, and send tidings to St Germain, and I promise you I shall meet you on your road to Paris. Now call my Lord Wilmot in to me again, for he holds for me a keepsake I desire you will take in memory of me.'

'It needs no keepsake, sir. I shall never forget.'

'It is my will,' he replied, smiling.

She moved to the door, and summoned my lord, who was waiting with Lassels at the stairhead. He came in, and the King said at once: 'Give me back my watch, Harry!'

'Your watch, sir! Consider, should you carry upon you so valuable a jewel?'

'I shall not carry it. Come, man, give it to me!'

Wilmot blinked, glanced at Jane, and said: 'Oh – ah! Why, certainly, sir!' He thrust his hand into the breast of his coat, and produced a silver-studded leather case, which he gave into the King's out-stretched hand.

Charles opened the case, and drew out a crystal watch, with a silver face engraved with roses and leaves. 'I would give you a prettier watch than this, my Life, and one day I will do so. Meanwhile, I give you this one, which I wore at Worcester, to remind you of Charles Stewart and his gratitude.'

He put both watch and case into her hand; she tried to thank him, but her voice failed, and she could only look up speakingly into his face. He bent, and kissed her cheek, and nodded to Wilmot, who came forward at once to escort her out to where Lassels waited with the horses.

Hardly had these two travellers left the house than Colonel Wyndham also set out, to ride to Melbury, in the hope of engaging Sir John Strangways's help for the King. When he arrived at the house, a big, sprawling mansion, with gardens running down to a lake, he was met by the intelligence that Sir John was away from home. This was an unexpected set-back, but even as the Colonel began to enquire whether either of Sir John's sons was at Melbury, Colonel Giles Strangways came walking across the hall, with a couple of spaniels at his heels, and instantly recognized him. He called out in a bluff voice: 'What, by God, is it you, Wyndham? I am right glad to see you, man! Come you in!'

He was a man in the late thirties, of rather a full habit of body, and a handsome, arrogant countenance. A permanent crease between his brows, and eyelids that fell steeply from the inner corners of his eyes, gave him a contemptuous expression, not in the least mitigated by the upward curl of his mouth under very neat mustachios. His lower lip strongly supported the upper; he had the suggestion of a double-chin; and a masterful, aquiline nose. His bearing proclaimed the soldier; he was brisk, and held himself well, and seemed to have the habit of command.

Wyndham clasped hands with him. 'I came to see Sir John, but I hear he is away from home. I daresay my business can be as easily told to you, however.'

'Never doubt it! Is it of importance? Must it be settled immediately?'

'Oh no!' Wyndham replied, slightly pressing his hand before he released it. 'It is merely that I promised to bring Sir John word if I heard of a good hunter that might suit him.'

'Is that it! Walk out with me, will you? What horse is this? Is he up to my father's weight?'

He thrust a hand in Wyndham's arm, and marched him out of the house into the sunlit gardens. Not until they were out of earshot of anyone in the house did he abandon his flow of cheerful, loud-voiced enquiries. Then he said in quite a different tone: 'Let me have it now! By God, I dare not open my mouth in my own house these days! A pretty pass we have come to, odd rot it! I know not which of the servants may not be spying and listening at key-holes. The whole country is putrid with disaffection! What's your need of my father? Are you in some trouble?'

'No,' Wyndham replied. 'Not I. But the King is at Trent.'

The hand on his arm gripped it most painfully. 'God's body, what's this?' Strangways rapped out. 'Man, are you jesting?'

'Jesting! On such a subject? I tell you, the King is lying hidden in my house, having made his way there in disguise from Worcester! Wilmot is with him, and I must procure a vessel to carry them both safe to France.'

'Good God!' Colonel Strangways's ruddy cheeks had grown suddenly quite pale. 'He's alive, then! But in this neighbourhood! 'Sdeath, he could not have chosen a worse to come to! It stinks of Puritanism. He must be got away, and that right speedily, Wyndham!'

'Ay, he must be got away to France, but I believe him safe at this present. There is a secret hiding-place at Trent, and not a soul I cannot trust knows of his presence there. I came seeking Sir John, thinking him the likeliest man to have the means in his power to render the King aid.'

Strangways gave a groan. 'Put it out of your head!' he said. 'My father would give his life for the King, but I tell you neither he nor I dare move in such a matter. We are watched, and followed every step we take! We should bring a veritable pack of those rebel knaves upon the King. Get you to Lyme, and try there for Captain Alford! He has interest with I know not how many mariners. If any can contrive the King's passage overseas, he can.'

'Ay, I know Alford, but heard that he had been forced to go overseas, being too much suspected. The man I had in mind is William Ellesdon, who fought upon our side in the late Wars, and is since turned merchant, and resides at Lyme. You'll recall Sir John Berkley's escape from Lyme: that was contrived by Ellesdon's brother, John, through Colonel Bullen Reymes – the same that married my wife's sister.'

'If Alford is still at Lyme, seek him out!' said Strangways. 'I don't doubt the Ellesdons, but it's in my mind that one of them is wedded to a damned Puritan woman.' A thought occurred to him; he asked abruptly: 'Has the King money for his needs?'

Wyndham said with a wry smile: 'The King has a few shillings in his pocket only, being disguised as a poor serving-man. My Lord Wilmot has a little more, but not much, I fear.'

'Oddsblood, man, if the King is to be carried overseas, money will be required to buy his passage! Come you back to the house, for that is one need I can supply!'

Wyndham began to protest that he himself would furnish the King with money; but Strangways broke in on his speech, to say: 'No, no, that shall not be! I know what expense you have lately been put to. You shall not deny me the right to do the only thing for the King that lies in my power!'

He grasped Wyndham's arm again, as he spoke, and marched him up to the house. When Wyndham presently took his leave, and rode back to Trent, he carried in his bosom a little bag containing three hundred gold pieces, which was all the money Colonel Strangways had by him.

The King received Strangways's messages of loyalty, and grief at being unable to wait upon him in person, with a careless nod; but when Wyndham put the bag of money into his hand, his brows flew up, and he burst out laughing.

'Harry, Harry, here is a man who sends me money un-asked! Faith, I begin to think this an age of new miracles!' He loosened the cord of the bag, and spilled the gold pieces out on to the table. 'Oddsfish! a fortune!'

'There is a hundred pounds there, sire, which was all Strangways had in the house. He sent it with his humble duty, that your Majesty might be able to buy your passage overseas.'

'Three hundred broad pieces!' said the King, spinning one of them into the air with a flick of his thumb. 'You shall be my steward, Harry. Put them up in your purse! What now, Frank?'

'With your leave, sir, I think I should lose no time in seeking out Captain Ellesdon. Lyme is some thirty miles from here, so that I may easily reach it before dark, and return to you tomorrow, when I trust I shall have accomplished the business.'

This plan receiving the King's approval, Colonel Wyndham was soon in the saddle again, his pass in his pocket, and a portmanteau strapped behind him. He left his Royal master teaching Juliana Coningsby to play some game of cards that seemed to afford both players considerable amusement, and to necessitate the King's black head being bent continually over the lady's glossy brown one. But beyond brushing one chestnut curl with his lips, and once pinching the lobe of her ear, the King attempted no familiarities. For Lady Wyndham remained throughout in the room, embroidering a length of stiff satin.

When Juliana presently went away, the King sat idly shuffling the cards, letting them drift in cascades between his practised hands. 'Madam?' he said presently.

'Sire?'

He looked at her, a laugh in his eye. 'You need not fear me, I do assure you, for though you may have heard some sad stories of me, indeed, I was bred a gentleman!'

She stuck her needle into the satin, and pushed the frame aside before answering him. 'I shall speak to you, sire, as an old woman to a young man – if your Majesty so permits?'

He got up and came across the room, seating himself on a

stool beside her chair. 'Nay, here is no King, but only one Charles Stewart, madam. Scold me, then – but not too harshly!' he added, with a melting glance up into her face.

'Has anyone ever scolded you harshly, sir?' she asked, shaking her head at him.

'My Chancellor, madam, and I know not how many godly Scottish ministers besides. The truth is I was always a sore trial to my preceptors.'

Lady Wyndham folded her lips rather tightly for a moment; and then said with unaccustomed asperity: 'You had a bad, unprincipled woman for your nurse, sir, as well I know!'

'Fie, madam! A kinswoman of your own!' protested the King, but blushing a little.

'Mrs Wyndham was no kinswoman of mine, sir, for I was born a Coningsby!' said her ladyship, sitting very upright in her chair.

'Do not let us talk about Mrs Wyndham,' he coaxed. 'I had thought it was a Coningsby you meant to speak of.'

She relaxed slightly. 'A pretty, fond wench, sir. Hearts mend easily at her age, yet I prefer she should not break hers.'

'What, over this ugly face of mine?' said the King, his eyes brightening with laughter. 'Do you think she will?'

'Yes, if you aid her to it,' replied Lady Wyndham bluntly.

'Eh, madam, I desire no woman to break her heart for my sake! I have no taste for tragedy.'

'Then you should take heed lest you smile too kindly upon foolish maids!' said her ladyship.

'But, madam, my Lord of Newcastle, who was my governor, laid it down as a maxim that to women I could not be too civil!' he pleaded.

'Fine counsel!' she said, considerably amused. 'Pray, what other useful maxims did my lord instil into your ears, sir?'

He reflected. Some of my lord's maxims, excellent though he had found them to be, could hardly be repeated to the King's faithful subjects. *'Believe it,'* my lord had said, *'the putting off of your hat and making a leg pleases more than reward or preservation, so much doth it take all kind of people.'*

Very true, thought the King cynically, but cast about in his memory for a more suitable maxim to repeat to Lady Wyndham. He found it. 'Madam, he bade me be courteous.'

'You conned that lesson well, sir.'

'Not to fall into a divine melancholy, to be an anchoret or a capuchin,' said the King demurely.

'I see no fear of your doing any of those things, sir. Had my lord no moral maxims to impart?'

*'Short prayers pierce the heaven's gates,'* had said my lord.

'My lord left such maxims to my tutor, the Lord Bishop of Chichester,' said the King. 'But he made me what I knew not then to be a true prophecy. *"If any be Bible mad, over much burnt with fiery zeal, they may think it a service to God to destroy you, and say the spirit moved them, and bring some example of a king with a hard name in the Old Testament."* '

This was apt enough to make her laugh, but to one who had known his father it was so odd to hear him making a jest of treason that she could not resist asking him if he found it easy to forgive his enemies.

'I could make the most of them like me very well if they would but let me,' he replied seriously.

She was too stiff-necked a Royalist to let that pass. 'You are the King, sir, and what has liking to do with duty?'

'Madam,' said the King, his eyes glinting, 'my Lord of Newcastle said he would not have me so seared with majesty as to think myself not of mankind; nor suffer others to flatter me so much.'

This was too modern a thought for her; she could only shake her head, mourning a little over the passing of the old order.

At the dinner-hour, the King being served in his own room by Joan Halsenoth, one of Lady Wyndham's Catholic maidservants, the Church bells suddenly began to ring, clanging forth such loud and joyous peals that the King wondered what could be the reason of such a commotion. That none of the household should suspect that a guest was hidden in Lady Wyndham's apartments, the King's meals were cooked in his room, himself, to while away the time, acting as master-cook. After the bells had been ringing for ten or fifteen minutes, Charles took the frying-pan out of Joan Halsenoth's hold, saying: 'This should portend some great event, methinks. Do you go out and discover what is going forward, Joan, while I toss the collops in the pan.'

'Oh!' she blurted out, 'your gracious Majesty will spoil the meat!'

'Not I, faith! Get you gone, now, for I am very desirous to know what all this rejoicing may mean.'

She was gone for some time, returning to find the meat fried, and the King busily engaged in eating it. Her sallow little face was set into lines of the most rigid disdain, and when the King asked what news she brought, she stood before him with downcast eyes, and compressed lips, and twisted her apron into a screw between her fingers.

Charles looked her over with a tolerant eye. 'Did they cut your tongue out, my girl? Come, why do they ring the bells so lustily?'

'I be not wishful for to tell your Majesty. They are rogues,' said Joan darkly.

'Oho! Now, what makes you say so?'

'There is some of Cromwell's soldiers come into the village, prating of the great battle that was fought at Worcester, and saying as how your Majesty's army was o'erthrown.'

'Well, so it was, indeed,' said Charles, with a grimace. 'Is that all?'

'No, your honour.'

'Let me know the rest, then.'

'There's one of them has on a buff coat, which he says your Majesty wore at the battle. And he is bragging of how he slew your blessed Majesty, and you was buried on the field; and the rebels here are so tickled they are building up a great bonfire, and drinking themselves silly, and ringing all the bells for joy!'

'Ringing the bells for joy!' repeated the King. 'Alas, poor people!'

'They had ought to be hanged, every one!' said Joan ferociously.

'That is what they say of me. I hope they may not come here to search for me – though I suppose, if they do indeed believe me dead, there is little fear of that.'

None of the soldiers did come to the house, but their presence in the village put my Lord Wilmot into a state of fidgeting alarm, and made him insist upon the secret hiding-place's being furnished with cushions and blankets in case the King should be forced to go into it. All that evening the window-panes glowed redly with the reflection of the huge bonfire burning in the village, and the sounds of shouting and of singing penetrated even to the King's chamber. Mrs Anne Wyndham's cheeks were crimson with shame, while Juliana, eyes flashing and breast stormy, enumerated the various fates she would like every one of the villagers to suffer. Lady Wyndham, saying calmly that they were but ignorant hinds, shut the windows, and drew the curtains across them, for although the King made a jest of the celebrations upon his supposed death, she thought he must be a very odd man who could listen unmoved to such rejoicings.

The troopers all left the village at nightfall, for they were upon their way to the coast; and upon the following day, which was Friday, Colonel Wyndham came back from Lyme.

Wilmot, who was taking the air with Mrs Wyndham in the garden, saw the Colonel first, and knew from the way he flung himself out of the saddle, and from the ring in his voice when he hailed them, that his mission had been successful. They hurried forward to meet him, Wilmot asking, as he grasped his hand: 'You found a vessel?'

'Ay! All is in train. I must go to the King at once with my news. He is well? Safe?'

'Safe enough, but I like not the humour of this village,' said Wilmot. 'The people spent yesterday evening dancing for joy, and all most beastly drunk, because a report came in that the King was killed at Worcester.'

'Oh, Frank, it was horrible!' Anne said, with a shudder.

'Better that than that a report should come in of the

King's being at my house,' responded the Colonel.

He and Wilmot went upstairs to the King's apartment, where they found Charles engaged in boring a hole through one of the gold pieces sent to him by Giles Strangways. He looked up as the door opened, and hailed his host with a cheerful wave of one hand. 'Come in, Frank! How did you fare?'

'Well, sir, as I do hope,' Wyndham replied. 'I could not discover Captain Alford, he having been forced, as I had heard, to leave England, but William Ellesdon I soon found. He is willing and anxious to aid you, sir, for all his wife is a most strict Puritan.'

'I give him thanks, and you too, Frank. Shall I go to France?'

'Upon Monday night, sire, if our mariner keep faith, which, please God he will do!'

'Not until Monday!' Wilmot exclaimed. 'Ah, that likes me not at all! I would not have his Majesty remain so long in this neighbourhood.'

'I am very well-pleased to remain,' said the King, intent upon his coin. 'Go on, Frank: tell me the whole!'

'Why, sir, there is little enough. I waited upon Ellesdon at his place of business, and, finding him apt, I opened to him the matter I had come upon, but withholding your name, sire, and calling you a Cavalier that was a fugitive from Worcester. He said at once, and very earnestly, that he was still of the same mind as he had ever been, and would do what lay in his power to help anyone who had fought upon our side. Upon his enquiring more closely who my gentleman might be, I told him one was my Lord Wilmot, and the other a friend of my lord.'

'Oh!' said Wilmot, with rather a blank look.

The Colonel smiled a little. 'There is worse to follow, my lord, for no sooner did Ellesdon hear your name on my lips than he started up with a most eager and joyful expression on his face, and demanded "Is it the King?"' He glanced down at Charles. 'Being very sure of my man, sir, I told him Yes, whereupon he was a good deal moved, and swore most solemnly that he would endeavour the execution of your commands to the utmost hazard of his person. After we had discoursed a little time together, he sent one of his fellows to the Custom-house, to make enquiry who had entered his vessel as bound for France. By great good-fortune, we learned that one Stephen Limbry, with whom Ellesdon has interest, Limbry being a tenant of his, had lately entered his barque, intending a voyage to St Malo. Ellesdon assured me that Limbry was well-disposed towards your Majesty, so without more ado we set off by road to Charmouth, which lies a few miles to the east of Lyme, and where this Limbry has his dwelling. Ellesdon sent for him to come to the inn there, which he soon did. When he was told that the end of our sending for him was to procure passages for two gentlemen who had had a finger in the pie at Worcester, he was at first startled – as apprehending more than ordinary danger in the undertaking. But upon my engaging to pay him sixty pounds, which I have promised to do when he shall return from having conveyed your Majesty to France, he cheerfully undertook to do the business. It is agreed, therefore, that he is to prepare his vessel with all speed, and to hale her out of the Cob on Monday next, and about mid-night to send his long-boat to a place appointed, to take you off. As soon as you and my lord board the vessel, he will immediately put out to sea, sir.'

'If the wind serves,' said the King. 'Does he know whom he is to carry to St Malo?'

'Nay, sire, he has not the least notion, nor would Ellesdon or I breathe a word of it to him, in case the reward that is being offered for your capture should prove too great a temptation to him. As soon as we had struck our bargain, Ellesdon and I rode back to Lyme, by the land road, so that I might, from the top of the hill between the two towns, become more perfectly acquainted with the lie of the land. Then it was that Ellesdon bethought him of the Fair which is to be held at Lyme, by ill-hap, upon Monday. He was fearful that the inn at Charmouth might, on account of this, be filled with other guests; so after some discussion we sent my man Peters into Charmouth, with an earnest of five shillings, to secure the two best rooms in the inn against

236

your Majesty's coming. And herein,' added the Colonel, with a look half-merry, half-deprecating, 'I fear I have compromised your Majesty shockingly.'

'Compromised him?' Wilmot said sharply. 'What's this? What do you mean?'

The King looked up, smiling. 'You're a rogue, Frank. What have you done?'

'Why, sir, I have informed the hostess at the inn, through Peters, that there will come to her house on Monday night a young man who has stolen a gentlewoman of fortune, to marry her against the will of her guardians.'

'Oddsfish, is that all? It seems you have bestowed a very proper character upon me, if I am to marry the damsel,' remarked the King, bending over his coin again. 'I hope your romantic fairy tale won the hostess's heart?'

'Ay, it did, sir, for she readily engaged to keep the house and the stables free for you. If you will be pleased to take my cousin up behind you, as you did Mrs Jane Lane, I believe it may serve as a very excellent disguise, besides satisfying the hostess.'

'So Mrs Juliana is my bride, is she?' said the King. 'It likes me well. But I fear the hostess will think Juliana has made an ill-choice, for besides being still so dark-complexioned, I look a mean sort of a fellow in this serving-man's gear. Will you lend me your fine cloak, Harry?'

'No, my dear master, I will not, for the meaner you look the less you will be suspected of being the King,' replied Wilmot affectionately. 'I had rather play the part of the bridegroom, taking you along as my servant.'

'Fie, you are too fat, nor will I relinquish my pretty bride. My thanks, Frank: you have done excellent well.'

'I do trust it may be found so,' the Colonel said, a worried look in his eyes. 'Any scheme must be fraught with danger, but I have tried to mitigate this by arranging with William Ellesdon to conduct you first to a country-house belonging to his father, which lies in a very private place, inland about a mile and a half from Lyme and Charmouth both. There Ellesdon will meet us, and there your Majesty may remain until nightfall.'

Wilmot's harassed frown lifted a little. 'Ah, that was well thought of! Yes, yes, that should serve! My dear master, the end of this weary pilgrimage is at last in sight! In less than a week now you will stand upon French soil, and know yourself safe.'

'If the wind is favourable,' agreed the King.

'And Limbry prove himself faithful,' muttered Wyndham.

CHAPTER XIV

A PRYING KNAVE

THE following day, which was Saturday, September 20th, passed uneventfully, the King whiling away the time by boring holes in some more of Giles Strangways's gold pieces, and enjoying some airy dalliance with Juliana Coningsby, who, to her good aunt's satisfaction, showed herself to be more in love with the adventure she was to take part in than with the King. On Sunday morning, the household was a little disturbed by a visit from a tailor, who lived in the village and owed the greater portion of his livelihood to the Colonel's patronage. He presented himself at an early hour, and seemed to be so anxious that none should spy upon his coming to the manor that Wyndham was put instantly upon his guard. He had the man brought into his private parlour; and after assuring himself that no one was listening at the keyhole, the tailor informed him in conspiratorial accents that he had come to bring him warning.

The Colonel laughed at this, and said: 'Warning? Warning of what, my man?'

The tailor jerked his thumb over his shoulder. 'Last night the zealots were discoursing together, saying as how your honour was hiding persons of quality in your house, and they would come to search the place, and seize them, they having seen the stout gentleman, which is staying privily with your honour, and suspicioning that he be of the King's party. Which is the reason of my taking the liberty of waiting upon your honour, me not being wishful that any harm should befall you.'

'Why, that was kindly done!' said the Colonel, thrusting a hand into his pocket, and drawing out a gold piece. 'But the gentleman you speak of is not private, but public in the house, being a kinsman of mine. The sectaries may make themselves easy, for I believe my kinsman will show himself in Church at the time of prayers, he being a very godly man. But I thank you for your care of me.'

The coin changed hands, and the tailor, a little abashed, bowed himself out. No sooner had he departed, than the Colonel made haste upstairs to the King's apartment, to tell him what had chanced, and to beg him to use his influence with my lord to induce him to go to Church.

'You will never prevail upon him to do so,' remarked the King. 'See, I mean to bestow this coin upon your mother for a keepsake! I am becoming very deft at boring my holes, I can tell you. Do you think she will like it?'

The Colonel could not help laughing. 'I think she will scold you for spending the money so wantonly, sir! But touching this matter of my Lord Wilmot, I know full well I may not prevail with him, so depend upon your Majesty's commanding where I can only implore. I am very sure his presence and mine in Church today will lull all suspicion to rest, for I have informed my tailor that my lord is my kinsman, and a very godly man. He need not fear to be known, for besides that none of the villagers have reason to recognize him: when I go to Church (which is not often) I sit in an aisle distinct from the body of the congregation. My hope is that the villagers will believe my supposed kinsman to have made a convert of me. For your own safety, sir, I beg of you, lay your command upon my lord!'

'He will think it very odd of me,' said the most easy-going King in Christendom.

But when my Lord Wilmot, informed of the engagement that had been made for him, roundly declared that nothing would induce him to expose himself in Church that day, the King, in obedience to a compelling look from Wyndham, sighed, and said: 'But you shall go, Harry. It is my will.'

Wilmot blinked at him. 'Your will, sir?'

The King held out his hand. 'Nay, go for my sake, my dear Harry!'

Wilmot kissed his hand. 'For your sake, anything!' he declared heroically.

No mishap attended his visit to the Church, nor did the fanatics fulfil their threat of coming to search the manor. The Colonel discovered, through Henry Peters, that the sight of my lord in the manor pew had indeed lulled suspicion to rest, whereupon the King, who had strenuously resisted all endeavours to make him go into the secret hiding-place, said: 'Then I can go to bed in comfort.'

On the following morning, he took a tender leave of Lady Wyndham, tying his pierced coin round her neck with a length of ribbon; and embracing her upon both cheeks; a more punctilious leave of Anne, and was ready at an early hour to set forward upon the journey to Lyme.

It had been agreed that the party should separate, to escape attracting too much attention; and, accordingly, Wilmot, escorted by Henry Peters, set out some little time later than the King, and followed a slightly different route. Juliana Coningsby rode pillion behind the King, with Colonel Wyndham going beside them.

The road chosen by the Colonel was not much frequented, nor did they encounter anyone on the way who accorded their small party more than a casual glance of curiosity. The journey was, in fact, so uneventful that Juliana complained that she might as well be riding behind a real servant.

The Colonel called her sharply to book for making such a speech, but the King said over his shoulder: 'If I were not sworn to good behaviour, you rogue, I would make you unsay those words!'

'Oh, but indeed, sir, I meant not *that*!' explained Juliana. 'Only where is the adventure I was promised? When you had Mrs Jane Lane behind you, you rode through a troop of horse, but all *I* see is a parcel of country-people who stare at us like cows. How, how can I be a heroine if not one shred of danger offers?'

'You are thoughtless and silly, Juliana!' the Colonel said.

She was both, but she suited the King's humour. He began to tease her, and she responded in kind, being excited by the part she was playing. His body felt light and urgent, but not for love; his secret mind was far away from Juliana, wandering in a future that now seemed sure. He was gay, and charming, but subtly withdrawn, in a way which she found tantalizing.

They arrived at their destination late in the afternoon, Colonel Wyndham experiencing no difficulty in finding Ellesdon's house in the hills behind Lyme. No one was at present staying in the house, but Captain Ellesdon had taken care to convey refreshment there earlier in the day; and himself met the party about a quarter of a mile from the gate. He was a sober-looking man, just now a little harassed by the charge that had been laid upon his shoulders, and rather overwhelmed at finding himself face to face with his sovereign. The King immediately made himself known to him, but disconcerted him by interrupting his formal speech of welcome with a request to be treated like a private gentleman. When Ellesdon began to tell him that all was in train for his embarkation that night, he said: 'Why, that is excellent hearing! You shall presently tell me the whole, but my present need is a drink, for I am parched.'

Since Colonel Wyndham had not thought it necessary to inform Ellesdon what manner of man his King was, Ellesdon was a good deal surprised by his careless good-humour, and his apparent unconcern with any possibility of danger. He saw that he need not have wasted any time on the preparation of set speeches, and abandoned them, inwardly congratulating himself on having had the forethought to bring some bottles of wine to the deserted house. When the King dismounted, he perceived that he was taller even than he had supposed, and whispered to Colonel Wyndham that such a height made him remarkable.

Wyndham nodded, but said: 'He is very well disguised, however, and there are, after all, other tall, dark men in England.'

'Oh, I do not think anyone could forget him that had once

laid eyes on him!' Ellesdon replied, looking worried. 'I have a great fear that he may be known, and wish that this house were by the sea, that he might not be obliged to go into a common inn. Surely, too, he is very careless?'

'Yes, very careless,' agreed the Colonel, smiling. 'I should have warned you, perhaps, that he is not at all like what his father was.'

'Well, I must own he has taken me by surprise. Such a very odd countenance! I had said ill-favoured, but his eyes have a strange brilliance that makes one forget the extreme ugliness — But I say too much!'

He made haste after the King, who had passed into the house by this time; and ushered him into a small parlour which had been prepared for his reception. Wine, biscuits, and fruit stood upon the table, the sight of which made the King clap his host on the back, telling him that he was a man after his own heart.

Wilmot and Henry Peters arrived at the house while the King was eating his light repast. As soon as he saw Wilmot, the King toasted him, bidding him sit down at the table, and fall to. Wilmot said: 'Yes, yes, my dear master, but are matters in good train? Will the boat be at the appointed place tonight? When must we go to Charmouth?'

'Be still, Harry, be still!' said the King. 'Matters are in excellent train, as I have been assured. Captain Ellesdon, advise me now what arrangements have been made between you and your mariner.'

'There!' said Wilmot in his ear. 'I knew you would not trouble your head to make the least enquiry! Well, Captain? Well?'

'Indeed, my lord, all has been most carefully attended to, I having repeatedly sought out the master of the barque, one Stephen Limbry, moving and pressing him so earnestly to the punctual performance of his promise, that he was even a little discontented at my importunity, as betraying in me a suspicion of his fidelity. But I excused it, on one count and another, to his satisfaction, and this morning he was able to give me very comfortable tidings, that he had victualled himself, taken in his ballast, and haled his vessel out to the Cob's mouth, for fear of being beneaped. For you must know, my lord, that the tides are now at their lowest.'

My lord showed plainly that tides meant nothing to him; but the King looked up from the apple he was peeling, and nodded. 'I know. When will the tide serve to take me off?'

'Sire, at midnight. The master will send his longboat to a very commodious place appointed between us, lying a full quarter of a mile from any house or footpath. And further, sire, Limbry has informed the sailors that my Lord Wilmot is a merchant, by name Mr Payne, and your Majesty his servant. Upon my advice, he has given as the reason for Mr Payne's taking ship at Charmouth at such an unseasonable hour, that he is a Town-Corporate, and fears an arrest, his factor at St Malo having broken him in the estate by his unfaithfulness to him.'

The King put the peeled apple into Juliana's hand. 'There, my bride: is it sweet? – I thank you, Captain: you have served me faithfully.'

'Then we need not go into Charmouth until it is dark,' said Wilmot.

'But when we do go,' suggested the Colonel, 'I think it were best Ellesdon should not accompany us, but should instead ride back to Lyme, where he may see Limbry, and assure himself that the man will not fail us. That is, if your Majesty pleases.'

Juliana had offered her apple to the King, and he was engaged in taking a bite out of it. A wave of the hand signified to the Colonel that he might make what arrangements he liked.

It was eventually agreed that the Colonel's plan should be adopted. Shortly after ten o'clock, the party set out, the King taking leave of Captain Ellesdon at the point where the road branched, the western fork leading to Lyme, and the eastern to Charmouth. He bestowed one of his bored coins upon him, bidding him keep it in remembrance of him, a circumstance which made Wilmot say, when the Captain was out of earshot, that it was as well that this pilgrimage was approaching its end, since such prodigality must soon leave them once more penniless.

The road to Charmouth led steeply down hill, the inn where the King was to lodge being situated at the bottom of the street, within sound of the sea. That the hostess's suspicions might not be aroused by the arrival of too great a company at her house, it was decided that only the King, Wilmot, and Juliana should alight at the Queen's Head, the Colonel, and his servant, going on to await the arrival of the ship's longboat at the place appointed.

'And now,' said the King to Juliana, 'do not you forget, sweetheart, that I am the man of your choice! I think you should hang fondly upon me.'

'Indeed, and so I will,' promised Juliana. 'But I misdoubt me the hostess will think I have run off with my groom. I am sure I am the first to elope with a King. Do you wish a meek bride, dear sir, or a bold one?'

'For God's love, no boldness!' implored Wilmot. 'The whole of this business mislikes me! I think you do not realize the danger of it!'

They had reached the inn-yard by this time. Wilmot heaved himself out of the saddle as an ostler came out of the stables with a lantern in his hand. My lord hailed him immediately. 'Come hither, fellow! Your mistress expects us. Take the horses in, and see them rubbed down and watered.'

The ostler held up his lantern, peering at the King. 'If you be the party as is making off with a rich heiress, you are looked for,' he said rather dourly.

'Oh, Will, shall we be safe here from my uncle?' demanded Juliana, clasping the King about the waist.

'Ay, upon mine honour!' he responded promptly. 'Mr Payne, lift down my mistress, if you please!'

As soon as Juliana had alighted, the King swung himself to the ground, and, pulling the bridle over the double-gelding's head, handed it to the ostler. The lantern swung level with his head, making him blink momentarily; he turned away, but not before the ostler had caught a glimpse of his face.

A warm hand stole into the King's. 'Take me in!' Juliana begged.

'With all my heart?' he said.

The ostler stared after them, holding the horses' bridles slack in his hand. 'That's a powerful big fellow,' he said slowly. 'Dark, too.'

'Ay, we breed big men in Devonshire,' Wilmot replied, hiding his uneasiness under a casual manner.

The ostler jerked up his lantern again, and by its light scrutinized Wilmot's countenance. 'What's your name, master?' he demanded.

'It's Payne, but what concern of yours may that be?' said Wilmot.

'No offence,' the ostler muttered.

Wilmot hurried after the King, who had reached the door leading into the inn from the yard. Here he was met by a stout woman with a shrill voice, who cast an appraising glance from him to Juliana, and said with a sniff: 'One man's meat is another man's poison! I doubt you might say the like of women. Come you in, mistress!'

Juliana stepped before the King into a dimly lit passage. Mistress Wade held a candle, and shaded its flame from the draught with her cupped hand. Beyond one cursory glance at the King, she paid no heed to him, but surveyed Juliana with evident approbation.

'Ay, I blame no man for being wishful to make off with you, mistress!' she said. 'I'll warrant you've never lacked for suitors! There's a fire lit in my parlour, and the whole house to call your own. Ah me! I doubt I do wrong, but I'm a feeling woman, so I am, and a couple of lovers, so star-crossed as you be, is what I could never harden my heart to, come what may!'

The parlour to which she led the star-crossed lovers was a little, square, low-pitched room on the ground floor, to the right of the main door of the inn. The floor was uneven, paved with stone; and the mullioned windows were all tightly shut. A lamp was slung from one of the huge beams supporting the upper floor, and a couple of candles in brass candlesticks gave a little added light to the room. The air was close, slightly acrid with the smoke which now and then belched out from the log-fire in the grate. A couple of straight-backed chairs, one or two joint-stools, a dresser, and an oak-table, which rocked on the uneven floor, made up the furniture of the room, but Mrs Wade looked round her with a satisfied eye, saying: 'It's the best parlour, such as I don't use in the ordinary way, but I grudge nothing. There's a decent bedchamber beside. Ay, ay,' she added, shaking her finger at the King, 'look naughtily at me if you choose, young master, but I'll have you know I'm a decent woman, and my house has ever been respected! I know full well the knot's not tied yet betwixt you and your mistress here, and you'll not put her to bed under my roof, be you never so hot a lover!' His harsh, brown face, and cropped locks seemed to strike her. She clicked her tongue, and shook her head. 'Eh, if ever I saw such a great, black fellow! And you the dainty little lady that you be, my pretty! Ah well! they do say as how a black man's a jewel in a fair woman's eye!'

'Oh, he is, he is!' declared Juliana, clasping her hands on the King's arm, and looking soulfully up into his face.

Charles bent his head, and kissed her. He shot one of his wicked, merry looks at the hostess, saying meekly: 'I know I am an ill-favoured fellow, but I swear I have a good heart, mistress. Do you fetch a bottle of wine, and you shall drink to our happiness!'

She was nothing loth; but when she had bustled out, Wilmot said peevishly: 'I wish you will not be so free, sir! A vulgar creature that will try to nose out all your business, I'll swear! I misliked that ostler, moreover, for he took particular note of your being a tall, dark man. Faugh, how that fire reeks!'

'My poor Harry! I do fear I shall never again prevail upon you to go adventuring with me!'

Wilmot's face softened; he replied: 'I pray God there may never again be the need for such a journey as this!'

'For my part, I could wish it might go on for ever!' said Juliana, putting off her cloak. 'I am not afraid, my lord, and I am sure the good woman has not the least notion who my bridegroom may be.'

Mrs Wade soon came back with a bottle, and four thick glasses, which she set down upon the table, after giving them a polish with her apron. The King knocked the top off the bottle, and filled the glasses. He raised his own to Juliana, saying: 'My pretty bride!'

'My black jewel!' returned Juliana, with a gurgle of laughter. 'Good mistress, shall I know happiness with my Will, think you?'

'Maybe you will, maybe you won't. There's more 'longs to marriage than four bare legs in a bed, my dove, and so I warn you!' She looked the King over, and added somewhat grimly: 'One thing I'll tell you, and that is certain: the maid that is wedded to a lad with a roving eye shall know no quiet all the days of her life.'

'Alas, Will!' mourned Juliana, catching the King's hand, and dropping her forehead on to his arm to hide her laughing face.

'Can you blame my eye to rove towards you?' demanded the King of his hostess. 'I warrant it is not the first eye to do so!'

She shook with comfortable mirth. 'Go to, I know you for a rogue.'

She drank up her wine, and at last went away, much to Wilmot's relief. He walked to the window, parting the curtains a little to look out. The moon was just past the full, but the night was cloudy, and nothing could be seen beyond the leaded panes but murk and vague shadows. The sound of waves breaking on the shore was muffled by distance; but the wind moaned a little round the angles of the house, and whistled under the ill-fitting door. Wilmot began to fear an approaching storm, and was only partly reassured by the King's saying that the breeze was but freshening, and was, besides, very favourable for their voyage.

Charles had brought a pack of cards with him from Trent House; he and Juliana began to play cribbage. Wilmot could not be persuaded to join them, or even to sit by the fire and take his ease. He was restless, his mind troubled by the chances of failure. He walked up and down, sometimes watching the card-players for a few moments; often begging them to be silent so that he could listen intently for some fancied sound.

His anxiety began to communicate itself to Juliana. Once, glancing up from her cards, she thought that she caught a glimpse of an eye looking at her through the chink between the curtains. She cried out in sudden fear, and dropped her cards, but when Wilmot strode to the window and peered out, he could see no one there.

'Doubtless, it was the eye of providence,' remarked the King. 'Come, my bird! it was naught but a trick of the light.'

She picked up her cards with shaking hands. 'It must have been that. Yet I could have sworn I saw something!'

'I will soon see that!' said Wilmot, drawing the curtains exactly together. 'Do you remain here, sir, if you please!'

'Oddsfish, what else should I do?' enquired the King, bored.

Wilmot went out of the room. There seemed to be no one stirring in the inn. A lamp burned low at the foot of the narrow stairs, but the taproom was in darkness. After listening for a moment, and hearing only the sigh and scuffle of the wind, Wilmot opened the street-door, and stepped out. The clouds hid the moon, but there was enough light to show him that the street was quite empty. He stood still for a few seconds, looking about him. No sound came to his ears but the rhythmic fall and drag of the waves; the wind was strong, but not as tempestuous as he had feared. He noticed that it was blowing off the land, and felt a little comforted. He went back into the inn, and was about to return to the parlour when the creak of a floor-board made him look quickly over his shoulder. The dim lamplight left the end of the passage in darkness, but he thought something moved by the door leading into the stable-yard, and strode forward, his hand instinctively seeking his sword-hilt. 'Who's there?' he said sharply.

A sullen voice answered him: ' 'Tis me, master. Who else would it be, this time o' night?'

Wilmot stopped, saying sternly: 'What's the meaning of this? Why are you skulking in the house? Your place is in the stables!'

The ostler came slowly into the light. He held his head

down, but shot my lord a covert look upwards under his pale-lashed eyelids. 'I bain't skulking. I come in for to tell your honour that the bay has a shoe loose.'

'At midnight, fellow?'

The man shifted his feet, muttering: 'Mistress, she did say you was going away afore morning. But you'll not go far without the bay casts his shoe.'

'When I want the horses I will call you. Get you to bed! What kind of a house is this, that has ostlers wandering about it at this hour?'

'I bain't doing any harm,' the ostler said sulkily. He turned on his heel, and slouched away towards the door into the yard.

Wilmot went back into the parlour. The game of cribbage had come to an end, and Juliana was sitting on a stool by the fire, with her cloak over her shoulders. The King was still seated at the table, idly shuffling the cards. He looked up as Wilmot came in, and raised his brows.

Wilmot said in a lowered voice: 'I saw no one in the street, but when I came back into the house I found that ostler lurking by the back door. He had some tale of having come in to tell me my horse has a shoe loose, but I think him a prying knave, sir, and greatly fear that he suspects your true estate. I have sent him about his business, but I don't disguise from you that I shall be right glad to get you away from this place.'

Juliana looked up, saying with a little shudder: 'I am afraid of this house. It is dark, and I hear queer noises.'

'You hear rats, my dear,' said the King. 'What o'clock is it, Harry?'

Wilmot pulled out his watch, and, opening it, found that the hands stood at ten minutes past twelve. 'It is after midnight. God send no mischance has occurred to prevent Limbry's keeping his appointment! We ought to have heard from Wyndham by now.'

'Patience, patience!' said the King.

Time lagged on. Wilmot kept on consulting his watch, sometimes standing for a few moments by the window, with his head bent, listening for the sound of a signal; at others leaning his arm on the mantelpiece, and tapping his foot on the stone hearth. The King pushed the pack of cards across the table, and refilled his wine glass from the bottle at his elbow. He leaned back in his chair, with his legs stretched out before him, the glass in his hand, and his unfathomable gaze fixed unseeingly upon the wall opposite him. He paid no heed to Wilmot's restless movements about the room; he seemed to be unaware of them, so lost in his own meditations that Juliana, watching him from under eyelids weighed down with sleep, was seized by an odd fancy that his soul had followed his thoughts miles away from this stuffy little room, and only his body sat there, immobile in the straight-backed chair by the table.

The scamper of a rat behind the wainscoting, or the tiny crack of furniture settling, from time to time broke the monotony of the noise of breaking waves, and the moan and sigh of the wind round the house. Juliana started, and glanced fearfully towards the King, but he gave no sign of noticing these sounds.

A board creaked softly in the passage. The King did not move, but Juliana saw that he was not lost, as she had supposed, to his surroundings, but very much on the alert, for his eyes turned swiftly towards the door, and remained watchfully upon it.

'Sweetheart, I must send you to bed,' he said. His voice startled her; she thought he had raised it a little above the ordinary. 'What o'clock is it, Mr Payne?'

Wilmot had taken a couple of hasty steps towards the door, but he stopped in obedience to a sign from the King, and once more pulled out his watch. 'It lacks only a few minutes to one,' he said.

'Oddsfish, so late? My heart, you must leave me, and seek your bed, or I shall have a yawning bride tomorrow.'

'Oh no!' she said imploringly. 'No, I cannot!'

He got up, scraping the legs of his chair on the floor. His deep, cheerful voice interrupted her protest. 'Sleep while you may, love: tomorrow night I shall entertain you too well for sleep, I promise you!'

He lifted her from the stool, holding her in the circle of

his arm, and covering her mouth with one brown hand for a brief, warning instant.

'Ay, she must certainly go to bed,' Wilmot said. He picked up one of the candlesticks, and walked to the door with it in his hand. He lifted the latch rather noisily, and pulled the door open. The lamp still burned at the foot of the stairs; there was no one in the passage, but the door into the tap-room stood ajar. 'Well, mistress, are you ready?' Wilmot enquired. 'Call a truce to your fondlings, Will! You will have her soon enough!'

'Do not make me go!' Juliana whispered. 'Let me stay here with you!'

'Nay, you will undo me,' the King replied under his breath. 'If suspicion is awake, it must be lulled to sleep. Go up, and get what rest you can upon your bed. I think that some hitch has foiled our plans, and we shall not leave this place tonight.'

She said bravely: 'I will do as you bid me. I am sorry to be foolish. I am not fearful for myself.'

'Eh, good sweetheart, if you leave me not now you may well be, for you are too cosy an armful for my virtue, look you!' he said, lightly kissing her cheek.

She blushed, but laughed too, a little uncertainly, and drew herself out of his embrace. Wilmot gave the candle into her hand, and watched her go up the steep stairs. As soon as he had heard the latch of the bedchamber door click into place, he drew back into the parlour, and turned an anxious face towards the King. 'That knave! He was spying upon us, I know full well. If he suspects you of being the King – Sire, I cannot conceal from you my great uneasiness!'

The King laughed. 'No, Harry, you cannot indeed!'

'If Wyndham comes not within the next half-hour we must go away from here. The master has played us false. He may betray our plans, for aught we know. It is not safe to linger here!'

'I am very sure it would be more perilous to go from here without waiting for word from Frank Wyndham,' responded the King. 'Courage, Harry! There are a dozen reasons why the master may not have been able to send his longboat ashore.'

Wilmot's mouth worked. 'Courage, say you? I have none where you are in the case.'

'Yea, but this is folly,' the King said. 'How far will you ride upon a nag with a loose shoe? Shall I go alone? I dare not, if I would. For your prying knave, he will keep until morning, when he may go hang himself, for I shall either be upon my voyage to France, or – oddsfish, where shall I be, Harry?'

'In the hands of the regicides!' Wilmot said with suppressed anguish. He sank down into a chair by the table, and dropped his head into his hands. 'In the devil's name, why does Wyndham send no word?' he groaned. 'If you tarry in this place you may be trapped here!'

'Oh, peace, peace!' said the King. 'If danger threatened, Frank would have contrived to send me warning of it. Think, if our plan of sailing to St Malo has miscarried, where next must I go?'

Wilmot's fingers writhed in the meshes of his long love-locks. 'My God, where? Where?'

The King sat down opposite to him, and filled both their glasses. ''Sdeath, if that is all you have to say, let us for God's sake play cards!' he commanded.

'Cards! If you can, I cannot, sir!'

The King put the pack down with a snap between them. 'Cut!'

Wilmot raised his head, looking resentfully into the King's mocking eyes. 'Will you laugh when you stand upon the scaffold, sir?'

'I do not mean to stand upon a scaffold. My lord, I am still waiting!'

'Oh, my dear!' The King's imperious tone dragged a laugh out of Wilmot. He cut the cards towards him, saying with an effort to regain his self-possession: 'It shall be as you please, sir. Deal, then!'

They played piquet for an hour, Wilmot's ears straining all the while to catch every sound that disturbed the night-silence. A little after two o'clock, Charles fetched a great yawn, and remarked that since there now seemed to be little chance of his embarking for France that day, there was nothing left for him to do but to try what sleep he could get on the settle by the fire.

To Wilmot's envious surprise, he did sleep, waking only when the daylight began to creep between the chinks of the curtains. The fire was a heap of grey ashes, and the candles were guttering in little pools of liquid tallow. Wilmot blew them out, and pulled the curtains back. The King woke, and sat up, remarking that it was very chilly.

'There can be no hope of our being taken off to that ship,' said Wilmot, with the calm of despair.

'None,' agreed Charles, stretching his cramped limbs. 'The tide no longer serves. What o'clock is it?'

'A little past five, sir. I wish to God Wyndham would come!'

'Is anyone stirring?' enquired Charles. 'My belly cries out for breakfast.'

'What tale must I tell the hostess? Our shot was paid, and we should have been gone hours ago.'

'Tell her the truth, that our plans miscarried. I must shave me,' he added, passing a hand over his chin.

Wilmot looked at him in exasperation. 'Shave! Good God, sir, to what good end?'

The King's eyes derided him. 'To the end that I may kiss my pretty bride. Go get me some hot water and soap, Harry.'

He was engaged in scraping the last of the black stubble from his chin when Wyndham arrived at the inn. The Colonel was looking haggard from anxiety, and lack of sleep. He paid no heed to Wilmot's flood of questions, but addressed himself to the King, saying in a worried tone: 'Sire, I know not what may be the reason, but no boat came ashore, though we waited until the last possible moment.'

The King dried his wet face with a napkin, and began to wipe his razor. 'Am I betrayed, think you?'

'I know not, sir, but I have sent Henry Peters to Lyme, to seek out Ellesdon, and discover from him why the master sent not his boat to take you off, and whether he may yet do so. There is one circumstance which puzzles me not a little.

As I was coming away from the appointed rendezvous, I saw a man who, I am ready to swear, was Limbry himself, walking by the shore. He recognized me, I am sure, but made no sign, his footsteps being dogged by three women. I thought it best to appear not to know him. My mind much misgives me, sire. I would you were gone from this place!'

'Ay, the dice are not falling towards me this bout,' remarked the King. 'Yet I believe I should do ill to run away without awaiting word from Ellesdon.'

'No, no!' Wilmot said urgently. 'He may have betrayed you, sir! What do you know of him, when all is said?'

The King glanced towards him, a sardonic gleam in his eye. 'Content you, Harry: I know when a man is honest. I will wait for a message from him. Let that ostler take your horse to the stithy to be shod, and do you bespeak breakfast for us all.'

Wilmot went out of the room. When he came back, he was looking pale, and spoke in an agitated manner. 'Sire, the ostler cannot be found. He is not in the stables, neither is he in his bed. He has gone off somewhere: I think, to lay information against you.'

'My dear Harry, why should you think so?'

'I have spoken to the hostess. She told me the man is a canting Puritan, a soldier of one Captain Macey's troop, which is quartered at Lyme.'

This intelligence, coupled with an account of the ostler's behaviour overnight, made Wyndham feel very uneasy. He began to think the King would do well to depart from Charmouth without loss of time, and when Charles enquired where he was to go, replied: 'To Trent, sir, if you will. There at least you may lie in safety while we make new plans for your sailing to France.'

The King was silent, turning it over in his mind. He still had not spoken when Mistress Wade came bustling into the parlour to set the table for breakfast. She seemed to have no suspicion of his being other than an eloping bridegroom, and after exclaiming at the mischance which kept him still kicking his heels in her house, she informed Wilmot that the ostler had come back to the inn, and was to take his horse to the stithy immediately.

These tidings made the King decide to remain where he was until Peters returned from Lyme.

Peters reached the inn an hour later, and, coming directly into the parlour, fixed his serious eyes on the King's face, and said bluntly: 'My liege, Captain Ellesdon bade me give you this message instantly, that he is astonished at the failure of our scheme, and greatly disquieted in mind. He begs your Majesty will not tarry any longer here, but instead will make all speed away from Charmouth. He bade me assure your Majesty that he is wholly ignorant of the cause of the master's breaking faith, unless it be that by reason of the great Fair that was held in Lyme yesterday, he was not able to command his mariners out of the ale-houses to work. He is going about speedily to search into it, but bade me very earnestly to conjure your Majesty not to stay longer here, but to ride away from Lyme, to Bridport.'

'I thank God for sage counsel!' Wilmot said. 'Sir, you must go at once, and Wyndham with you! I will keep Peters with me here until we learn from Ellesdon what he has discovered, and will then ride after you to Bridport.'

The King nodded. Colonel Wyndham interposed to suggest that he should stay behind in Wilmot's place, but this my lord would not permit, deeming the Colonel, from his knowledge of the country, the better guide. Peters went out to saddle the horses, the ostler being gone with Wilmot's nag to the stithy; and in a very few minutes the Royal party was riding up the steep, cobbled street, Juliana seated behind the King upon the double-gelding, and Wyndham going ahead to lead the way.

Wilmot watched the horses out of sight, and then turned to Peters. 'Now, my man, as soon as my horse is shod, you and I will go to Lyme, and confer a little with Captain Ellesdon!'

## CHAPTER XV

# 'TAKE NOTICE OF HIM TO BE
# A TALL MAN'

THE ostler, when he slipped out of the inn that morning, had betaken himself to the house of one Mr Westley, who was minister of Charmouth. Here he was confronted by the parson's housekeeper, a rigid Puritan, who, upon his demanding speech with her master, told him austerely that Mr Westley was at his morning-exercise, and might not be disturbed. She lifted a warning hand, and the ostler could plainly hear the minister's voice issuing from his study.

He hesitated. There was no thought in his mind of disturbing the parson at his prayers, for he was himself a pious man, and the sound of a man wrestling so fluently with his own soul filled him with too much respect to allow of his intruding worldly matters into such a godly communion. The question that teased him was whether he should wait for Mr Westley to end his prayers, and so – for he knew the parson delighted in long prayers – lose his chance of a reward from the mysterious strangers at the Queen's Head when they should take horse. Gentlemen of Mr Payne's stamp could nearly always be counted upon to leave a gold piece in the bottom of the stirrup-cup, and gold pieces were not easily come by in such hard times as these.

Half-formed suspicions were revolving mazily in his head. He had heard stories of noble gentlemen escaping from their enemies in female disguise, and he wondered whether the lady at the inn were perhaps a man. It did not seem very likely. He had not been able to look closely at her, but his memory retained a brief vision of a full, exquisitely rounded bosom, and of a dimpled cheek too smooth ever to have known the touch of a razor. Her waiting-man's great height, and swarthy complexion, had startled him, and an unbidden thought had crossed his mind that the King of Scots was a tall, black-avised man. But he had not seriously supposed that the waiting-man could be the King of Scots. It was only when he saw how private the strange visitors kept themselves, and had been told that their horses were to remain saddled and bridled all night, that he began to wonder whether his mistress might not be housing Malignants, who were fugitives from the great battle which had lately been fought at Worcester. He had thought it odd that one who was dressed as a serving-man should spend the night with his master in the parlour, but when he had set his eye to the keyhole he had seen the big, black man lounging in a chair by the table, and he had not been able to believe that anyone so easy, so shabby, and so tanned of face could be the King. Yet, some uneasiness still possessing his mind, he had presently resolved to lay the matter before the parson. With the housekeeper's severe eyes upon him, and the prosaic daylight making the night's mysteries seem unreal, doubt shook him. He remembered that one of the horses must be taken to be re-shod, and thought he might lose more than the visitors' reward if his mistress should discover him to be absent from his post. He muttered something about coming again presently, and turned away from the minister's house.

Mistress Wade rated him shrilly when he entered the inn's stableyard, and told him to take the horse with the cast shoe to the stithy at once. He asked her who these guests of hers might be, but she was in a morning-humour, and bade him mind his own business. He went off up the street, leading my Lord Wilmot's horse, secure in the conviction that the party could not leave the inn until he returned.

The blacksmith's forge was situated some little distance up the street. Hammet, the smith, was working on a broken ploughshare, but when he learned that a gentleman's horse had been brought to him to be shod, he laid the ploughshare aside, and bade the ostler lead the horse in. His experienced eye at once recognized breed; he said with casual interest: 'You'll be having noble guests at the Queen's Head, seemingly.'

'I know not that,' the ostler replied cautiously.

'This is a right good horse.'

'Ay, that's so.'

The smith picked up one of the gelding's feet, and studied the size and shape of the shoe. 'Come from the north, have they?' he remarked. He walked round the horse, and inspected each of his hooves in turn. 'I'll tell you something about this nag, friend,' he offered.

'What's that?'

'Why, he has but three shoes, and they were set in three different counties, and one of them in Worcestershire.'

The ostler stared at him. Behind the mistrustful blankness in his eyes, his brain felt hot with suspicion. He said slowly: 'Nay, how can you tell that?'

'Trust me, I can tell!' replied the smith, moving away to the back of the forge. ' 'Tis the way the nails are, look you.'

'Worcestershire,' repeated the ostler, ruminating. 'They kept themselves mightily private. One of them is a powerful big fellow.'

Hammet began to blow up his furnace. 'Ay?' he said absently.

The ostler watched him for a minute or two in silence. His suspicion fought in his head with caution, and the dread of making himself a laughing-stock. 'They do say as he's a serving-man. He came riding before a wench. He's a queer-seeming fellow, black as a coal. 'Tother's a fat gentleman, and high-stomached. I was wondering —' He paused, looking at the smith in a little indecision.

Hammet thrust a horseshoe into the heart of the furnace with his long tongs. 'Private, was they?' he said.

'Ay. Like as if they was afeard to be seen. The big 'un has on a plain grey suit, withouten any lace. He has his hair cut short, like a countryman.'

The smith turned his head; the ostler saw that the stolidity of his countenance was disturbed by some sudden glimmer of comprehension. 'Was you to Lyme Fair yesterday?'

'Nay, I don't hold with such. There's a mort of ungodliness at fairs.'

'Ay, that's true.' The smith relapsed into silence, inaccessible behind his own consuming thoughts. He began to hammer the red-hot shoe, seeking refuge from conversation in the clanging din he set up.

The two men eyed one another furtively. A new suspicion was seething in the ostler's brain. He made no attempt to shout above the noise of hammering, but stood in fretting silence until the shoe was nailed in place. He paid for the work, and led the horse back to the inn. A vague intuition quickened his brain: he felt that he had been able to read Hammet's mind; the vision of a great reward filled his eyes. When he discovered that only one of the party of three travellers still remained at the inn, his heart bounded sickeningly in his breast. He pocketed the coin that was tossed to him, and went in at once to his mistress to get her leave for his going to Lyme. She grumbled, but, having no visitors in the house, told him he might go, and a good riddance to him for a lazy gadabout.

The smith, meanwhile, had scarcely waited until the ostler was out of sight before he strode off at a smart pace towards the minister's house. *A queer-seeming fellow, black as a coal . . . a powerful big fellow . . . his hair cut short, like a countryman's.* The recollected phrases stirred him to a greedy excitement. He had heard a proclamation read in Lyme upon the previous day. Its words echoed in his head: *Take notice of him to be a tall man, above two yards high, his hair a deep brown near to black, and has been, as we hear, cut off since the destruction of his army at Worcester, so that it is not very long.* When it had presently been nailed to a wall, he had spelled the proclamation out laboriously, not dreaming it might concern him. *Whosoever shall apprehend the person of the said Charles Stewart, and shall bring or cause him to be brought to the Council of State, shall have given and bestowed on him or them as a Reward for such service, the sum of One Thousand pounds.*

The thought of such a fortune made his senses stagger, and his breath come quickly and painfully. He hurried on up the hill.

When he reached the minister's house, Mr Westley had just come to the end of his morning-exercise, and received him without delay. He was a spare, thin-faced zealot. He saw nothing absurd in the tale the smith unfolded, but listened to it attentively, and offered to go with him at once to the inn. No thought of earthly reward tainted his zeal, as Hammet knew. He would have scorned to touch a groat of the blood-money offered for Charles Stewart's capture, but he saw a heavenly crown in the business, being, as my Lord of Newcastle would have said, Bible mad.

Together, the two men strode down the steep, cobbled street to the inn at its foot.

Mistress Wade met them at the door, and gave the minister a civil good-day. Her gaze flickered over the blacksmith, and he drew back a little, for she was a redoubtable woman, with a scathing tongue in her head.

Westley went breezily to work with her. 'Why, how now, Margaret?' he said. 'So you are a maid-of-honour now, as I learn!'

Her eyes narrowed mistrustfully; she set her arms akimbo, thrusting out her chin. 'What mean you by that, Master Parson?'

'Why,' said Westley, watching her like a cat, 'Charles Stewart lay last night at your house, and kissed you at his departure, so that now you can't but be a maid-of-honour!'

She remembered the kiss, and the smile that had gone with it. She had slapped the tall man's tanned face, yet fondly, feeling a stir in her blood which belonged to youth, not to staid middle-age. She flew suddenly into one of her quick rages; her palm itched to slap in good earnest, but she controlled the impulse. 'Strangers lay in my house last night. I know not who they were, nor would not demean myself to pry into what's no concern of mine.'

'Was there not a tall, dark man amongst them?' he persisted.

'And what if there was?'

'Woman, that was none other than the traitor, Charles Stewart!'

She was for a moment stupefied. She thought of the big, lusty young man who had lounged at his ease in her parlour, and had girdled her round the waist with a strong arm, and kissed her, and murmured a lewd jest in her ear. She had been a rollicking lover in her time, bringing to the business something of the same carnal, carefree zest which she had seen in the King's eyes, and felt, with a faint, delightful shudder of the flesh, in the touch of his hand, and the strength of his hard, male body. None of your prim, shy, newfangled lovers, that young man, but a rare, hot lad that would take his pleasure gaily, as nature meant him to do, and waste little time between meeting and bedding.

Suddenly her rage flared up, as she looked at Westley's thin form, his cold eyes, and pale, tight mouth. There was not as much red blood in all his undesiring body as there was in one of that wicked, black lad's fingers, she thought scornfully. She shook her fist at him. 'So it was the King that lay in my house, was it?' she said. 'You scurvy, ill-conditioned rogue! You'll go about to bring me and my house into trouble, will you? But let me tell you this, Master Parson: if I thought it was the King, I would think the better of my lips all the days of my life! And so, Master Parson, get you out of my house, or else I'll get those that shall kick you out!'

He recoiled, as much from the glimpse he caught of some primitive excitation of feeling in her as from the menace of her clenched fist, and flashing eyes. The skirt of his black gown was all but nipped between the door and the wall, as she slammed the stout oak in his face. He turned round, and saw the blacksmith hiding a grin behind his hand. He said with what dignity he could muster: 'The mouth of a strange woman is a deep pit. We will go to the magistrate.'

The smith agreed, but rather doubtfully, seeing the reward for the King's apprehension begin to slip out of his reach. He thought if the magistrates were to move in the matter they would very likely claim the reward. His footsteps lagged a little behind Westley's impetuous strides; he remembered his deserted forge, and half-wished that he had not led the parson on this chase.

When they reached Commer, the home of Mr Butler, the nearest Justice of the Peace, they were taken, after a short delay, into a parlour where the squire awaited them.

He was a short, stout man, rather red of face, and inclined

to be choleric. He was, by conviction, a Parliamentarian, but although he was forced to suffer them, he had little liking for the rigid Puritans. He favoured Westley with a bow, but when his full blue eyes alighted on Hammet, they started alarmingly, and caused the smith to shift his feet upon the polished floor-boards, and to look all ways but one.

'Ha!' said Mr Butler, straddling before his empty hearth, his hands linked behind his back.

This exclamation much discomposed the smith. He was sorry now that he had come with the minister, for it was plain that the squire thought he had taken a liberty.

Westley said: 'I have come to you, sir, with this honest man, whom you may know for Hammet, the blacksmith —'

'I know him very well,' interrupted Butler, still keeping Hammet under the stare of his fierce blue eyes. 'I marvel that he can leave his trade to come a-visiting upon a working-day!'

'He is a godly man that puts the Lord's business before earthly gain,' said Westley.

A snort escaped the squire. He hoped he was a decent, God-fearing man, but he held that the place for parsons was in Church, and not in his house at ten o'clock on a Tuesday morning. 'Does he so?' he said, with grim scepticism. 'Be short with me, parson, if you please, for I am not one who has the whole day to waste!'

'I will be short, yea, and pungent too! Sir, the traitor Charles Stewart lay in Charmouth yester-night, and left the town a bare hour since!'

The squire was no King's man, but Westley's words awoke in his breast a feeling of strong dislike. He would not have a Stewart back upon the throne; no, but, God's death, it made him mad to hear a scurvy rogue of a canting, low-bred, sour-faced, upstart minister speak so insolently of his betters! He opened his mouth to deliver a blistering reproof, and shut it again, as he recollected the changed times, and his own professed politics. He drew breath, and rapped out: 'What's this? The King at Charmouth? Pho! Pho, I say! Don't believe it!'

'Friend, recount to Mr Butler what the ostler told you!'

Westley commanded.

Butler whipped round upon the blacksmith. 'Ha, so this is your work, is it? Out with it, then! Let me have this story which brings you from your trade at such a time.'

The blacksmith moistened his lips, and began haltingly to recount all that the ostler had told him. The story sounded lame, even to his own ears, and when he came to the end of it he was not much surprised to find the squire incredulous.

''Sbud!' said the squire, spitting out the expletive. 'I marvel at you, parson, by God, I do! What a-pox ails you to come plaguing me with this parcel of nonsense? May a party of travellers not be private in an inn without your smelling them out to be Cavaliers? Are there not tall, dark men in England but the King? What the devil brings you to me?'

Westley looked sternly at him. 'I believe that man to have been Charles Stewart. I see your duty plain, sir, and am come to put you in the way of it.'

'Plain, d'ye say? So do not I, by God! Come be brief: what would you have me do?'

'I would have you issue a warrant to raise the country for the apprehension of the traitor!'

The squire gave a short crack of laughter. 'Make a laughing-stock of yourself if you please, Master Parson: you shall not make one of me!'

'Do I understand that you will not do it, sir?' cried Westley.

'Look 'ee, parson, I know my duty, and am a good Parliament-man, and so you know! But to set up a commotion for the sake of a tall fellow whom a silly ostler tells the blacksmith (which is as big a fool as himself!) is the King, comes not within any duty of mine. If you had seen the man, and suspicioned it was the King, I would have lent an ear, maybe. Upon such testimony as I have, I'll issue no warrant. And so I bid you good-day!'

'You will rue this, squire,' Westley said in a sombre tone.

The squire waved him away. He did not believe that the King had been at Charmouth; he did not want to believe it. He was the King's professed enemy, wholehearted for the

Parliament; but he thought it would be better, since, unhappily, the King had not been killed at Worcester, that he should escape out of England. For himself, he heartily wished him dead, but he wanted to have no hand in bringing him to the block. It was an ill business, chopping off a King's head. He had not been in London upon that bleak January day, two years and more ago, but he knew those that had. Yes, an ill business: when the King's head had been lifted up by the locks for the crowd to see, from behind the thick hedge of pikes a groan had gone up that had turned a man's guts to water. He knew one, not a squeamish fellow either, who had vomited where he stood. Queer, that, for he had been no King's man. Well, what was done could not be undone: but better not to have it done again. The squire pushed the thought of the tall, dark visitor to Charmouth out of his mind. After all, there was little chance of the fellow's having been Charles Stewart.

The squire's disbelief, after a few minutes' reflection, began to have some effect upon Mr Westley. He feared that his zeal had led him into too precipitate action. On their way back to the village, Hammet talked of the bills posted up in Lyme, and the suspicion that Hammet and the ostler both had allowed their greed to make them leap to unproved conclusions took strong possession of his mind. He answered the smith shortly, and presently parted from him, going back to his own house to pray for guidance.

The ostler, meanwhile, was half-way to Lyme, trudging along the coast-road. He wondered what signal reward would be bestowed upon the man who brought about the King's capture. Gold filled his vision: enough gold to keep a man in comfort all the days of his life, he thought. No more soldiering for him; no more sweating in a red-coat through a long day's march; no more easing of his rump in the saddle after hours of riding at a jog-trot under a blistering sun; no more work in stables, ekeing out a bare living. He would buy him a good alehouse, or maybe an inn, the kind of inn that gentlemen patronized, and get him a comfortable wench to wife, besides; and live soft at last.

When he reached Lyme, he saw one of the bills, nailed up

in the market-place. He could not read it, being an un-lettered man, but seeing a group of citizens standing by it, he asked to have it explained to him. When this was done, by a stout man in a frieze coat, he felt the palms of his hands grow suddenly damp with starting beads of sweat. A power-ful excitement made him tremble; he found himself repeat-ing: 'One thousand pounds, one thousand pounds!'

'Ay, that's what it says. Three thousand broad pieces for him as lays hands on Charles Stewart! Well, it's a mort of money, sure enough.'

'Or lays information!' the ostler said anxiously. 'That's what it says, don't it?'

'Ay, that's it. But who's to know him, that's what I'd like to know? Ah, there's many an honest poor man as would be glad of the money, but it's not the likes of us as'll see the colour of one of them broad pieces.'

'I dunno as I'd want to, not when all's said,' remarked an elderly man on the outskirts of the group. 'Seems to me it wouldn't be well come-by. King or no King, it's blood-money. I warrant it'll do no good to them as gets it.'

'There ain't no King nowadays. You read what it says there: the traitor Charles Stewart: that's what it says. It's different, laying your hands on a traitor.'

'Maybe it is. I wouldn't like to have it on my conscience, though. Seems to me, I wouldn't sleep easy in my bed, knowing as I'd sold a man to his death.'

'But he's an enemy to the Commonwealth!' protested the stout man. 'You'm talking like you was a King's man, Henry Daw!'

'Well, I ain't. All I say is, let the Commonwealth catch the King, if it can, and make an end of him, without putting dirty work on to honest men's shoulders. Blood-money's blood-money, say what you will.'

The ostler edged his way out of the group. He thought how the fools would stare, and that cavilling fellow change his tune to one of envy, if it were known that he had it in his power to earn the promised reward.

He hurried up the street, walking so fast that the sweat from his body made his clothes stick uncomfortably to his skin. An obscure dread that someone might be before him with his news drove him on; when he reached the guardhouse he was red with heat, and panting so that he had to pause to get his breath before he could speak intelligibly.

The troopers lounging about the door were unimpressed by the urgency of his demand to have speech with their Captain. His greed made him over-cunning; he would not divulge the nature of his business; and when he said that it was a matter touching the State, he was laughed at so loudly that he lost his temper, and hit out at the nearest grinning face.

The arrival of the sergeant put an end to the brawl before it was fairly started. Discipline in Cromwell's New Model was a real thing, not lightly set aside. The troopers looked abashed, mumbled excuses, and drew off; and the ostler, trying to straighten his tumbled clothes, and smooth his shock of short hair, repeated, but in humbler accents, his request to speak with the Captain.

He was told that he must wait; and left to kick his heels in the guard-room for half an hour. His body grew cool again; his rough shirt now felt clammy, and had rucked itself up round his stomach; he was thirsty, too: the vision of gold had no power to ease his bodily discomforts.

When he was taken to the Captain, his brief excitement had waned; he was sullen, for he thought if the Captain heeded his story it would be for his own ends. There was little a poor man could do, if one of his betters chose to claim the reward that properly belonged to him. He scowled when the Captain sharply asked him his business, and said: 'If I tell what I know, shall I have the money?'

Captain Macey subjected him to a hard stare: 'What money, rogue?'

He jerked his thumb over his shoulder. 'For taking up Charles Stewart.'

Macey started up out of his chair, with his square blunt-fingered hands resting heavily on the table before him. 'What's this? Speak out, man!'

'Shall I have the money?' the ostler repeated obstinately.

'We'll see that! If you speak not what you know, I'll loosen your tongue with a stirrup-leather!'

The ostler shot him a rancorous look. But he had guessed how it would be, after all. 'He was in Charmouth last night, at the Queen's Head.'

Macey's baldrick was slung over the back of his chair; he reached a hand behind him, fumbling for it. 'Are you certain of this? Is he there now?'

'Nay, but I know where he's gone to.'

'Where, then? What proof have you it was Charles Stewart?'

'Nay, I know not that, but he was a great, black fellow, with his hair cut short, like a countryman's. But he spoke very fair, mince-mouthed, like he was town-bred, and kept himself private all night in the parlour.'

A flush rose to Macey's cheeks; he put on his baldrick, saying: 'It may well be! It may well be! Where is he gone, fellow? Who is of his company?'

'Bridport way. He's gone with a wench riding behind him, but the fat lord set out for Lyme.'

'When was this?'

'It was early, eight o'clock, may be.'

'Fool, do you know it is already noon?' shouted the Captain.

He did not wait for an answer, but snatched his hat from a chair, and went stamping out with a great jingle of spurs, and clatter of his scabbard swinging against the lintel of the door. The ostler ran after him, calling out: 'Shall I have the money?' He was thrust out of the way; the Captain was shouting orders to his troop. In a very few minutes horses' hooves were clattering on the cobbles outside the guard-room. The ostler, elbowed this way and that, ran into the street in time to see the Captain hoist himself into his saddle. ''Twas me brought the news!' he cried despairingly.

'If I catch up with the traitor you shall not lose by it,' called Macey, over his shoulder, as the troop began to move forward.

The ostler stood still, glowering after him. If I get a hundred broad pieces out of the whole three thousand, it'll be the most I'll see, he thought. Then he remembered that he was a poor man, and had told his tale without witnesses, and he thought ten pieces would be as much as Macey would give him, or maybe five.

## CHAPTER XVI

## 'I KNOW WE ARE PURSUED'

THE King's little party, climbing the hill out of Charmouth, rode at an easy pace towards Bridport, following the direct road through Morecamblake and Chideock. Juliana, who had not been able to sleep much during the night's interminable hours, but had tossed restlessly from side to side in the smothering billows of a feather-bed, was looking pale and a little heavy-eyed; but once the last straggling cottages of Charmouth had been left behind, she began to revive, her spirits, which had been oppressed by the night's alarms, lifting with all the resilience of youthful optimism. She roused the King by her chatter from the fit of taciturnity which had descended upon him. Not very sensitive to impression, nor fully appreciative of the danger the King stood in while he remained in England, she did not feel the melancholy that made him silent, and was not altogether sorry to know that he meant to return to Trent. The Colonel, more perceptive than she, felt the King's melancholy like a wound in his own flesh. He made a movement with his hand as though to check Juliana's prattle. She did not notice it; he saw then that the King was not teased by his cousin, but rather diverted, and he held his peace. By the time they had covered the seven miles that lay between Charmouth and the larger town of Bridport, the sombre look had vanished from the King's eyes, and he had begun to discuss with the Colonel new plans for his escape.

Upon their entering Bridport, the most unwelcome sight of a red-coat met their eyes. A few hundred yards farther on they saw more red-coats, and discovered, to the Colonel's dismay, that the town swarmed with them.

Juliana was afraid of night, of stuffy inns and guttering candles, and the moan of the wind under the door; danger in the form of prosaic soldiers lounging through sun-lit streets, looking homely, and rather hot in their muddied uniforms, quickened her nerves only to a fright that had in it something of enjoyment. She stole her arms round the King's waist, murmuring: 'Ah, this is what I was promised! This is as it was when you rode with Mrs Jane Lane! I can be as brave as she, I promise you!'

'And we will follow the same course as we did then, and press on boldly,' said the King.

'There can be no turning back,' the Colonel muttered. His knee jostled the King's as the horses pressed close in the narrow street. 'Ride on, sir, straight through the town!'

'Nay, what would become of my lord?' said the King. 'I have appointed him to meet me here.'

'You will not stop here!' The Colonel's voice sharpened with horror.

'Yea, and at the best inn,' returned the King. 'I shall not be looked for in this host of rebels.'

A frightened giggle broke from Juliana. The Colonel said: 'It is true, but you have set my knees shaking. What will you do?'

'I shall play the serving-man. When we reach a decent inn, go you in with Juliana, and bespeak dinner in a private parlour. I will join you there when I have seen the horses safely bestowed.'

'O God, my mouth feels as though a sow had farrowed in it!' said the Colonel, with the humour of despair.

'Craven!'

'I am indeed. Do you see that building ahead? It is the Town Hall, and the George Inn lies directly opposite it. Stop there, if only the best will do for you, sir.'

The street was so crowded that they made slow progress. There were soldiers everywhere, and when they presently reached the George Inn, they found its courtyard full of troopers, and their horses.

The Colonel dismounted, and lifted Juliana down from

the pillion. He dared not linger by the King, though every instinct urged him not to leave him alone amongst his enemies. He said: 'See to the nags, and don't stand gossiping, Will, do you hear me?'

'Yes, master,' said the King, taking his horse's bridle from him. 'I'll be with you straight.'

The Colonel led Juliana into the inn; her hand trembled a little in his, and might have trembled more had she waited to watch the King's behaviour.

Beyond a cursory glance or two, and a few nudges of the elbow to call a friend's attention to Juliana's ripe charms, no one paid much heed to the arrival of the King's party. A serving-man – even an uncommonly tall serving-man – excited no interest, nor did any honest red-coat perceive a need to make room for such an one to pass. The King led his horses forward, thrusting a rude passage through a group of soldiers, who stood with their tunics unbuttoned, and tankards in their hands.

He was cursed, but good-naturedly. 'Pox on you, where be you going?'

'You son of a bitch, who gave you leave to elbow your betters?'

'The toe of my boot to your arse if you jostle me, my lad!'

'None of your holiday-terms to me!' retorted the King, entering whole-heartedly into the spirit of this. 'Odd rot me, what times we live in when a pack of herring-gutted militiamen think they may lord it over a gentleman's groom!'

'Militia-men!' A red-headed trooper made a grab at his arm. 'Ditch-begotten knave! We'm of the New Model!'

'God save the mark!' The King made Wyndham's horse rear, and the red-headed man was forced back a pace. 'Come from Worcester fight, I warrant! Ay, ay, and swollen with sinful pride because ye beat a parcel of dirty Scots there. Let be: there's no Scots to beat here, and soldiers in peace are like chimneys in summer.'

'Marry, there's a saucy rogue for you!' remarked one of the troopers admiringly. 'Take care your tongue cuts not your throat, friend!'

The King winked broadly, and thrust forward with his

horses. The troopers let him pass, and he reached the stable-door without incurring any worse harm than a parting insult hurled after him by the red-headed man.

He led the horses into the cool of the stable, and called to an ostler who was sweeping out one of the stalls. The man came forward as the King began to loosen the saddle-girths. 'Good-day to you: do ye stay long?' he enquired.

'Nay, to bait only.'

The King lifted the saddle off his horse's back as he spoke. Over it his eyes encountered the ostler's, which had narrowed suddenly in an effort of memory. 'Sure sir, I know your face?' the ostler said.

'Ay, do you?' replied the King coolly. 'Where do you live?'

'Well, I'm only come here of late. I was born in Exeter, and was used to work at an inn there, hard by Mr Potter's, which is a merchant of the town. Seems to me it was in Exeter I saw you, but I misremember when that would have been.' He frowned, knuckling his chin, and evidently searching his memory more strictly.

The name of Potter had made the King's eyelids flicker, as though a lightning-flash had suddenly startled him. He remembered that he had lain at Potter's house once, during his father's life-time. He said quickly, hoping to put an end to the ostler's mind-searchings: 'Oh, certainly you have seen me, then, at Mr Potter's, for I served him a good while, above a year.'

Apparently the ostler's memory was still recalcitrant, for he replied in a satisfied tone: 'Oh, then I remember you as a boy there. That'll be it.'

'That'll be it,' agreed the King, beginning to rub his horse down with a wisp of hay, and so contriving to keep his head bent.

'You'll not recall me,' said the ostler. 'My name's Horton: what's yours?'

'Will Jackson.'

The ostler shook his head. 'Nay, I can't seem to remember that name. However, it don't signify. We must drink a pot of beer together, friend.'

'I would, with all my heart, but I must go wait on my master.'

'No haste: you can bide long enough to drink a toast.'

'Nay, I dare not for my life. My master's an ill man to cross. We're on our way to London, but I'll tell you what: upon our return we'll have that pot together, and so I promise you.'

With this the ostler seemed to be content, and the King managed to escape from him, and to make his way across the yard to the inn-door. The soldiers were still lounging in the yard. One of them called out: 'Here's our dunghill cockerel come back to crow again! You'd best take heed lest the sergeant clap his eyes on that bay horse you was leading. We're in need of likely nags, look'ee!'

'Sing small, sing small, friend!' said the King, with a disarming grin. 'There's peace since Worcester fight, and they say though war makes thieves peace hangs 'em.'

A shout of laughter greeted this sally. The King leaned his shoulders against the door-post and enquired of a stout fellow with button-black eyes what his regiment might be.

'Colonel Haynes's, bound for Jersey for to subdue the Malignants there,' replied the stout man.

'Jersey,' repeated the King in a queer voice.

'Ay, if so be we don't get drowned at sea. They do say as the place fair stinks with Malignants. The Scots King lived there, not so long since.'

'Not he, he lived in furrin parts,' interrupted a long-nosed man, wiping his mouth on the back of his hand.

'So 'tis furrin. He were there! 'Tis an island.'

'Go teach your father to get children! He were not there. He were in France.'

The noise of contentious voices, more and more of them joining in the foolish argument, sounded to the King's dreaming ears like the roar of the sea. His eyes stared straight before him, seeing not red faces, and red-coats, but an island that was dear to him, and a yacht that skimmed the waters of a great bay, with the sun on her sails, and an eager boy who knew nothing of bitterness or of defeat at her helm. The vision faded; he caught his underlip between his teeth, and turned and went into the inn, while the soldiers still argued amongst themselves.

He found Colonel Wyndham and Juliana in an upper parlour overlooking the street. At sight of him, the Colonel heaved a sigh of relief, and exclaimed, 'Thank God!'

A smile flickered in the King's eyes. 'My poor Frank! I am still at large. What's for dinner?'

'Mutton, sir!' said Juliana, uncovering the dish. 'Trust me to remember your Majesty's favourite meat!'

'If you love me, no Majesties, good sweetheart! There are upwards of a thousand rebels quartered in this town.'

'It's the most damnable mischance of this whole ill-starred journey!' said the Colonel, setting a chair for him at the table. 'What do they here, sir?'

'They are upon their way to Jersey,' replied the King curtly.

His tone seemed to indicate that he did not wish to discuss the matter; he began to eat his meat, washing it down with sack.

Before he had finished his dinner, the Colonel, who all the time stood in the window, keeping a watch on the street, saw Lord Wilmot ride past with Henry Peters behind him. My lord cast a searching glance up at the windows of the George Inn; his eyes encountered Wyndham's for a moment, but he rode on, making no sign.

The Colonel turned away from the window to tell the King that my lord had entered the town. The King nodded, and went on eating. It was not long before Henry Peters presented himself at the George, bringing an urgent message from Wilmot that the King should join him without loss of time at a smaller inn, at the eastern end of the town.

Having by this time finished his dinner, Charles made no objection, but got up, remarking that since an ostler knew his face, and some fifteen or twenty red-coats had stared him out of countenance, it might be as well for him discreetly to leave the town.

Horton was not in the stables when he arrived there. Another ostler, untroubled by memories, helped him to saddle the horses; and in a few minutes the little party had left the George, and was proceeding sedately along the street in the wake of Henry Peters.

Wilmot, who was awaiting them at a mean little ale-house on the fringe of the town, no sooner caught sight of them approaching than he hurriedly paid his shot, and went out to mount his horse, which he had kept ready saddled in the hen-ridden yard. The King had scarcely had time to draw rein before my lord joined him. Wasting no time on ceremony, he said: 'Go on, sir, go on! For God's sake, will you make haste out of this town?'

'No,' said the King. 'I will not. I shall ride at a decent sober pace, and so, by God, shall you, Harry!'

'Well, I did not mean you to go at a gallop!' said Wilmot crossly. 'Though how you can be so crazed as to linger in a town swarming with rebels is a matter passing my poor comprehension! When I saw Wyndham's face at that window I thought I must have taken leave of my senses!'

'Why, then, you should be thankful to discover that you are still in possession of them,' said the King in a rallying tone.

'You should have stopped him!' Wilmot flung at the Colonel.

'I think I would have done so had I known the trick of it,' Wyndham agreed. 'But he was right, my lord: no one would look for him in the midst of a whole regiment of rebels.'

'I would we had never ventured into this infernal country!' Wilmot said. 'It's the most damnably disaffected part I ever was in! Also, I greatly fear that I have been recognized, for a man doffed his hat to me as I rode into the town. And who the devil is Reymes? Someone called "Good-day, Reymes," to me in Lyme.'

The Colonel turned in the saddle to look at him. 'Odds-blood, did they so? Why, yes, I suppose you might be mistaken for him, for you have a great look of him. He is a native of Dorsetshire, and married my wife's sister. It will serve very well! We will pass you off as Colonel Bullen Reymes.'

'I see not the least need for me to change my name yet

again,' snapped his lordship. 'It does nothing but confuse me.'

The King, who was riding a few paces ahead, looked over his shoulder. 'I wish you had stayed to dine at that alehouse, Harry, so it might have put you in a better humour. Leave disputing with Frank, and tell me what news you learnt in Lyme.'

'The worst!' said Wilmot. 'There are bills posted up in the town, offering a thousand pounds for your capture, and describing you so exactly that it is plain some traitorous dog has been talking. The rebels even know your hair has been cut short!'

'That would be the Cornet who told them I was at White-Ladies,' remarked the King. 'But what of Ellesdon? Did you have speech with him?'

'Yes, I had speech with him, but he knew no more than I did myself. It was not his doing that the boat came not to take you off: I never saw a man more shocked! He went immediately to seek out the master of the vessel, and came back presently to me with a tale so fantastic you would scarcely credit it! It seems Limbry had no thought but of keeping faith with us, and so hailed out his vessel to the mouth of the Cob, as we heard. But going back to his house to put up his necessaries, his wife took a suspicion into her head that he was engaged upon some dangerous, secret business, and importuned him so unceasingly to tell her why he was going to sea before his time, and with no goods aboard, that at last the fool confessed that Ellesdon had provided him with a freight which would be more worth to him than a shipful of goods. Whereupon the woman, having been at Lyme Fair, and heard the proclamation read there, at once suspected him of having engaged himself to assist – not, indeed, yourself, sir, but some of your party, to escape out of England. Limbry had not the wit to deny it, and the end of it was that the woman and her daughters bolted him into his chamber for fear he should risk his life upon the business. He durst raise no outcry, for if he did so the woman swore she would go instantly to the Captain of a rebel troop quartered in Lyme, and inform against him and Ellesdon both, and so make sure of a reward for herself and her daughters. There, sir, is the history of last night's misadventure in a nutshell!'

His voice was edged with exasperation, but the King thought the tale so comical that he burst out laughing.

'Yes, yes, you may laugh, my dear sir, but all our hope of setting sail from Lyme is at an end!' said Wilmot. 'Moreover, if that woman was ready to betray her own husband we don't know but what she may even now have informed the rebels of our having been at Charmouth. Nor can I banish the remembrance of that prying knave of an ostler from my mind. I consider that you stand in no small danger, sir.'

'So do I,' said the Colonel unexpectedly. 'Call me craven, if you like, sir, but I find myself wanting all the time to look behind me. If you will be guided by me, we will leave the highway, and thrust up through the country to Broad Windsor, where there is an inn which is owned by an honest fellow, always heartily well-disposed towards your cause. You may lie in his house tonight in safety, I think, for we shall not reach Trent, that's sure.'

'My dear Frank, do with me as you will: I am entirely in your hands,' said the King.

Juliana, who had been oddly silent for some time, looked at the Colonel with eyes that were darkened by fear. '*You* feel that?' she said in a hushed voice. 'Someone coming behind us? Oh, make haste, make haste, for I have *known* that we are pursued all the way from Bridport!'

'Fie, a sick dream!' the King said.

'Sick dream or sober truth, make haste off the highway we will!' said Wilmot, spurring forward to ride abreast of the King. 'Come, sir! Your person is a little too precious to be hazarded so wantonly. We are upon the road to Dorchester, and too many travellers have already seen you.'

The King quickened his pace, but remarked placidly: 'But they have not known me, I think. How far must we go before we leave the highway, Frank?'

'Less than a quarter of a mile now, sir.'

They rode on at a trot, the King taking care to keep his

hat pulled low over his brow. There were many travellers on the road, and one or two whom he recognized as old acquaintances, but no one paid much heed to his party, and within a short space of time the Colonel had led him off the highway into a narrow lane, which wandered northwards, twisting erratically between steep, hedge-crowned banks.

Here they encountered no one but an occasional farm labourer, plodding along with his dog at his heels. For once, my Lord Wilmot forbore to complain of the roughness of the track, or of the stench arising from the deep miry pits, full of water, that lay in their path, and made their progress necessarily slow. The more impassible the track became, the more content he grew, for he believed that if the pursuit was up, the King's enemies would be more likely to follow the highway to Dorchester than to scour every lane and cart-track that diverged from it.

He was right. Half an hour after the King had ridden quietly out of Bridport, Captain Macey's troop galloped into the town at a breakneck pace that sent the townspeople scuttling for safety into the kennels at the side of the street. Macey drew rein at the George, and flung himself down from his foaming, trembling horse. He stamped into the yard, his spurs clanking on the cobbles, and set up a shout for the innkeeper. A little crowd began to gather about him, open-mouthed and pop-eyed. 'A tall, black man with his hair cut short! Has any seen a big fellow pass this way? A big, black fellow above two yards high?'

As might have been expected, so sudden a question was unproductive of anything but blank looks. By the time it had been repeated twice, with gathering emphasis, the inn-keeper and two ostlers had joined the group. 'A tall black fellow?' said the innkeeper. 'What would you be wanting with such an one, master?'

The Captain shot out a hand and grabbed him by his doublet. 'You fool, have you set eyes on him? It is the traitor, Charles Stewart!'

The innkeeper let his jaw sag, but recovered himself in a moment, replying: 'Well, I ain't seen him, that's certain. The only tall, black fellow I've seen was nowt but a serving-man as come here with his master and a lady, a while back.'

Macey shook him to and fro. 'Dunderhead! That was none other than the traitor himself! Where is he? Speak, can't you?'

'I'll speak fast enough if you'll give over shaking me!' responded the host, pardonably incensed. 'I dunno where he be, and what's more he didn't look like no King to me, no, nor talk like one, neither!'

'The King?' Horton repeated stupidly. 'The King?' He clapped a hand to his brow. 'It were the King! And him standing there as bold as Beauchamp! Lordy, Lordy!'

His words passed unheeded, the other ostler, smelling a reward in the business, having pressed forward to tell Captain Macey that he had heard the gentleman that was with the King say that they were off to meet someone at another inn in the town. He had seen the party ride towards the Dorchester road, a bare half hour before.

Macey waited for no more, but strode back to his troop, shouting orders to them to separate at once, and scour every inn and alehouse in the town.

The search, which occupied some time, yielded nothing but the information that a tall, dark man had been seen riding before a lady on the Dorchester road.

'Making for Portsmouth!' Macey exclaimed. 'Sound the recall, sergeant! We shall overtake him yet!'

The troop swept out of the town as stormily as it had entered it, and settled down to ride in close formation along the highway to Dorchester.

The King's party, meanwhile in happy ignorance of his hairbreadth escape, rode gently on to Broad Windsor.

It was some hours before they reached the village, for it lay about six miles to the north-west of Bridport and they had ridden eastward out of the town and had to work their way back by circuitous lanes, and over ground too rough to allow of their horses going at a faster pace than a walk. Several times one or other of them would put a foot wrong, and come near to foundering in some unsuspectedly deep pool of standing water, but no accident befell, and the party rode into Broad Windsor towards the end of the afternoon, tired, hungry, and plentifully splashed with mud.

The George was the only inn so small a village could boast. It was a pleasant half-timbered building with a thatched roof, standing upon the village street, with a cluster of outhouses in its rear. As soon as the travellers drew rein, the host came out to welcome them. He was a big, muscular man, with a merry twinkle in his eye. He recognized Colonel Wyndham at once, and strode up to his knee, a beaming smile irradiating his countenance. 'Good-day to you, sir, and to you, my lady! And a right good day it is that brings your honour to my house! 'Deed, and it's a weary while since you rode this way, sir! Will it be a stoup of ale for your honour, or a jug of sack, or maybe some good canary that I have in the cellar?'

The Colonel set his hand on the man's shoulder, looking down into his frank upturned face. 'More than that, Rhys Jones, if I can trust you!'

The landlord's smile widened. 'Your honour knows full well you can trust me.'

'I count upon it. For I have strayed farther afield than our new masters permit, look you, and I want none to spy upon me here and tell the magistrates I was beyond the limits of my parole upon such-and-such a night.'

Rhys Jones nodded. 'Trust me, none shall come nigh you, sir. Do you mean to lie in my house this night?'

'Ay, and my brother-in-law with me, who is in a like case. You know him, I think.'

The host turned his head, looking at Wilmot with a slightly puckered brow. His frown cleared, he exclaimed: 'Why, surely! If it is not Colonel Bullen Reymes of Waddon! You be most heartily welcome, sir. And my lady too!'

'My cousin, Mrs Coningsby,' explained the Colonel. 'Have you two chambers where we may lie hid from prying eyes? My groom must come in with us, for he is as well known in these parts as myself.'

'Ay, surely! I have two chambers at the top of the house, if your honour must be private. But they are attics, and not fit! Will ye not condescend to my best chambers? It will be a hardy rogue that comes spying in my house!'

'Nay, we will lie in your attics and be well content,' replied the Colonel, dismounting and going to lift Juliana down from her pillion. 'But see you provide us with a good supper, my friend, for we are all of us hungry!'

'Have no fear, your honour! My wife's a redoubtable cook, I warrant you! Come you in, you know well my whole house is at your orders!'

'Have you other guests putting up in the house, fellow?' demanded Wilmot.

'Nay, sir, there'll be none but yourselves that I know of, save them as comes to the taproom.'

'Nevertheless, we will still sleep in your attics,' said the Colonel. 'I'll run no risk of being clapped up in prison again.'

'Pretty times we live in, when a gentleman like your honour's prisoned for serving his rightful King!' said Jones, with a snort. 'But there! Talking pays no toll, as they say. The rebels may be up today, but wait till the King comes to his own again, and we'll see whether the first laugh's better than the last smile!'

The King had swung himself out of the saddle; he said abruptly: 'Do you look to see him come to his own, friend?'

Jones glanced towards him curiously. 'Every honest man does. He'll do it, mark me! He's a likely lad, by what I hear. See if he don't spit in his hand, and take better hold!'

The King's teeth gleamed white in the brown of his face. 'Oddsfish, I hope he may!'

Wilmot trod heavily on his foot. The King remembered that he was a groom, and rolled an apologetic eye towards his lordship.

'Will,' said the Colonel, 'when you have helped Peters to stable the nags, you may come up to my chamber. Lead us in, Jones, lead us in!'

The attics at the top of the house were sparsely furnished and rather stuffy, but as they were approached by way of a secluded backstair, even Wilmot agreed that they would serve their purpose better than the guest-chambers on the lower floor. The landlord bustled about, bringing up chairs, a finer coverlet for Juliana's bed, a cloth to spread over the scarred table, and some good wax candles in place of the common lamps that were ordinarily kindled there. On one of his journeys in search of more suitable furnishings, he encountered the King, who had come in from feeding the horses, and at once thrust a chair into his hands, bidding him make himself useful, and carry it up for his master to sit upon.

The King obeyed him meekly enough, but when he appeared in the doorway of one of the attics with his burden, Wilmot started towards him with a shocked exclamation: 'My dear master! Good God, what next will you be obliged to do! There, let me take it!'

'Who trod on my foot?' demanded the King, setting the chair down by the table. 'It is my turn to tread on yours now, methinks.'

'When we are alone there is no need for you to demean yourself, sir, nor for us to forget your state!'

'Harry, only you could remember my state in such surroundings as these!' said the King.

'Alas, they are very mean, but I dare not let you have better!'

'I care less for my surroundings than for the capon I am to have for my supper. Frank, this fellow, Jones, is a man after my own heart. Spit in my hand, and take better hold! Why, so I will, God willing! I swear there is not one amongst my Councillors has given me better advice.'

Wyndham smiled, but lifted a finger to his lips. Footsteps, and the rustle of a dress, were to be heard on the narrow stairs; some one scratched softly on the door; and, a moment later, lifted the latch, and peeped into the attic. My Lord Wilmot found himself looking into a plump, comely face that was wreathed in smiles. Mistress Jones came in, her eyes beaming with tender welcome, her cheeks blushing a little. 'Eh, love, they told me 'twas yourself come to trouble my poor heart!' she said. 'Ay, ay, I see 'tis indeed you! But alack the day, you've grown stout, Bullen my dear!'

My lord cast one anguished glance towards Colonel Wyndham, standing by the dormer-window with the King, but finding that there was no help to be got from that quarter, swallowed and stood his ground. He saw the hostess advancing towards him with her hands held out, and mechanically stretched his own to meet her. Mistress Jones walked straight into his arms, and embraced him. The brown hand resting on Wyndham's arm suddenly closed on it, gripping it quite painfully. The King began to shake.

'Beshrew your heart, what make you here, my dove?' demanded the Mistress Jones, scolding fondly. 'Have you come to undo me, you naughty rogue? Nay, nay, I'm a sober woman these days, and have got me a good husband besides. Eh, but I'd scarce have known you, for all the sweet traffic we had together!'

My lord, clasping this warm armful to his bosom, said manfully: 'I may have grown older, but I swear you have not altered a whit!'

'Ay, you had ever a false, cozening tongue!' she said. 'Go to, I know you for a very knave! And so they clapped you into prison, them dirty Puritans? I would I had the hanging of them!' She began to stroke his cheek, crooning over him, and murmuring so many reminders and endearments that the Colonel thought it prudent to stand between her and the King, for fear of her catching sight of his face.

My lord, finding no help for it, kept his eyes averted from the two by the window, and did his best to respond adequately to the caresses lavished upon him. He was delivered from the lady presently by her recalling to mind the capons twisting on spits in the kitchen. Promising to return anon, she went away, with a blush and a wink at the Colonel, and a provocative look cast over her shoulder at my lord.

'Harry, oh Harry!' gasped the King. 'Alack the day, you've grown stout, my dear!'

My lord wiped his brow with a handkerchief. 'God's death, Wyndham, you might have warned me what manner of fellow this brother-in-law of yours is!' he exclaimed.

'On my soul, I knew no more than you!' replied the Colonel, in a quivering voice. 'Thank God, Juliana is in the other attic! This tale must not come to my wife's ears! Bullen! Oh, if I roast him not for this! Truly, if the bed could tell all it knows, it would put many to the blush!'

The sound of laughter brought Juliana into the room, but tease as she would neither the King nor her cousin would disclose the cause of their mirth. Lord Wilmot, who knew enough of his Royal master to be sure that his discomfiture would not be soon forgotten, smiled in a world-weary fashion, and suggested that they would all of them be better employed in discussing new plans for the King's escape than in holding their sides over lewd jests.

'We are agreed, I suppose, that there can be now no question of our setting sail from Lyme or Charmouth,' he said.

This reminder sobered the Colonel at least. 'None indeed, my lord. We must look farther afield. I have been thinking, since Lyme has failed, Southampton must now be the likeliest port.'

'Good God, Wyndham, his Majesty cannot ride all the way to Southampton without certain help there! Where might he stay? Is there any loyal subject there who will serve him?'

'That I do not know, nor was it in my mind that his Majesty should venture his person upon this chance. All must be in good train before he again leaves the safety of my house. If I were not upon my parole, I would go myself to seek out a vessel, but you know well I dare not, my lord. It must be for you to do.'

Wilmot's strained eyes flashed. 'For what other purpose do you think that I accompany his Majesty? I will do my possible, rest assured. Yet, though you talk so glibly of riding to Southampton, Colonel, I would have you know that to charter a vessel for such a cause, in a town where I have no acquaintance, is more easily spoken of than done!'

'Indeed, my lord, I am well aware of it,' Wyndham replied. 'If you will listen to me, I have a plan that I hope may answer.'

The King who had seated himself by the table, stretched out his hand to Wilmot with a faint smile, but addressed the Colonel. 'Let me hear your plan, Frank.'

'I would have my lord go without loss of time to Salisbury, sir, taking with him Henry Peters, who will lead him to the King's Head, which is a hostelry very well known to many of us Royalists. I dare not say how many of us have not lain there in time of trouble. When my lord is safely housed there, I would have Peters seek out a kinsman of mine that resides in the Close, one John Coventry, whom your Majesty may know.'

'A son of Lord Coventry?' asked the King.

'The eldest by a second marriage, sir. I need not tell you that he is very well disposed towards you. Indeed, I would stake my honour on his hazarding his life in your service. With his assistance, I do think that my lord need not despair of finding the means to transport your Majesty to France.'

The King's hold on my lord's delicate hand tightened. 'Will you go, Harry?'

Wilmot looked down at him, his mouth twisting a little wryly. 'Do you think I will not, my dear?'

'No.'

Wilmot lifted his hand and kissed it. 'Anywhere for your sake!' he said, under his breath.

### CHAPTER XVII

## A VERY HOT CONFLICT

Rhys Jones carried his guests' supper to the attic with his own hands. The darkness was setting in, and the candles had been lit some time earlier. An appetizing smell of roast capon escaped from the big covered-dish; Rhys Jones bustled about, wiping the trenchers with a napkin, placing bottles of sack upon the table, and trimming the candles. He promised himself the pleasure of waiting upon the company, and the Colonel had only just assured him that the supposed groom would perform that office, when a noise in the street startled them all, and sent the innkeeper to the window to peer down into the dusk.

'I know not what this may mean,' he remarked. 'It sounds

to me like there was a rare mob coming down the road. I'd best get me downstairs, your honour.'

'Ay, do so,' said the Colonel. 'And if they should be Parliament-men, take care you do not disclose my presence here tonight!'

'Trust me, master, there's none shall get so much as a sniff of your honour!'

The King, who had been standing behind the Colonel's chair, pulled up a stool as soon as the innkeeper had left the room, and sat down. He saw that Juliana was looking rather frightened, and smiled reassuringly at her. 'We do not know yet that these newcomers are searching for me, good sweetheart,' he said, with a gleam of amusement. 'You know, you and my lord are well-matched, for you are for ever starting at shadows.'

'The truth is, sir, that we are not blessed with your hardihood,' remarked the Colonel, who had gone over to the window, and was trying to obtain a glimpse of the street.

'My dear Frank, custom breeds contempt. It is three weeks now since I fled from Worcester, and I suppose I have never been out of danger once during all that time.'

'I think God has you in His care, sir.'

'Why, yes,' agreed the King. 'I begin to think so too. Leave looking out of the window, and come to your supper before it is cold. I don't doubt but that our friend Jones will soon bring us tidings who these visitors may be.'

It was not the innkeeper, however, but his wife who presently came up the attic stairs. She was out of breath from the climb, and stayed only long enough to tell the company that the men who had come to the inn were rebel soldiers, brought by the Parish Constable, to be quartered for the night.

'No less than forty of the rogues!' she panted. 'Eh, I shall be hard put to it to find enough for such a pack of wolves.' She saw Wilmot's face of consternation, and smiled at him. 'Nay, now, don't you be fretting, my dear! They'll not find you, no, nor your friends neither! If I know aught of soldiers, they'll all be as drunk as wheelbarrows come midnight.'

The King laughed. 'Fie, are they not godly men?'

'Soldiers are soldiers all the world over,' she retorted. 'As for these, I would I had the sorting of them. Godly! Oh, ay, mighty godly to come roistering into a decent house with their drabs behind them – saving your presence, mistress!'

She dropped an apologetic curtsey to Juliana, and whisked herself downstairs again.

My Lord Wilmot's eyes met Wyndham's across the table. 'Have you any more fine plans, Colonel?' he enquired with ironic civility. 'No doubt you will now tell me how to extricate his Majesty from this trap?'

The King wiped his fingers on his napkin. 'Peace, Harry! There is nothing any of you can do to extricate me."

Wilmot got up, thrusting back his chair. 'If they should take it into their heads to come up to this room —'

'You are alarming my pretty bride,' said the King.

Juliana gave a gasp. 'No, sir! Indeed, I am not afraid.'

'Why, that is well!'

Wyndham said in a shaken voice: 'I have led you from danger to danger, sir. Before God —'

'Before God, Frank, I acquit you of blame.'

'You are generous, sir. But if any harm should befall you, think you I could acquit myself?'

The King yawned.

Wilmot said in a mollified tone: 'There is no blame, but only hideous mischance. Yet that woman spoke truly when she said that soldiers are soldiers all the world over. I will admit that I have encountered some plaquily pious ones in my day, but I think, from the sounds we hear, that these are not of their number.'

The noise that rose from below did indeed seem to be rather boisterous than godly. During the ensuing half-hour it swelled appreciably in volume; and when the strains of a catch being lustily sung reached Wilmot's ears, he drew a long breath of satisfaction and said: 'Excellent! When the liquor's in the song will out. Mrs Juliana may seek her bed without misgiving.'

Juliana looked imploringly at her cousin, but he told her that she could do no good by forgoing a night's sleep, and bade her make her curtsey and be off into the adjoining attic.

She pouted, but obeyed him. She had not been gone many minutes before Rhys Jones came into the room with a bottle of wine under each arm, and a broad grin on his face. 'All's well, your honour!' he told the Colonel. 'But I made bold to bring up a couple more bottles, for dang me if those pesky rogues below won't drink the cellar dry, the way they've settled down to it.'

'What make they here?' demanded the Colonel. 'Where do they come from?'

'There's no saying where they come from, master, but I can tell you where they be bound for and that's Guernsey. They're on the march to the coast, and all drinking confusion to the King's party. Let 'em! Words are but wind, and his blessed Majesty will take no harm along o' such.'

'Well said!' smiled the Colonel. He poured out a glass of sack and held it out. 'We'll have a health to his Majesty, and see which of the two toasts shall be the more potent. Drink up, man!'

Rhys Jones took the glass. 'Ay, so I will, and gladly! The King, God bless him, and may his enemies rot in hell!'

'Amen!' said the Colonel, and drank.

Rhys Jones set his glass down, and drew the back of his hand across his lips. He seemed to be on the point of making some observation when a fresh noise arose from the lower floor. It made my lord jump. 'God's death, what's that?' he exclaimed. 'It sounded like the scream of a wench!'

'The devil fly away with those rascally red-coats!' said Rhys Jones wrathfully. 'I'll be off down to 'em, with your good leave, my masters.'

He went out, but the screams, instead of abating, grew rather more piercing. The King cocked an intelligent eyebrow. 'I think, gentlemen,' he remarked, with a primness wholly belied by the laughter in his eyes. 'I *think* that is a case for the mid-wife.'

'Good God, sir, no!' said Wilmot, outraged.

But the King was right. Rhys Jones came back in a few minutes, torn between anger and amusement, and flung up his hands at the Colonel's look of enquiry. 'Oh, it's a rare gallimaufry, sir, and never a wink of sleep shall any of us get this night! It's one of them light-skirts, crying five loaves a penny in the kitchen. She'll be worse before she's better, but if there comes not a brawl out of the business, trust me never! What with my Nan scolding, and every one of them red-coats trying to clap the dish at the wrong man's door, there's a new Civil War starting below-stairs.'

'I wish the wench would make less noise over the business!' said his lordship, with a look of deep disgust.

'Short pleasure, long lament,' murmured the King.

Rhys Jones gathered the platters together into a pile. 'They say where there are women and geese there wants for no noise, and a true saying it is! But 'deed I'm mortified there should be such a commotion when I have noble company in the house!'

He bore off the pile of platters, encountering Juliana in the doorway, who had jumped up out of her bed, and come in some alarm, and a good deal of curiosity, to discover what the din downstairs betokened. The Colonel told her shortly that a woman was in labour, and commanded her to go back to bed, and draw the blanket over her head. She remarked with considerable asperity that it would take more than blankets to muffle such loud cries, but since she was young, and tired, and had slept little during the previous night, it was not long before her ears grew accustomed to the noise, and she dropped into a sleep from which not all the disturbances of that fantastic night had the power to rouse her.

There was a naked bed in the front attic, and the King was presently persuaded to lie down upon it. He lay with his hands linked behind his head, drowsily watching Wyndham and Lord Wilmot, who sat at the table with their heads close together. The murmur of their voices discussing plans for his escape made his heavy lids droop lower and lower over his eyes; he was sliding into sleep when the tramp of hasty footsteps in the street jerked him awake.

Wyndham jumped up and went over to the window, but could see nothing but a few lanterns bobbing along below him. These disappeared one after the other into the inn, and there arose almost immediately the unmistakable sounds of an altercation. To the three men, listening in the attic, it soon seemed as though a Civil War must indeed have broken out. The noise increased momently in volume; voices shouted unintelligible abuse: sundry thuds and crashes indicated the overturning of furniture; and more than one inebriated gentleman hurtled through the door of the inn, propelled by some unseen agency into the street. The courtesan's cries ceased when the racket in the tap-room was at its height, and a little later Mistress Jones came up to the attic, looking hot and dishevelled. She accepted a glass of wine from the supposed Colonel Bullen Reymes, and announced that she had delivered the drab of a lusty male child, but that the trouble was only just beginning.

'What, is the father still undiscovered?' asked Wyndham in some amusement. 'Has the wench nothing to say on that matter?'

'God save your honour, a woman must conceal what she knows not! That cockatrice below is as common as the highway, never doubt it! The brat will be cast on the Parish, if those eightpence-a-day soldiers get their way. They've set to brawling with the Parish officers, which came hot-foot as soon as they got wind of there being a wench in travail in the kitchen. For they want no bachelor's children dumped upon them to be a charge on the Parish, look you. The Lord knows what will be the end of it, for there's a-many below-stairs which has got a cup too much, and when the malt's above the water men will start fighting, no help for it.'

She soon went away, but with such a roguishly inviting look cast over her shoulder at Wilmot, that the King mocked him for being only half a man to sit in the dumps when such fair entertainment was offered him. 'After her, Harry! I swear it's a scurvy trick to take a man's name, and betray his reputation!'

'Oh no!' said Wilmot plaintively. 'Oh 'sdeath, sir, no! She has been eating largely of onions, as you would know if you had been obliged to fondle her!'

'Go to, you are too nice! I would she had cast her naughty eye in my way. A pox on this walnut juice which has made me so hideous that as merry a wench as any I have seen will not look twice upon me!'

'I thank God for it!' said Wilmot, with a little show of severity. 'Your affairs at this present are ill enough, without your making them worse by becoming entangled in a woman's toils, sir.'

'Eh, Harry, I never knew what a dull dog you could be until I took you with me upon my travels!' said Charles, pulling down the corners of his mouth.

'Nor I,' replied my lord, sighing. 'I would I knew how we may escape unseen from this house! Why that trollop belowstairs must needs choose this of all the hostelries in England for her lying-in is a matter passing my comprehension!'

'It seems my path is to be strewn with women in child-bed,' said the King idly. 'First it was Mrs Norton of Abbotsleigh, and now a red-coat's doxy. Oddsfish, what are they at now?'

This last remark was caused by a sudden recrudescence of noise coming from the taproom. It continued with occasional lulls until the early hours of the morning, when the disputants, too much fuddled with liquor to retain any very clear notion of the reason of their quarrel, gradually ceased from blows and arguments, and either staggered off to their homes, or fell asleep on the taproom floor.

To Wilmot's relief, Mrs Jones did not come up to the attic again, but her husband appeared from time to time to regale the company with accounts of the brawl's progress. By two o'clock he was able to report all quiet below, and to prophesy that the soldiers would not rouse up from their drunken sleep until an advanced hour of the morning. As for anyone amongst them having enough wit left in his head to suspect the presence of other guests in the inn, he begged Colonel Wyndham not to trouble his mind over such a contingency.

It was agreed that the King should leave the inn before any of the soldiers were stirring; he lay down on the bed again to snatch a few hours' sleep, and Wilmot and Colonel Wyndham, wrapped in their cloaks, dozed uncomfortably in two straight-backed chairs.

As soon as it was daylight, Rhys Jones carried up some beef and ale for his guests' breakfast. Henry Peters, who had slept peacefully over the stables, brought the horses to the door; and, while the red-coats still snored in their several quarters, the party mounted, and rode quietly out of the village.

Remembering that my lord's presence in his house had given rise to some unwelcome suspicions in Trent, Colonel Wyndham was determined not to let him return there with the King. It had been arranged between them, during the night's discussion, that my lord, having reached Salisbury, and, through the Honourable John Coventry's agency, set matters in train towards the King's escape, communication should be maintained with Trent by messengers and letters. The King had not got his cypher with him, but Wyndham proposed to give his own, which he used when writing to Coventry, to my lord. Partly to enable him to do this, and partly on account of my lord's flat refusal to go as far without Robert Swan to wait upon him, Wilmot did not set out with Peters towards Salisbury immediately, but rode with the King as far as Sherborne, in which town he proposed to await the arrival of Swan, with Wyndham's cypher.

When the moment of parting with Charles came, his heart misgave him. His too-vivid imagination pictured nightmarish contingencies, and had it not been for the impossibility of Wyndham's journeying as far from Trent as to Salisbury, he would have insisted on the Colonel's going there in his stead, and leaving him to guard the King. The tears sprang to his eyes as he kissed Charles's hand; he begged him to take good care of himself, and told the Colonel, with a little flash of jealousy, that he should hold him answerable for his master's safety.

Robert Swan arrived at the inn in Sherborne later in the day. He was able to report the King's safe return to Trent, but although he expressed a prim regret at the failure of the Charmouth plan, he was more shocked by the muddied condition of my lord's dress, which had not been changed since his leaving Trent, two days previously, than by the King's misadventures. He at once unpacked the portmanteau he had brought; laid out fresh linen; and stayed up long after his master had retired to bed, cleaning and ironing his doublet and breeches.

Henry Peters watched this activity with a tolerant but rather amused eye. 'A dainty gentleman, your master,' he observed. 'Does he set such store by his clothes that he cannot abide a speck of mud though he go in fear of his life?'

'My master,' replied Swan coldly, 'is a nobleman, and is used to go in velvet and lace. You are country-bred, I dare say, and do not understand the ways of us as have lived always in Courts.'

'No, faith, I don't understand 'em, nor want to. But I've lived next and nigh the King these last days, and never a murmur did I hear from him that his linen was foul, or his coat bemired.'

'His Majesty is above all, and may go as carelessly as he will,' said Swan in an expressionless voice.

'Careless? Ay, I warrant you! He's the man for my money: a right jolly lad is the Black Boy!'

Swan winced at this familiar way of speaking of Royalty. 'His Majesty is young and has mixed much with vulgar company. He will amend in time, yet I fear we must not look to see his father live again in him! Ah, there was a great and worshipful gentleman for you! I never saw him lose one jot of his majesty, no, not when his affairs were at their worst!'

'God save you, d'ye think none but yourself ever laid eyes on the old King? I saw him often, and I'll tell you this, friend: he played wily beguiled with his fortunes, but his son was not born when wit was scant. I'd lief as risk my life for the Black Boy, for he'll ever give you a smile and a thank you for what King Charles the Martyr would have taken for his right.'

Swan gave a sniff, but declined to argue the point. He folded up my lord's doublet, laid a clean lace-edged collar upon it, gave a final rub to his high boots, assured himself there was no hole in the fine stirrup-stockings, and went off to bed.

My lord set out early upon the following morning to ride

the thirty miles to Salisbury. He encountered no adventures upon the way, and after trotting along for some time in a mood of despondency, his spirits began to rise. He remembered that Dr Henchman, who was ever a staunch supporter of the King's Cause, was a Prebend of the Cathedral, and determined to take him into his confidence.

The sight of Salisbury spire in the distance seemed to him like a sign of hope. He spurred on faster, and was soon riding through the twisting, narrow streets in the direction of the Cathedral Close.

The King's Head was a tall, gabled house, standing just outside the Close, not far from St Anne's Gate. Immediately opposite to it, upon the other side of the street and within the Cathedral precincts, was a mansion built of mellow red brick, which, Peters informed my lord, was Mr Coventry's home.

Upon my lord's riding into the courtyard round which the King's Head was built, Hewett, the landlord, came out in person to receive him, and had no sooner exchanged half-a-dozen sentences with Peters, with whom he was well-acquainted, than he conveyed my lord into the house, and upstairs to an oak-panelled parlour upon the first floor. Here he lost no time in disclosing a secret place behind the panelling, which, he assured Wilmot, had never yet been discovered.

Thinking it wisest to keep his identity concealed, Wilmot described himself merely as a distressed Cavalier who was seeking the means to escape out of England, and was glad to find that Hewett showed no disposition to enquire further.

'You may lie safe in my house, sir,' he said. 'Indeed, your honour is not the first Royalist gentleman I have hidden here, for you must know I have been a King's man all my life, and mean to continue so to the day of my death.'

He went off at once to order his guest's dinner to be prepared, and my lord, with a sigh of thankfulness to find himself once again in civilized surroundings, sank down in a cushioned chair before the fire, and permitted Robert Swan to draw off his boots. By the time he had partaken of an excellent meal, and the covers had been withdrawn, Henry

Peters had contrived to get speech with Mr Coventry, and, confiding to him my lord's name and business, had conducted him across the street to the inn.

Upon his coming into the parlour and addressing my lord by name, Wilmot was at first inclined to be very much on his guard, but John Coventry's frank, easy manners, and evident good-will, soon allayed his qualms, and he opened to him the whole business, giving him so vivid an account of the King's movements during the three weeks that had elapsed since Worcester fight, that Coventry was held spellbound with wonder. In common with many others, he had feared that the King had indeed fallen in the battle, and his joy at learning that he was alive and quite overcame the horror he could not but feel at the thought of the hardships Charles had undergone. He was unable to give Wilmot, in return for his news, any tidings of the lords who had parted from the King at White-Ladies, but he said that there was no doubt that the Duke of Hamilton had died at Worcester.

Wilmot thought that the King's mind was prepared for this sad news; he sighed a little over it, but almost at once banished it from his thoughts, and asked Coventry what chance there was of the King's being able to set sail from Southampton.

Coventry replied that he hoped to arrange the business safely, even though he himself had no interest with any merchant or mariner in Southampton. After walking about the parlour for a few minutes, plunged in thought, he asked my lord's permission to despatch Henry Peters to summon one Colonel Robert Phelips to the inn. He assured Wilmot that he and his brother Edward were wholehearted for the King, both having fought upon his side in the late Wars; and Wilmot, after begging him very earnestly not to divulge his name or business to the Colonel, consented to his being brought to him.

It was not long before Peters brought Phelips to the King's Head, and conducted him upstairs to the private parlour. He was a thick-set man, obviously country-bred. His face was heavy-featured, with a craggy nose, slightly pouched eyes, and a fleshy jowl. He did not smile very readily, his habitual expression being one of stolid severity, but his regard was unwavering, and he looked to be honest as well as rather dull.

He entered the room with a firm tread and held out a square hand to Coventry, who had risen to greet him. He said in a deep, rough voice: 'Good-day to you, Mr Coventry. I'm told ye have need of my services. You're very welcome.'

'Great need,' Coventry replied, shaking him by the hand. 'But first I must present you to this gentleman, who was at Worcester fight, in the King's service, and is seeking to escape out of England.'

Phelips's eyes travelled past him to where Lord Wilmot stood with his back to the fire. They remained fixed on Wilmot's face in a hard unfathomable stare, but the Colonel uttered not a word.

Not knowing how much of the truth my lord meant to divulge, and thinking that he might prefer to be alone with the Colonel, Coventry said, with his pleasant smile: 'Well, I will go into the next room to take a pipe of tobacco with my good friend Hewett, and leave you together for a while.'

Colonel Phelips gave no sign of having heard this remark. He continued to stand stock-still in the middle of the floor, looking at Wilmot, who found his fixed gaze so embarrassing that he gave a forced laugh, and said with more bluntness than he had meant to use: 'Can you help a gentleman in distress out of the kingdom, sir?'

The Colonel replied after a chilling pause: 'I will give you the best directions I can, my lord, since it is a duty one gentleman owes another.'

Wilmot coloured, and said quickly: 'You know me, then?'

'Yes, my lord, I know you very well.'

'You do not seem much pleased to see me!' exclaimed Wilmot, the flush mounting in his cheeks.

'I am sorry to see any gentleman in such straits,' replied the Colonel, picking his words with laborious care.

'I am obliged to you! Yet this coldness, sir —'

'My lord,' interrupted the Colonel bluntly, 'I will be open with you, and tell you plainly that we have heard strange news here in the south, that your lordship was too warmly engaged with Argyll's faction in Scotland.'

Wilmot's eyes fell before the accusing stare that never wavered from his face. His beautiful, disdainful mouth quivered; he replied with a touch of hauteur: 'If you have heard that I was ever engaged with Argyll's faction to the prejudice of his Majesty's affairs, rumour has most grossly lied, sir! However, I do not mean to burden your ears with an account of our policies in Scotland. I have not heard that his Majesty is dissatisfied with my part in these.'

The Colonel responded only with a little ungainly bow. Wilmot glanced at him frowningly, and said, trying not to betray his discomfiture: 'Well, Colonel, I see that you are not minded to assist me. But since I am commanded to be free with you, I will tell you what I hope may make you more eager to engage upon the business, which is that your services are required not for myself, but for the King.'

He had the satisfaction of knowing that his words had shocked the Colonel out of his disapproving stolidity. The ruddy, rather pendulous cheeks blenched, and an expression of incredulity started to the heavy eyes. The Colonel repeated in an altered voice: 'The King?'

'Yes, sir, none other. He is at this present at Trent, in the house of Colonel Wyndham, with whom I think you are acquainted, and knows not how to dispose of himself. If you can provide for his security, he will commit himself to you, knowing you to be a gentleman of proved loyalty.'

'Ay, I hope I am so indeed, but alack, this is a fearful business to engage upon!' said Phelips, aghast. 'My fortune, my life, the fate of my whole family is the forfeit! I must consider well, my lord! Give me a moment, I beg of you! This is a promise not to be lightly given!'

'Not lightly, but readily, I hope!' Wilmot said sharply. 'I perceive that I have not made myself plain to you. His Majesty is in a situation of the direst necessity. By God's grace, he has so far escaped the fury of his enemies, but if those whom he deems his friends fail him in his extremity he must perish as his father did before him!'

'God forbid!' exclaimed Phelips, with a shudder. 'If this

heavy burden is laid upon my shoulders, do not doubt that I will bear it! Yet I should do less than my duty if I did not warn you most earnestly, my lord, that I consider the risk very great, as things now stand. If the King should miscarry in my hands, the sacrifice of my own life must bear testimony to my truth and sincerity. I see clearly that I have no choice but to do my possible for his Majesty. But I think your lordship does not appreciate the difficulties which must beset any one wishful of assisting the King.'

'*I* not appreciate them?' Wilmot said, with a blank look. 'My good sir, the truth is that you are far from appreciating the difficulties which have been overcome throughout these painful weeks!'

This remark led Phelips into making a more particular enquiry into the circumstances of the King's escape, and by the time Wilmot had favoured him with a brief relation of Charles's adventures, John Coventry had come back into the parlour, and was anxious to discover whether my lord had reached a good understanding with the Colonel.

Over a bottle of wine, various plans were made and rejected, it being finally agreed that the Colonel should ride to Southampton upon the following day to seek out a merchant of his acquaintance, who, he believed, might be able to hire a barque to carry the King to France. It was plain however, that he thought the chances of success slim. John Coventry, after taking counsel with my lord, decided to wait next day upon Dr Henchman, and to open the whole matter to him.

Henry Peters took his leave of Wilmot early the following morning, and rode back to Trent. He found the King in the best of spirits, and was given the Royal hand to kiss when he had related all that had passed at Salisbury.

'I thank you, I thank you: I think no King of England was ever so well served as I am,' said Charles, adding with a gleam of merriment: 'And I am sure none was ever so plaguey a burden to his poor subjects!'

## CHAPTER XVIII

## CÆSAR'S MAN

IF any apprehension possessed Colonel Wyndham's anxious mind that the King would be cast-down by the failure of his plans, this was soon banished. 'Indeed, I am very glad to find myself back at Trent!' Charles told Lady Wyndham.

'Ah, dear sir, I would I could say that I am glad to welcome you back,' she replied. 'But this mischance is a sad blow, and my mind much misgives me.'

'Oh, don't waste a thought on it!' he said. 'I am sure that I shall contrive to escape from my enemies soon or late. Meanwhile, I think myself very safe in this house, besides being exceedingly well-entertained.'

Neither Lady Wyndham nor her daughter-in-law could share this feeling of certainty, but they concealed their inward qualms, and applied themselves to the task of keeping the King's presence in the house a secret, and the King himself amused.

The return of Peters from Salisbury, with the news of Lord Wilmot's activities, made them hopeful of seeing the King soon set sail for France, but for two days nothing more was heard, a circumstance which made Colonel Wyndham feel uneasy enough to beg the King to permit him to take into their confidence a neighbour of his, one Captain Littleton, who, he believed, had interest with sea-faring men. The King seemed to be more interested in a new fashion of cooking eggs, which he said that he had discovered, but he gave a careless permission, with the result that Captain Littleton, immediately set off for Hampshire, to try certain sea-ports there.

The rumour of the King's having been at Charmouth spread swiftly over the county. Captain Macey, losing the trail at Dorchester, cast about in all directions to pick it up again, scouring the countryside for some miles north of the coast, and ransacking several known Royalists' houses. The first intelligence of this to reach Trent was brought by the Colonel's uncle, Sir Hugh Wyndham, who lived at Pilsdon, seven miles inland from Charmouth. He arrived at Trent, two days after the King's return, snorting with rage, and burning to recount his wrongs. The thought of the indignities to which he had been exposed overcame him to such a degree that it was not until he had drunk two glasses of burnt claret that he became calm enough to tell his woes to his nephew with any coherence. His house had been invaded by rebel soldiers, who had seized him, his lady, his daughters, and all his household, and had set a guard over them in the hall while they searched the house from loft to buttery. Not a chest, not a cupboard, not a trunk (he said) but had been ransacked; and, finally, discovering nothing, the rebels had taken a more particular view of their prisoners, had singled out the loveliest damsel in the bevy confronting them, and had declared that she was the King, disguised in female apparel.

At this point, Sir Hugh had recourse to the claret. 'The King!' he ejaculated. 'My daughter! I ask ye, Frank, why? Why? Tell me that!'

The Colonel replied with as good a countenance as he could: 'Nay, how should I know? It is the veriest nonsense!'

'Nonsense? Ay! For, from all I've heard, he is a big fellow, above two yards high, and ill-favoured to boot! But those rogues – those damned rascals, I say! – took my poor girl, and stripped her! Nothing else would satisfy them she was not the King! God's blood, if I have not their heads for it! It was only when they discovered their mistake with their own lewd eyes that they desisted from offering any further violence to my family! But look 'ee, Frank, it's in my mind you know somewhat to the purpose, and I'll thank ye to tell me this instant what's in the wind!'

The Colonel refilled his glass. 'Nay, uncle, indeed, I know nothing. It's some silly notion the rebels have taken into their heads, doubtless, and no rhyme or reason to it.'

Sir Hugh fixed him with an accusing stare: 'Ha, is it, indeed? Then tell me this! – why did William Ellesdon come to Pilsdon two days since, demanding of me, where was the King?'

The Colonel took a moment or two to reply to this, being somewhat aghast at Ellesdon's imprudence. He raised his eyes presently to Sir Hugh's plethoric face, and said: 'I cannot tell you that, sir, and do most earnestly entreat you to forget that Ellesdon ever came to your house.'

Sir Hugh's eyes started at him. 'By God, so you're mixed up in it indeed! You're a fool, Frank, d'ye hear me? You'll lose your head in the business, as sure as check! Don't tell me what you're about! I don't want to know! I'll have naught to do with it! And I'll thank 'ee not to drag me into your coils, for I'll none of 'em, no, nor for twenty kings!'

The Colonel hastened to reassure him, but it was plain that the poor man had taken fright. He could not be persuaded to dine at Trent House, but called for his horse within a very short time, and rode away very much as though he expected to be caught in the meshes of some plot if he remained another instant under his nephew's roof.

When the story of the ransacking of Pilsdon was recounted to the King, he tried to preserve a decorous demeanour, for Lady Wyndham and her daughter-in-law were both in the room, but the thought of a young and beautiful damsel's being unable to convince the rebel soldiers that she was not himself in disguise proved to be too much for his gravity. He bit his lip, but his shoulders shook; and when he unwisely caught the Colonel's eye, he gave one gasp, and broke into a roar of laughter.

Mrs Anne Wyndham blushed, and turned her face away, murmuring: 'Oh, how could even rebels make such a gross and rude mistake? How can you laugh, sir?'

He begged her pardon, but with such an impenitent gleam in his eye that she was a little shocked. The Colonel, although he thought the Pilsdon episode comical, was perturbed by it, and made it his business to see that the secret hiding-place in the house was prepared for the reception of the King at a moment's notice. No news reaching Trent of Captain Macey's activities, Mrs Wyndham went to the neighbouring town of Sherborne one day, ostensibly to do some marketing; and returned presently with a great many rumours to relate, and the alarming tidings that a troop of horse had entered the town, and was quartered there.

The only person to remain unmoved by this information was the King himself, who refused to believe that the troopers had come to Sherborne to search for him, but supposed instead that they were upon their way to the coast. As nothing more was heard of the troop, the Wyndhams were at last persuaded that he was right, and, much to his relief, relinquished a little of their anxious care.

'Look you, Frank, if you mean to wear that frown upon your face I must believe you do not relish having me for your guest,' said Charles in his lazy, provocative way.

The Colonel's thin cheeks flushed, but he answered only by a smile and a shake of his head. His mother laid a hand on the slim brown one resting on the arm of her chair. 'My liege, do you know that there is a price upon your head?' she asked.

'Why, yes, madam, but I think none will claim it.'

'But you cannot blame us for our anxiety, sir.' She smiled at him, for he had lifted her hand to his lips. 'Yes, yes, you may coax as you please, my dear, but you are too careless. I would we might hear that my lord has made safe arrangements to carry you overseas.'

But it was not until the 28th September, five days after the King's return to Trent, that a message came from my Lord Wilmot, at Salisbury. The day was a Sunday, and evening was drawing on, when a stout, heavy-jowled man, dressed in grey breeches and a weather-stained leather coat, rode up to the manor house and desired speech with Colonel Wyndham. He was led into the winter-parlour, and upon the Colonel's joining him there presently, he got up from a chair by the window, saying bluntly: 'Good day to ye! I should tell you I am Colonel Phelips: Colonel *Edward* Phelips, brother to Robert Phelips, whom ye know of.'

Wyndham started forward with his hand held out. 'You are very welcome, sir! You have come upon – a certain matter?'

'Ay,' responded Phelips. 'That's it. It's upon my brother's business I've come, or, to put it more properly, upon the King's business.' He added gruffly: 'The which I am right glad to do, though it is a fearful business, and very perilous. But I don't regard that.'

'Nor he,' said the Colonel, with a wry smile. 'I will take you to him, for I know well he will desire to hear your message himself.'

'Well,' said Phelips, giving a jerk to his leather coat, 'I should like to see his Majesty, for I have never done so; but I am no courtier, look ye, but a plain soldier, and if it's knee-bendings, and pretty speeches he's accustomed to, I shall maybe offend him, for I am not versed in such, and that is the truth.'

'You need not fear to offend him. He is very easy, and uses little ceremony,' replied Wyndham.

Colonel Phelips, whose stolid countenance admirably concealed some inward trepidation, followed him upstairs, straightening his lawn collar on the way, and trying to rub a mud-stain from the sleeve of his jacket. He hoped that he would acquit himself creditably, but set not much store by his host's reassuring words. It was not until he found himself looking up at a tall, ugly young man in a much plainer suit of clothes than his own, who held out a hand to him and smiled in the friendliest fashion, that his fears were banished. He went down heavily on to one knee to kiss the King's hand, saying awkwardly: 'Your Majesty!'

'Oh, get up, man, get up!' said Charles. 'Never kneel to me! What news do you bring me? How does my Lord Wilmot?'

'Well,' said Phelips, rising to his feet, 'I doubt he is in good health, but he can't be at ease, sir. Mr Coventry was telling me that he mislikes his quarters too much to bide in them, the King's Arms being a place well-known to harbour us Cavaliers. But I have a deal to tell your Majesty, and that's neither here nor there.'

'You shall tell me the whole presently, but first let me know this: shall I set sail for France?'

'Ay, your Majesty, God willing!'

'Why, that is excellent hearing, and calls for a glass of Frank Wyndham's sack!' declared the King.

By the time several glasses of sack had been drunk, and the King had been prevailed upon to recount some of his adventures, Colonel Phelips had become quite at his ease, and was able to tell his own tidings as fluently as a naturally silent man could be expected to do. His brother, Robert Phelips, had not found it an easy task to hire a barque in Southampton, but after sundry vicissitudes he had compounded with the master of a sailing-vessel to carry two gentlemen to France for the sum of forty pounds. This had been accomplished through the agency of a merchant of his acquaintance, and the final arrangements were to be made upon the following Wednesday, when Robert Phelips and the mariner were to meet at the Bear Inn, beyond the gates of Southampton.

'But I must tell your Majesty,' added Phelips, 'that my brother was forced to pay half the moneys to the master of the barque at once, the times being so chargeable, and no man willing to risk aught save he feel the gold already tickling his palm. And this my lord was not very pleased at, misdoubting the master's honesty, which, however, I will vouch for, knowing him to be a decent fellow, very well disposed towards your Majesty's cause.'

The Colonel interrupted to ask how soon the master would be ready to set sail, but beyond saying that no extraordinary delay was anticipated, Phelips could give him no definite answer, the date of sailing being one of the details to be agreed upon at the Bear Inn on Wednesday.

The King seemed to be satisfied with this. He enquired after my Lord Wilmot, which made Phelips scratch his head, and wrinkle his brow as he tried to render a coherent account of my lord's starts.

He left both the King and Wyndham with a hazy picture of my lord's calling upon first this loyal gentleman and then that to render all the assistance that lay in their power. Besides Mr John Coventry and old Dr Henchman, he seemed to have summoned to his side one Lawrence Hyde, of Hinton Daubnay, who was a cousin of the King's Chancellor, Sir Edward Hyde; and a Mr Henslow, of Burchant, who, in his turn, had drawn into the affair the Earl of Southampton.

'Oddsfish!' exclaimed the King, with a comical lift of one eyebrow, 'how many more heads does Harry mean to thrust into my noose?'

'Into your noose, sir?' repeated Phelips, bewildered and a little shocked.

'Why, yes,' said the King, 'for to render me the least assistance is to place your head in a noose, or to receive a bullet through your chest: I know not which.'

Upon the following morning, Colonel Phelips took leave of the King, and rode back to Salisbury. Since matters now seemed to be in good train for the King's escape out of the country, Colonel Wyndham thought it advisable to recall Captain Littleton from his search for a likely vessel at some other Hampshire port, and to depend upon the success of Robert Phelips's plans.

Two days later, on Wednesday, 1st October, another messenger arrived from Salisbury, in the person of one Mr John Selleck, who announced himself to be Mr Coventry's chaplain.

He was a nervous little man, very zealous to serve the King, but fearful of betraying him through some unwitting slip or carelessness. He told Colonel Wyndham that he had been at pains to approach Trent by devious and unfrequented roads; and spoke in hushed tones, as though he suspected spies to be lurking even in the Colonel's sunny parlour. He had brought with him a letter in cypher from My Lord Wilmot, which had been rolled into a pellet no bigger than a musket-ball. 'To be swallowed at need!' he whispered.

This made the King laugh, but Wyndham, spreading the paper out, applauded such caution, and said that if his Majesty desired to send a message back to my lord it should be in the same fashion. While he transcribed the cyphered letter, the King leaned on the back of his chair, looking over his shoulder. It was soon discovered that my lord wrote not from the King's Arms at Salisbury, but from Hinton Daubnay, the home of Mr Lawrence Hyde. 'And where the devil may that be?' demanded the King, raising his head, and bending an enquiring look upon the chaplain.

Mr Selleck made him a little bow. 'It is not far from Hambledon, if it please your Majesty, and near to the coast, about thirty miles from Salisbury, as I judge – to the south-east, of course.'

'Thirty miles from Salisbury!' said the King in lively astonishment. 'What in the name of all that's wonderful took my lord so far from Salisbury?'

'If it please your Majesty, my lord rode over to take counsel of Mr Hyde,' replied the chaplain, with another bow. 'My lord deemed his lodging in Salisbury too public, and Mr Hyde's house being very convenient, and Mr Hyde pressing him to remain there, he thought it wisest to be gone from Salisbury.'

'My lord in the toils of his own alarms!' said Wyndham scornfully, under his breath.

'Fie on you, Frank, you are too severe!' said the King, with a chuckle. He bent again over the Colonel's shoulder. 'What's this? I am to lodge where?'

'At Heale, the home of Mrs Hyde, a few miles north of Salisbury,' replied the Colonel, after wrestling with the cypher for a moment or two. 'Who is Mrs Hyde, Mr Selleck?'

'A very trustworthy gentlewoman, sir, I do assure you, the relict of Mr Lawrence Hyde of Heale.'

The King blinked. 'The relict? I thought my lord was the guest of Lawrence Hyde?'

'Oh no, your Majesty! That is to say, yes, your Majesty. But Mr Lawrence Hyde of Hinton Daubnay is but the nephew of Mr Lawrence Hyde, deceased, of Heale, being the son of Nicholas Hyde, that was the eighth son of Sir Lawrence Hyde, a worshipful knight that was an uncle of Sir Edward Hyde, your Majesty's Chancellor.'

The King flung up his hands. 'No more, I beseech you, Mr Selleck! You have named me three Lawrence Hydes already, and my poor head reels.'

'But two are deceased, your Majesty,' explained the chaplain helpfully.

'I give them thanks. What more, Frank?'

The Colonel, who had by this time finished his transcription, rose, and gave it to the King. Charles read it, remarking, when he came to the end: 'My lord is mighty urgent to convey me to Heale, it seems. I wish he had sent me tidings of the ship which is to carry me to France.' A cough from the chaplain made him look up. 'Well, Mr Selleck?'

'Mr Coventry, sir, charged me most particularly to assure your Majesty that he and Colonel Robert Phelips are hopeful of all being in train for your Majesty's setting sail next week. And this also I am commanded to say, that Mr Coventry thinks your Majesty may lie safe in Mrs Hyde's house, Heale being distant from Salisbury a few miles, and very secluded.'

'I think myself safe where I am,' replied the King, sitting down at the table, and picking up the Colonel's pen. 'Give me that cypher of yours, Frank: I must send Harry an answer to his letter. I shall tell him not to seek to remove me from your house until he is sure of a vessel to carry us both to France. I have had my fill of wandering about the country.'

The Colonel watched his hand travel across the paper, filling it with his bold characters, with the cypher numbers lavishly interspersed between the words. There was a little trouble in his face, and after a moment's reflection, he said slowly: 'I think my lord's advice is wise, sir. It is in my mind that too many people know of your presence in my house.'

The King paused, raising his head, and looking meditatively at the Colonel. 'Would any of them betray me, think you?'

'Nay, I think not, but how can I be sure of it, sir? When too many persons share a secret, it is a secret no longer, and I own to some uneasiness. Besides myself and my family, there are three servants who know you, and beyond the walls of this house there is my uncle, Sir Hugh Wyndham, who has a shrewd notion that you are here; Giles Strangways, who knows it for certain; and now Littleton, whom we sent into Hampshire. Furthermore, sir, the rebels had wind of your having been at Charmouth. It is my constant dread that at any moment they may descend upon us, and ransack the house in the hope of finding you here.'

The King sighed. 'Well, then, I must truss up my baggage and be off, I suppose; for I would not play the knave so grossly as to bring you into danger of your life, my poor Frank.'

'We are not talking of my life, dear sir, but of yours, which is of a little more importance, believe me!'

'Indeed, sir,' ventured the chaplain, 'it will be a strange thing if the vessel Colonel Phelips has hired does not take your Majesty off.'

'A great many strange things have befallen me in the past month, Mr Selleck,' said the King somewhat dryly.

The chaplain rode back to Salisbury upon the following morning, bearing the King's letter to my Lord Wilmot, and the King resigned himself to another period of waiting.

Since the Wyndhams dared not let him step outside the apartments set aside for his use, he was unable to stretch his legs, except by walking up and down his room, a restriction which he found hard to bear with patience. To his hosts, he was invariably cheerful, making light of his troubles; but when he was alone the weight upon his spirits occasionally overpowered him, and he would sit lost in gloom, unable to see any hope in the future. With a bitter curl to his lips, he reflected that those who begged him not to risk his person could scarcely have looked ahead to see what he saw so clearly: a life worn out in exile. At other times, the optimism of youth would assert itself, and he would think that although his twenty-one troubled years had culminated in the crushing defeat of Worcester, he would yet prevail over his enemies, and one day ascend his throne. Nothing of his hope or of his despair would he confide to his hosts. He had learned to keep his own counsel.

As the days dragged past, he began to fret inwardly at his inaction. No soldiers rode into Trent to search for him, but rumours of his presence in Somerset were flying about the countryside, and he knew that it was time he slipped out of the county. When, upon the following Sunday, the 5th October, Colonel Robert Phelips arrived at Trent, he greeted him with hardly restrained eagerness, and, giving him his hand, asked swiftly: 'What tidings do you bring me? Where is my lord?'

'Sir, I am come to beg you will remove to Heale,' replied Phelips.

'Well, and so I will, but what of the vessel which is to carry me to France?'

'Alas, sir, all our schemes have miscarried,' said Phelips heavily. 'When the master of that vessel came to the appointed place on Wednesday, it was but to tell me that his barque had been pressed to carry provisions to Blake's Fleet, which is lying before Jersey.' He saw the King's underlip begin to pout, and added: 'I would not have your Majesty despair, however. Dr Henchman has put my Lord Wilmot in the way of finding other means whereby you may escape out of England.'

'What are these means?'

'There is a very honest man living at Racton, by Chichester, sir, with whom Dr Henchman is well acquainted, and who, we believe, may help your Majesty to a ship at some port in Sussex. He is one Colonel George Gounter, who married Kate Hyde, that was sister to Lawrence Hyde of Heale. We believe him to have interest with sea-faring men, and my lord will go to Racton, with your Majesty's permission, to solicit his aid.'

'What security for his Majesty is there at Heale?' demanded Wyndham.

'The best, for Dr Henchman knows of a secret hiding-place there, which, in case of a surprise, his Majesty may enter into.'

'And how many more know of it?'

Colonel Phelips regarded him solidly. 'None but those who wish his Majesty well.'

'I like it not!' Wyndham said impulsively.

A faint smile warmed the King's eyes. 'Nay, but it was yourself told me I should go to Heale, Frank.'

'When I supposed you would be upon your journey to Southampton, sir! Does this Mrs Hyde know that it is the King who comes to her house?'

Colonel Phelips shook his head. 'She has been apprised

only of a distressed Cavalier's being wishful to find safe shelter for a space, Dr Henchman not choosing to take it upon himself to disclose the secret without his Majesty's leave. But I warrant her to be a very staunch, loyal gentlewoman, and one whom his Majesty may depend upon.' His rather dull eyes travelled from Wyndham's face to the King's. He added: 'If your Majesty will be pleased to go with me, it will be more convenient than your Majesty's remaining so far removed from Salisbury. I have made a particular study of the roads, and will engage to lead your Majesty by very safe ways.'

The King nodded. 'I will go with you.'

'I also will go,' said Wyndham grimly.

This, however, the King would not permit. 'If you have forgotten the limits of your parole, I have not,' he said.

'I care not *that* for my parole!' Wyndham exclaimed, with a scornful snap of his finger and thumb.

'You may not, but I have a better regard for my head,' said the King frankly. 'If you should be stopped upon the road and found to be beyond your boundaries, a pretty coil we should be in!'

The Colonel was silenced. Bitterness at his helplessness welled up in him; he turned away, and walked over to the window, his face clouded and his mind much troubled. Phelips said with rough sympathy: 'We live in noisome times, Colonel, but 'deed, it will not serve his Majesty to have you taken up in his company for a parole-breaker. There's another scheme which my lord is anxious his Majesty will comply with, but which is none of mine. He would have your Majesty ride before Mrs Juliana Coningsby, as you did before.'

'He is right,' said the Colonel briefly. 'She shall go.'

Phelips, who thought the presence of a female would be more likely to add to the dangers of the journey than to mitigate them, looked glum, and said in a reluctant tone: 'Well – and if his Majesty so desires!'

'You will take her, sir? You know it is a disguise which has served you better than any other. No one thinks to look closely at a groom riding before his lady!'

'I am willing,' the King replied, 'but I'll not have Juliana constrained to go with me, mind!'

Juliana, however, needed no persuasion. She was no sooner asked if she would ride pillion again behind the King, than she jumped up out of her chair, clapping her hands together, and exclaiming that there was nothing in the world she would like better.

It was decided that the King should leave Trent upon the following morning, and that Henry Peters should accompany the party, for the purpose of escorting Juliana home again from Salisbury, where she was to part from the King. Once more Charles bade farewell to the Wyndhams, bestowing upon the elder lady so fond an embrace that tears sprang to her eyes, and trickled down the cheeks he kissed. 'My dear boy – my blessèd liege!' she whispered.

'Nay, I beseech you! Let it be *my dear boy*!' he said. 'Indeed, I like it better.'

'God keep you safe!' she said, with a catch in her voice. 'Go now, but if these new schemes they have made for you should miscarry, give me your promise that you will come back to Trent!'

'Madam, you have my word that I will do so, yet I hope not to serve you so scurvy a trick. Why, what a guest have I been, who came to spend a couple of days in your house, and remained for nineteen! I swear you are well rid of me.'

She shook her head, clasping him in her arms once more before she could bear to let him go. He turned from her to her son, grasping both the Colonel's hand in his. 'Frank, I cannot thank you as I would, but I shall never forget. God be with you, my friend, and when next we meet, may it be at Whitehall, and I your host!'

He bowed over Mrs Wyndham's hand with a grace startlingly at variance with his rough clothes, and cropped hair, and in another few minutes was gone.

'I am more fortunate than my cousin, for I am still in your company,' murmured Juliana, behind his shoulder.

'Do you count that good fortune, sweetheart? I had thought the good fortune was all upon my side.'

'I shall not know how to support life when I come back to

Trent,' she said disconsolately. 'Oh, it will be so flat and weary!'

He laughed. 'Why, I think you flatter me! Or were you ambitious to play the heroine while I skulked in the secret place?'

She smiled, but said thoughtfully: 'Mrs Jane Lane wept when she left us, and I wondered at her.'

'Did she?' The image of Jane's sweet, grave face glimmered before his mind's eye. He remembered the steadfast look she had, and the cool touch of her lips on his. He hoped she was safe at Bentley Hall, and suddenly felt impatient with the pretty, childish creature riding behind him. He turned his head towards Phelips, and began to ask him about the way they were to follow.

Phelips had studied it to some purpose, and would have conducted the King all the way to Salisbury along country lanes and by-paths, had not Charles upset his careful plans by demanding, after riding some miles, where they were to dine.

'Dine, sir?' repeated Phelips, taken aback. 'Your Majesty may be assured of a good supper at Heale.'

'I hope I may,' said the King, 'but dinner comes before supper.'

Phelips began to see that the task of escorting this fugitive King was fraught with more peril even than he had supposed. 'But sir, I must humbly remind your Majesty that to stop anywhere upon the road would be so imprudent that I dare not think what the consequences might be!'

'You may think instead of the consequences of my swooning from hunger,' said the King cheerfully.

'But your Majesty will surely not swoon for the lack of one meal!'

'Nay, I'll take care of that. Come, man, you are too fearful! Where shall we dine?'

'Sir,' said the Colonel, 'if dine you must, we shall be forced to enter some town upon the highroad! What if you be recognized?'

'Robin Phelips,' said the King, 'I dined in Bridport when the whole town, ay, and the inn itself, swarmed with Noll

Cromwell's men, and not one of them looked at me twice! Now tell me where I shall dine today, and trust me not to betray myself, for I shall not.'

Colonel Phelips, who had carefully planned to skirt every town, refrained with a strong effort from telling his Royal charge what he thought of his reckless conduct, and replied in his dourest voice: 'If your Majesty is determined, there is a house at Mere where the host is said to be honest.'

'Then lead me there,' said the King.

'Oh, I am glad that I am to have my dinner!' sighed Juliana, with a naughty glance cast at the Colonel's rigid profile. 'Indeed, and I am quite famished!'

Phelips swallowed a testy retort, and rode on in silence. Presently the King said softly: 'Pray do not look so crossly, Colonel. I shall never amend my ways, tell me till Doomsday.'

The Colonel's head was jerked round; flushing deeply, he met the King's quizzical eyes, and stared into them. An unwilling smile crept into his own; he said in a mollified tone: 'Nay, but such a spurt as this, sir —! You know I must obey you, but I like it not at all – not at all!'

'My dear Colonel, I have been hunted dryfoot through half England, and have come off scatheless. Be of good cheer! I am not so ill a manager of my affairs as you think.'

The Colonel shook his head, pulling down the corners of his mouth, but attempted no further remonstrance. Another couple of miles brought the party to the outskirts of Mere; they rode slowly along the main street, between two rows of plaster-faced houses turned to gold by the autumn sunlight, and pulled up at a roomy-looking inn which stood on the corner of the street.

Making the best of a bad business, the Colonel bespoke a private parlour, and tried to divert the innkeeper's attention from the King by talking to him himself. He let a great sigh of relief when the landlord shut the door of the parlour on them, but his peace of mind did not last long, for the landlord came back while they were still eating their dinner, anxious to know whether everything was to his guests' liking. He was a pleasant fellow, with a taste for gossip, and, since he did not seem to see anything suspicious in the King's height or dark complexion, the Colonel, as the custom was, invited him to drink a glass of wine with them. He complied very readily, sitting down at the end of the table, and asking the Colonel what the news was.

'I know of none,' Phelips replied. 'They say there are soldiers being sent to Jersey, but I know not if it be true.'

'Well, and a pox go with them: they are rogues all! The best news that has come this way these many days is of them men at Westminster being all in a maze, notwithstanding their victory at Worcester.' He chuckled, and drank some of his wine. 'Proper mazed they are, and wherefor? Why, because they can't discover what has become of the King! They say the most received opinion is that he has gone in a disguise to London, so now every man jack amongst 'em is as busy as a good wife at oven, and neither meal nor dough, a-hunting for the Black Boy in all the likely houses. What I say is, here's a health to the King, and may he confound every snuffling Puritan of them all!' A laugh escaping the King made him look across the table at him. 'You look like an honest fellow,' he said, with bluff familiarity. 'But ye don't drink, I see. Are you Cæsar's man, or have I a rascally Roundhead under my roof?'

The King filled his glass from the bottle at his elbow. 'Nay, I am no Roundhead, but wholly Cæsar's man, I do assure you.'

'Then drink a health to his Majesty!' commanded the landlord, raising his own glass. 'Here's to the King, God bless him!'

'The King!' said Colonel Phelips, draining his glass.

'The Black Boy!' said Charles, with a laugh quivering in his throat. 'And may you not be hanged for wishing him well, friend!'

## CHAPTER XIX

## GUESTS AT HEALE

I<small>T WAS</small> dusk when the King reached Heale. Colonel Phelips having represented to him in the strongest terms the folly of his passing through Salisbury, he had parted from Juliana at the village of Lower Woodford, less than a mile from Heale House. Juliana had wept a little, but the King, drying her cheeks with his own handkerchief, and planting the lightest of kisses on her mouth, had coaxed her back to smiles, bidding her look forward to the day when she would come to Court in her best gown, and find herself the prettiest lady there. He had exchanged horses then with Henry Peters, had lifted Juliana into the pillion with his own hands, and stood in the road with Colonel Phelips, to watch her ride away towards Salisbury.

'Now we shall do very well,' said the Colonel, with frank relief, when Juliana was out of sight. 'It mislikes me, taking women along on such a journey as this.'

'Without one woman's devotion I should not be standing here today, Robin Phelips,' said the King.

'Well, and I wish your Majesty would not stand here, but would mount and ride on before some prying fellow comes upon us,' replied the Colonel, unimpressed.

The King swung himself up into the saddle, remarking, more to himself than to his companion: 'They seem to be lost in the past, all who have helped me. I wonder, shall I see them again?'

'Ay, fast enough, when you come to your own, sir,' replied the Colonel.

The rest of the way to Heale led winding beside the river Avon, which here ran through a pretty, lush valley, and was bordered by pollard-windows. Heale House was situated with the river in its front, and a belt of tall cedar trees sheltering its gardens. There were no other houses within sight of it, a circumstance which the Colonel took care to point out to the King.

Upon their arrival, their horses were taken in charge by a groom, and they were admitted at once into the house, and led across a wide, panelled hall to a parlour, where several persons were gathered round a small wood-fire. An elderly lady, wearing widow's weeds, rose at their entrance, and came forward to greet them. The Colonel, who had walked in before the King, bowed to her, and, having kissed her hand, begged leave to present his friend, Mr Jackson. She turned towards the King with a pleasant smile, and, held out her hand, saying: 'I bid you welcome, sir, and am very glad to see you here.'

The King pulled off his hat, and took her hand in his to kiss it. He found that it was shaking, and, raising his head, saw that the smile had been wiped from her face, and that she was gazing at him as though he were a ghost. He said easily: 'You are very good, madam. I warrant you, Robin Phelips and I are mighty glad to be here.'

She moistened her lips. 'Yes,' she said. 'Indeed, sir —' She broke off, and seemed to swallow some obstruction in her throat. 'You must let me make you known to my sister, Mrs Mary Tichborne, and my good brother-in-law, Sir Frederick Hyde, and Dr Henchman here.'

A younger woman, who bore a marked resemblance to the widow, curtseyed; Sir Frederick, who was shaking hands with Phelips, looked a little curiously at the shabby figure beside Mrs Hyde, but bade him a civil good-evening. The King glanced beyond him towards Dr Henchman, a twinkle in his eye. The doctor, a stately Churchman with a neat beard, and carefully curled white locks, slightly inclined his head, and made a gesture with one thin hand to invite the King to a chair beside his own. Charles walked across the room to him, and held out his hand. 'Sir, I am happy to see you here. You must know, madam,' he added, turning his head towards Mrs Hyde, 'that I have the honour to be a little acquainted with Dr Henchman.'

She replied, with a faint gasp: 'It is a fortunate chance

which brings you both here to sup with me tonight. Will you not be seated, sir?'

Her sister looked at her in some surprise, for she was in general a very calm woman; but before she could make any remark, Mrs Hyde had begun to talk to Colonel Phelips, rather fast, and breathlessly, but with a good deal of vivacity. Sir Frederick was soon drawn into the conversation, a circumstance which enabled the King to exchange a few sentences with Dr Henchman. Leaning a little sideways in his chair, he said softly: 'Where is Wilmot?'

'At Hinton Daubnay,' replied Henchman, blandly surveying his finger-tips.

'A ship?'

'Patience, sir: you are being watched.'

The King saw that Mrs Mary Tichborne was looking at him, and relapsed into silence.

Supper being presently announced, the company withdrew into an adjoining parlour, and sat down to table. Mrs Hyde, after a moment's hesitation, asked Dr Henchman to sit at her right hand. Her sister taking the other end of the table, the King chose a chair beside her, and began to converse with her in his pleasant, easy way. Since she knew him to be a Cavalier travelling in disguise, she found nothing to astonish her in his air of breeding, and his knowledge of the world; but Sir Frederick Hyde, who was sitting on his sister-in-law's left hand, several times broke off his talk with Dr Henchman to turn and look at the shabby stranger beside him. His attention was always gently recalled by the doctor, but his curiosity soon got the better of him, and he contrived to find an opportunity to whisper to Mrs Hyde: 'Who is this fellow beside me? Is he not a servant?'

'No, but a very poor man: one who lost his fortune in the late Wars,' she replied.

'He is not dressed like a gentleman. What is his name?'

She whispered: 'It is Jackson. Pray do not let him overhear you!'

The King, however, was not listening to Sir Frederick. He was lending a polite ear to Mary Tichborne's complaints of the weather.

''Deed, I never remember such a rainy October,' she said, shaking her head. 'I fear you must have got wet upon your ride?'

'No, no, we met nothing worse than a little Scotch mist at one place,' he assured her, adding with a twinkle: 'They have a saying in Scotland that a Scots mist will wet an Englishman to the skin, but we did not find it so today.'

'Are you a Scotsman?' suddenly demanded Sir Frederick.

'Not I, faith!' answered the King.

'You have travelled in Scotland, perhaps?'

'Ay, for my sins.'

'I have never visited that country. By all accounts, Argyll's faction is grown very great there. I know not which may be the worse: a Scotch Presbyter or an English Puritan.'

'I have no acquaintance with English Puritans, but Scotch Presbyters I know very well, and if there is anywhere in the world a more hypocritical set of rogues I hope it may not be my ill-fortune to encounter them,' said the King roundly.

'Ah, madam, here is a treat indeed!' said Dr Henchman. 'A dish of larks! You will agree with Mrs Hyde's friends, Sir Frederick, that nowhere is there to be found such good entertainment as at Heale House.'

'Now, if there is one thing I esteem more than another it is a fat lark!' declared Colonel Phelips.

The widow began to serve her guests. 'You see I remember what you like, dear Dr Henchman. Colonel, you glad a hostess's heart! Frederick, you will let me give you a lark?'

'Indeed, I like them very well,' said Sir Frederick, taking his plate from her, and noticing, with a jaundiced eye, that although one lark was all that fell to his lot, Mr William Jackson, alone amongst the company, received the two best birds on the dish.

Mr William Jackson noticed it too, and did not fail to observe the jealous look cast at his plate by his neighbour. 'Why, madam, I see that to the biggest man comes the biggest portion. I was never more glad of my inches!'

'Oh!' she said, with a flustered laugh, 'you must know that I have a fine, lusty son of my own, sir, and know what a stomach a young man has!'

'Ay, they say a growing youth has a wolf in his belly,' contributed Colonel Phelips, made desperate by trepidation.

Sir Frederick cast a measuring glance over the big frame beside him. 'It's to be hoped Mr Jackson has done with growing,' he remarked dryly.

'Tell me, Sir Frederick,' once more interposed Dr Henchman, 'are your peaches this year as good as ever? Mine were quite spoiled by a blight earlier in the season.'

Since Sir Frederick was an enthusiastic gardener, his attention was at once diverted, and a discussion was begun that lasted until his hostess and her sister withdrew into the winter-parlour. The gentlemen remained seated round the table for some time, drinking the widow's excellent wine, and discoursing on a number of different topics. Neither Colonel Phelips's scowl, nor Dr Henchman's mild glance of warning, had the desired effect of imposing silence upon the King, who bore his share in the conversation with an entire disregard for the incongruity of his servant's dress, and well-informed speech. When he betrayed, by entering into an argument with Sir Frederick on the several ways of cooking partridges, that he had lived in foreign parts, Colonel Phelips abruptly put an end to any further disclosures by yawning loudly, and announcing that he for one was forespent, and would seek his chamber.

'And I daresay you will be glad of your bed too, Jackson,' he said firmly.

This put Sir Frederick in mind of the time. He glanced at the clock over the fireplace, and at once got up, saying that he must take his leave of his good sister, if he was to reach his own home before dawn.

The three gentlemen, accordingly, removed into the winter-parlour, Colonel Phelips explaining to his hostess that he and his friend had come to crave her leave to retire, being wearied by their journey.

She made no demur at such an early breaking-up of her supper-party, but at once requested her sister to escort the Colonel and Mr Jackson to their bedchambers, and turned to bid farewell to Sir Frederick.

Dr Henchman having left the parlour on a murmured

excuse, Sir Frederick was able to speak frankly to his sister-in-law, which he did, saying earnestly: 'My dear Amphillis, I know not who this fellow may be whom Phelips has brought into your house, but there is something mighty odd about him, which puts me in a little disquiet. From his dress, which is very mean – not a shred of lace to his collar, and no wristbands, my dear sister, and his suit much worn! – one would suppose him to be a serving-man. That cropped head, besides, and his complexion, which is as sun-burned as any hind's! But his voice is good, and he can converse sensibly on all manner of subjects, which gives me a suspicion of his being one of these soldiers-of-fortune which have jumped-up in the late troublous times, and do now infest the country. You know, you should be more careful whom you admit into your house, sister. I say it in all brotherly kindness, you understand!'

'Yes, Frederick, but indeed you wrong the poor man! He is perfectly respectable, but has fallen upon evil days, like so many honest gentlemen! Dr Henchman is acquainted with him, and Robin Phelips besides.'

'Jackson!' said Sir Frederick, pursing up his mouth. 'I cannot call to mind any gentleman of that name. Well, have it as you choose, but if you will be advised by me you will keep a sharp watch on him. He seems to me a very plausible rogue.'

The King, meanwhile, had been led by Mary Tichborne to a bedchamber in the front of the house. It was a fair-sized apartment, hung with green damask, and furnished with a four-poster bed, two oak chests, and several chairs. Mrs Mary thought it a very good chamber for an ugly young man in a worn grey suit, and was startled, upon her going downstairs again, to be met by her sister, who asked her in an agitated voice where she had bestowed Mr Jackson.

'Why, in the green bedchamber, sister, as you bade me!' she replied, staring.

'No, no!' said Mrs Hyde. 'The crimson room, Mary! Stay, I will lay out the Holland sheets, and my best down pillow!'

'The crimson room for that poor man!' exclaimed Mary. 'The Holland sheets! Nay, you are out of your senses! I warrant he has not often lain in such an elegant room as your green bedchamber. And he has a feather-bed to lie on, besides, which —'

'Hens' and capons' feathers!' said Mrs Hyde, in a stifled voice. 'Will you stand there disputing all night with me? Run quickly, and fetch the Spanish blankets out of the chest in my chamber! And the counterpoint of crimson plush that is lined with taffeta, and the down pillows, mind!'

'Well!' said her sister. 'One would say you were making ready to receive the King at the very least, instead of a shabby young man who, I daresay, has never set foot in as fine a house as this in his life!'

Mrs Hyde grasped her by the wrist. 'Mary, he *is* the King!' she said in a shrill whisper.

'Sister!' gasped Mary, gazing at her in the liveliest alarm. 'You must be crazed!'

'No, I tell you! I am sure of it! I could not mistake! It is the King himself!'

Mrs Mary Tichborne was so surprised that she felt quite faint, and had to lean against the balusters for support. All she could think of to say was: 'Mercy on us, what shall we do?'

The housewife in Mrs Hyde supplied the answer to this question. 'He must have the crimson chamber, and the Holland sheets! Oh, that such an honour should have befallen me! I do not know whether I am standing on my head or my heels!'

Mary recovered her presence of mind. 'The Holland sheets, if you will, but good God, sister, not the crimson bedchamber! Think what suspicion it would give rise to amongst the servants! And you putting two larks on his plate! Was there ever such folly? I could see Sir Frederick wondering at it!' A footstep on the landing above made her look up. Dr Henchman had come out of the green bedchamber, and began slowly to descend the staircase. She said in a hurried undertone: 'I will lay out the sheets. Do you ask the doctor if it is indeed the King!'

Dr Henchman stood still to let her pass him on the stairs. His eyes surveyed her with a good deal of comprehension in their calm depths. As soon as she was out of sight, he went on down the stairs, and said with a slight smile to Mrs Hyde: 'I have been commanded to make known a very secret matter to you, madam, but I see that you have guessed it already. You may say that I have done very ill by you to bring that gentleman into your house without apprising you of his true estate, but you must understand that without permission I might not disclose so dangerous a secret.'

She clasped her hands together. 'Oh yes, indeed I do understand, and not a word shall cross my lips! But such a wretched chamber as I have given him, and the bed stuffed only with hens' feathers! But the Holland sheets he must and shall have!'

'Will you come in to him?' Henchman asked. 'I know nothing of sheets, nor he either, I daresay. But he wishes to speak privately with you.'

'I will come at once,' she said, lifting a hand to smooth the bands of hair just visible under the veil she wore over her head.

She paused at the top of the stairs to recover her breath, for she was stout, and panted easily, and then allowed the doctor to usher her into the green bedchamber.

The thick damask curtains had been drawn across the windows, and the candles lit. Their little tongues of flame cast the King's shadow grotesquely on the wall behind him, and touched one of the steel buttons on his coat with a pin-point of light.

The widow curtseyed deeply, the joints in her knees cracking. 'Sire, you are very welcome, and I greatly honoured,' she said.

The King moved forward to raise her. 'Madam, madam, I thought you would betray me with your larks!' he said, laughing. 'Did you know me at once, then? Was that why your hand trembled so in mine? Yet how could you do so? Have we met before? I do not think it.'

'Nay, sire, but seven years ago I saw you ride past Salisbury, with your Royal father. When I laid eyes on you this evening I recognized you at once, and was ready to drop where I stood, not having had the least suspicion that your

Majesty was the gentleman Colonel Phelips was to bring to my house.'

'Recognized me at once!' repeated the King. 'Oh, this face of mine! It will undo me yet!'

'Not in this house, sire!' she said, holding herself very erect. 'There is only one other who knows of your presence here, and that one is my sister, and she is as honest a woman as I am, and I will vouch for her.'

Colonel Phelips, who had been standing by the bed, half-hidden from the widow by the folds of the curtains, stepped into the candlelight, saying in his forthright way: 'The case is, madam, can you hide his Majesty so securely that none may get a sight of him?'

She replied without hesitation: 'There is a secret place in the house, which few know of. It is hidden behind the wainscoting in a small chamber which we do not use in the general way.'

'Softly, softly!' said the King. 'It is not *can* you hide me, madam, but *will* you hide me?'

Her breast swelled; she lifted her chin. 'It needs not to ask that question of one who bears the name of Hyde, sire.'

He seemed to be a little amused, but he bowed with a kingly grace that matched her dignity. 'Madam, I thank you! But will you not be seated? My good friend, Dr Henchman, will tell us then what we must do, eh, doctor?'

'Sire, I do not sit while my King stands,' she told him.

At that, a laugh escaped him. 'Do not use me with such ceremony, madam, for I am a very threadbare King, and one, moreover, that has no Kingdom to reign over.'

She let him lead her to a chair, but said with a very speaking look cast up into his face: 'Sire, that is not so, for you have a Kingdom in the hearts of your loyal subjects, and there you will ever reign absolutely.'

The laughter vanished from his eyes; a tinge of colour stole into his lean cheeks; he raised her hand to his lips, and kissed it. 'Madam, none has ever said a kinder thing to me than that, nor one more comfortable to mine ears in my present straits.'

'My son, you have heard no less than the truth,' said

Henchman. 'If there are rebels in England, there are also many loyal subjects, as I think your Majesty knows.'

'Ay, and the day will come when every snuffling Puritan will be utterly confounded,' said the Colonel. 'I shall live to see your Majesty at Whitehall, that's sure.'

The King sat down in a chair beside Mrs Hyde's, and laid his hands on the carved wooden arms. 'Why, I believe you will, Colonel, but first get me out of England! Dr Henchman, what's the news from my Lord Wilmot?'

'Not as good as I had expected to be able to tell you, sir, but still hopeful. Colonel Phelips will doubtless have informed you of the unhappy miscarriage of the Southampton plan. My lord being sadly cast-down, and not knowing which way to turn, I bethought me of a loyal gentleman of my acquaintance, one George Gounter of Racton, in Sussex.' He inclined his head towards Mrs Hyde. 'Your good hostess, sir, will answer for his faithfulness, for he is married to her sister-in-law, and she knows him well.'

'Yes, indeed,' Mrs Hyde said. 'He fought for your Majesty's sainted father throughout the late Wars, and has suffered grievously in your cause.'

'Ay, and that is what has cast some new rubs in the way,' said the Colonel. 'It's not fourteen days since Gounter was confined upon pain of imprisonment not to stir five miles from Racton, sir; but at the very time the doctor here hit upon the notion of using him to your service, he was summoned to appear before the Commissioners in London to pay his fine of two hundred pounds. And the devil's in it, as the doctor has been telling me, that he is still jaunting betwixt London and Chichester, first seeking to compound with the blood-suckers for a hundred pounds, and then to borrow the money, which is not easily done in these sickly times.'

'The marrow of the matter, sir, is this: that my lord has not yet been able to meet with Colonel Gounter. But a young kinsman of the Colonel, one Thomas Gounter, to whom I made my lord known, under the name of Mr Barlow, does positively expect to see the Colonel at his own house again tomorrow, and thither will escort my lord. I do not doubt he will find the Colonel very apt and ready to serve you. He will send to tell me how the business progresses, and I, in my turn, will engage to keep your Majesty punctually informed.'

'And your Majesty will stay hid in this house until we have all in train for your embarking for France,' interpolated Phelips anxiously.

'I seem to have heard those words before,' said the King, with a humorous cock of one eyebrow.

'This time there shall be no miscarriage, sir, I promise you.'

Mrs Hyde, who had listened in silence, suddenly said: 'I must think! This must not be carelessly contrived. None but my sister and myself must know of his Majesty's presence in the house. I will not trust such a secret to any of my servants.' She paused, her brow puckered. After a moment she nodded briskly, and sat bolt upright in her chair. 'Your Majesty must seem to leave the house tomorrow, in company with the Colonel. I will give my servants leave to go to the fair in Salisbury, and so have none here to spy upon your return. That must not be until dusk, if you please, sir, when I will instantly convey you to the chamber I spoke of. There my sister and I can wait upon your Majesty, and none be the wiser, for we do not use that chamber.'

'Ay, but where must I take his Majesty?' said Phelips dubiously. 'I dare not go to Salisbury, nor to any house in the neighbourhood.'

Dr Henchman raised his eyes from the contemplation of a ring upon his finger. 'Nay, that would be too perilous, certainly. But you might take his Majesty where it will be strange indeed if you encounter anyone, and that is upon the Downs, towards Stonehenge.'

'But what if it should be a rainy day, and his Majesty be thus exposed to the weather?' objected the Colonel. 'And where shall he dine?'

The King remembered the dripping of the rain in Spring Coppice, and the mess of butter and milk and eggs that was brought him in a wooden cup by Eleanor Yates. It seemed a long time ago, but his face grew sombre as he thought of it, and a little shiver ran through him, as though he could still feel the chill in his flesh.

He looked up. 'Nay, I like it very well, and will engage to eat bread and cheese for my dinner at Stonehenge.'

The Colonel, with a lively recollection of his obstinacy in riding into Mere for his dinner, looked sceptical, but raised no further objections. It was, however, in the expectation of being commanded to lead his master to a decent inn for dinner that he set out with him from Heale next morning, and he was not a little relieved to find, presently, that Charles was apparently in a docile mood, ready to be escorted as far from any village as the Colonel thought proper.

The day was fine, though with a sharpness in the air; and when their horses climbed the chalk downs to the north of Salisbury, a strong wind met them. For as far as the eye could see, nothing but the lift and fall of the bare downs was visible. The King sat with one hand resting on his saddle-bow, looking about him. The wind slapped the brim of his hat against his cheek, and whipped his horse's mane into a tangle. He turned his head towards the Colonel remarking: 'Well! you have certainly brought me to a very remote place, Robin Phelips!'

'It is very bleak, sir, and I fear there is no shelter to be found from this wind.'

'I like it,' said the King. 'I have been so cooped-up of late that this suits my humour exactly. Lead me to Stonehenge! I have never seen it, which is, I think, a shocking thing for a King of England to be obliged to confess.'

'If we follow this track, sir, we shall come upon it over the next rise. Your Majesty must count the stones, for there is an old saying in these parts that they can never be told twice alike.'

'I will put that to the test,' the King promised, and pricked his horse to a canter.

His arithmetic gave the lie to the fable, presently, which, he said, was a sad disappointment. He sat down by one of the huge stones and in its grim shadow ate his dinner of bread and cheese. The Colonel sat beside him, sharing his meal. At first a little stiff still, and ill at ease, his tongue

grew gradually looser, and his manner less stilted. He found
the King very merry and conversable, and by the time they
set out to retrace their steps to Heale he had forgotten that
Charles could be obstinate, and foolhardy, and would have
been ready to swear that he had the sweetest and most
reasonable disposition of any prince in Christendom.

There was not a soul to be seen at Heale House but Mrs
Hyde and her sister, and Dr Henchman. After delivering
the King into their charge, the Colonel kissed hands, and
rode away, taking the King's horse to be stabled against
his future need at the house of a friend living some nine
miles distant from Heale.

<br>

CHAPTER XX

## 'I MUST ENDEAVOUR'

WHEN Colonel Phelips escorted the King to Heale, my
Lord Wilmot was gnawing his nails at Hinton Daubnay. The eleven days he had spent in alternating fits of hope
and despair had left their mark upon him. He had lost
weight, and his weak, handsome face was beginning to wear
a perpetual look of strain. A frown lived in his eyes; he found
it hard to sit still; and every day knew that his temper was
growing shorter. Lawrence Hyde and his lady bore with
his humours with great good-nature, but found him a difficult guest, for he could neither divorce his mind from the
terrible responsibility resting upon him, nor decide upon
any one course of action to be followed. No sooner had he
sent to implore Southampton's aid, than he became obsessed
with the fear that the Earl was too noted a figure to engage
upon the business without attracting unwelcome attention.
He eagerly embraced Henchman's plan of confiding in
Colonel Gounter, yet when Henchman put him in the way of
meeting Captain Thomas Gounter, he took fright, and, re-
gardless of the fact that the Captain had once served under

his command, would not permit Henchman to disclose his identity to him. While the King remained at Trent, dreadful nightmares of his being searched for there made him start up night after night out of his troubled sleep, his body bathed in sweat, his limbs rigid with horror. The thought that sixty miles lay between him and Charles filled him with self-reproach at having consented to leave him at Trent; the face of the ostler at Charmouth, the blur of red-coats encountered in Bridport, the thick black characters of a proclamation nailed to a wall in Lyme, haunted his mind. He began to think of Trent, not as a secure refuge, but as a trap out of which he must somehow contrive to steal the King. But when he had despatched Phelips to fetch Charles to Heale, doubts assailed him. Wyndham he could trust, but what, after all, did he know of Mrs Hyde? The need to set the King safely aboard a vessel bound for France seemed to be more urgent than ever before, and Colonel Gounter's continued absence from his home filled him with an irrational fury that made his hands shake, and his voice rise to a shrill note.

Thomas Gounter, an unimaginative young man with a strong sense of duty, thought him an odd, impatient creature, but forbore to pry into his affairs. It was quite evident that he was engaged upon some secret and dangerous business, for no man, thought Tom Gounter, could live in such a sweat of fear merely because he was being hunted by Roundheads. He called himself Barlow, and said that he was a native of Devonshire, but Tom Gounter did not think that his name was Barlow, or that he came from Devonshire. His countenance seemed to him vaguely familiar, but since he did not wish to be known, Tom Gounter was not the man to try to discover his identity.

Upon the 7th October, the day following the King's arrival at Heale, Gounter arrived at Hinton Daubnay, late in the afternoon, for the purpose of escorting my lord to Racton, which lay four miles from Chichester, and was the home of his kinsman, Colonel George Gounter. He found my lord in a fret of impatience, and was greeted by a testy demand to know what had made him so late.

Captain Gounter explained, for perhaps the fourth time, that since his kinsman was not expected to reach Racton until the evening no good purpose would be served by their making an early start. 'My cousin will come home for his supper, I daresay, and will be glad to house us for the night,' he said. 'You'll remember that so it was agreed between us, Mr Barlow.'

Wilmot tried to curb his impatience, but soon fell to walking about the room, every now and then pulling out his watch to compare it with the bracket-clock on the mantelpiece. Captain Gounter, who would have been pleased to have smoked a pipe with Lawrence Hyde, decided, after a very little of this restlessness, that the only thing to be done was to set out for Racton at once and let Mr Barlow do his pacing there.

Robert Swan, impassive as ever, rode with them, with my lord's yellow-hair sumpter-trunk strapped on to the crupper behind him. The distance, which was less than ten miles, was soon covered, and the travellers came within sight of Colonel Gounter's house at a little before seven o'clock. It was a rambling, two-storeyed mansion, standing in its own orchards some way back from the south bank of the river Ems. It was enclosed by flint walls, and approached by an avenue of pollard-ash trees, stretching to the Chichester road.

When the visitors entered the house it was to find, as Tom Gounter had expected, that the Colonel had not returned yet, but was looked-for in an hour or so. His wife, a thin, anxious-eyed woman, seemed rather taken-aback at the arrival of company. She explained that she had given her servants leave to go out for the day, but if she cherished a hope that the visitors might decide not to put her to the trouble of providing for their entertainment that evening, she was soon disappointed. With an airy, male lack of comprehension, Captain Gounter begged her not to put herself out, for they would be content with the simplest fare, and desired her to make no change in her arrangements upon their account. She was too well-bred a woman to disabuse his mind of its evident belief that three men could be as easily fed as one, and, putting a good face on it, invited him and Wilmot into one of the parlours, and fetched some sack and biscuits for their immediate refreshment.

She looked curiously at Wilmot, and, upon hearing that he wished most particularly to have speech with her husband, grew rather pale. An attempt to elicit from him the nature of his business failed. After a pause, she said in a faltering voice: 'My husband has only just been released from his parole, and that upon payment of a fine that can only be raised through his going to an usurer. I do trust, sir, that your errand to him is not such as must again undo him?'

'No, no!' Wilmot said hastily. 'But it is about a reference which none but he can decide. I am directed to him by Mr Hyde of Hinton Daubnay, who is, I believe, related to you.'

'He is my cousin,' she said, not appearing to derive much comfort from this introduction.

It was not until some time after eight o'clock that Colonel Gounter reached his home. He was met in the big, wainscoted hall by his wife, who had been preparing supper in the kitchen, with the assistance of Robert Swan. She came hurrying across the hall, as the Colonel tossed his plumed hat on to a chair, and began to unbuckle his sword-belt. He looked up when he heard her footstep, and smiled, and held out his hand. 'All's well, Kate! You see before you a free man. What's the news with you, good sweetheart? Whose nags are those, put up in our stable?'

She stood on tiptoe to embrace him, for he was a tall man. 'It's your cousin, Tom Gounter, with a gentleman from Devonshire, who is wishful to have speech with you. But, oh, my dearest, my heart much misgives me, and I fear they mean to draw you into some dangerous coil of theirs!'

'Your heart misgives you because Tom is come to see me?' he said, holding her away from him, and looking down into her face in surprise.

'No, but this Mr Barlow! I am sure he is other than he appears, for he has such an air, and a fine London servant besides! Oh, George, promise me you will not engage upon any rash undertaking!'

'Why, Kate, what's this farrago of nonsense? What rash undertaking should I engage upon? I promise you, I know of none. Go you in now, and tell Tom I will be with him as soon as I have pulled off my boots.'

He gave her shoulder a little pat, and let her go. She went reluctantly, and delivered his message. Ten minutes later, his firm, brisk tread was heard crossing the hall towards the parlour door; he came in, a soldierly figure, with a tanned face, a swift smile, and rather stern grey eyes. 'Well, Tom! Give ye good den!' he said, shutting the door behind him. 'You are come in a good hour, for I am just arrived from settling my plaguey affairs.' He clasped his kinsman's hand, as he spoke, and looked keenly at Wilmot, who had risen from a chair on the opposite side of the wide fireplace. My lord stood just outside the circle of light cast by a branch of candles upon the table, but as Tom Gounter spoke his assumed name, he moved slightly, and the Colonel saw his face. A startled expression leapt to his eyes; he stood quite still for a moment, and then went up to my lord, saying: 'You are very welcome, sir.'

Wilmot took his hand, and contrived to draw him a little apart. 'I see you know me,' he muttered. 'Do not own me!'

The Colonel cast a wondering glance at his cousin. Apparently he really was in ignorance of his old commander's identity, for his countenance was quite disinterested, and he very slightly shrugged his shoulders as he met the Colonel's puzzled eye.

The Colonel turned to the table, which had some bottles and glasses upon it. 'You'll take a glass of sack, Mr Barlow? Have you ridden far?'

'No, from Mr Lawrence Hyde's, where I am staying. I believe we have some friends in common, Colonel. You are acquainted with Dr Henchman, are you not?'

'Yes, I know Dr Henchman,' the Colonel replied, drawing the cork out of one of the bottles. ' 'Sdeath, what's this?'

A couple of small hornets most unexpectedly flew out of the bottle. They created a not unwelcome diversion, no one being able to decide how they had got into the bottle in the first place, or had managed to survive there. While these problems were under discussion, Mrs Gounter slipped out of the room to lay the covers in the dining-parlour. She presently summoned the gentlemen to supper, and, when they sat down at the table, again looked very closely at Wilmot.

Robert Swan waited upon the company; and, when the meal came to an end, the Colonel almost at once offered to conduct my lord to his bedchamber. The hour was already considerably advanced, and my lord, saying that he would be glad indeed to seek his bed, followed his host upstairs to the room which had been prepared for him.

Tom Gounter, yawning prodigiously, said that he also would go to bed; and Mrs Gounter, who was more than ever suspicious of her unknown guest, took up a candle and accompanied the three men to Wilmot's chamber. Here she made a parade of turning back the coverlet, of snuffing a candle, of assuring herself that the windows were all shut to keep out the night air; but when she had performed these tasks, the Colonel told her to seek her own bed. 'I will follow you there very soon, for I promise you all this riding about the country has made me mighty sleepy. Tom, do you be off too! I will wait upon Mr Barlow.'

The younger Gounter needed no persuasion, but Mrs Gounter went very reluctantly, lingering in the doorway to whisper a warning to her husband. 'I am positive of a disguise! Do not let yourself be drawn in!'

'I shall be with you before you have had time to get between the sheets, good sweetheart,' he replied lightly. 'Nay, go now, Kate: enough!'

He shut the door upon her, and, turning, showed Wilmot a face from which the smile had quite vanished. He said abruptly: 'My lord, how may I serve you? How do you come to be in my kinsman's company, and how is it possible that he knows you not?'

'But I am travelling in disguise!' Wilmot said, a little hurt. 'You see how plainly I am dressed, surely! I have put off my ornaments, and have no lace upon my collar, besides having my hair almost uncurled.'

'I think my cousin should have known you,' replied the Colonel, with a slight smile. 'Indeed, you may trust him, my lord. But how came you in his company?'

'I was directed to him, and to you, Colonel, by Dr Henchman,' said Wilmot, looking anxiously at him.

The Colonel met that look rather searchingly. 'Yes, my lord? To what end?'

Wilmot hesitated for a moment, and then, drawing a long breath, blurted out: 'Colonel Gounter! The King of England – my master, your master! the master of all good Englishmen! – is near you, and in great distress. Can you help us to a boat?'

The Colonel stood perfectly still, his eyes fixed on Wilmot's face. He did not answer immediately, which a little discomposed my lord, and when he did speak it was to say: 'Is he well? Is he safe?'

'He is both,' Wilmot replied guardedly.

'God be blessed!' Gounter ejaculated. He saw that Wilmot was watching him suspiciously, and added: 'I asked, because if he should not be secure I don't doubt I could secure him till a boat he got. Now tell me the whole, my lord, and show me wherein I can serve his Majesty! Where is he lodged?'

Again Wilmot hesitated, but after a little pause he said: 'I do trust he is out of danger at this present, having gone to Heale, with Colonel Robin Phelips, but I know not what course has been taken for securing him there. Indeed, what security can there be for him in all this ungrateful country? Oh, my dear sir, if you but knew the danger he has passed through, the checks we have met with!' He sank down into a chair by the table, clasping his head in his hands. 'It is more than a month since we bore him off from Worcester, and still I can find no means to transport him overseas! Sometimes I think I must grow mad with the fear, always with me – yea, waking and sleeping! – that he will be taken!'

His voice had risen; he broke off, shuddering. The Colonel repeated: 'Tell me the whole, my lord.'

His quiet, the firm note in his voice, seemed to inspire Wilmot with confidence. He raised his head from between his hands, and began to recount some part of the King's adventures. He found the Colonel a silent, but a sympathetic listener, and was soon impelled to unburden his mind of its fears. 'No one knows what I have lived through during these weeks!' he said, at the end. 'He chose me to go with him: me alone, mark you! *He* laughs at his danger, but he is young, and of that disposition which — He does not comprehend the dreadful burden which I must carry every moment of every day! But let that go: if I can bring him safely off, I shall be content. Three times our plans have miscarried! Now I come to seek your aid, believing you to be one who can help the King to a boat, as knowing many sea-faring men.'

'My lord,' the Colonel said seriously, 'I will be very plain with you. For all I live so near the sea, I must believe there is no man living so little acquainted with these kind of men.'

A groan broke from Wilmot. 'O God! What to do, then?'

'Will you trust me? I, as you, am bound to do my utmost to preserve the King. I give you my word that somehow I will acquit myself of this duty, and that with all possible expedition, which I account to be the very life of such a business.'

Wilmot embraced him, kissing his cheek, his own wet with tears. 'Oh, my friend, God will surely reward you! But where will you go? how will you find an honest seaman?'

'Nay, my lord, leave that to me, and do you rest secure. You are overwatched, and wearied out. You may sleep in my house without fearing to be taken in your bed.'

'But you? What shall you do?' Wilmot persisted.

'I shall seek my bed too,' said the Colonel, with a smile. 'In the morning, I will ride to the coast, to a little port, called Emsworth, which is some two miles from this place, and see what fortune I meet with there.'

'Shall I go with you? Would it be wise, think you?'

'No, your lordship were much better to remain here,' Gounter replied in his decided way. 'For I shall go very early, and take with me only one John Day, that is a trusty man and a very loyal subject, and was formerly my servant. He is related to seamen of good account, and I think he may serve our turn. Your lordship must await me here. I will return to you as speedily as I can, I promise you.'

'Well, I will do so,' Wilmot said, sighing. 'But to stay kicking my heels is the hardest thing of all to do, Colonel.'

'Ay, that is true, but your going with me will serve no purpose, my lord. Be patient! In good time, all will be well.'

He took up his candle as he spoke, and bidding Wilmot goodnight, went away to his own chamber. He found that his wife was sitting up for him, still fully dressed, and with an expression in her face that boded no good. He smiled at her. 'What, Kate? Not abed?'

'Who is that man?' she demanded. 'What is his business with you, George?'

'My dear heart, it is nothing concerning you, nor am I at liberty to disclose it to you.'

She twisted her hands together. 'You cannot put me off so. I know there is more in it than you would have me believe, enough, I doubt not, to ruin you, and all your family! And in that, George, I am concerned!' Her face puckered; she burst into tears suddenly, rocking herself to and fro, and sobbing that they had had trouble enough, and she would rather he killed her than let her live to see him utterly undone.

His attempts at soothing her only made her weep the more, and after a minute or two he took up his candle, and went out of the room, back to my lord's chamber.

Wilmot was undressing, and looked round with instinctive alarm as the Colonel's knock sounded on the door. When he saw who it was, his suddenly stiffened limbs relaxed, and he said: 'Oh, it's you! Why, what's amiss?'

'This is amiss,' said the Colonel, 'that my wife suspects you of being other than you seem, and is put into a very passion of weeping for dread lest I engage myself upon some unlawful business. I know her, my lord: there will be no appeasing her, except I disclose the truth to her. I dare pass my word for her loyalty, and, indeed, for myself, I would acquaint her with the whole. But it is for you to decide. Without your allowance, she shall know nothing.'

Wilmot, a little dismayed, but thinking that a woman labouring under a suspicion would be more dangerous than one in possession of the truth, replied hastily: 'No, no; by all means acquaint her with it!'

When he entered his chamber again, the Colonel found his lady still sobbing, and wringing her hands. He went to her, and took her in his arms, removing her handkerchief from her grasp, and drying her cheeks with it. 'Enough, Kate! I will tell you the whole, but you must leave crying, and keep a still tongue in your head. I am going upon the King's business.'

'The King's business?' she faltered, her voice thickened by her tears. 'Oh, George, what can you mean? How can you be going upon his business?'

'Listen now, my heart! The King is lying concealed in your good sister-in-law's house at Heale, in what desperate plight you may guess. Unless a ship be found to carry him to France, he must soon or late fall into the hands of his enemies.'

She was rigid with shocked surprise. Involuntarily, she exclaimed: 'Ah, that, God forbid! But you – you are to find a ship?' He nodded. She said, looking searchingly up into his face: 'Who is that man?'

'He is my Lord Wilmot. He has been the King's sole companion in this perilous adventure, and was sent to me by Dr Henchman, who believed that I could help him to a boat. You know the truth now, Kate: what would you have me do?'

There were still tears on the ends of her lashes, but she blinked them away, and forced her lips to smile. 'Alas, alas that you should have been singled out! I must say, Go on, and prosper! Yet I fear you will hardly do so.'

He pressed her hand gratefully. 'I must endeavour, Kate, and will do my best, leaving the success to God Almighty.'

She shook her head sadly, but said nothing to dissuade him from his duty. He told her in what a state of breaking nerves he had found Lord Wilmot; and discussed with her for some time which of the Sussex ports would be the likeliest for his purpose. She lay awake for long after he had fallen asleep, torn between loyalty and fear; but when he left her side very early in the morning to ride to Emsworth, she did her best to conceal her dread, and sped him on his way with resolute cheerfulness.

The Colonel's old servant, John Day, was delighted at receiving a visit from his master, but when the reason for it was disclosed to him, his jaw dropped, and his eyes grew round with astonishment. He heard the tale out in complete silence, and for several moments after the Colonel had finished speaking said not a word, but stood staring. But some thought seemed to be stirring in his brain, for a slow grin gradually crept over his face. A chuckle escaped him; he slapped his leg delightedly, and said: 'Well, dang me, if I ever heard the like! Here's you not seven days released from your parole, and as brisk as a bee in a tarpot to make them Roundheads' noses warp already! You'll go up the ladder to bed, master, no question!'

'Well, if I hang for it, what will you do, John?' demanded the Colonel.

'Oddrot me, I'll hang alongside ye, master! But lordy, to think of your honour getting your parole took off, and a-paying of that wicked fine, all as meek as a nun's hen, only to 'broil yourself again in the King's business straightway! Master, master, you'll go from little good to stark naught!'

'I do as I must. If the business mislikes you, stay you here, but tell me what sea-faring men you know that are honest!'

'Nay, nay, if it's for the King, I'll go through stitch with it!' Day declared. 'But if there is any sea-faring crony of mine which has his ship lying up at Emsworth, I know not, nor if such would come up to squeeze neither.'

The day was cloudy, and when they reached the bleak little port, a boisterous wind was whipping into a surge of grey billows the long tongue of sea that licked the land. A few cottages, and a squat alehouse, were the only houses Emsworth boasted, nor were there many vessels riding at anchor in the harbour. While the Colonel smoked a pipe in the alehouse, John Day went out to discover whether any of his acquaintances were to be met with. He returned presently, wearing a glum look on his face, and informed the Colonel that there was no ship at present lying in the harbour whose master he durst trust. He suggested that they should ride on westward to Langstone, a port south of Havant, and there try their fortune; but although Gounter thought this advice good, he determined to go back first to Racton, to acquaint my Lord Wilmot of his intention. Wilmot had promised not to stir out of the house until his return, but the Colonel, knowing him to be in a condition of jangled nerves that made it impossible for him to be still, feared that if his own return to Racton were postponed my lord might take it into his head to fly off somewhere at a tangent. So he rode back to his house, to find that his fears had been by no means groundless. He met Wilmot half a mile from Racton, coming, with Robert Swan, to search for him.

'You were so long gone I feared some mischance!' Wilmot told him.

'No mischance, my lord,' Gounter replied, 'but Emsworth will not serve our purpose, and I must go farther, to Langstone, where, haply, I may find a vessel.'

'I will come with you,' Wilmot said. He looked narrowly at Day, and, drawing nearer to the Colonel, whispered: 'Who is that fellow? Can you trust him?'

'He is my old servant,' explained the Colonel patiently. 'You have no need to fear him: he is steel to the backbone.'

Wilmot seemed to be satisfied with this answer, and rode for some time beside the Colonel in apparent peace of mind. But presently, putting his hand into his pocket to pull out his handkerchief, he discovered that the purse containing Giles Strangways's broad pieces was not there. He reined in immediately, pale with dismay, exclaiming that he had left a hundred pounds belonging to the King under his pillow. Nothing would do, in spite of the Colonel's assurance that his wife would by this time have found the purse, and would keep it safely for him, but that Robert Swan should return instantly to Racton to look for it. This arrangement met with John Day's approval. 'A good riddance to him!' he said, as Swan rode off. 'He's as dull as a beetle, and looks besides like one which has eaten his bedstraw. I warrant we shall fare better without him.'

There was, however, no likely vessel lying in Langstone

harbour, nor could Day, whilst his master and my lord consumed a dish of oysters in a tavern by the sea, discover any trustworthy mariner in the town. Wilmot fell into a mood of despair, but the Colonel rallied him, saying: 'Good luck comes by cuffing: we must about, and try again. But I would suggest that your lordship should return now to Hinton Daubnay, where I promise I will bring you news presently. Leave this business to me!'

'You will never succeed in it,' Wilmot said wretchedly. 'I think I ought not to leave you with all at odds like this. Yet I have appointed Robin Phelips to bring me tidings of his Majesty to Mr Hyde's, and I am in the expectation, besides, of receiving a message from my Lord Southampton. But to go away with nothing settled, and no immediate hope of removing the King from Heale – no, no, how can I do so?'

'My lord, upon my honour you can do no good by remaining,' said the Colonel, who was anxious to be rid of a companion very imperfectly disguised, and too nervous to be helpful. 'I will do nothing without advising you, but if you go not back to Lawrence Hyde's house I know not how you may contrive to keep his Majesty informed of our plans.'

This argument at once prevailed upon my lord to go. He instructed the Colonel to send Swan after him from Racton, and, after conjuring him most solemnly to send him word that very evening how he had fared, he mounted his horse, and rode away.

The Colonel then went home to Racton, and, having sent Swan off to join his master, sought out his kinsman, whom he found walking in the orchard. Captain Gounter greeted him placidly, enquiring, but without much interest, what he had done with Mr Barlow.

'He has gone back to Lawrence Hyde's.'

'Good!' said Tom Gounter simply. 'He frets for all the world like gummed taffety.'

The Colonel took him by the arm, and began to walk beside him under the laden trees. 'Where have your wits gone begging?' he said. 'That was my Lord Wilmot!'

'Lord Wilmot?' repeated Tom. 'Well, I did think I knew his face. But what ails him that he must needs cut so many cross-capers?'

'This much ails him: that he has the King hidden at Amphillis Hyde's house, and must find a ship to carry him to France, or go hang himself!'

This disclosure had the effect of startling Tom out of his imperturbability. He appeared much shocked, and no sooner learned that his cousin was engaged upon the task of hiring a vessel for the King, than he offered at once to lend all the help of which he was capable. He thought that a kinsman of his, one who had served in his regiment in the late Wars, had interest at certain ports, and proposed that he should seek him out immediately. This the Colonel agreed to, appointing his cousin to meet him in Chichester upon the following morning. He himself went off once more with John Day, but again to no purpose; and later rode to Hinton Daubnay, a distance of about ten miles from Racton.

Wilmot was eagerly awaiting him, and although he brought no welcome tidings, seemed to be in a more sanguine humour, having heard from Robin Phelips that the King was safely hidden at Heale House. My Lord Southampton, too, was anxious to do his possible, and had sent to offer his help in procuring a boat; an offer which Wilmot could not make up his mind whether to accept or to decline. He thought that Southampton might possess influence in Portsmouth, but was at the same time afraid to employ him for fear of his being too well-known a Royalist to escape being under suspicion. Colonel Gounter begged him not to move in the matter until he had seen his cousin next day; and after discussing the question with Lawrence Hyde, Wilmot decided to follow this advice.

The Colonel stayed to supper, and was pressed both by his host and by Wilmot to remain the night. The weather had been growing steadily worse all day, and by the time supper was ended a boisterous wind was driving the rain against the window-panes. Wilmot could not conceive of anyone's venturing out in such dismal weather, and was quite amazed when the Colonel declared that since the business of transporting the King out of England would brook no delay, he must return to Racton that evening.

'But, my dear sir, it is, besides all else, extremely dark!'

'I know the way too well to miss it,' Gounter replied. 'I will come to you again as soon as I have anything to tell you – certainly within the next twenty-four hours.'

'But if you cannot discover any seaman willing —'

'I shall discover one,' Gounter interrupted.

Wilmot blinked at him. 'You are very sure, Colonel!'

'My lord, when a thing *must* be done, there is always a way,' said Gounter.

He reached his home between one and two in the morning, and snatched a few hours sleep on his bed before setting out again. He would not stay for breakfast at Racton, but left the house soon after sunrise, and rode to Chichester, where, in a quiet inn not far from the Market Cross, he had appointed his cousin to meet him.

While he discussed cold beef and ale, Thomas Gounter recounted the tale of his own endeavours. These had been as unavailing as the Colonel's, the only conclusion to be drawn from them being that there was no chance of success at any of the coast-towns within reach of Chichester.

The Colonel said with decision: 'I must seek out some French merchant.'

'Do you know any?' asked Tom. 'I am woefully sure I do not.'

'I don't, but it's in my mind I have met one Francis Mansel, in company, and that it was told me that he was a merchant that had considerable traffic with France. I believe him to be honest: it was in a loyal house that I met him.'

'I have heard of him,' said Tom. 'He may be honest, for aught I know, but you'll scarcely break such a matter to one who is no better than a stranger!'

'Nay, no need to speak of the King. I'll hatch some tale that shall satisfy him.'

Tom looked rather dubious, but since he had no better plan to suggest, he made no further demur, but went with his cousin as far as to Mr Mansel's door. Here they parted, Tom going off to await his kinsman in a neighbouring inn, and the Colonel being admitted into Mansel's house.

The merchant, who was a middle-aged man, with quiet

manners, and a rather chilling pair of grey eyes, received his guests courteously, but with a hint of surprise in his face. When the Colonel recalled to his mind the occasion of their former meeting, and gave as a reason for his visit a desire to become better acquainted with him, he bowed, but directed a long, speculative look at him. He sent for a bottle of wine, and some Spanish tobacco, and said that he was glad to know the Colonel better, and they must drink a glass of French wine together.

'Ah, you usually trade into France, do you not, sir?' asked the Colonel casually.

'Usually,' agreed Mr Mansel, delicately pouring the wine into two glasses. 'Not always.'

While they drank the wine, and smoked their pipes, the Colonel kept up a flow of idle talk which was yet designed to lead his host into betraying his politics. These seemed to be satisfactory, and after perhaps half-an-hour's chat, Gounter said, with an air of frankness: 'I think you have guessed that I do not come only to visit you, but have to request a favour of you.'

'Anything in my power, my dear Colonel,' said Mansel politely.

'I hope and believe that it may be in your power. To be plain with you, there are two special friends of mine who have been engaged in a duel, and there is mischief done, so that I am obliged to get them off if I can. Can you, for a sum, freight a barque?'

Mansel took a moment to answer this. He sipped his wine, looking inscrutably at the Colonel over the rim of the glass. He said after a meditative silence: 'I daresay I could do so, if I went to Brighthelmstone.'

'Then, sir, will you do it?' asked the Colonel bluntly.

Mansel set his glass gently down on the table. 'Yes, Colonel, since you ask it of me and I know you to be an honest man, I will do it – for a sum.'

'There is fifty pounds in it, if you can effect the business, and will do so speedily.'

'A fair price,' said Mansel, with an inclination of his head. 'I think it can be accomplished.'

'I thank you! Now, will you go to Brighthelmstone today, and take me along with you?'

A thin hand was lifted. 'Ah, I am sorry! Tomorrow, with good will, if you please, but today, my dear sir, is Stow-Fair-day here, as you must know, and my partner being out of the way I must not absent myself – indeed, I cannot absent myself.'

The Colonel tried to persuade him, but soon saw that he was wasting his breath.

'Tomorrow,' smiled Mansel. 'Positively tomorrow, sir, and that I will faithfully promise. Come for me here, early, and if you will lend me a horse to go upon, I will take you to Brighthelmstone, and put you in the way of striking a bar-gain with an honest mariner there, who, I think, will be glad to serve you.'

With this the Colonel had to be content. He got up to take his leave, saying as he shook hands with his host: 'I need not enjoin you to keep this matter to yourself, I know.'

'No,' said Mansel, faintly amused. 'You need not, indeed, Colonel. I am persuaded that it would be very foolish – ah, very dangerous, perhaps? – for me to mention that I have agreed to freight a barque to carry your – er – duelling friends – out of England.'

The Colonel looked at him, his face a little grim. Mansel's smile grew. 'Oh no, Colonel!' he said. 'You need not fear me, nor do I wish to know the names of these – er –unfor-tunate gentlemen, whom I am to have the honour of assist-ing.'

'Oh, as to that, I think you would be little the wiser!' replied the Colonel. 'Tomorrow, then; and I will not fail to bring a horse for you.'

He then left the merchant's house, going first to the inn where Tom Gounter stayed for him, and, presently home to Racton, where he ate his dinner, and a little rested his horse before setting out once more for Hinton Daubnay. The weather was very bad, sheets of rain being driven across the countryside by a wind that brought the yellowing leaves down from the trees in swirling drifts. The Colonel's horse was nearly done, and he was forced to ride more slowly than he wished, arriving at Lawrence Hyde's house only in time for supper.

Wilmot as overjoyed to hear of his transactions with Francis Mansel, his approval being tempered only by regret that the merchant had been unable to go that very day to Brighthelmstone. He had had word from Dr Henchman that the King was well, and in good spirits, his presence at Heale quite unsuspected; but the fact of his being confined to one small room, with only two elderly ladies to wait on him, made my lord extremely anxious to remove him. When he learned that the village of Brighthelmstone was situated nearly thirty miles to the east of Chichester, he began to fret again, foreseeing that it would be impossible for the Colonel to go there, and return to Hinton Daubnay in one day. The Colonel, however, promised to come to him again with all possible despatch, but was forced to beg Lawrence Hyde for the loan of a good horse, his own being quite spent. As ill-luck would have it, the only horse in Hyde's stables that could be spared, or was up to the Colonel's weight, was the falconer's a sturdy beast, but no flyer. Mounted on this animal, Gounter left Hinton Daubnay late that evening, once more declining a most pressing invitation to remain there for the night.

A few hours' sleep was all that he allowed himself when he reached Racton. He rose from his bed at dawn, heavy-eyed, but denying any extraordinary fatigue, and set out for Tom Gounter's house, there to borrow a horse for Francis Mansel. This accomplished, and Tom promising to repair to Hinton Daubnay, to assure Wilmot that the business was in train, the Colonel rode into Chichester, to Mansel's house.

The merchant was ready for him, but insisted that before they set out on their long ride, the Colonel should partake of breakfast. 'You are not one who lets the grass grow under his feet, I perceive,' he said, with his thin-lipped smile. 'But fair and softly goes far in a day, my dear Colonel. Eat first, ride after!'

They reached Brighthelmstone by two o'clock in the after-noon, and repaired immediately to the only inn so mean a village possessed. It had been agreed between them that

Mansel should conduct the negotiations with the master of the barque he had in mind, and upon their arrival at the George he left the Colonel to smoke a pipe in the parlour while he went out to look for the mariner. He returned in a short while with the unwelcome tidings that Stephen Tattersal had already bargained for a freight in Chichester, and was gone there. This was a bitter set-back, but when Mansel further disclosed that Tattersal had touched at Shoreham, a port four miles to the west of Brighthelmstone, and was in all probability there still, the Colonel at once persuaded him to send off a messenger, begging Tattersal to come to him upon urgent business.

Mansel raised his brows slightly, but obeyed. While they waited together in the inn, he asked the Colonel what price he was willing to pay Tattersal for the business.

'I will pay what I must, but I beg of you to get it as low as you may,' replied the Colonel.

'You need have no fear of that,' said Mansel.

It was dark before an answer to his message was received, but it came at last in the person of Captain Tattersal, who rolled into the inn as the Colonel and Mansel were sitting down to supper.

Mansel at once invited him to join them, and he sat down to table, declaring that he was very willing. He was a thick-set man with a weather-beaten complexion, and a bluff voice that could easily make itself heard above the howling of any gale. He announced that he would not have broken his journey for any other than Mr Mansel, and demanded to be told why he was sent for.

'I have a freight for you,' replied Mansel.

'Then I'll compound with you, and let my other bargain go hang, for you and me has dealt together oft-times, and I know you for a warm man,' declared Tattersal, helping himself liberally from the blackjack full of sack that stood on the table. 'Is it coals?'

'No,' said Mansel, in his calm way.

'What then?'

'That,' said Mansel, 'you shall know when the time comes.'

''Sblood, what's this?' demanded Tattersal, his little, quick eyes bright with suspicion. 'I'll know what I'm to carry, or I'll not treat!'

'Presently, presently!' said Mansel.

But it was no until two o'clock upon the following day, which was Saturday, 11th October, that a bargain was finally struck. Mansel, although unwilling to do so, was forced to disclose the Colonel's story of the mythical duellists before Tattersal could be brought to enter into any agreement; and after this there was still much haggling to be done.

Finally, Tattersal pledged himself to carry the unknown passengers to France for the sum of sixty pounds, to be paid to him in hand before he took them aboard his vessel. He agreed to hold himself in readiness to set sail upon an hour's warning, and to bring his boat to the little hamlet of Southwick, which lay between Shoreham and Brighthelmstone. Mansel, upon being privately assured by the Colonel that, besides receiving his fee of fifty pounds, all his charges should be defrayed, consented to remain at Brighthelmstone, under pretence of freighting the barque, so that he could keep a watch over Tattersal, and be certain that all was in readiness for whenever the Colonel should bring his friends to Brighthelmstone.

The Colonel took leave of him at about three o'clock, and set out to cover the forty miles to Hinton Daubnay before nightfall. Since he had his portmanteau strapped to the saddle behind him, and had warned his wife that he might be absent for some days, he wasted no time in calling at his own home, but pushed on as speedily as he could to Mr Hyde's house, arriving there shortly before nine o'clock in the evening.

Lawrence Hyde himself came out to greet him, exclaiming: 'Well, George! If you are not dead of fatigue, you should be! Come you in, man! How have you fared?'

'Well, as I hope,' the Colonel answered, easing his aching limbs. 'I've left Mansel at Brighthelmstone to see all prepared. The bargain was not concluded until two o'clock this afternoon, which has made me later than I wished to be. How is my lord?'

Hyde took him into the house, with a hand thrust in his

arm. 'My lord is – very much like himself,' he said. 'He is not here at this present.'

The Colonel turned his tired face towards Hyde. 'Not here?' he said sharply. 'Do you mean that something has gone amiss?'

'Nothing in the world that I know of,' replied Hyde. 'But some friends chancing to visit me yesterday, my lord took fright, believing he might be recognized, and that my house was, besides, too public for safety. He could not be at ease, so your cousin Gounter removed him to his sister's house, where he awaits you.'

'To Anthony Brown's?' said the Colonel, in rather a blank voice. 'Well, I suppose he is secure there, but —' He broke off, and, happening to catch Hyde's eye, could not help laughing. 'Nay, poor man, it's no wonder that he goes like a cat upon a hot bakestone! But I must not stay here, if he is gone.'

Hyde opened the door into one of the parlours, and thrust him in. 'My dear George, not one of us looked to see you back this night, so you may be easy! Go you in: I swear you shall not leave my house until you have at least drunk some sack, and eaten a biscuit. I have Robin Phelips with me, who will be glad to hear how you have fared.'

He made the two men known to each other, and went off to fetch refreshment, while Colonel Gounter sat down, stretching his muddied boots to the fire, and answered Phelips's anxious questions.

The two Colonels were in odd contrast one to the other, Phelips being stockily framed, and of a fleshy habit, slow of mind and of speech; and Gounter a tall man, with a body hardened to the temper of his own sword, and movements that were as quick as his brain, and as decided. He gave Phelips a brief account of the arrangements he had made. It was evident that he saw nothing remarkable in his own driving energy, but Phelips, quite lost in admiration of the man who could not only, without apparent discomfort, spend four days in ceaseless searching, but who was also not in the least afraid to take upon himself the direction of the whole, dangerous affair, could only stare, and ejaculate: 'You shall be a saint in my almanack for ever! I had not thought it possible you could have concluded the business in so short a time!'

'Ah!' said Lawrence Hyde, smiling. 'It's plain you don't know my kinsman, Robin.'

He turned to Gounter, to suggest to him that he should postpone his departure for Brown's house until the following morning. This, however, Gounter could not be persuaded to do, for he knew that although Hyde might not have expected him to return so soon from Brighthelmstone, Wilmot would certainly be looking for him. He finished his sack, and got up.

'Well,' said Phelips, heaving himself out of his chair, 'I doubt you are right to go, and I will come with you, for it seems to me that you and I have some things to discuss, my lord being no more fit to have the ordering of his Majesty's removal from Heale than my spaniel. Let him have his way, and there will be a dozen men pulled into the business, and all with a different plan.'

The Colonel laughed, but said quickly: 'He has not let my Lord Southampton set about the finding of a ship, has he?'

'No,' replied Phelips, with a grim little smile. 'He has not, for he sent me to discover the King's will in the matter, and the King, hearing that you had gone to Brighthelmstone with a very fair hope of engaging a vessel there, said he would not put my Lord Southampton to the danger of having anything to do with it. I can tell you, Gounter, that's a man of quite another kidney for you.'

'Southampton?' Gounter asked.

'Nay, the King. I'll own, when I first clapped eyes on him, I was sadly taken aback, for he is a damned ugly lad, you know: no more like his father than chalk is to cheese. 'Deed, I knew not how to take him, for I never saw a man so merry, not one that cared less for danger. Well, I'll not deny I came nigh to forgetting my duty when nothing would do for him but he must ride coolly into Mere all for the sake of his dinner! But the truth is he's like a cat: fling him which way you will, he'll light on his legs!'

'Merry?' Gounter said. 'Is he indeed *merry*?'

A reluctant grin stole into Phelips's eyes. 'As merry as cup and can,' he asseverated.

## CHAPTER XXI

## BROTHER ROUNDHEAD

AFTER consultation with Wilmot, it was decided that Phelips, and not Gounter, should go to Salisbury upon the following day, which was Sunday, to inform Dr Henchman that all was in order to the King's escape; and, through him, to provide for Charles's leaving Heale very early upon Monday morning. Although Gounter was responsible for the arrangements, and was considered by Wilmot the better man to send upon such an errand, he was plainly so tired-out that if he was to be of any further use to Charles, he must be allowed to rest for a day. When he found that Phelips, no less than Wilmot and Tom Gounter, looked to him for orders, and that all three of his companions were relying on him to direct every detail of the King's journey to Brighthelmstone, the Colonel himself realized that it was extremely necessary that he should clear his head of the befogging effects of weariness. Before he retired to rest, he sat with the others round a table in Anthony Brown's parlour, and forced his brain to grapple with the new problem presented to it. His eyes were bloodshot, and he found it difficult to keep his weighted lids from sinking over them; but after he had drunk a glass or two of wine he was able to hammer out a plan that met with Wilmot's approval. Phelips had provided himself with a rough map of the district. He and Gounter bent over it, deciding upon the route along which he was to lead the King, and the precise point where it would be most convenient for Wilmot and both the Gounters to meet them.

'And where is his Majesty to be housed on Monday night?' demanded Wilmot.

'Why, at Lawrence Hyde's, surely?' said Phelips, raising his head. 'It is the fittest place I know, besides that Hyde has engaged himself to provide absolute security for him.'

'No, no, I like it not at all!' Wilmot said, with a quick frown. 'It is too public, and has no secret place. Moreover, I myself stayed there over-long, so that the news of it may have spread abroad. I'll not expose his Majesty to that risk.'

'For my part, I see no risk,' growled Phelips. 'I warrant his Majesty will be pleased enough to go there. It's but for one night, and Hyde positively expects him.'

'I know not why he should, for I gave him no such assurance,' said Wilmot, with one of his haughty looks.

'Then where is he to go?' asked Phelips.

Tom Gounter removed his pipe from his mouth to say in his slow way: 'You will not bring him here, my lord, will you? For I have not opened to my brother-in-law the real reason of your coming here, and he knows nothing of the King's being at hand. George! Do you think the King would stand in any danger at Lawrence Hyde's house?'

'No,' said the Colonel wearily.

A flush mounted to Wilmot's cheeks. 'It is to no purpose, think what you will! I would remind you, gentlemen, that it is I who am responsible for his Majesty's safety! Some other house must be found for him.'

'I will take order to it,' said the Colonel, finding that three expectant pairs of eyes were turned towards him.

'Yes, my dear sir, but do you know of any secure house? Have you any in mind?' persisted Wilmot.

The Colonel's eyes watered with his efforts to suppress a yawn: his sudden smile dawned. 'To tell you the truth, my lord,' he confessed, 'at this present I have nothing in mind but a longing for my bed.'

'Ay, and small blame to you!' said Phelips, folding the map, and stowing it away in his pocket. 'Look ye, my lord: we are using our good friend mighty scurvily! As well go rabbit-hunting with a dead ferret as call upon a man that has not had above eight hours' sleep in four nights to do your thinking for you! Go you between sheets, Gounter! I have it all pat, and will look for you to meet us in the neighbourhood of Warnford, as agreed.'

Wilmot looked dissatisfied, but it was evident that Colonel Gounter could scarcely keep himself awake, so he was forced to allow him to go up to bed, and to trust that when he was rested he would be able to think of some house where the King could lie in safety.

His trust was not misplaced. The Colonel slept like a log until it was almost dusk next day, but when he did come downstairs he looked perfectly refreshed, and was ready to bend his mind to any problem which my lord chose to put to him.

'Was I abominably stupid last night?' he asked apologetically. 'I could hardly hold my eyes open. But I do remember that you asked me if I could find a safe resting-place for the King hereabouts.'

'Yes, for I would not have him venture to Mr Hyde's,' replied Wilmot. 'Beyond all else, his is too great a house for security.'

'If he would be content with quite a small house, I think I can escort him to one where he will neither be known nor looked for,' said the Colonel. 'But it is not such a house as he has been used to stay in, my lord, being the home of one who is but a yeoman.'

'My dear sir, he will not care a fig for that! Where is this house?'

'At Hambledon, not three miles from here. It belongs to my brother-in-law, one Thomas Symons, that married my sister Ursula.'

'It is the very thing!' Wilmot declared. 'But can you trust him? Are you sure of him?'

'I daresay I might trust him, for he is a very honest man, but it is not my intention to put him to the test,' replied the Colonel coolly. 'I think I know how I may contrive to take the King there without Symons's knowing him for any other than plain William Jackson.'

Upon the following day, which was Monday, 13th October, the Colonel's energies, throughout the morning, were directed towards keeping my lord from riding to meet the King long before there could be any possibility of his being within twenty miles of him. Wilmot was thrown into a fret of anxiety, and spent his time looking at his watch, blaming himself for having allowed Phelips to go alone to fetch the King from Heale, and urging the Colonel to ride to Hamble-don to arrange for the King's sleeping there that night.

Gounter, while appreciating, with ready sympathy, the thousand dreads that made my lord so importunate, refused to swerve from the agreed course. 'Only trust me, my lord!' he said. 'Indeed, I know what I am about.'

'Yes, yes, I know you do!' Wilmot replied remorsefully. 'Do not heed me! Can my watch be right? I am certain it must be later!'

'What the pox ails this fellow you have brought into my house?' demanded Anthony Brown of his brother-in-law. 'He's like a frog on a chopping-block!'

'Well,' said Tom Gounter, 'he is anxious to be gone. You know I told you he has had his finger in the pie that was baked at Worcester.'

'Then I wish he would be gone, for he frets me more than a louse in the bosom!' said Brown, with some asperity.

But it was not until they had eaten their dinner that Colonel Counter would permit my lord to call for his horse. He consigned him then to Tom Gounter's care, instructing Tom to lead him up on to Warnford Downs, and himself rode ahead to his sister's house.

Hambledon lay in a cup of the hills two miles from Hinton Daubnay. Mr Thomas Symons's house was a little way from the timbered cottages that constituted the village, and was a comfortable manor, standing in its own neat, though small demesne. When the Colonel rode up to the door, his sister, who had seen his approach from an upper window, came out to meet him, her sleeves rolled up (for she had been busy in her stillroom), and an apron covering her stuff gown.

'Come you in, George, come you in!' she cried, holding out her hands to him. 'It is a weary while since you have been able to visit me! Is your parole taken off? Are you free at last?'

He dismounted, and kissed her cheek. 'Ay, I have compounded with the Commissioners, and am enlarged. How do you go on, sister? Is your good man well?'

'Very well, but as ill-luck would have it he is gone to Portsmouth, and I don't expect him back till supper-time. But come in, George, and tell me how Kate does, and the children?'

'All well. But I may not remain with you at this present, for Tom Gounter and some other gentlemen stay for me. The devil fly away with your good man! I came to beg he would lend me a brace of greyhounds, for we have a mind to have a course at a hare, upon the Downs.'

'You may take them, and welcome!' she returned. 'But this is scurvy usage, brother, to come not nigh me for a year, and then only to borrow Tom's dogs!'

He had his arm round her waist, and gave her a hug. 'Nay, I knew you would say so, but being promised to Cousin Gounter, what can I do? I'll tell you what, Ursula! If we stay out late, and do not beat too far, we will all of us come and be merry with you tonight.'

'If you do, you shall be heartily welcome,' she said. 'How many must I expect to supper?'

'Why, there's Tom Gounter, and a Mr Barlow, from Devonshire, and two others, besides Barlow's servant. You will wish such a company at the devil, I daresay!'

'Nay, how can you say so?' she replied indignantly. 'If you are to please me, you will come with your friends, and you shall be sure of a good supper, and good beds after it.'

'Well, if I can, I will come,' he said. 'In any event, tell Tom Symons he shall be sure of his dogs.'

He would not stay to taste her March beer, but, having collected a brace of greyhounds, rode off to join Wilmot and his cousin on the Downs.

It was a fine day, and for an hour or two even Wilmot allowed himself to be diverted by the excitement of beating for hares. When the time of the King's probable arrival approached, the Colonel left the dogs with him and Tom Gounter, and rode on alone towards Warnford.

He went at an easy pace, but he had reached Warnford before he met the travellers. As he trotted gently down the main street, he saw two horsemen approaching him from the other end of the little town. In another minute he recognized Robin Phelips, and directed his eager, searching gaze towards the tall man riding beside him.

The first thought that struck him was that the King had the best seat in the saddle of any man he had seen; the second, that however meanly he might be dressed, his whole bearing so plainly proclaimed his royalty that it was little short of miraculous that those who saw him ride past them did not know him at once for what he was.

God save the mark! thought the Colonel, half aghast, half amused, let but a man pull off his hat to scratch his head, and the King will bow his thanks for the salute!

He was almost abreast of the two other riders by this time, and could clearly see the King's face. Beyond one quick glance, however, he did not look at it, but met Robin Phelips's questioning stare instead. He made no sign, thinking it very imprudent to recognize him in the middle of a town, but rode past, and dismounted farther up the street, at a decent ale-house. Out of the tail of his eye, he saw that Phelips and the King had not checked, but were riding on at an ambling trot.

He called for some beer, and a pipe, and sat down in the taproom as one who had the whole day to waste. It was nearly half an hour before he would permit himself to leave the ale-house, and when he did get up he forced himself to move in a leisurely fashion, strolling out to his horse, and riding off in the King's wake at a slow trot.

Once clear of the town, and sure that no suspicious eye observed his movements, he set spurs to his horse, and made what speed he could up on to the Downs.

He overtook the King and Phelips on the top of Old Winchester Hill, where they stayed for him. As he reined in his horse, and pulled off his hat, a merry voice said: 'Is this my new and careful guardian that will not know me in the street? I am very glad to see you, Colonel Gounter.'

The Colonel saw that a hand, brown enough for a country-fellow's but by far too shapely, was being held out to him. He pressed his horse up close to the King's, and took the hand in his, and kissed it. 'Your Majesty! God be praised that you are come, and safely!'

'Why, certainly, but from what Robin here tells me, I must praise one George Gounter also,' responded the King.

'Ay, that's true,' agreed Phelips. 'But it's by God's mercy we did not miscarry, Gounter! I can tell you, I have never been in such a sweat in my life, for when I brought the horses to the meadow-gate at Heale, close on three o'clock this morning, what must that jade his Majesty is mounted upon do but break his bridle, and run I know not how far up the river! I thought I should never recover him!'

'Broke his bridle!'

'Yes,' said the King, 'but when Robin had done swearing, all was very tolerably amended by my good hostess, who fetched us a length of strong ribbon, with which we contrived to secure the bit, as you may see.'

'Well, and if I swore I am sure it was no wonder, sir,' said Phelips. 'At least I did not stand laughing fit to break my sides while all went to rack! Gounter, tell me, is all provided for against his Majesty's coming? Where's my lord?'

'I left him running a course with my cousin not far off. If you will lead his Majesty on towards Hambledon, I will soon bring my lord after you.'

'Will you go, sir?' Phelips asked the King. 'I think it not wise to linger.'

'My dear Robin, did I not promise to do as you bad me?' said the King meekly.

'Saving my respect, I'd say your Majesty is a mighty careless promiser,' replied Phelips, with blunt honesty.

'Fie on you, I swear you wrong me! Lead on: I will go with you most obediently.' He smiled at Gounter as he gathered up his bridle, and added: 'Tell my lord to leave his sport, for I have a great desire to see him, Colonel.'

It was not necessary to tell my lord to leave his sport. He no sooner caught sight of Gounter riding over the Downs towards him, than he spurred forward to meet him, anxiously demanding whether he had seen the King. Upon hearing that he had ridden on with Phelips in the direction of Hambledon, he could scarcely wait for Tom Gounter to call the dogs to heel before starting in pursuit of his master.

They came up with the King upon Broadhalfpenny Down, above Hambledon. Wilmot let his bridle fall and caught Charles's outstretched hand in both of his, patting and fondling it. 'My dear!' he said in a broken voice. 'You are safe! What I have suffered since I parted from you! But you are well, you are safe!'

'I was never better in my life,' declared the King. 'But as for you, Harry, I swear you have become as gaunt as a greyhound!'

'If I had, it were small wonder!' said Wilmot, laughing. 'But alas, I am not yet as slender in the middle as I could wish!'

He released the King's hand, and rode beside him at a walking pace for some way, a little ahead of the others. They fell back out of earshot, but presently the King looked over his shoulder, and called Colonel Gounter to him. When the Colonel came up, he said: 'I have been holding some discourse with my lord, Colonel. Can you get me a lodging hereabouts?'

'Yes, sire, very easily,' replied the Colonel. 'My lord will have told your Majesty that my cousin Hyde's house at Hinton Daubnay is heartily at your disposal, for one.'

'But it seems that my lord will not have me go there. Know you of no other?'

'There is my sister's house at Hambledon, where your Majesty will be right welcome. It stands privately, and out of the way, but it is not as proper a lodging as Hyde's sir.'

'I like it better!' Wilmot said quickly. 'None will look there for you, sir!'

'Then let us go there,' said Charles, deciding the matter without more ado.

The Colonel sent his cousin and Robert Swan scouting ahead, and the whole party reached Symons's house, by a back way, at about candle-lighting time.

The master of the house had not returned from Portsmouth, but provision had been made for the visitors, and they had no sooner alighted from their horses than the door was opened, and a servant was begging them to step within.

The Colonel went first, with Lord Wilmot. As he greeted

his sister, who came across the hall to meet him, he heard the King say: 'Go before me, Robin: you look the most like a gentleman now!'

The Colonel kissed his sister, devoutly trusting that she had not heard this irrepressible sally, and said: 'Well, you see how I have taken you at your word! Let me make Mr Barlow known to you, and Colonel Robert Phelips here, and Mr Jackson. I warrant you, we have all of us very good stomachs, and are like to eat you out of your house!'

'You are all most welcome!' she assured them. 'A strange thing it would be if I could not provide supper for your friends! Please to come into the parlour, gentlemen. There is a good fire there, and you shall have some biscuits and sack presently.'

She ushered them into a cosy room where the curtains had been drawn and the candles lit, and bustled about, setting stools and chairs for them, bidding them come close to the fire, and enquiring what sport they had had. My lord's fine air at once impressed her, and she was careful to offer him the best chair. She turned her hospitable attention next to the King, and for one anxious moment the Colonel feared that she had recognized him, so solicitously did she beg him to take the chair opposite my lord's. But it seemed that she was prompted only by kindness, for she presently found the opportunity to whisper in her brother's ear: 'The lad looks quite tired-out, and has not a bit of colour in those brown cheeks of his! So shy and silent as he is, too! I daresay he feels awkward in company, for he seems a very poor man, by his dress.'

'Oh, let him be! He will speedily forget his shyness, if you pay him no extraordinary attention,' replied the Colonel. 'He is a tenant of Mr Barlow, and unused to going into company.'

She soon saw that this must be so, for upon some wine and biscuits being brought into the room, although her brother and Tom Gounter both got up to hand the glasses for her, Mr Will Jackson remained seated, and apparently thought no shame to allow his seniors to wait upon him. Such manners did not suit Mrs Symons's notions; she thought that if he knew no better he might well be taught, and so said in a kind but firm voice: 'Come, Mr Jackson, you may pass the wine for me, if you will, and let my brother take his ease'

'Nay, he is tired!' said the Colonel hastily. 'Do not plague him, sister!'

The King, however, got up at once. Mrs Symons noticed that although he had the grace to blush he seemed to be a good deal amused, for his heavy, dark eyes brimmed with laughter. She received a look from them which quite startled her, since it was not in the least the look of a shy youth, but rather that of an extremely audacious young man. 'I was dreaming,' he apologized, smiling at her in a way she found hard to resist. 'Sit down, Colonel, and leave all to me!'

It seemed to Mrs Symons that her brother hesitated for an instant, but before she could be sure of it, he had sat down, and Will Jackson was taking one of the wine-glasses out of her hand.

It was not long before she was forced to alter her opinion of Will Jackson. He was certainly not shy. Indeed, the shyest member of the party seemed, unaccountably, to be Tom Gounter, who made himself as small as he could in one corner of the room, and did not utter a word unless directly addressed. Will Jackson, on the other hand, though not talkative, had not the smallest hesitation in advancing any opinions he might chance to hold on the various subjects under discussion. He stood leaning his great shoulders against the mantelpiece, and slowly sipping his wine; and whenever he chose to speak, in his surprisingly musical voice, the three older gentlemen broke off whatever they were saying to listen to him. Mrs Symons shook her head over the freedom accorded to the younger generation, and went away to superintend the preparations for supper.

'I wish you would not all be so damned civil to me,' said the King. 'You will betray me yet.'

The Colonel replied, with a pronounced twinkle in his eye: 'Well, sir, it is very hard for us to forget that you are the King, when *you* do not remember that you are a poor tenant of Mr Barlow.'

A responsive laugh sprang to the King's lips. 'Very good,

Colonel! But what have I done?'

The Colonel shook his head. 'Alas, sire, it is no one thing, but everything you do. Even when you say nothing, your very looks are enough to betray you.'

'Oddsfish, so high in the instep am I? This is very ill-hearing!'

'No, no!' said Wilmot. 'He means not that. The truth is, sir, you are too careless.'

'I will amend my ways.'

Mrs Symons came back into the room just then to summon the company to supper. She led her guests into another, and larger parlour, where covers were laid upon a round table, and begging them to sit as they pleased, called upon her brother to carve the cold capons. 'Indeed, I do not know what is keeping my goodman,' she said. 'However, he will be home presently, and there is no need to wait supper for him.'

Halfway through the meal, the slam of a door, and the sound of a man's voice upraised in song proclaimed the return of Thomas Symons. He came across the hall to the dining-parlour, and thrusting open the door, stood blinking at the guests, and swaying a little on his heels. There was not the least need for anyone to enquire what had kept him: Mr Symons had plainly been in company that day.

'Oho!' murmured the King, in Phelips's ear. 'Our host has been playing the goodfellow at the tavern methinks!'

Symons released the door, and trod carefully into the room, exclaiming: 'This is brave! A man can no sooner be out of the way than his house must be taken up with I know not whom!'

'Husband!' said his wife. 'Mind your manners, I pray you!'

'Capons, and hams, and sour prunes, and I know not what beside!' he said bitterly. 'This is what it is to live under the sign of the cat's foot! Ay, ay, when the goodman's from home the goodwife's table is soon spread!'

Colonel Gounter pushed back his chair, and rose. 'Brother,' he said in some amusement, 'I think you have been in the sun!'

Symons looked at him closely. 'Oh! Is it you?' he said.

'Well, you are welcome.' He added handsomely: 'And, as your friends, George, so are they all!'

Wilmot muttered to his neighbour, Tom Gounter: 'This turns out very ill. The man may be dangerous to us.'

'No, sir, indeed!' Tom said earnestly. 'It is a pity he should come home disguised tonight, but when he is sober he is as honest a man as any I know.'

Symons, who had been shaking the Colonel by the hand, released him, and began to walk round the table, owlishly inspecting the rest of the company. The sight of Tom Gounter made him say with a comprehensive sweep of his hand: 'These are all Hydes now. They are welcome.' He came next to the King, and stared very hard at him. He was apparently much struck by his short hair, for he announced in an indignant tone: 'Here is a Roundhead!' He turned to look reproachfully at his brother-in-law. 'I never knew you keep Roundheads' company before!'

'It's no matter,' said the Colonel soothingly. 'He is my friend, and, I'll assure you, no dangerous man.'

Either this remark satisfied Symons, or a hazy notion of his duties as a host entered into his head, for after looking at the King again he suddenly sat down beside him, and grasping him by the hand, said: 'Brother Roundhead, for his sake you are welcome!'

My Lord Wilmot sighed, for he had caught the gleam in the King's eye, and knew him too well to entertain the smallest hope of his bearing himself discreetly. He saw that Colonel Phelips had grown alarmingly red in the face, and was evidently on the point of bursting into an indignant protest, and frowned at him. Phelips muttered something inaudible, and bent resolutely over his plate.

The King, meanwhile, allowed Symons to shake his hand up and down, and said: 'Brother, I thank you! I see you are an honest man.'

'If any man says I am not, they shall answer for it!' declared Symons. 'By God, I am so honest a man that the sight of a cropped head affects me like a wasp in the nose! But if you are George Gounter's friend, no matter for that! I'll cut you a slice of capon.'

'Nay, I pray you! no more, for I have eaten my fill,' said the King, recovering his hand.

'One slice off the breast!' begged Symons, picking up the carving-knife. 'I warrant you, you shall find it as tender as a parson's leman.'

'Nay, cut it for yourself, friend,' replied the King. 'I have come to the sweetmeats.'

'Well, if you will not eat you may drink,' said Symons, grasping the blackjack. 'I'll give you a toast.' He refilled the King's glass, and rather unsteadily poured himself another. 'There's no deceit in a brimmer,' he remarked, as some of the ale spilled over the top of his glass. He winked broadly at the rest of the company, and, lifting his glass, said: 'Here's to all good Roundheads! Drink up, drink up!'

'I had rather knock under the board!' growled Phelips.

The King's foot found his under the table, and trod upon it heavily.

'I'll have no such toasts drunk in my house!' said Mrs Symons in a mortified voice. 'As for you, Thomas Symons, you have drunk enough!'

He drained his glass, and set it down with a disgusted exclamation. 'This is poor stuff! Oddsdeath, it goes against the shins with me to set such thin ale before guests! Wait now, I'll fetch down that which shall ease your stomachs!'

He rose precariously to his feet as he spoke, and wended his way to the door. His wife said: 'Indeed, gentlemen, he is not often so, but having been to town, and run against his cronies, I daresay, you see how it is!'

Lord Wilmot, who was seated beside her, said in his light, bored way: 'My dear madam, the man who had never a cup too much is no man for me.'

'But I am concerned that he should take your tenant for a Roundhead!' she whispered. 'I hope he may not be offended!'

'You need not be concerned on his account, madam,' replied Wilmot, casting a glance at the King, who was laughing at something Colonel Gounter had said to him.

'I assure you, he has been a Royalist all his life,' persisted Mrs Symons. 'I know not what maggot can have got into his head to make him pretend otherwise!'

'Why, madam, I take it he means to put Mr Jackson at his ease. Never heed it!'

Symons came back into the room with a dusty bottle in his hand. He declared that he would shortly amend all, and in spite of his brother-in-law's protests, insisted upon lacing the ale with the brandy the bottle contained. 'That'll make a cat speak!' he said, with satisfaction. 'Fill up, Brother Roundhead, and we'll drink some more good healths!'

'If you will drink a health, let it be the King's!' said his wife.

'What, madam!' exclaimed Charles, throwing up his hand. 'Drink the health of that rogue, that brought the Scots in! Fie, fie!'

'You say well!' approved Symons, with yet another wink round the table. 'Ay, does your nose swell at that, cousin Tom? Go hang yourself for a pastime! we are all snuffling – nay, I mean we are all godly Puritans here.'

He filled up the King's glass again, bidding him drain it, for there was plenty more. Colonel Gounter emptied his own glass, and swiftly exchanged it for the King's, while his cousin drew off Symons's attention.

Mrs Symons, quite unable to sit by in quiet while her husband by his fits aped the manners of a Puritan, excused herself, and went off to rage unavailingly in her kitchen.

'Now we may be merry!' said Symons. 'Commend a married life, Brother Roundhead, but keep thyself a bachelor!'

'Yea, we bachelors grin, but you married men laugh till your hearts ache!' responded the King, edging yet another full glass towards Colonel Phelips.

Tom Gounter, who was profoundly shocked at the turn events had taken, tried to engage his host in conversation, but only partially succeeded in diverting his attention from the King. The more he drank, the more convinced Symons became that he had a Roundhead in his house. The King did nothing to disabuse his mind of this belief, and whenever an oath escaped Symons, which was often, he rolled his eyes upwards and exclaimed: 'Oh, dear brother, that is a 'scape. Swear not, I beseech you!' Occasionally Symons forgot his rôle, and not only uttered sentiments startlingly at variance with it, but tossed off bumpers to the King, wishing damnation to his enemies.

'Nay, nay, he is a godless young man, and woundily ill-favoured besides!' the King assured him.

'If a lie could have choked you, that would have done it!' said Symons, with the sudden ferocity of the drunk.

'Alas, brother, I fear you have a kindness for Malignants!' mourned the King.

'What I say, and hold to, is this!' said Symons, wagging a finger at him. 'If the King had kept his foot out of Scotland, he would have done better, for do you know what they did to him there? They held his nose to a grindstone, which was the Covenant, and the more fool he to suffer them! But a ragged colt may make a good horse, and if any gainsay it he shall have a cup of ale thrown in his face!'

'A man of Belial!' groaned the King, covering his eyes with his hand.

'Will you hold your peace?' whispered Phelips indignantly. 'You'll bring yourself to ruin, sir!'

'Retro me, Sathanas!' said the King in a hollow voice.

'You're out, sir: that's popish stuff!' murmured Colonel Gounter.

Time wore on. By ten o'clock, Symons had passed from querulousness to a mood of rollicking good-fellowship, and showed no sign of abating his hospitality. Since the King had ridden forty miles that day, and must ride as far upon the following day, it became a matter of some importance to get him to bed. His glass was still being replenished, and as regularly passed to Colonel Phelips, who was hard put to it to know how to dispose of its contents; and whenever he made a movement to retire, his host thrust him back into his chair, declaring he should not let him go, for he was a good fellow in spite of his cropped head.

Finally, Colonel Gounter solved the difficulty, by ousting Tom Gounter from his place on Symons's left hand, and sitting himself down there in his stead. Plucking Symons by the sleeve, he whispered to him: 'I wonder how you should judge so right! The fellow is a Roundhead indeed.'

'It's as plain as a pack-saddle,' replied Symons, wisely nodding his head. 'But to see a canting Puritan so dagged would make a cat laugh! Do you mark him? He is as drunk as David's sow!'

'So he is,' agreed the Colonel, refusing to meet the King's eye. 'But he is a melancholy fellow! If we could get him to bed, the house were our own, and we could be merry.'

'By God, you are right!' said Symons, much struck by this idea. 'But how to be rid of him? He sits there as full as a piper's bag.'

'Leave it to me: I think I know how to persuade him.' The Colonel got up, and walked round behind Symons's chair to the King's. He bent over him, and spoke softly in his ear. 'Will you come, sir? It's time and more that you were abed.'

'But I have never been so well-entertained in my life!' objected the King.

'I don't doubt it,' agreed the Colonel. 'But you have a very hard ride before you, sir.'

The King laughed, but rose. Colonel Phelips followed suit, announcing that he kept no late hours. Symons, deciding that it behoved him to escort his guests to their chambers, lurched out of his chair, and would have gone with them, had not Wilmot intervened, calling attention to his glass, and telling him that he was hanged that left his drink behind him. While Symons disposed of what was left of his ale, Colonel Gounter removed the King and Phelips out of his sight, and took them upstairs to a chamber where there was a truckle bed at the foot of a roomy four-poster.

'This is what comes of my lord's whims and crotchets!' exploded Phelips. 'We should have taken his Majesty to Mr Hyde's, and so I held from the start!'

'And you'll hold to it, buckle and thong, to the end,' remarked the King. 'I would give much to see your brother-in-law's face if ever he discovers the truth, Colonel Gounter!'

'I promise you, he will be ready to cut his throat, sir,' replied the Colonel, helping him to pull off his coat. 'But you may sleep here in safety, for there is none would think to look for you in this house. Tomorrow, at daybreak, we must set out for Brighthelmstone, where I have left my merchant to see all prepared against our coming.'

'If only we do not again miscarry!' said Phelips.

The King's slumbrous eyes rested thoughtfully on Gounter's face, a smile lighting their darkness. 'I do not think we shall miscarry,' he remarked.


## CHAPTER XXII

### 'I KNOW HIM WELL'

WHEN Colonel Gounter went to rouse the King at day-break, he found him sleeping peacefully with his cheek on his hand. Phelips was already up and dressed. He saw Gounter looking half in wonder, half in admiration, at the King, and gave a grim little smile. 'I told you he was of a different kidney from my lord,' he said. 'Did ye think to find him wakeful that has half England hunting him through the length and breadth of the land? Not he! he has not stirred since he dropped his graceless head on the pillow. It's I who have slept a dog's sleep, starting at every rat that gnawed behind the wainscot.' He stood looking down at the King, with a mixture of severity and lurking affection in his face. 'Well, you may take him, and welcome!' he said gruffly. 'He has brought my bones to water with his wilful spurts. And now, when I look to be rid of him and the whole dangerous business, what must he demand of me but that I shall risk my neck in London to provide that moneys may be sent to meet him at Rouen!'

'Will you do it?' enquired Gounter.

Phelips smiled sourly. 'If a man's fool enough to let that lad put his spells on him, he must give himself up for lost, no help for it! He'd coax Noll Cromwell himself, if he did but come face to face with him, plague take him!' He bent over the bed, and laid his hand on the King's shoulder, and shook it. 'Rouse up now, sir!'

The King stirred, and opened his eyes. When he saw Phelips leaning over him, he smiled sleepily, and stretched himself. 'What, Robin, is it dawn already?' he murmured.

'Ay, long since, sir, and Gounter here waiting to carry you off.'

The King sat up. 'I was ever a very sound sleeper,' he said apologetically.

Colonel Gounter, conscious of Phelips's sardonic eye upon him, looked across the bed at him, and said frankly: 'Yes, I am lost, and care not a jot what may come of it.'

Phelips gave vent to a short laugh. 'I told ye!'

But when he parted from the King on the Downs above Hambledon, he gripped that slender hand to his lips in the most uncourtier-like fashion, and said in a voice that was thickened by emotion: 'God keep you safe, sir, and bring you to your throne at last!'

'God keep you safe, also Robin, and when I come to my throne, let me see you!'

'I shall do so, and hope it may be soon. Have a care to him, Gounter!' Phelips said roughly, and saluting, rode off at a smart trot.

'And now,' said the King, 'the last stage in my adventures!'

'I trust so, sir. But it is in my mind that we are too great a company to escape notice. With your good will, I would have my cousin leave us as soon as we reach Stanstead, and my lord's servant too, if he is not to take ship with you.'

'What!' exclaimed the King, with a comical expression of amazement. 'You will never go without Swan, Harry!'

'Yes, yes, I think I must do so,' replied Wilmot seriously. 'I shall not be without a servant for long, after all, and he would not do to go to France with me.'

'But, Harry, do you look to me to wait on you? I give you fair warning I shall not do it!'

'Now, my dear master, I beg of you, leave jesting!' Wilmot implored him. 'You may count yourself safe, I daresay, but I shall not do so until I see you set foot on French soil. I do trust, Colonel Gounter, that you mean to lead us away from the highroads?'

'I do indeed, my lord.'

'Ah! No dinner,' said the King. 'I would someone would

protect me from my friends.'

The Colonel's eyes twinkled. 'Content you, sir, you shall have your dinner, for I have put a couple of neats' tongues in my pockets, which you may eat of when you will. I have also made provision for your Majesty to rest awhile, if it you would be pleased to do so, at a very loyal gentleman's house at Beeding, which is near to Brighthelmstone.'

The King said, with a glancing smile: 'My friend, is there anything you have forgot to make provision for?'

'I hope not, sir,' answered the Colonel, frowning in an effort of memory. 'Upon consideration, I thought it well to arrange for your going into some secure house while I ride ahead into Brighthelmstone to assure myself that it is safe for you to enter the village.'

'I thank you, Colonel, and begin to wonder how I came so far without you to manage my affairs.'

The Colonel flushed. 'Your Majesty had others to serve you.'

'Yes, many others,' said Wilmot, 'but he speaks truly: you have done excellent well, my dear sir!'

'I have tried to do my duty,' replied the Colonel briefly, and made an excuse to fall back to ride beside his cousin.

At Stanstead, Tom Gounter kissed hands, and rode away to his own home. Robert Swan kissed hands too, but although he uttered a prim hope that God would preserve his Majesty, it was only when he bade farewell to his master that a tremor of emotion shook his voice. 'My lord,' he said, overcoming it, 'I have placed your lordship's lace-bands between your handkerchiefs in the trunk, and laid the Holland shirt over all. And the roots for the cleaning of your lordship's teeth will be found wrapped in a napkin, alongside your lordship's comb, and the phial containing the musk, which we have not broached.'

'Harry,' said the King, when Swan had ridden away, 'if I did not mean to claim that clean shirt the instant we set sail for France, I swear I would have your head! Do you know what there is in my bundle?'

'Alas, very little, dear sir!' said Wilmot, sadly shaking his head.

'You say sooth!' returned the King with deep feeling.

Colonel Gounter, a good deal amused by this interchange, begged leave to remind the King that if they were to reach Brighthelmstone that evening, they had no time to waste. The three men accordingly rode on, Gounter acting all the time as guide.

The way led across country, and the only people they encountered, until they drew near Arundel, a little after midday, were country-folk, who displayed no interest in them. Even Wilmot's fears began to be sensibly allayed, and after a few hours of riding over lonely uplands his spirits became quite gay. But as they came abreast of the steep hill leading down into Arundel, the noise of hounds baying reached their ears, and in another instant a company of horsemen came into sight, riding at full-butt towards them.

The Colonel, who had caught a glimpse of the foremost rider, a stocky man with very smartly curled mustachios, and a voice of brass, said quickly: 'In amongst the trees, and dismount!'

The King at once swung his horse round; Lord Wilmot followed him, and by the time the hounds swept by in full cry, the three travellers were hidden from the huntsmen's view, all of them standing on the ground, and gripping their horses above the nostrils to prevent their betraying them by neighing.

If any of the hunt had noticed three travellers on the road they were either too much absorbed in their sport to wonder at their sudden disappearance, or they supposed them to have ridden down the hill into the village. They galloped by without a check, and were soon out of sight over the brow of the hill.

The Colonel removed his hand from his horse's nostrils, and said devoutly: 'Thank God! Did you see the man who rode first behind the hounds, sir? He was none other than Captain Morley, who is the governor of the Castle, and as rabid a schismatic as you may find in the whole of England!'

'Oddsfish, was he indeed?' said the King. 'I did not much like his starched mustachios!'

He spoke merrily, and did not seem to be at all disconcerted by his narrow escape; but Lord Wilmot's peace of mind was shattered. His gaiety fell away from him, and when the little village of Houghton, just south of Amberley, was reached, and the Colonel proposed to the King that he should stop for some beer at the ale-house, and there eat his neats' tongues, he reprimanded him sharply for suggesting such a thing.

But the King, being both hungry and thirsty, hailed the suggestion with acclaim. 'If you are afraid, ride on, Harry!' was all the answer he had for Wilmot's protests.

Wilmot flushed angrily, and said in a low voice: 'If I am afraid, it is upon your account! Do you think I would leave you?'

'Nay, I did but jest,' Charles said soothingly.

'If you would jest less and give more heed to the danger you stand in, I might be spared some part at least of the anxieties you make me to undergo!'

'Alas, poor Harry! I use you damnably,' said Charles.

He sounded remorseful, and the caressing note in his voice won Wilmot over; but he stopped at the ale-house for his dinner. As a concession to my lord's fears, he ate it in the saddle; but Colonel Gounter, an appreciative spectator of his King's methods of getting his own way, remembered Robert Phelips's words, and smiled to himself.

When they had finished the bread and neats' tongues and drunk their beer, they rode on, crossing the Arun by Houghton Bridge, and proceeding due east, in the direction of Bramber. They reached Bramber between three and four o'clock in the afternoon, and were riding down the street, past the first thatched cottages, when they discovered that the village was full of soldiers.

Wilmot was aghast, and the Colonel hardly less so, for no soldiers had been quartered at Bramber when he had ridden through it on his way from Brighthelmstone to Hinton Daubnay.

'For God's sake, sir, stop!' Wilmot said. 'We dare not go on! We must turn back, and go by another way!'

The Colonel, though shaken, still kept his wits about him, and interposed quickly, saying: 'If we do, we are undone!

Let us go on boldly, and we shall not be suspected!'

'God's death, are you mad?'

'Nay, he says well,' said the King. 'We will go on.'

'Sir, I implore you —'

'My dear Harry, this is not the first time I have ridden through a troop of Roundheads,' said the King calmly. 'I warrant you they will not look twice at me.'

He rode on down the slight hill, with Gounter's knee brushing his. When they reached the centre of the town, where the soldiers were lounging outside an ale-house, there was only room in the road for a single horseman to pass, and Gounter pushed ahead, touching his hat in civil acknowledgment when a couple of troopers drew aside to let him go by. There was not much disposition shown to make way for travellers, and once or twice the Colonel had almost to force his passage. There was just enough good-humoured authority in his voice to carry weight, and by dint of a well-chosen jest or two, he brought the King through the town without incurring anything worse than a few grumbles.

Once clear of Bramber, Wilmot spurred up to ride beside the King. He was inclined to blame the Colonel for having led them into a nest of Roundheads, and had been roused to a good deal of impotent fury by the conduct of the troopers in taking up the whole street; but the King said that all soldiers were very much the same, whether Roundheads or Royalists, a remark which annoyed Wilmot, but drew a laugh from Colonel Gounter, who knew it to be true.

They had not ridden far out of Bramber when they heard the thunder of hooves. The King cocked an eyebrow at Gounter, and cleared his throat in a warning hem. The Colonel looked swiftly over his shoulder, and saw, to his dismay, a troop of thirty or forty soldiers riding down upon them at a purposeful trot.

'Slacken, sir, slacken!' he said, his throat suddenly dry. 'My lord, for God's sake keep your hand away from your sword-hilt!'

'Swords won't help me, Harry, but wits may,' said the King, riding with a slack rein, as one who was ambling homewards at his leisure.

The noise of the troop's approach grew louder. Wilmot began to talk to the King, his light voice a little higher-pitched than usual, but wonderfully careless.

In another minute the troop was upon them, and they were jostled almost into the ditch, nearly losing their seats as the soldiers thrust rudely past them. But the troop had not come in pursuit of them, which was all that signified, and in a very short time it had swept by, freely spattering them with mud, but mercifully heedless of them.

'Well!' said the King, gentling his snorting mount. 'I think those were the worst few minutes of any I have so far endured!'

The Colonel pulled out his handkerchief and wiped his face with it. He said in a shaken voice: 'I make you my compliments, sire. I thought at last I must see you make some sign of fear.'

'My dear sir, I was much too fearful to betray myself!' replied the King.

'We must get away from this road!' said Wilmot urgently. 'At any moment that troop may return, and look more closely at you! Colonel Gounter, you are his Majesty's guide! Where must he go?'

'If his Majesty will be advised by me, he will continue along this lane to Beeding, which we have nearly reached, and there rest himself, at Mr Bagshall's house, where I have provided a treatment for him. I will then ride on alone to Brighthelmstone, and see to it that all be in readiness for his Majesty's arrival at nightfall.'

The King seemed to be quite willing to follow this advice, but Lord Wilmot was loud in his condemnation of it. Nothing would do but that he should carry the King away from the high road, and keep him hidden, till dusk, somewhere on the lonely slopes of the Downs. For once, he was proof against the King's coaxing, and when Charles said, half in jest, half in earnest: 'Harry, it is my will,' he replied with an unaccustomed note of grimness in his voice: 'It is not mine, sir, and though you may have my head tomorrow, today you shall obey me!'

In the end he had his way, the King yielding with the

easy-going sweetness of disposition which caused his Chancellor so much anxious foreboding. He and Lord Wilmot left the high road for the lonelier lanes, and Colonel Gounter rode on over the Downs to Brighthelmstone.

When he had covered some eight or nine miles, a windmill, standing against the cloudy sky, came into sight, and a little farther on he could see a stone blockhouse perched on the cliff. He rode gently into the little fishing village, passing its one church, and made his way between some straggling, tumbledown cottages to the George Inn, a small hostelry by the sea.

Wilmot, after the encounter with the soldiers at Bramber, and with a lively recollection of the events at Charmouth in mind, had been so reluctant to consent to the King's risking his person in a public inn, that Charles, to silence his protests, had agreed to seek some other shelter, if any might be had, and to send word where he was to Gounter, at the George.

The Colonel found the inn free of any other company, and, knowing that my Lord Wilmot would not discover any more convenient lodging for the King in such a mean village, engaged the best room in the house, and bespoke supper. Francis Mansel had promised to meet him at the George, and to bring Tattersal with him, but as it was too early yet for the Colonel to expect him, he called for a pipe, and some wine, and sat down before the fire in the parlour. The landlord, who was a pleasant fellow with a ready tongue, lingered to talk to him for a while. He accepted, without apparent disbelief, the Colonel's explanation of having come to Brighthelmstone to do business in connection with a cargo of merchandise, and said that he was well acquainted with Captain Stephen Tattersal, who was accounted an honest man, and a good seaman.

He presently withdrew to order the preparation of supper, but it was not long before the sound of horses stopping outside the inn brought him out of the kitchen. He looked into the parlour on his way to the front-door, to say: 'More guests, your honour, but I'll take them into the next room, so you'll not be disturbed by them.'

'Ay, do so,' replied the Colonel, knocking out his long pipe in the fireplace. He remained lounging in his chair until the sound of voices in the adjoining room reached his ears, and the landlord came back to tell him that a couple of gentlemen had arrived to supper.

'Leastways,' Smith corrected himself, 'a gentleman with his servant, maybe, for one of 'em – a great brown-looking fellow – is very meanly clad. But the stout gentleman's Quality, no question!'

The Colonel got up, and walked towards the table to pour himself another glass of wine. This movement brought him close to the door between the two parlours. He heard the King's voice say clearly: 'Here, Mr Barlow, I drink to you!' and at once jerked up his head, as though much surprised, exclaiming: 'I know that name! I pray you, host, go and enquire whether he was not a major in the King's army once!'

Smith went off at once on this errand, returning in a few minutes with the expected reply that Mr Barlow was indeed the man Gounter supposed him to be. The Colonel then bade Smith invite both Barlow and his companion to the fellowship of a glass of a wine with him, and in this way contrived to join forces with the King again, without arousing any suspicions in the landlord's breast.

Francis Mansel arrived at the George with Captain Tattersal as supper was carried into the parlour. The King was sitting in one corner of the wooden settle by the fire, a little out of the candlelight, and remained there while the Colonel greeted the newcomers, and made Wilmot known to them, under his assumed name of Barlow. They all drew round the fire for a few minutes before sitting down to table, the sea-captain telling them that he had hailed his barque into the mouth of the Adur, off the hamlet of Southwick, two miles west of Brighthelmstone.

'This wind won't serve us,' said the King abruptly.

'Nay, you say right, my master,' replied Tattersal, looking at him with a little curiosity. 'I warrant you're no landsman?'

'I have done some sailing in my time,' admitted Charles.

The landlord then called them to supper, and they moved towards the table, Mr Mansel taking one end, and the King the other. As the King stepped into the full candlelight,

Colonel Gounter kept his eyes watchfully on the merchant's face, but could not detect in it the slightest quiver either of surprise or of recognition. His attention was diverted by the landlord's clumsily letting a platter fall, and when he looked round again Mr Mansel had seated himself, and was conversing calmly with my Lord Wilmot. Then he saw that Tattersal, instead of applying himself to his supper, was staring fixedly at the King, and, with a sinking sensation in the pit of his stomach, he sat down beside the captain, and began to talk to him of his calling.

The answers he received were rather curt, and every now and then Tattersal would steal a sidelong look at Charles. The King gave no sign of apprehending any danger, but soon entered into my lord's conversation with the merchant. The landlord, who seemed to be subdued by his clumsiness in dropping the platter, remained in the room throughout the meal to wait on his guests.

When supper was finished, and chairs pushed back from the table, Tattersal plucked Francis Mansel by the sleeve, and whispered that he desired a word with him apart. Mansel looked a little surprised, but after excusing himself to the rest of the company, withdrew with the Captain into the taproom.

The King had strolled over to the fire, and was standing with his hand resting on the back of a chair, exchanging a few casual words with the landlord. Smith looked round cautiously as Mansel and Tattersal went out, and no sooner saw the door shut behind them, than he broke off in the middle of what he was saying, and quickly bent his knee to kiss the hand on the chairback. 'God bless you, wheresoever you go!' he whispered. 'I do not doubt, before I die, but to be a lord, and my wife a lady!'

The King withdrew his hand, and turned aside, saying with a laugh: 'I hope you may, yet I know not why you should!'

Smith said no more, but set about clearing the dishes off the table; and, after a few minutes, the King removed into the next room. The Colonel, who had observed the whole episode, followed him almost immediately. His face was drawn into rather worried lines; he met the King's eyes with a great deal of concern in his own, and said bluntly: 'Sire, I know not how that fellow should have known who you are. I beg your Majesty to believe me he learned it not from me. I am indeed so altogether ignorant of the cause —'

'Peace, peace, Colonel!' interrupted the King. 'You are in no way to blame!'

'While I have the ordering of your affairs, sir, I must think myself responsible for what goes awry,' said the Colonel. 'The man said no word to me of having recognized you. It may be only a suspicion that has entered his head, but —'

'The fellow knows me, and I know him,' said Charles. 'Unless I mistake him, he is one that belonged to the backstairs to my father. I hope he is an honest fellow; but I came away, thinking it not wise to hold more discourse with him than I need.'

A gentle knock upon the door made him break off. Before the Colonel had time to take more than two steps towards the door, it had opened, and Mr Mansel had come into the room.

He was looking grave, and upon the Colonel's greeting him, he shut the door behind him, and said in his precise way: 'I desire to have speech with you, sir, or – more particularly,' he added, with his eyes on the King, 'with this gentleman.'

'I am heartily at your disposal,' replied the Colonel.

Mansel glanced at him. 'Ah, yes, Colonel!' he said dryly. 'So, I think, have I been at yours.' His cold grey eyes passed on to the King's face. He said with precision: 'I shall crave your leave, sir, to ask you one question – ah, a delicate question, I apprehend!'

'Why, what's this?' said the King. 'You have my leave: let me hear your question!'

A thin smile flickered on the merchant's lips. 'I shall ask you, sir – but indeed, you have answered me – if I have the honour to stand in the presence of my King?'

The Colonel, who had foreseen this question from the moment of Mansel's entering the room, burst out laughing, and exclaimed: 'God pity all tall, dark men! My friend, you are sadly out. If you must know, this gentleman is Mr Jackson, who, as I told you, has lately been concerned in an unchancy duel.'

Mansel bowed slightly. 'I shall of course accept your assurance, my dear Colonel, and will do my possible to convince Tattersal that his suspicions are groundless.'

'Does he say I am the King?' asked Charles.

'He says, my liege, that he is positive it is you,' replied Mansel calmly.

The King smiled. 'Mr Mansel, can I trust you?'

'I hope your Majesty will be pleased to do so – ah, if Colonel Gounter permits!'

The Colonel was standing with his back to the door, his hand resting suggestively on his sword-hilt, two circumstances which seemed to amuse the merchant. He replied, in a level tone: 'I believe you to be an honest man, sir. I should not else have employed you in this business. What reason had Stephen Tattersal to say this gentleman is the King?'

'Why, it seems he had a very good reason, sir, for upon my denying it, he answered that he knew him well, for his ship had been taken by him, along with other fishing vessels, in the year 1648.'

'That was when I commanded the King my father's fleet,' remarked Charles thoughtfully. 'But, as I remember, I very kindly let them go again.'

The Colonel laughed at this, and, letting his hand fall from his sword-hilt, came forward into the middle of the room. 'I hope your kindness may now stand you in good stead, sir. Mr Mansel, the King is in your hands. Will you serve him?'

'I think,' said the merchant, 'that it is better for Mr Mansel to have the King in his hands than for Mr Mansel to be in Colonel Gounter's hands.'

'Faith, this is a man after my own heart!' said the King. 'My friend, tell me what kind of a fellow is Stephen Tattersal?'

'As the world goes, he is honest, sire. Yet, the risk of any way assisting your Majesty being very great, I would humbly suggest that you do not make yourself known to him, but will permit me instead to do what I can to reassure him.'

'Go, then,' smiled the King. 'But see to it you do not let him leave this house, for it may be that he has a wife, and I am not minded to lose him as I lost one other that was pledged to carry me to France.'

'I will do my possible, sir,' replied Mansel, and, bowing, went back to Tattersal in the taproom.

The King and Gounter rejoined Lord Wilmot in the larger parlour. When he heard that, besides the landlord, Tattersal had recognized the King, and that Mansel had been admitted to the secret, Wilmot gave a groan, and clasped his head in his hands, saying that all would yet go to rack. 'Again and again have our hopes been dashed!' he declared. 'Alas, under what evil star were you born, sir?'

'But, Harry, my hopes are not dashed, I do assure you! I am very well pleased with this merchant who has a sting under his tongue, and as for the master of the sailing vessel, we have him safe, and shall not let him go until we go with him.'

'We shall fail!' Wilmot said gloomily.

'Well, we have failed before. Keep a high heart: I was not born to lose my head on a block!'

'Your Majesty must forgive my lord, and all your poor servants,' said the Colonel, with the hint of a smile. 'Though you may be like Elisha's servant, that saw an heavenly host about him to guard him, to us it is invisible. We must think every minute a day, a month, until we see your sacred person out of reach of your enemies.'

'Yes!' said Wilmot. 'That is what he shall not understand!'

'I thank you, I thank you! But indeed you are too fearful.'

Mansel coming back into the room with Stephen Tattersal at that moment, the King strolled towards the window, and stood there, holding back the curtain, and looking out into the moonlit yard.

The Colonel observed that the corners of Mansel's mouth were slightly pulled down, but without seeming to notice it, he stepped forward, saying: 'You come in pudding-time! Now, tell me, Captain, in what readiness are you to set sail?'

Tattersal cast a glance towards the tall figure by the window, but the King's back was turned to him. He said gruffly: 'Nay, there's no getting off without the tide. Look 'ee, master, to your better security I hailed the *Surprise* into the creek, and the tide has forsaken her, so that she lies aground. I know not when I may set sail, for the wind's contrary, besides.'

The King had opened the casement. 'The wind had turned,' he said.

'If you will get your boat off tonight, you may have ten pounds more than was promised you,' said the Colonel.

Tattersal shook his head. 'Nay, I tell ye she's aground, master! The tide must take her off, and that'll not be till eight in the morning at soonest.'

'But you could take us aboard before dawn?' Wilmot demanded.

'I could do so,' said Tattersal, 'if, maybe, your honour was wishful none should see you step aboard.'

'Well! Then we will go aboard with you, and there await the tide!'

Tattersal looked under his brows at him. 'Ay, and you may do so, if the Colonel will insure the barque,' he said.

'Insure the barque!' exclaimed Gounter. 'What maggot have you in your head to think I should do so? You are being handsomely paid for your pains, so let that be the end of it!'

'Your demand, my friend,' said Mansel, 'is, as I have told you, out of all reason. You have had many freights of me, but I have never yet insured your vessel, nor shall not, believe me!'

'I have not had a freight the like of this one,' replied Tattersal sturdily. 'If I'm to take dangerous stuff aboard, I'll be insured, or I'll not set sail, do what you will.'

Nothing could move him from this resolve, and after arguing it for ten fruitless minutes, the Colonel, at a warning look from Mansel, yielded. Tattersal valued his boat at two hundred pounds, which Mansel admitted to be a fair price, and the Colonel promised, much against his will, to stand surety for that amount.

'And I will have your bond, master,' said Tattersal, with a stubborn look about his mouth.

'No,' said Mansel coldly. 'That you shall not. The

Colonel's name shall not appear in the business.'

The Colonel's eyes began to sparkle. 'You have my word, and if that should not content you, there are others whom it may!'

'I'll not sail without I have your bond.'

'There are more boats besides yours, Captain Tattersal. If you will not act upon the word of a gentleman, I will find those that will!'

'That's as you please, master. I'll have your bond, or go my ways.'

The King shut the window, and turned, and came deliberately into the full candlelight. He met Tattersal's searching stare with a faintly satirical gleam in his eyes, and said with a smile curling his mouth: 'The Colonel says right: a gentleman's word is as good as his bond – especially before witnesses,' he added, somewhat naïvely.

There was a moment's silence. Tattersal drew in his breath, and said in an altered tone: 'I'll carry you to France, master.'

'Why, that is very good hearing,' said the King. 'We will drink to the bargain. Mr Barlow, call up the landlord, if you please!'

His decision having been made, Tattersal began to be in a better humour, and by the time he had drunk a glass or two of wine, he talked no more of going away to provide further necessaries for the voyage, but took a pipe, and was soon lured into a game of cards with Wilmot and Francis Mansel.

When he had seen him fairly settled, the King went apart with Colonel Gounter, to take order for the moneys to be expended. Giles Strangways's broad pieces were not enough to defray both Tattersal's and Mansel's fees, so the King wrote out a bill of exchange drawn upon a certain London merchant, saying, as he scrawled his name across the paper: 'For God's sake, be rid of this as soon as you may, Gounter! They say a King's signature has the power of life or death. I know not what power of life mine may hold, but I assure you it is very potent for death.'

The Colonel put the scrap of paper in his pocket. 'I will keep it safe, sir, have no fear! But I am a little uneasy, and upon a different count. Dare we trust the boatman? His stomach came down mighty quickly – too quickly for my peace!'

'Yea, for I let him see my face, and he very well knows me for the King,' replied Charles.

'That brings me no comfort, sir,' said the Colonel.

'I think him honest enough. We will keep him with us, making merry, until we go aboard his barque.'

'You may leave that to me, sir. Will you not rest awhile?'

'Nay, I'll take a hand at cards,' replied the King, adding with one of his droll looks: 'You and my lord are so high in the instep you will very likely frighten the poor man.'

He went back into the parlour, and soon joined the card-players. His coming infused the game with a spirit of good fellowship which had been lacking from it. He lounged at his ease, as though he had not a care in the world, and straightway won Tattersal's heart by letting fall a jest coarse enough to double the mariner up.

It was not until two in the morning that the party set out for Southwick. The horses were brought round to the back of the inn; Lord Wilmot paid the shot; and the sleepy land-lord contrived once more to kiss the King's hand, declaring that it should not be said that he had kissed the best man's hand in England.

Francis Mansel then took leave, since his part in the business was done, and he had (he said) little desire to hazard his life unneedfully; and the three other men left the inn, taking Tattersal with them.

Colonel Gounter being the lightest man in the company, Tattersal climbed up behind him on to the back of the sturdy nag barrowed from Lawrence Hyde. They made their way along the shore in the moonlight, and arrived at South-wick to see the *Surprise*, a barque of not more than sixty tons, lying high and dry on the mud in the creek. Tattersal having directed the Colonel to a derelict hovel a little re-moved from the huddle of cottages that constituted the hamlet, the horses were stabled in it, and the Colonel accom-panied the King and Lord Wilmot to the ship.

The crew were all sleeping, and Tattersal at once led the King (who seemed inclined to inspect the vessel more thoroughly) down the steep companion-way to a little stuffy cabin that was lit by a lantern hanging from a beam.

Lord Wilmot looked about him with an expression of patient long-suffering, but the King saw nothing amiss in his surroundings, and said, stretching himself out on the bunk: 'Harry, how long is it since I was upon the sea! Mark me, if I do not sail this barque to France!'

'You are not upon the sea, sir,' replied Wilmot tartly. 'You are heeled over upon the mud, and in a cabin which stinks! And if so wretched a boat can reach to France, I for one shall deem it miraculous!'

'Nay, she's a right seaworthy vessel!' said the master, who had come into the cabin in time to hear these remarks. 'Your honour's no seaman, I see plain.' He looked at the King with a smile hovering about his mouth, and trod over to the bunk and knelt down beside it. 'Your Majesty knows better,' he said simply, 'I would not tell ye so, back in that inn, but I know ye well, my liege, ay, and I will venture life, and all that I have in the world to set you down safe in France.'

'I thank you, friend,' the King said, giving him his hand to kiss.

'Look 'ee, my liege, it's thought I'm bound for Poole, with a load of sea-coal,' said Tattersal. 'I am not wishful the folks at Shoreham should take note that I don't go upon my intended voyage, so if your Majesty pleases, we'll stand out with an easy sail towards the Isle of Wight till afternoon, and then make for Fécamp.'

'It pleases me well,' the King replied.

It did not please my Lord Wilmot, but the King told him that he was a landlubber, and bade him hold his peace.

The tide was creeping in, and it began to be time for Colonel Gounter to go ashore. He would have knelt to kiss the King's hand, but Charles swung his legs to the ground and stopped him, grasping both his hands in his, and saying: 'Nay, you shall not kneel to me, who have preserved my life! How may I think you, Colonel?'

'Sire, by pardoning me for all that has gone amiss in our journey, and believing it was through error, not want of will or loyalty,' the Colonel said, a little unsteadily.

'Nay, none has served me so well. It is my earnest prayer

you may not hereafter suffer for it, my dear friend.'

'It imports little. Yet, if I may beg one favour of your Majesty, it is that when you come to France you will conceal the instruments in your escape.'

'Have no fear: until I come to my throne, I will not divulge to any the names of those who have helped me, and so I promise you!' the King said.

The Colonel lifted one of his hands to his lips, and gripped it there for a moment.

'God bless and preserve your Majesty, and bring you back to us!' he said, and releasing the King's hand, turned sharp on his heel and left the cabin.

At eight o'clock, the incoming tide lifted the *Surprise* off the mud, and the Colonel, seated before the hut where he had stabled the horses, saw her on sail. Slowly she drew away from the land, a dingy little barque, carrying a precious burden to safety.

The wind was cold, but the Colonel sat on, watching the *Surprise* move slowly seaward. It was lonely on the shore, with only the screams of the gulls wheeling against the dull sky, and the breaking of the waves on the sand, to break the silence. A deep thankfulness filled the Colonel's breast, but he felt a little sad as well, and suddenly very tired. His life, which had been quickened for a brief space by peril and sharp care, and made bright by the magic of an ugly young man's smile, now seemed empty, and rather bleak.

All day long the *Surprise* stood out into the Channel, but as the afternoon wore on she grew smaller in the distance, till at five o'clock she was a speck upon the sky-line, sinking slowly out of sight.

The Colonel got up stiffly, and went into the hut, and saddled the horses. When he came out again, only the grey sweep of the horizon met his straining gaze. He mounted Lawrence Hyde's horse, and, leading the others, turned his back to the sea, and rode soberly home to Racton.

# BIBLIOGRAPHY

AIRY, Osmond. *Charles II.* 1901.

BOSCOBEL TRACTS, reprinted in the works of A. M. Broadley, Allan Fea and J. Hughes:

*A True Narrative and Relation of His Most Sacred Majesty's Miraculous Escape from Worcester.* 1660.

*A Summary of Occurrences from the Personal Testimony of Thomas Whitgreave and John Huddleston.* 1688.

*An Extract from Dr Bate's Elenchus Motuum Nuperorum in Anglia.* 1662.

*Captain Alford's Narrative.*

*Letter from a Prisoner at Chester.* (Clarendon State Papers.)

*An Account of His Majesty's Escape from Worcester, dictated to Mr Pepys by the King Himself.* 1680.

*Boscobel, by Thomas Blount.* 1660.

*Mr Whitgreave's Narrative.*

*Letter of Mr William Ellesdon to Lord Chancellor Clarendon.* (Clarendon State Papers.)

*Claustrum Regale Reseratum, or The King's Concealment at Trent, by Anne Wyndham.* 1667.

*Miraculum Basilicon, or The Royal Miracle, by A Jenings.* 1664.

*White-Ladies, Faithfully imparted for the Satisfaction of the Nation by Eye-witnesses.* 1660.

*The Royal Oak, by John Danverd.* 1660.

*Mr Robert Phelipps's Narrative of the Occurrences between September 28th and October 15th, 1651.*

*The Last Act in the Miraculous Story of His Majesty's Escape, by Colonel Gounter.*

BROADLEY, A. M. *The Royal Miracle.* A Collection of Tracts, Broadsides, Letters, Prints, and Ballads. 1912.

CARY, Henry. *Memorials of the Great Civil War in England.* 1842.

CHARLES II: *The Letters of.* Ed., Arthur Bryant. 1935.

CLARENDON, Earl of. *History of the Rebellion.* Books XII and XIII. Ed., W. Dunn Macray. 1888.

COATE, Mary. *Social Life in Stuart England.* 1924.

*Domestic State Papers: Petitions.*

EGLESFIELD, Francis. *Monarchy Revived.* 1822.

ELLIS, Sir Henry. *Original Letters.*

EVELYN, John. *Diary and Correspondence.* Vols. I and IV. *Incorporating The Private Correspondence between Sir Edward Hyde and Various Members of the Royal Family during the Commonwealth and Protectorate; and The Private Correspondence between Sir Edward Hyde and Sir Richard Browne.* Ed., William Bray.

FEA, Allan. *The Flight of the King.* 1897. – *After Worcester Fight.* 1914.

GODFREY, Elizabeth. *Home Life Under the Stuarts.* 1925.

*Harleian Miscellany.* Vol. IV.

HOSKINS, J. Elliott. *Charles II in the Channel Islands.* 1854.

HUGHES, J. *The Boscobel Tracts.* 1830.

IMBERT-TERRY, H. M. *A Misjudged Monarch.* 1917.

*Journals of the House of Commons.* Vol VII.

LYON, C. J. *Personal History of King Charles II.* 1851.

PEPYS, Samuel. *Diary.* Ed., Lord Braybrooke. 1825.

SCOTT, Eva. *The King in Exile.* 1905.

TRAILL, H. D. L., and MANN, J. S. *Social England.* 1903.

VERNEY, Margaret M. *Memoirs of the Verney Family.* Vol. III. 1894.

# Constance Heaven

Winner of the Romantic Novelists Association's award for the best romantic novel of 1972.

## THE HOUSE OF KURAGIN          30p

What is the mystery that haunts the house of Kuragin? Against the background of one eventful Russian summer, Amaryllis Weston, a young English governess, discovers the loves and hates that motivate the Kuragins and witnesses the first, faint stirrings of the revolt that will one day sweep away great families such as this. And as the fruit ripens, the lark sings and the corn grows high, she falls desperately in love . . .

## THE ASTROV INHERITANCE          35p

'I could feel his gloved hand burning through the lace of my gown. I was so small I barely reached his shoulders but as we swung round in the dance, I could see his white uniform stiff with gold braid and catch a glimpse of the fine-boned face . . .' A simple English girl visits Russia and marries a dashing aristocrat. The ingredients of this novel are adventure, love and a carefully researched historical background.

This superb historical romance is due for major promotion by Pan in February 1974.